PALADIN'S HELL

MANDA MELLETT

Published 2018 by Trish Haill Associates
Copyright 2018 by Manda Mellett

Edited by Maggie Kern
Proof reading by Astronima's
On Pointe Proofreading

Book and Cover Design
by Lia Rees at Free Your Words
(www.freeyourwords.com)

www.mandamellett.com

Disclaimer

This is a work of fiction. Names, characters,
businesses, places, events and incidents are either
the products of the author's imagination or used in a
fictitious manner. Any resemblance to actual persons,
living or dead, or actual events is purely coincidental.

Warning

This book is dark in places and contains content
of a sexual, abusive and violent nature. It is not
suitable for persons under the age of 18.

ISBN: 978-1-912288-34-2

AUTHOR'S NOTE

The Satan's Devils are a fictional outlaw MC. Their mother chapter is based in Tucson, Arizona, and they have chapters elsewhere including California, Utah and Colorado.

Paladin's Hell is the first book following the exploits of the members of the Colorado Chapter, and is a standalone novel.

If this is the first Satan's Devils novel that you've picked up, you may like to know that the Arizona Chapter have their own series, which starts with *Turning Wheels* (Satan's Devils MC #1). There is some crossover between the two series. The full story of how Jayden and her sister Ella come under the protection of the Satan's Devils can be read in *Slick Running* (Satan's Devils MC #3), and more background as to why Paladin and Jayden have to leave to come to Colorado is contained in *Mouse Trapped* (Satan's Devils MC #9).

There will be more books about the Colorado Chapter, as well as continuing the exploits of the Tucson chapter. In future, the other chapters may well have their own series too.

If you're new to MC books you may find there are terms that you haven't heard before, so I've included a glossary at the end to help along the way.

CAST LIST OF CHARACTERS

COLORADO CHAPTER	
ROAD NAME	ROLE/STATUS
Hellfire	President
Demon	VP
Buzzard	Treasurer/Secretary
Thunder	Sergeant-at-arms
Mace	Enforcer
Sparky	Road Captain
Blackie	Previous President
Furnace	Previous VP
Ingot	Previous Enforcer
Bomber	
Cad	
Dan	Prospect
Ink	
Lizard	
Pyro	
Runt	Prospect
Rusty	
Smithy	Failed Prospect
Taser	
Wills	Prospect
Bella, Breezy, Sheila, Titsy, Tulia	Sweet Butts

Other Name	Old Lady	Children
Carter Black	Moira	
Dave Black		
	Sindy	
	Jeannie	
Stephen Bartlett		
Jesse Devin		

ARIZONA CHAPTER	
ROAD NAME	ROLE/STATUS
Drummer	President
Wraith	VP
Heart	Secretary
Dollar	Treasurer
Peg	Sergeant-at-arms
Blade	Enforcer
Joker	Road Captain
Mouse	Computer expert
Adam	deceased
Beef	
Bullet	
Buster	deceased
Dart	transferred
Fergus	Prospect
Hyde	
Jekyll	
Lady	
Marvel	
Matt	Prospect
Paladin	(was Marsh)
Roadrunner	
Rock	
Slick	
Shooter	(was Spider)
Tongue	deceased
Truck	Prospect
Viper	

Other Name	Old Lady	Children
Rick Felis	Sam	Elijah (Eli)
Scott Remington	Sophie	Olivia
Dale Norman	Marcia	Amy, Jacob, Isabel
Todd Bishop		
Ronald Rinter	Darcy	Noah
Jack Sharples		
Josh Wilkinson		
Tse Williamson		
	Carmen	
Colin Lowe	Alex	Tyler
Scott Flintstone		
	Becca	
Jeff Andrews	Ella	
	Sandy	

CONTENTS

Prologue

Two and a half years ago...

Standing, with my back against the wall, I watch the girl lying on the bed. Observing the slight differences, changes in her breathing, little twitches of her muscles that signify she's stirring, waking up. My gut clenches in sympathy, half wishing she could continue sleeping, knowing her nightmare is still to come.

Jayden, Ella's younger sister, who'd been groomed by much older men, members of the Herrera family who had forced themselves on her time and time again. I hadn't been in the house when the Satan's Devils had found her. As a dutiful prospect I'd been standing guard outside. My role began when I'd been called in to carry her out and take her back to the safety of the compound.

I'd seen enough of what she'd been through from the state she was in. I'd gritted my teeth and stilled my hands to stop rushing in and gunning them down myself. Had to be satisfied with the knowledge that all her abusers would die. Once she was out of the way, they'd be killed at the hands of the men I hoped one day to call brothers.

Even sleeping, she fills me with pity. As she wakes, I wish I could take all her pain, both physical and mental, away. What she's gone through will stay with her for years, for all her life. Her pallor pale, her eyes sunken, there's drool at the side of her mouth, but it doesn't detract from her beauty. My stomach tightens again. Will, can, she ever recover?

"Marsh, could you leave us, please?"

"Sorry, Ella. No can do. Slick told me to stay put so here's where I'm stayin'." Even if I hadn't been given the instruction, I couldn't move from this spot. Not bothering to analyse the reasons why, I just know I want, need, to stay close, to protect her, even if all I can do now is help save her from those thoughts in her head.

"Can't you stand outside the door? You can guard us from there just as well."

As I wonder how I can refuse Ella's reasonable request, Jayden takes one of her sister's hands in hers, and points the other toward me. "You. You were there. You rescued me." Rather than immediately correct her assumption, I give her a smile and a quick nod. She looks at Ella and pleads, "Can he stay?"

Unable to keep my distance, I walk to the bed, now admitting the truth. "I didn't have much to do with it. I just carried you out. I didn't think you'd remember." She'd been drugged and out of it.

Ella's hovering as though she's her mother, not her sister, but I ignore her. It's me who passes Jayden the painkillers the doc had left. It's me who carries her into the bathroom and holds back her hair as she vomits. Something about her calls to me. Already, I care.

I stay, listening to her story. Feeling my eyes water as she goes into the horrific details. How she'd been groomed, threatened, isolated. Forced to do things no fourteen-year-old—scrap that, no woman should ever have to do. Telling myself it might be hard hearing, but it had been devastating for her to live it. She's the same age as my sister. Not that I have any contact with her, just know of her existence, we'd both been entered into the system after my mom had died. But she's out there somewhere. I'd hate to think anything like this would happen to her.

Jayden latches onto me. Although I'm almost five years older, I'm the closest to her age on the compound. It's me she turns to, and I try to help heal her, showing I don't give a damn what had happened. It hadn't been her fault, she hadn't done anything to attract the unwanted attention, been naïve perhaps, but that was because she was so young. She'd had sex, yes, but she had never been an active participant. Broken and shocked, she tries to find her own way to recover. Eventually I have to spell it out, letting her down gently when she tries to take our relationship further.

I wouldn't take advantage of a traumatised girl, even if Slick, Ella's man or Drummer, my president, hadn't read me the riot act. They'd seen where things were heading even then. I was to be hands off until she was of the age of consent which, in Arizona, is eighteen. I knew I'd wait for her. Watch over her, keep her safe, give my life for her if that's what was needed.

When I'd been patched in, she was the reason I was given my handle. Paladin. Jayden's knight in black leather armour.

CHAPTER 1
PALADIN

I don't like this, Slick." I grab a couple of beers from Paige, one of our sweet butts who's minding the bar. Luckily now I've turned twenty-one no one can make snarky comments about underage drinking any longer. Yeah, while I've indulged in alcohol since I was a prospect, being the youngest member made me the butt of many jokes, brothers enjoying yanking my chain. Now there's one less thing to tease me about. But it's all good. It's what family does.

Taking one of the bottles from my hand, Slick's eyes narrow. "You and me both, Brother. Thought the Herreras were long in our rear view. Or at least, where Jayden is concerned, that is."

Looking across the clubroom I see Slick's old lady, Ella, and her sister Jayden, heads bowed talking together. Reckon they'll be discussing baby shit. Ella's pregnant after a couple of years of trying, and Jayden couldn't be more excited at the prospect of being an auntie—she adores kids. The promise of soon having one that's truly blood family seems to have gone to her head. Having got to the end of that apparently risky first trimester, Ella's glowing and excited, and it seems she and Jayden talk of nothing else.

Slick must be able to read my mind. "Hate for Ella to lose Jayden now. They're both excited as fuck about the kid."

"As you are," I smirk at him. Slick's a real softie where his old lady's concerned.

He takes no offence. "As I am," he confirms with a grin. Then his face grows serious. "You know, as well as anyone,

Brother, what a hard time those girls have had. Everything that happened to Jayden that led to us being in this mess, Ella's fuckin' run-in with the Rock Demons, then thinking she wasn't going to be able to have a baby of her own. Those girls need each other."

I grit my teeth. We've been through this often enough. I know what he's saying, but the time's approaching when I want to be the one Jayden leans on, the one she looks to instead of running to her sister all the time. Trouble is, according to the rules I'd been given, I've still got eighteen months to wait. Too fucking long.

I raise my bottle, taking a long swallow, thoughts of when I first met Jayden coming back into my mind. I hadn't been the one going into the house to find her about to be raped by a group of much older men, or one of the brothers who'd stopped them. Unfortunately, it hadn't been the first time it had happened to her, girl had got caught in a trap. The fuckers had carefully groomed her, sucked her in, then kept her from telling her mom or her sister with a barrage of threats. Only fourteen and already abused on many occasions.

My involvement began when I'd been called in from my guard keeping duties outside. It had been me who'd carried her drugged-up, almost lifeless body out of the way of the carnage that would be wreaked once she was gone. I'd been that man, a boy really, just turned nineteen myself. She'd woken up, luckily all she remembered was me carrying her.

That she wanted more from me than a girl her age should was clear, as were her reasons. To wipe away all that had happened to her, she wanted to replace her ordeal by making fresh memories with a man she had chosen herself, instead of living with those that haunted her.

God knows I was tempted. But I couldn't go there. She pushed, tried to make me show my interest. Fuck, was I interested. But Drummer put a stop to that. He forbade me to touch her for three and a half years, until she was legal in the eyes of Arizona.

Jayden had felt slighted, but even then, I knew Drummer was right. Let her have what remained of her childhood, a time to regroup, to recover from her ordeal before pushing her into becoming a woman too soon.

You're still a virgin, I'd told her. To me, you are. You've never had a first time the way it should have been.

I've been waiting over two years, still more than a year to go. In all that time, I've thrown myself into being there as her friend, have dedicated myself to watching out for her.

But things are changing. Word on the street is that the Herreras might be coming for her again. In their eyes, she was the one who got away, the one who caused multiple deaths in their family. When the rumours had been raised in church, Drummer went as far as to suggest I should take her some place safe, away from Tucson, away from her brother-in-law and sister. After we'd left the meeting, he said he'd give Hellfire, the prez of the Colorado chapter, a shout to see if he'd be on board with the idea of us relocating to their base in Pueblo. Hellfire being chosen because he was a family man.

Drummer's suggestion was a step too far for Slick and his old lady. Knowing the danger threatening Jayden, though, they'd left their home in Tucson, and had moved back to the compound, taking two adjacent suites that were made empty for them. It wasn't an ideal situation, not with a baby coming along. But for now, living amongst the Satan's Devils was the most we could do to ensure Jayden was kept out of danger.

Breaking free from my reverie, I return to the conversation, reassuring the man seated opposite me. "Slick, both you and I have Jayden's best interest at heart."

"I think there's another part of you more involved than your heart, Brother." Slick sneers. "I can read you like a fuckin' book. Moving to Colorado would hold attraction for you. You're thinking it brings the end of your waitin' time forward a year. Not happy about that, Brother, not happy at all."

I can hardly remind him she lost her innocence a long time ago. Ella and Slick have never treated her as anything other than virgin and pure, as I've done myself. Fuck, I've not taken such liberty as to kiss her, not touched her except for a brotherly hug. Sometimes I wonder whether she still wants me that way, or if she's changed her mind over the past couple of years. Once the boundaries had been established between us, they were never referred to again. I've acted as her friend. Nothing else.

My feelings for her haven't dulled in the interim. Like I told her that long-ago night, I'd wait for her. And I have. She's filled out, looks like a young woman now. A woman I'd be proud to have on the back of my bike.

As if our conversation has in some way summoned her, Jayden gets up, says something to her sister and then crosses the room. Reaching us, she plops herself down on the couch beside Slick, leaning in when he holds out his arm to place around her. If you didn't know different, you'd think she was his daughter. Sometimes I get scared when she looks at me, she views me only as something akin to a brother.

"What are you two old women gossiping about?" she asks cheekily, her brow raised toward me.

"Just shootin' the shit," I tell her. Noticing the pool table's free, I nod that way. "Want to play?"

"You've been talking about me," she says firmly. As I wonder whether she knew from her female intuition, she adds, "One or the other of you kept looking my way."

"Ella," Slick says firmly. "We were talking about Ella and the baby. But there is something else I want to talk to Paladin about.

Go get the balls set up, will you?" I tilt my head slightly as she gets up and goes. Slick's lips press together, then he nods. "Ella and I have been talkin'. You and Jayden? No idea where that's going to go. Most girls her age by now would be going to the movies with a boyfriend, a walk in the park holding hands. Innocent stuff, but maybe the basis of a relationship in the future. If she had a normal life, she'd be playing the field."

I can't suppress the growl that comes out of my throat at the thought of her with another boy.

He barks a laugh; it sounds a bit strangled. "Reckon Drummer and I might have tied your hands too much. Perhaps we should cut you some slack. Start slow though, maybe we should allow you to take her on dates. Think we could trust you enough not to take advantage. Proved yourself, Brother."

I raise my chin at the compliment. My heart rate speeds up as I consider what he's offering, but then I shake my head, pointing out the problem. "Now's not a good time, not with the Herreras about."

"Yeah, been doing some thinking. You take her anywhere, she needs to have brothers around her." Rolling my eyes, I glare at him. Sure. Sounds like a great date. "Nah," there's a twinkle in his eye as he continues, "also thought about that. Why not take her to the Wheel Inn? Treat her to a decent meal?"

It's a thought. More than I've been allowed up to now. It's a decent restaurant in Tucson, and one which is owned and run by the club. Sufficient culinary reputation that any young girl would be excited to go there for a dinner date, and with the benefit that a couple of members are normally there in the background. If they're loosening the reins a little, who am I to object?

"If I do, would a goodnight kiss be out of the question?" I ask eagerly, already anticipating the touch of her lips, while thinking I may have pushed my luck.

Slick looks around, shrugs, smirks then leans forward, puckering his lips. "If you insist, Brother."

I stand abruptly, waving him back, grinning like a loon. He may have deliberately misunderstood me, but he hadn't shot me down.

As she sees me walking over, Jayden's got the balls set up, and at my nod, takes the first shot. She's learned quickly, it's fifty-fifty whether I'll beat her or not. Me? I just enjoy watching her stretched out over the pool table, her breasts, small but perfectly adequate, hanging low over her cue. My cock twitches as I think on the benefits of Colorado. If we ended up there, in a few months I could make her mine. Yeah, that's a definite plus.

At last I get a turn. As I line up the cue, I ask casually, "Wanna go on a date, Jay?"

Her squeal makes me miss my shot. Chuckling, I look back over my shoulder. "Is that a yes?"

She pouts. "Slick wouldn't allow it."

Moving away from the table, I stand, leaning on my cue, indicating that she should take her turn, then explain. "He actually suggested it. Thing is, Jay, you, me. We made promises for the future. I like you, you seem to like spending time with me, but we need space to explore if there could be anything between us."

She seems to have forgotten the game. For a second her face is unreadable. I feel my heart skip a beat. Having expected her to leap at the chance, her non-reaction is worrying. But then, she lights up with a smile. "I thought Slick was going to make us wait the full time before you were allowed to take me anywhere." Now she's beginning to get excited. "Can we go on your bike, Pal? Always wanted to ride on the back."

"Whoa, slow down." I'm laughing at her enthusiasm. "Nah, I know what you girls are like. You'll want to get dressed up all fancy. Don't think the bike goes with that." And while I want her, I'll need to know a relationship will be for keeps before I have her on the back of my bike. I'm nowhere prepared for that level of commitment, and there's practicalities to consider first. I'll need to get a pillion pad.

Whether Ella's so content with her life at the moment, she wants everybody to be as happy as her; not only does she agree to Slick's suggestion, but she helps Jayden to get organised with clothes and makeup. On the following Saturday evening when Jayden appears, she completely blows me away. I have never seen anything so fucking gorgeous in my life. That includes my Harley.

I think my mouth drops open. For a moment, I stand and stare. That's until the smile she's wearing starts to slip from her face. That's when I step up. "Doll," I can barely get the words out. "You're fuckin' beautiful." She also looks at least five years older, definitely not jailbait.

I want to reach out, to hold her, hug her close. But Ella's standing behind her with her arms crossed, a brow raised as though in challenge. It's probably one of the most stupid fucking things I've ever done, but I reach for her hand, bring it to my lips and kiss it.

I hadn't noticed Slick coming up behind me. He barks a loud laugh. "Chivalry's not dead, eh? Knew there was a reason we named you after a knight."

Jayden seems as confused as myself. She giggles awkwardly at my gesture and Slick's words and takes her hand away quickly. I notice she's softly caressing the place my lips touched with her fingers.

How do we do this? How do we go from friends forbidden to be anything else, to a couple who are courting? I don't want to fuck this up. Apart from how Jayden feels, I've got to do right in front of Slick and Ella.

"Shall we go?" I want to take her hand, put my arm around her shoulders, but what does she expect? And is that too far for her brother-in-law and sister?

"I'm ready." Her eyes sparkle, letting me know she has expectations of this evening. I just hope I don't disappoint.

We walk down to where the club's SUV is parked behind the garage. Gentleman like, I open the passenger door, and help her in. Then, leaning over her body, I fasten the seat belt. Doing so, my hand brushes against her breast. At her sharply inhaled breath, I apologise. "Sorry." Smartly I step around to the driver's side and get in.

"Have you ever been to the Wheel Inn before?" I ask her as we wait for the gate to be opened.

"No." Her response is stilted.

"It's got quite a good menu." *Why the fuck did I say that?* Conversation that usually flows easily between us feels awkward.

"Ella's excited about the baby."

I already know that, you couldn't be in the clubhouse and not see for yourself. Seems Jayden's struggling for things to say as well.

I'm relieved when we draw up to the restaurant that the Satan's Devils own, driving into the rear parking lot. She reaches for the door, I tell her to wait, and again, acting the gentleman, go around and help her out.

As I start for the entrance, she gently rests her fingers on my arm. I turn around to see her lips curving.

"If I don't tell you later, I had a good time tonight."

My fist softly makes contact with her bicep. "You watch that darn film too much." And I've watched it with her, many times. Sometimes worried she's reading some of her situation into *Pretty Woman*, how a whore can find redemption. *She isn't a whore. Far from it.* Not for the first time, I'd love to know what's going on inside her head.

I've booked a table, and I'm glad I did. The restaurant is full, in the bar area it's standing room only. With my hand gently resting on her back, I lead her over to the table. There's only one other table empty, and that's the one closest. My eyes are focused on seeking out the location I'd reserved, and nodding to the bartender who knows me. When I go to pull out her chair, I freeze. The prez and his old lady are seated behind us. *Coincidence?* It's unlikely. I can't do anything except acknowledge Drummer's raised chin lift, though I don't fail to notice the way his lips quirk.

Martha, the assistant manager, comes over and hands us menus. "Can I get you a drink?"

I look at Jayden. She smiles. "A coke, please."

"I'll have a beer."

I want to say something that shows my brain's not tied up in knots, but all I can stammer out is, "See anything you'd like to try?" The menu's got a number of gourmet dishes on it, things she might not have come across before. As well as a good variety of simpler fare.

Her brow creases a little as she reads. "I think I'll just have the fried chicken. What are you having?"

I'm not here for the food. "The T-Bone steak." It's a quick decision with no thought behind it.

"Good evening." The familiar voice startles me. Looking up I see Sandy, Viper's old lady, and the manager of the restaurant delivering our drinks. I didn't think she worked in the evenings. Just when I'm about to ask her, I hear the chair being pulled out at what was the empty table next to us. *Oh fuck no.* I feel like putting my head in my hands. *This can't be happening to me.* Slick and Ella are taking their seats.

A laugh from behind me gets me turning, in time to see a glass being raised as if in toast toward me. *It's fucking Bullet and Carmen.* That's not all. Blade's standing at the bar, half paying attention to something Beef is telling him. Just behind are Joker and fucking Lady.

Now I do place my elbows on the table and sink my head down into my hands. *Every word we speak will be overheard. Any hopes I'd had of covering her hand romantically with mine, playing footsie under the table, have been dashed.* I don't have a chance.

"Pal? What's up?"

I look up to see Jayden's concerned eyes watching me.

"Did you know about this?" I hiss softly.

Her focus has been on the menu. As I jerk my head to one side, her eyes widen when she spies Slick and Ella. I then nod to something over her shoulder. She turns, when she looks back having seen Prez and Sam, she's shaking her head, her eyes wide with disappointment. "Of course I didn't know."

My first inclination is to get up, throw enough cash on the table to cover the drinks and get out of here. But Jayden deserves a night out, I'll just have to be on my best behaviour.

The food, when it arrives, tastes like cardboard in my mouth. I can see Jayden's uneasy, her eyes flicking around to our audience which is watching us like hawks. I'm finding it hard to start any topic of conversation. All the things I'd wanted to say to her go unsaid. My anger begins to rise. *She's sixteen, almost seventeen. She should be allowed to date.* Fine, send one brother or two to provide protection. *But half the fucking club?*

"Can I show you the dessert menu?"

"No." I say fast. Then want to withdraw my sharp reply. "Jayden?"

"Not for me." She leans forward. "Can we go, Pal?"

I ask for the tab, pay it, then stand, seeing brothers at the bar hurriedly finishing their drinks, then following us out of the restaurant.

The bikes surrounding the SUV as we drive back may have been an escort to ensure Jayden's safety. That Blade, instead of me, escorts Jayden back to her suite is not. Unless it's me, he's protecting her from.

This can't go on. Watching him walk *my date* away makes my body tense with frustration. I've been offered a chance, only to have it snapped away.

CHAPTER 2
HELLFIRE

"What?"

Moira's clipped tone conveys her annoyance that she's caught me staring. I shrug. Nowadays I'm not certain whether it's better to keep quiet or change the subject. Commenting or making an observation, is likely to get my head snapped off. Deciding the sensible option is probably to keep my mouth shut, I grab a sweater that's hanging on the back of one of the chairs in the kitchen. Saying nothing, hoping not to draw attention to what I'm doing, I casually slip it on over my head. It's mid-February, and while I admit it's not the coldest it has been, it's still too chilly to have windows open all over the house. It seems, though, even actions have consequences.

"I can't fucking help it," she snarls, as if I'd replied using words. With a loud huff, she leaves what she was doing and walks out of the room.

After closing the wide-open window, I follow her. Moira's now in the living room, idly flicking through a magazine. Her face red and glowing. *How can I make her realise I hate to see her going through this?*

"What do you want, Hell?" she sighs, tiredly.

To right the world for her if I could. But some things are beyond me. I go and sit on the armchair, she's taken the couch. Right now, she won't want me near her. It's as though the thermostat of her body is faulty, one moment she's feeling normal, the next she can be out in the snow wearing just her nightie. It embarrasses her, I know it. So, pulling the sweater more firmly around me, I ignore the temperature in the house.

"Had word from Drummer."

"The National Prez?"

I nod to confirm it, while thinking it's probably better we're here in Pueblo, Colorado, rather than Tucson where the mother chapter of the Satan's Devils is based. At least Moira can get cool here if she wants to.

Closing her magazine, she tilts her head to one side. "What does he want? You going to be making a trip down to Tucson? They got trouble again?"

Quickly I reassure her. "Nah, nothing like that." My lips curve briefly as I recall the conversation I'd had with Drummer. "He was feeling me out as to my views on something."

Her eyes narrowing, she states, "You don't usually discuss club business with me, Hell."

She's right, I don't. I've been the prez of the Colorado chapter of the Satan's Devils for twenty years now, VP ten years before that. Moira's been mine since I got my patch, a few years before I started to work my way up the ranks. She's known the score for a very long time. What the club does remains secret from old ladies and anyone who isn't a patched member.

I sit forward and place my elbows on my knees, clasping my hands together. "Think I need a woman's advice on this one, and it's possible that I'll need you to get involved."

Getting up she, *thank fuck*, closes the window, shivers, then comes back and sits down. I keep my face impassive, but she gives a sheepish grin, then a look full of apology. I wave it off.

"What's going on, partner?"

Yeah, she's my partner. Always has been, constantly having my back. I raise my chin. "Bit of a long story…"

Another curve of her lips. "I've got time." She has. Now that our youngest has gone to college, she's often at a loss for things to do.

I acknowledge her statement with a nod and take a breath. "Trouble is, where do I start?"

"At the beginning?" Moira suggests as she settles back to make herself comfortable.

Another raise and dip of my head. "Okay, the way I understand it, he's got a member wanting to transfer… Nah." I break off. "It doesn't start with him; it begins with what happened to Jayden." As Moira's eyebrow rises, I resume. "Jayden's the young sister of one of the brothers, Slick's, old lady. Couple of years ago she got caught up in a child-grooming ring. Can't put this any other way but to say it as it is. She was drugged, raped, forced to have sex with multiple men, and on more than one occasion." My eyes go to hers to see how she's taking it. If I'm to do what Drummer has requested, I need Moira on my side, but I'm wary of throwing her back into her own painful memories.

Moira's hand is covering her mouth; her pupils look large on her face. Of anyone, I know how much she'll understand what happened to Jayden and will be sympathetic. "How old was she then?"

"Fourteen," I tell her.

My old lady settles back on the couch, drawing her legs up under her. I take a second to admire the way she's still as supple as she was when she was seventeen. "Poor kid. Sad story. What's it got to do with us?"

"Drummer and his brothers broke up the child-grooming ring. But it had been run by members of the local crime family, the Herreras. The fuckers who were molesting kids were all taken out, but the Herreras still seem to have the Tucson Devils in their sights. If it hadn't been for Jayden, the lucrative business might still have gone on, and those responsible, their family, still alive."

"After all this time, they still want her?"

It's hard discussing this shit with her, knowing what to say and what to hold back. This is new territory for me. "There's been changes with the Herreras at the top, Drummer might be being overcautious, but he knows enough to be worried. He wants to be prepared."

Her head tilts as she examines me. "I don't understand where we come in, or what you want from me? You know, Hell, if there's some way I, or we, can help, you don't have to ask." Creases appear on her brow. "You mentioned someone wanting to transfer."

This is the bit where she might get upset. Our personal history is all water under the bridge now. But it's not as easy to dismiss as that. Though years might have passed, my old lady still dwells on what had left a permanent scar. "Paladin. He was just a prospect at the time, but he carried that young, drugged girl out of the house. When she came around, she remembered it was him, latched onto him. Paladin, well, he was taken by the kid. Seems a mutual attraction developed between them."

Quickly she sits forward. "I know Satan's Devils don't do everything legal, but shit, Hell. Drummer shouldn't have allowed…"

My hand slashes through the air. "He didn't." I snipe. "Let me fuckin' finish, woman. Paladin was nineteen, Jayden fourteen. At the risk of losing his patch, Paladin had to promise to keep his hands off her until she reached the age of consent. Which in Arizona, is eighteen."

"In Colorado it's seventeen." She purses her lips, and I can see her mind whirling. "How old is the girl now?"

"Sixteen, approaching seventeen, Drummer said." I'd asked to estimate how much supervision she'd need. Knowing Mo, though, I can see why she'd think it significant, that's confirmed by her next words.

"Paladin wants to bring her here so they can have sex."

"No, Mo. Drummer wants Jayden to come here for protection. Paladin wants to come with her so she isn't alone." My hand sweeps back through my grey/white hair. "Fuck, Moira, I don't know much more than what I've told you. But there's more to this shit than a boy wanting to get into a girl's pants. Don't forget the need to hide her. Reckon Paladin just wants to get her away from Tucson and somewhere she'd be safe."

"They could have gone to Vegas if they just needed to get out of Arizona." Moira stands and goes to open the window again, sweat glistening on her face. "I reckon the legal age limit has a lot to do with it."

"Nah," I contradict. "It's because of *us*. You and me. San Diego is too close so that's out of the question. Neither Utah or Las Vegas are anything approaching family clubs…"

"And we are?" she scoffs, incredulously.

"Not the club. Us," I emphasise again. "We've raised a family. We've got experience with teenagers. That's the way Drummer's thinking."

Again, her lips press together, clearly unconvinced. Yeah, Drummer had walked me through his reasoning. But I have to wonder if my old lady's on track as to what's in those youngsters' heads. There's not a lot I can do about it. I've had a request from the National Prez, I need to get my woman, and my brothers, on board with it. Hard to say no to Drummer.

Standing, I approach, laying my hand on her shoulder. "They're still assessing the risk in Tucson, don't want to upend a kid's life if there's no real reason. If they come here, and at this point, it's still a big if, my suggestion is that they stay with us where we can keep an eye on them, and not at the club."

Moira stares outside, there's a squirrel searching for something to eat in the yard. Suddenly she turns around to face me. "*She* can," she agrees. "But not him. Not until I know what the score is, Hell. I won't be complicit in a young girl being forced to do anything she doesn't want, or she's not ready for."

A compromise, and a good one at that. The direction of my woman's thoughts doesn't surprise me one bit. Gently turning her around to face me, I place my lips to her forehead. "Agreed, Mo. We'll see how the land lies before throwing them together."

We stand like that for a minute, then she pushes me away. "You going to be coming home tonight?"

Moving my head side to side I think. "We've got church, then I'll have to be sociable and have a drink with the boys. I might need to stay at the club if the roads get iced up."

Her face tightens. "Do what you've got to do, Hell. I won't bother to wait up." She turns fast, but not before I see her eyes glistening.

I say a goodbye to her back, then go grab my jacket, thick winter gloves, and a warm beanie, then back my bike out of the garage. A steady rain is falling, and by the look of the sky, it could turn to snow later. If it does, the sun rising tomorrow should quickly melt any that settles, good thing is, this time of year, snow doesn't tend to hang around long. But the overnight temperatures will likely freeze it. Hate leaving my old lady alone, especially as our talk is bound to have dredged up thoughts of the past. But I can't neglect my duties, and that means putting in an appearance at church. Only been a couple of times I've missed it in the twenty years I've sat in that chair.

I put on the goggles I wear in cold weather and start the engine of my Harley Dyna Glide. Its rumble echoing from the garage whose motion sensor fitted doors are automatically closing behind me, then, facing it in the right direction, shift up through the gears and I'm off.

It only takes twenty minutes for me to ride to the small steel mill that closed when the market collapsed in the early eighties. An appropriate setting for our compound, seeing as it was the resulting unemployment that led to the start of the motorcycle club which, eventually, threw in their lot with the Satan's Devils. We had to knock the chimney down as it had become structurally dangerous, but the furnace remains. It's a huge pit, large enough to melt down a train. We kept it, in part as a memorial to the mill's origins, and by having placed our grills within it, as a talking point when weather permits and we hold club barbeques. In the factory alongside, brothers have rooms and the lower floor has been stripped out to become our club-house.

Over the almost four decades that we've been in existence, we've had the opportunity to mould it just how we like.

Mid-afternoon and the road's relatively clear, I let my mind wander back, the plight of young Jayden bringing the past back to me, just as much as I suspect it had done to my wife.

In the beginning the clubhouse had been a makeshift affair. Crooked shelving housing drinks behind a couple of planks suspended on brick blocks which had been our bar top. Mismatched tables and chairs, a pool table which had seen better times. But the members, who in time would become Devils, were even then bonding together as a brotherhood, and while the MC was just the bare bones, it was slowly shaping up.

Black Plate, more commonly known as Blackie, had started the club, and had assumed the position of Prez. His friend, another steelworker kicked loose when the steel market plummeted, Furnace, joined him as his VP. Members have come and gone, usually via coffins, over the years. The only two remaining original members, other than myself, are Bomber and Rusty.

Blackie also happened to be my father. Showing me, his son, no favours, I'd joined at the bottom as a prospect. Absolutely no preference given for, or acknowledgement of, our relationship. I'd probably have been treated better if I hadn't carried his genes. Maybe things might have been different had my mother lived. She'd died with complications from blood loss after having her only child, me. Something I'd felt he'd always blamed me for.

Drug running and moving guns had taken the place of earning an honest wage. Money in your pocket rather than eking a living from whatever you could. I didn't like it, but had no alternative, with the crash of the steel industry, there were too many people unemployed and chasing after the few available jobs.

It was on one of the days I'd just finished making a delivery to a local dealer, when I first saw her. A sweet girl, walking arm and arm with a giggling friend. As they approached, I saw I was the target of their mirth, or, rather, interested, slightly nervous laughter.

Seeing them eyeing my bike, and the cut that I'm wearing, I pull out a pack of cigarettes, light one, and watch them draw closer.

My greeting, of, "Ladies," accompanied by a grin and a chin lift has them giggling all over again.

They seem to be in awe as they approach. The one who'd first caught my attention, hangs back a little behind the other who's got a more hardened seen-it-all look in her eyes.

It's the bold one who's assessing me. "You're one of those bikers, aren't you? In the new gang?"

"Not a gang, sweetheart. We're a motorcycle club. We're just men who love riding motorcycles." It's a practiced statement, one I find myself saying often.

The bold one inches nearer. "My name's Jeannie. This is Moira."

Moira peers out from behind her, waggling her fingers. She's fucking adorable, and my cock hardens just watching her. Jeannie's okay in the looks department, but while I can't put my finger on it, Moira's got an aura of innocence about her which, strangely, I find appealing.

"Jeannie, Moira," I raise my chin and shake out my thick, dark and curly shoulder-length hair.

"You have parties up at your clubhouse, don't you?" Jeannie brazenly asks.

I grin, answering, "Sometimes." At least once a week and often more than that.

Jeannie looks at Moira, whose eyes have gone large in her face. Although she tugs at Jeannie's arm, it has no effect, nor does it stop Jeannie from almost making a demand, "Can we come?"

I'm more interested in Moira, who resembles a rabbit caught in the headlights. A thought hits me. "How old are you babes?"

"I'm eighteen, she's seventeen." Again, it's Jeannie who answers.

I nod, pleased. At least they're both of the age of consent. Jeannie, I could take or leave, my cock doesn't seem bothered at all. But Moira? Don't know what it is, but there's just something about her. My cigarette's burned down to the stub, I put it out against the heel of my boot. "Tell you what, you give me your numbers and maybe I'll call you sometime."

I'm not promising anything, but Jeannie's grin looks like she's scooped the jackpot. Quickly she delves into her purse, takes out some paper and writes on it, handing me just one number. Uh uh, not yours I want honey. I stare at Moira. "What about you, sweetheart?"

Jeannie glances at her friend, and her grin widens. Then as Moira's mouth forms a shocked O; Jeannie takes back her note and jots down a second number.

I pocket the paper, and start the engine, it roars loudly making both of them jump. "Later, ladies," I call out, as I kick down into first, let out the clutch and twist the throttle, and disappear down the street.

Chapter 3

MOIRA

Of course Hellfire's going to stay at the club tonight. Oh, if I'm honest, I wouldn't want him riding in this weather. Already the rain has turned to sleet, and I expect there will be a covering of snow by late evening. The probable condition of the roads is a perfectly rational explanation, and one I would readily accept were it not that it seems he's staying overnight at the club more and more lately, hardly ever coming home. *Or is that just my imagination?*

I close the window, the sensation that I was going to explode from overheating having dissipated for now. God, how I hate the changes happening to my body. No wonder Hell doesn't want to sleep with me, most nights I wake up dripping with sweat and throwing off all the bedcovers. He'll be in luxury lying by himself in the king-size bed in his room in the compound, no one tossing and turning beside him.

Or will he be alone?

I'm not blind. I know the breasts he used to admire are sagging, my tummy's no longer flat, and my waist has started disappearing. It's no wonder he's not approached me for sex in ages. I couldn't match up to the sweet butts and hangarounds that throw themselves at my man, all wanting to be the one to bed the president.

It's unfair. The years haven't changed him at all. He might have gone grey, but his figure's the same as it always was, his muscles still firm, his stomach like a washboard. It looks like I've let myself go, but I haven't. It's just these useless female hormones causing changes I didn't sign up for.

I'm scared I'm going to lose my man. And that there's nothing I can do to stop it.

I go to the bathroom, take out the hair dye I bought earlier, and start to apply it on the roots. Why does grey on a man make them look distinguished, while on a woman it shows their age? Life's so unfair. I check the instructions as it's a new brand, and see I've got to wait half an hour.

When was the last time he took me on the back of his bike? Christ, I can't remember. *Will he leave me?*

Why the hell did I let myself think that? I've been with him for thirty-six years, I'd had his children. Now they've grown and left home, is my job done? Have I out served my purpose?

For Christ's sake, Moira. Stop over-thinking things. Tonight may be the first time I've allowed such thoughts to surface, but they've been bubbling around for a while.

Nowadays I don't put in many appearances at the clubhouse where once I used to be a fixture. Hell no longer has an old lady he'd like to show off. He'd much rather be seen with one of the attractive hangarounds on his arm, proof of his virility. *Well, it seems he can no longer get it up for me.* It's been so long, I barely remember what his cock feels like.

In an action more violent than it needs to be, I grab a magazine, and go sit on the couch, checking the time. *Fifteen more minutes.* I turn the pages. *Christ.* Story after story of cheating men. Seems it's not just me that's in this situation. Ah, here's an article about how to keep your man interested. I give up reading halfway. How can you be sexy and alluring in a body that's determined to be the opposite? It's okay to suggest sexy underwear, but when the clothes come off, it's to reveal stretch marks and sagging skin.

If there was a way to turn back the clock, I'd do it.

I shower, wash the dye out, then dry my hair, not bothering to style it. I pull on my comfy pyjamas and settle in front of the TV. Flicking through the channels, there's nothing that catches my attention. *Maybe I'll read.* Having left my reading glasses in the bathroom when I'd checked instructions about washing out the dye, I get up to go and retrieve them. Reaching the bathroom, I do a quick pee, then return to the sofa, only then realising that I'd forgotten what I'd gone to fetch.

Rolling my eyes, I suspect if I go to fetch my glasses again, I'll probably only return with something different. I put away my book, and rest my head back on the chair.

What was it Hell had been talking about earlier? Oh, yeah. That poor kid from Tucson. If she ends up coming here, I'll do everything I can to help her. I know only too well what it's like to be forced to do something against your will. I, too, had my virginity stolen. Her situation brings it all back. I let my mind drift, dredging up memories.

"Look!"

"What?"

"Oh, my. He's a real hunk."

"Who you looking at? Oh." My eyes alight on a man who's just come out of a club and is getting on his bike. Wow. If I was going to give him a score he'd easily be a ten, if not an eleven or twelve. He's got darkish, curly, thick hair that reaches his shoulders, he's moving so smoothly he seems to glide, strong, long steps. He's tall, slim but muscular.

"He's one of those bikers. From that new gang. The one everyone's talking about," Jeannie hisses. "Let's go and say hi."

"Let's not," I toss back. But it's like Jeannie's on a mission. To my horror, the biker's looking straight at us. He's lighting a cigarette and seems to be waiting.

"Ladies," he calls out, as we approach. Nerves make me giggle. Up close I can see he might be young, but he's all man.

He's got a swagger and confidence about him. I slip myself behind Jeannie and let her do the talking. Jeannie's asking about parties at their clubhouse, it sounds terrifying to me. She can go if she wants. Just leave me out of it. Hey. What's she doing?

As the biker pulls away, I tug the arm of the person I thought was my friend in horror. "You gave him my number?"

Unrepentant she replies, "I gave him both of ours. That way one of us might be home when he calls."

"He won't call," I tell her optimistically. "And if he does, you're going to any party they hold alone." I've been her wingman before, but not at a gathering of leather-clad bikers...

Jeannie. As I emerge from my memory, I realise it's been a while since I've spoken to her. I ought to make more of an effort to stay in touch, though, to be honest, she still spends most of her time at the clubhouse, while I hide away at home. Yes, hide. Not wanting to be confronted with the temptation placed in front of my man there. Not wanting to face it head-on. Though lately, secreting myself away, pretending nothing's changed, isn't working as well as it used to.

Though years have passed since we first met the handsome biker on his bike, I still put some of the blame on Jeannie. If she hadn't given my number away, my life would have been very different, and things wouldn't have happened the way that they did. Of course, it's impossible to imagine how it would have turned out instead. But she had.

Using the information Jeannie had so helpfully supplied, Hell had indeed called me. Of course he wasn't named Hellfire then, hadn't yet got his road name. He'd been a plain and simple Carter. Yeah. He'd called me, not Jeannie, turns out it wasn't her he was interested in. Something I could never understand. And it wasn't a party he'd invited me to, instead he asked me to go for a ride on the back of his bike. In my naivety then, I had no idea what that meant to a biker like him.

Carter had turned up at my door, helmet in hand, while he wasn't wearing one himself. It was the one time I was grateful I had parents who didn't give a damn, Dad normally lost in an alcoholic fugue, with Mom not far behind. They didn't seem to find anything odd in a biker ringing the doorbell.

I'd been nervous. Of going somewhere with a man I didn't know, and on transport I'd never been on. But Hell, well, from the start he was dominant, knew what he wanted. He swept me away, and before I could have second thoughts, I was climbing on behind him, obeying his instructions, putting my hands around his waist. It wasn't long before I knew I could become addicted to this, the most exciting thing I'd ever done. It was the feeling of freedom, seeing the scenery as if I was part of it, smelling the air. So much better than being trapped in a car.

Hell rode confidently, even then. Not for one moment did I have concerns about him losing control and crashing. His warm leather-clad body encircled in my arms, the power seemed to emanate from him, installing a confidence in me.

I'd felt alive. For the first time in my life. I felt me. As if in covering those miles took me on an internal journey. *I hadn't wanted it to end.*

After a while he pulled into a little-used picnic spot. When he took my hand and led me away from the bike, I suddenly became nervous. I'd been on dates with boys, of course I had. But Hell wasn't a boy, he was all man. He might want to go further than I'd been before.

Jeannie wasn't a virgin, but unlike her, I'd never seen my virginity as a burden or something I felt in a rush to lose. It was partly down to the casualness of her relationships with the opposite sex, that had made me vow, I wanted my first time to mean something. And I didn't want it to be over a picnic bench with a virtual stranger.

Out of sight of the road, Hell stopped, pulled me around to face him. As I looked up, I saw his eyes flaring, and when he pulled me against his body as he lowered his lips to mine, I felt a hardness against me.

I'd jumped back.

"Carter. I…"

He turns away sharply. I've made him angry, I know I have. But when he swings back, he's wearing a lopsided grin. He takes a step toward me, I stand my ground as he shakes his head. "Moira, I'm sorry," he says sheepishly. "But you're to blame. Felt too fucking good with you on the back of my bike. Ain't gonna treat you like a whore, babe. You deserve better than that. We'll take this slow. Slow as you want. You'll let me know when you're ready."

"I'm sorry." I don't know why I'm apologising.

"Babe. You're young. You've not done this before, have you?"

Feeling more confident, I ask. "What gave it away?"

"Babe." He grows serious, his brow creased as though thinking. "Bitch feels a hard cock against her, if she wants it, she doesn't pull away."

"I'm sorry," I tell him again.

"Hey, don't fucking apologise. To anyone, okay? You choose me when you're ready? I'll be over the fucking moon. When it's time, you'll know."

Now it's me who closes the distance between us. Raising my hand, I place it against his cheek. He's made me confident, made me trust he won't be taking what I'm not offering. "You could kiss me."

"Fuckin' right I could," he chuckles. "And I will. Just ignore… him… if it seems he wants to play. I've got him under control, okay?"

I smirk, finding it funny he's talking about his dick as though it's a separate entity. Then I stop thinking about anything at all and just start feeling as he lowers his head and his mouth touches mine.

He might have said we weren't going to be having sex, but this kiss is almost criminal. His tongue probes, his teeth nip, my mouth opens. Every part of me starts to tingle as he explores and ravishes. That he knows what he's doing is certain. I'd heard Jeannie talking about boys who'd made her wet, but had never understood she'd meant it literally until my own panties feel sticky in my jeans. I'd be embarrassed were it not that I was fighting to prevent myself from rubbing against him.

He pulls back, I want more. Now it's me who goes on a hesitant attack, the growl in his throat tells me that's what he'd wanted.

Men like him should come with a warning.

When we finally part, my lips are swollen, my face burns. He pulls my head onto his shoulder, and gently cradles me with his huge hand. "Babe, love your taste, love the smell of you. If we don't do something else, gonna forget my promise to you. Let's walk."

It wouldn't have taken much for me to give in. At the time I was pleased that he hadn't pressured me. Later, well, that was another story. We'd walked, talked about everything and nothing. He'd told me some of his dreams, explained his father was the president of the club he was in, had started it along with some of his friends. Despite the familial relationship, Carter wasn't having anything handed to him on a plate, having to start at the bottom as a prospect. He'd had me laughing with some of the jobs he was asked to do, or at least those he could discuss. Other things he wouldn't talk about, but that was fine with me. I simply enjoyed listening to his deep, sexy voice.

When he asked me what I wanted from life, I came up with a long list that young girls often have. I wanted to travel. See other states. Other countries. No real idea how I'd be able to afford it, but not having had the best home life myself nor attending much to my education, I was thinking of perhaps at least quali-fying as a nanny, and getting a job with a rich family.

He listened as if my dreams were perfectly achievable, offering no judgement at all. It was one of the best afternoons of my life.

I went home with stars in my eyes and dreams filling my head of my handsome biker.

Chapter 4

JAYDEN

Thank you very much!" I round on my sister as she comes in with Slick. For now they're sharing the suite opposite mine. We used to live off the compound in a nice house, but now we're cramped in this small building. I've no idea of the reason why we moved, I wasn't included in the decision.

Like I hadn't been involved in them turning up tonight and spoiling the first date of my life.

"Why did you help me get dressed up and ready? You knew it was a sham all along." After I've thrown that at Ella, I turn to Slick, the man who's been like a father to me. It's times like these I wish he hadn't stepped into the role.

"Jayden," Slick starts, his hand smoothing over his bald head. "Wanted to make sure you were safe."

I feel like stomping my foot, but manage not to. "I was with Paladin! How could I be safer than that? If you're talking about my fucking virtue—which I haven't got by the way—Paladin wouldn't make one wrong move. He respects his patch too much to risk losing it. And me." I add the last as an afterthought. But it's true. I know Paladin would do everything by the book.

Ella's blanched at my comment about my lack of innocence. I almost want to apologise but I don't. I lived it, had the therapy to learn to cope with it. For the most part, I've managed to put it behind me, but El, well, she can't seem to lose the guilt that she'd been too wrapped up in herself at the time to do anything to prevent it. No matter how often I tell her I'd probably have done the same stupid things, even if she'd been around.

Yeah, I've put it behind me, as much as I can. The memories don't overpower me anymore, but I still can't quite shake them. The loss of control, the way my virginity was bought and stolen, as if I was no more than a piece of meat. I wasn't valued as a person, just a body to abuse. What actually happened, men putting their hands, their cocks, where I didn't want them, well, I've locked those memories in a box and have thrown away the key. It only opens occasionally in my nightmares. The only way to move forward is to try to forget what I'd gone through.

Paladin is safe. He'd never hurt me or force me to do something I didn't want to. I'm certain of that. When I eventually come of age, he'll give me the choice, let anything we might do be my decision. Which is why I'm so angry that Ella and Slick don't trust him. My judgement tells me he's a good man, my eyes do to. Since he brought me to the compound almost three years ago, I'm sure he's remained true to his word and as far as I know, has stayed faithful. I know Slick would delight in telling me if he hadn't. I can also tell he hasn't betrayed me by the way Slick has grown to admire him.

I'd never admit it to Ella, but I'm scared deep inside. Afraid that the box holds things that would stop me moving forward, becoming a real woman. The idea of having time to get to know Paladin, not just as a friend, but as a man, has been comforting. Dating with no expectations. I could do that. But it was ruined. Take things slowly? Hell, if tonight was anything to go by, any slower and we'd be moving backward.

"Jayden," Ella starts.

I'm still furious. I interrupt. "I'm sixteen, El. Nearly seventeen. Yet I'm not allowed to have any type of life. I'm kept captive on this fucking compound."

"Don't swear," she says automatically, tempting me to give her the finger. Keep me among bikers, well, I'm going to pick up some stuff. "Jay, you go to school…"

"Yeah," I huff. "Escorted there and back."

Slick clearly doesn't like the tone I'm using with Ella. Ella's looking upset, and it's making her old man annoyed. "Jayden," he starts, sharply. "Don't raise your voice with Ella. She's pregnant."

I snap my mouth closed to prevent the words escaping which would tell him we all know that. We're reminded every day. If he could wrap her in cotton wool, he would.

"We're just watching out for you, Jayden." Ella's soft voice sounds behind me.

I swing around. "Well you can stop. Think about the baby, not me. I'm not a young kid anymore."

To my surprise, Slick agrees. "No, you're not." He pinches the bridge of his nose between forefinger and thumb, and seems to have a silent conversation over my head with Ella. A suggestion, an answer. I sigh. Seems like I might be in for a lecture.

"Come sit down, Jayden." Ella indicates the bed, the fight now leaving me, I go and sit on it. She seats herself by my side while Slick paces the room.

"Jayden, sweetheart. We didn't explain why we moved back to the compound."

"You did," I contradict. "You said it was easier for Slick to be near his brothers. And that you wanted to be with the other old ladies. It was all for you." My temper hasn't abated as much as I thought. "You never think about me. What I wanted. The house wasn't a prison like this place is."

Slick moves so fast I rear back as suddenly he's to my front, leaning over, his arms straight, palms on the bed either side of me. "It wasn't for us, Jayden. Not for one minute. It was for *you*."

For me? "I didn't ask you to." I can't stop.

"Because we didn't tell you the fuckin' reason," Slick shouts. "If you knew, you'd have been beggin' us to bring you here."

I try to push him away. It's like he's an unmovable object and doesn't budge. "What the fuck do you mean?"

This time Ella doesn't admonish me for swearing. With one hand and a gentle nudge she gets Slick to straighten up and at last stop crowding me. Then she half turns, pulls her leg onto the bed, bending her knee. "Jayden," she starts gently. "There's no easy way to tell you this, but the club's had word the Herreras might be looking to take you again."

What? The wind now completely gone out of my sails, I bow my head, then shake it. In the back of my mind I can almost hear demons trying to escape the box. I swallow hard, fighting to keep those thoughts out of my head. The most terrifying thing that haunts me are wrapped up in the words Ella's just spoken. That I could be taken and abused all over again. It takes a moment before I can even attempt to speak. "Why?" I clear my throat and start again. "Why? Why would they want me? The men who took me are dead. You told me that." I look at Slick accusingly. *Has he been lying to me all this time?*

"They are." Slick takes a deep breath then lets it out on a sigh, his shoulders relaxing as he does so. He kneels at my feet, taking both my hands in his, then waits until I meet his eyes. "It's us, the Satan's Devils they want to punish for killing them. There's been a change of command, the old head of the family is gone, the new one? Well, we don't know a lot about him. Seems he wants vengeance, and the way he wants it is to take something precious from the club. To take back the one who got away."

"Me? But I can't be that important, surely?" My eyes silently beg for confirmation. When I don't get it, I start to feel sick.

"Jayden, I'm so sorry."

I turn to my sister. "Why didn't you tell me? I have a right to know."

"Sweetheart. We didn't want to worry you."

My teenage mood swiftly changes. Unable to cope with my fear, I swap it for anger once again. "I'm not worried. You wouldn't let them take me. It's that you lied to me and that's what I don't like." Yeah. That's what I got out of that. I should have been included. I don't feel a part of this family, just some baggage they have to carry around. An inconvenience they had to take on after my mom got shot of me just as soon as she could. She's living with a new man now, neither Ella nor I know who or care.

"Jayden…"

"No, Ella." I swing around. "Why don't you go back to the house? I'll be okay here on my own in the compound. You're here every day anyway. Wouldn't you be more comfortable back at home?" Maybe then I'd be able to spend more time with Paladin without their interference. Hmm. That sounds like a really good idea. He'll keep me safe. He wouldn't let anything hurt me. I try to persuade them. "I'll be fine. You can start decorating the nursery." I pause. Damn, I wanted to be part of that. I shake off my burst of remorse. "You'll be better off there than here."

Slick looks like he's veering between anger and compassion. In the end, it seems sympathy wins out. "Sweetheart. Wouldn't be anything wrong with that if we could guarantee you'd be safe on the compound."

What does he mean?

"Of course I'm safe," I scoff. "I'm part of the club. You've told me that. So all the Devils would protect me." Especially Paladin. No one would get through him. *Would they?* Again that box rattles.

Once more there's a loud sigh from Slick. Ella's shaking her head, but he narrows his eyes at her. "You heard the girl, El. If she's not armed with the facts, she can't make any choices. She's right, she's old enough to have some say in decisions concerning herself."

I frown, biting my lip to stop the words, 'I didn't mean it,' coming out of my mouth. I love living with Slick and Ella, don't really want them to go back to the house in Tucson and leave me alone here. I'm scared enough as it is.

"Okay." Ella looks like she's going to cry.

Slick's head dips up and down, then he draws up a chair and sits in front of us. "If the Herreras decide to launch an attack on the compound, Devils might not be able to hold them off. They outnumber us, sweetheart."

The implications sink in quickly. An attack on the compound? The men could be injured, or worse. The children. All the babies and toddlers I babysit and watch so often. They could be at risk. The men, the old ladies. While to me, my own safety is paramount, I couldn't live with being responsible for any of them getting hurt. There's only one solution. "If that's the case, it's best I go away. Away from Tucson."

To my surprise, while Ella lets out a sob, Slick nods. "That's the gist of it, sweetheart. Wish things were different, but it could be safer for you, and everyone else here."

Where would I go? My hands are trembling. *How far is far enough to be out of danger?*

"We could go somewhere with you," Ella suggests. "All of us, start over."

"We could," Slick agrees. "But there is another option on the table."

"One I don't like, Slick." Ella doesn't often glare at her man. She does now.

"Ella," Slick groans. He throws up his hands. "Don't you think she should make her own choice? Have the chance to say no for herself?"

For a moment they have a staring match, then Ella turns away. Slick seems to take it as permission as he resumes.

"Paladin is prepared to transfer to the Colorado chapter. Their prez, Hellfire, is happy for you to go with him."

I can feel the lines on my brow deepening. "Me go, with Paladin?" There's a little buzz of excitement inside me which I try to hide all visible signs of. "Why Colorado?"

"Why exactly," butts in Ella. "I'm sure Red would have them in Vegas."

Again Slick frowns at her. "Because Hellfire has brought up a family. Red, hasn't. Nor any of the other presidents. We all know what could happen if Jayden and Paladin go off together without a chaperone."

A chaperone? They're saying I couldn't be trusted? But I trust Paladin. *Don't I?* My eyes go to one then the other.

As my mouth opens wide, Ella purses her lips. "Then we all go. Together."

Slick places his hands over hers. "El, darlin'. I know you want to keep Jayden close by forever, but you've got to let her fly on her own sometime."

"But Colorado…" Ella protests.

"What's wrong with Colorado?" I butt in, thinking it must be something significant. *A warning? Something I need to know before I decide?*

"What's wrong with it," my sister answers, folding her arms and staring into the eyes of her husband, "is that the age of consent in that state is seventeen."

Again, my jaw drops. Various thoughts whirl around my head. Only a few more months and if I move states, Paladin and I could be together. But it's too soon. I'm not ready. I thought I'd have far longer. What if Paladin wants to bring the agenda forward? I thought I had time before I needed to open that box.

Slick stands up and pulls Ella with him. "Why don't you sleep on it, Jayden? Give it some thought. There are pros and cons. As El said, we could all make a fresh start somewhere different. Timing could be better, but hey, we can make it work. Talk to Paladin if you want."

"He knows?" Of course he does. One thing about bikers, they know how to keep their mouths closed. I don't have to see Slick's nod.

The door shuts behind them, and I'm left stunned. A lot's been laid on me tonight. I've gone from being a tantrum-throwing teenager to a woman who's been given the choice, an opportunity to be with her man. My head's reeling at all the possibilities. *What would the Colorado club be like? Would I like it there? Would Paladin and I live together? And if so, how could he wait?* How could I explain my nervousness to him? Everyone seems to expect we'll, *he'll* take advantage.

Going into my bathroom, I go through the normal motions of preparing for bed. Exiting, I leave the light on as I always do, unable to sleep in the dark. Tonight there's even more reason. I'm scared of just closing my eyes, worried the conversation I've just taken part in will result in a nightmare.

Instead of sleeping, I do some soul searching. Had I set my sights on Paladin simply because I decided he was what I wanted when I was fourteen? When I'd just come around from experiencing the worst that can happen to a young girl, had I focused on him because he was handsome and kind? How do I know that it's him who gets my blood rushing, in the way the women do in Ella's novels I sneak from time to time? I've never been allowed to get close to him. We haven't touched or kissed. Tonight's experience at the restaurant showed how overprotective not just Ella and Slick were, but all the brothers here. If it had been just for my safety, men could have been there but stayed discreet.

Paladin's been a good friend, but how can I, with what I lived through, allow that friendship to develop into anything further? With him, or with any man?

I need to know where his head's at. Find out his expectations. *Talk to Paladin tomorrow* I resolve.

CHAPTER 5

HELLFIRE

The decision for me to have a houseguest or two is mine and mine alone. But the suggestion of Paladin patching over needs a club vote.

As I reach the clubhouse, I walk in shaking sleet off my hat and jacket, and strip off my waterproof riding trousers in the foyer, putting them over my peg. I smile quickly to myself, wondering if the lad knows what he'll be giving up for this. Sure, it rains in Tucson, but it's always a lot warmer.

"Hey, Prez. Getting nasty out there."

"Bomber." I slap my hand on his back. "Yeah, reckon it will start freezing soon." Apart from myself, Bomber's one of the other two remaining members from the original club. He's older than me, and sometimes you can hear his bones creaking, though he swears it's the weather and nothing to do with his age. We all turn a blind eye to the fact he drives a truck in the winter months rather than riding his bike.

"Jeannie was wonderin' how Moira is. Been some time since she's visited the clubhouse, Hell."

It has. His comment makes my brow furrow as I try to remember when she was last here. Moira used to be a fixture in the club, over the past year, she's hardly visited at all. "Moira's…" Fine, I was going to tell him. But he's married to her best friend. "Fuck it, I don't know Bomber. She says the right things, but she's breaking inside and I don't know what to do to help her."

"Brother, have you talked to her?"

Sure, we talk all the time. *Don't we?* "I think it's just we're all growing older, things changing. *Bodies changing.* That shit can hit hard."

"Sure can." Bomber's nodding. "Just asked, 'cos Jeannie wants to know if there's anything she can do."

"You know Moira, Brother. Deals with shit by herself." She'd cut Jeannie out when *it* had happened, as though it had all been her fault—which it had in a way. Took years to get back to being friendly with her. Girls seem good enough friends nowadays, but don't live in each other's pockets.

He gives me a hard look. "Well, if it would help, we could all go out together. Not here, somewhere neutral. Give the girls a chance to catch up."

I nod slowly, thinking. A night out might give Moira something to look forward to. "Might take you up on that, Brother."

Side by side we enter the clubroom. Jeannie waves from her space at the bar, she's laughing at something Sparky, our road captain has just said. Bomber makes a beeline for her, making her laugh harder as he bends her over his arm and kisses her. I hide my grin when his hands discreetly go to the middle of his back as he straightens up. *Getting older, Brother. Sucks doesn't it?*

"Prez? A word?"

"Sure, VP." Demon, *my son*, comes over. "What's up?"

As he starts an explanation of an incident at our tattoo parlour the previous night, I listen, my first impulse is to laugh, but then I realise it could be serious. "Shit," I say when he's finished. "Didn't they notice he was drunk off his ass?"

"Didn't appear that way."

"He's going to sue?"

"He's going to try. Lizard's offered to ink it over for free."

I shake my head, "Didn't the fact he wanted a naked pussy tatted over his heart give away he wasn't all there? Fuck. Labia and all?"

"It was done delicately," Demon stands up for the tattooist. "The outside was a flower. Some of his best work he says."

"Jeez." I'm just hoping we don't get bad publicity. Mind you, if the tat was done well, might start a new trend. "Thanks for the heads up, VP."

"Sure." I watch him step away. I'm proud as fuck of him. Like me, he had no helping hand or favours. Was voted in as he was popular with the men, and they all trust him. Deserves to be at my right hand. I'm pleased I had the honour of watching him grow from a baby into a man. Time comes I ever step down, there's no doubt he'll be taking my place at the head of the table. Also, no doubt, that since he's well aware of the shit I deal with daily, I know he's in no hurry to get there.

Putting my fingers to my mouth I blow a loud whistle, then point my hand toward the back of the room, and the doorway leading to church. One by one my brothers follow me in.

Thunder, our sergeant-at-arms takes his seat to my right, Mace, who's been the enforcer since Ingot was killed six months ago, sits next to him. Opposite is Buzzard, our secretary-come-treasurer. Sparky is next, then Rusty, the other old-timer with predictable red hair which hasn't started to grey at all. Beside him is Ink, inaptly named as he's got no tattoos anywhere on his body, not even the Satan's Devils' patch. On the other side of the table sits Lizard, Cad, Taser, Pyro and last, at the end, Bomber.

I bang the gavel. "Over to you, Buzz."

Buzzard quickly runs through the state of our businesses. The tattoo parlour, the strip club, the bowling alley we've not long opened, and, of course, our auto-shop. Got a good rep for building custom bikes there. I listen carefully, all seems well and good.

Pyro raises his hand. "Prez, got more discrepancies with the stock take."

This isn't the first time he's mentioned it. "Thought you'd decided it was someone taking out a part and not recording it."

A quick smirk covers his face. "Well, mechanics are good at the shit they do, not so much on keeping paperwork up to date." He nods, considering. "Still prefer that explanation, rather than thinking there's someone with light-fingers."

"Much going missing?" asks Buzzard, concerned. "High or low value?"

"Low," Pyro confirms. "And it's not regular, just occasionally."

Buzzard raises his chin at me. "I've not seen anything in the books to worry me. Yeah, so sometimes it doesn't tally, but not by much."

My brow creases, then I make a decision. "Keep an eye on it, Pyro. I hope it's just someone making a genuine mistake." I don't add that if it isn't, stealing from the club, even if it's just the odd oil filter, would be taken very seriously. I wait for Pyro to acknowledge the undercurrent in my words, when he gives a sharp nod, I know he'll be on it. "Okay, other business."

Cad waggles his fingers in my direction. He's so light skinned and his hair so fair, if it wasn't for his dark brown eyes you might think he was albino. Brothers gave him his handle, Cadaver. His complexion is his own fault, he spends most of his time inside all but hooked up to his computers.

When I nod, he speaks. "Got a new police chief coming in. I'm working on getting some background."

It's information, not a question, I just nod. "Anyone got anything else?" When no one speaks, I prepare to raise the topic I need to. Reaching into my pocket I take out my smokes and light one up, pulling one of the ashtrays toward me. Then I begin to explain about Jayden and Paladin. They listen carefully, then start asking questions about the new member I'm proposing to bring on board.

Thunder is suspicious. "Any bad blood in Tucson?"

Valid question. "None at all. Brother's about as trustworthy as they come," I explain.

"He's young." Demon puts in.

"Yeah, patched in when he was nineteen. Held his patch just over two years."

"Permanent move?" questions Thunder.

I shrug. "Depends if they can sort out their problems in Tucson." There's a round of laughter at this. I've lost count of the times we've had to help the Arizona club out.

"Need a vote, Brothers. Or has anyone got anything more they want to ask?"

"Not a question, but this is my view if anyone's interested." All eyes go to Mace, a few chin lifts too. "We've never had someone patch over before. Tucson had their own problems when they let that fucker from San Diego in."

I nod, he's right to bring that up. Though we're not in the same chapter, we're all well aware that man turned out to be a rapist. "They've been more cautious since. Haven't had issues with anyone else."

Bomber raises his hand. He's not a man to speak much, but when he does, we all listen. Experience counts for a lot. "People prospect for a reason. To earn trust. You're saying we rely on our Tucson brothers having sussed out this Paladin for us?"

"Talking about the mother chapter, Brother. Got no reason not to trust Drummer." I can understand their reluctance. Club here is close knit. Hard for even prospects to patch in. Only recently we turned away Smithy who'd prospected nearly a year, but we'd decided he hadn't made the grade.

"You happy with this, Prez?" Demon asks, knowing my word will count for a lot.

I take a moment, draw on my second cigarette of the meeting, and let smoke out, giving time for a considered answer. "I am," I say firmly.

"Well let's vote," the VP suggests. "Unless anyone else wants to say something?"

They don't. We vote. A few reluctantly, but all say aye in the end. Paladin can transfer as a full member.

Sparky suddenly remembers he wanted to bring something up. A run he's organising in a couple of months when the weather grows warmer. We spend a few minutes thrashing around the details. Then, sensing brothers are getting restless, I bang the gavel for the millionth time in my life, and church breaks up.

"Having a beer or headin' home, old man?"

I throw a punch at Demon, well-practiced, he jumps back and evades it. "Less of the fuckin' old, *son*." I warn him. "Could still take you down with a hand tied behind my back."

"That I'd pay good money to see," Mace cuts in.

"Beer," I belatedly answer Demon's question, and pointedly ignore the enforcer, not wanting to acknowledge his point that nowadays, it's questionable who'd win out of me and the VP. "I'm staying here tonight. Roads are icing up out there."

"Prez. Want some company?" Bella, one of the club girls, has overheard me. Her arm snakes around my waist. "Maybe later," I tell her, watching her pert ass sway as she walks away at my answer.

"Really?" Demon raises his eyebrow.

I shrug, not deigning to answer. Nor reminding him what goes on in the club, stays in the club. Nothing a son should tell his mother. The tightening of his face conveys his opinion.

I rap on the bar top. Runt, our newest prospect comes running over, quickly fulfilling my request for a drink. I'll only have a couple, even if I'm not riding tonight. Being president I'm always on call, and need to stay relatively sober.

"Prez."

Swinging around I greet my brother. "Pyro. How's it going?"

He grimaces slightly. "Yeah, well, I might have picked up a ticket."

"Might have, or have?" My eyes roll. Seems it should be pretty clear-cut one way or the other to me.

His mouth curves, "Have."

"You get caught carryin' or something?"

"Nah, only had just under an ounce on me." He's over twenty-one, he can legally carry an ounce of marijuana in Colorado.

"So what's the problem?"

A shrug, "Left me a bit short, that's all. Can I get an advance on my wages?"

I jerk my head toward the treasurer standing in a group across the other side of the room. "Ask Buzzard." Why the fuck he came to me is beyond me.

It's always the same when I stay in the clubhouse. One by one brothers approach, all wanting to share their problems. Lizard's got a bitch problem, Ink's bike's got a weird noise, and Rusty, well, the winter's making his arthritis act up. Yeah, they all look to me as some kind of god who can solve all their problems. It starts to grate that there's no one here who wants to know mine.

Another slowly drunk beer, and I feel I've given about as much of myself as I can. "Runt. Get a bottle of whisky up to my room." I'll only drink one or two, but feel I deserve a nightcap.

"Shall I send Bella up?" Demon asks through gritted teeth.

Slapping his back, I take pity on him. Leaning into him, I speak quietly into his ear. "How many times have I cheated on your mom, Son?"

His eyes narrow. "Not seen you with anyone, Dad. But Mom thinks…"

"I know what your mom believes," I reply with a sigh. "Gonna have words with her soon."

"Don't like seeing her upset."

Demon, despite his name, has always been a good son. I'm glad to know he sticks up for his mother, but in this case, there's a good reason he's got no need to worry at all. He couldn't be barking up a more different tree. I just haven't yet decided how to explain it to my wife, and she's the one who needs to know first. It's no one else's business.

Runt's left the bar. A good prospect, there'll already be a bottle of my favourite spirit waiting for me. One more nod toward Demon, and I'm making my way across the room to the stairs, my progress happily unimpeded.

I half-smile as I watch Bella giving Mace an enthusiastic blow job on the couch. Guess she hadn't been waiting for a summons from me after all. Then, none of the club girls would expect anything different. For thirty-six years I've remained faithful to my wife.

I climb the steps and make my way to the President's Suite. It's not the same one my father used, and doubles as my bedroom and office. *My father.* There's not been a word invented to describe just how much of a bastard he was, I reflect, stripping out of my clothes. I take the bottle and glass over to my bedside table then pull back the covers, pouring myself a shot before getting into bed, and leaning back against the pillows, my arms folded behind my head.

I've never cheated on Moira. I never would. There's a good reason that when I became president, I had all the shit in my father's room burned, the room turned into storage. The memories can still make me seethe with anger, a rage that will never be quenched. *It should never have happened.*

I hadn't waited long to call Moira after I'd first met her that day when she'd been with Jeannie. Our first date, a ride where I had no problem having her up behind me on my bike. I already knew she was special and was going to mean something to me. I also quickly realised she was no club girl, and I needed to take things slow.

So I'd dated Moira. Courted her. Yeah, me, a burly biker. From the moment she first rode with her arms held fast around my waist, she was going to be mine. She'd have to wait, I was only a prospect. Prospects weren't allowed near club girls, or permitted to take an old lady. Instead they had to make do with their hand until they were patched in. With my father being President, all eyes were on me to slip up. I needed the members to be certain my sole focus was gaining my patch and becoming a full member of the club.

I wouldn't have started anything with Moira had I not known I was close, I knew it, sensed it. Even though Blackie, my father, had ensured I was given a rough ride, I'd come through every piece of shit tossed at me with flying colours.

Soon I would be patched in, and then I'd bring Moira to the club as my old lady, and everyone would know she was mine.

She was a virgin, I wanted her first time to be special, was willing to wait, even though my cock tried to persuade me differently every time I saw her. I was proud of the way I held back, but she was unlike anyone I'd ever met. That look of innocence and wonder in her eyes? Never wanted that to go out. Never wanted her to feel anything other than the only person in the world to me. She was precious. Priceless.

CHAPTER 6
HELLFIRE

Thirty-six years ago

Bartending. Not my favourite pastime, but one I stoically undertake, ignoring the full-patched members partying around me. The air thick with the smoke of illegal substances, men partying hard in all different ways. Sweet butts casting snide glances toward the hopeful hangarounds flooding in from nearby Pueblo, some already being fucked in the open, some being taken into brothers' rooms. Drinks are flowing freely, I'm rushed off my feet to supply them. A couple of brothers who've started early are already swaying on their feet. But I won't be cutting them off, not in the bar of an MC. In the morning I'll just clean up the mess, clear away anything broken, mop up any vomit or blood that's been spilt. It's all in a day's work for a prospect. I'm just hoping my time of being at everyone's beck and call is drawing to a close.

I'm pouring shots when my eyes are caught by two girls entering the clubhouse. Surprised, and more than a little concerned, when I recognise Moira, Jeannie, her friend, leading her by the hand, well, almost dragging her. As soon as I saw the other girl, I knew this hadn't been Moira's idea. I didn't need that look of apology when she caught my eye to explain it to me.

Jeannie pulls Moira toward the bar. "Hey, lover boy. The mountain wouldn't come to Mohammed, so I brought her to you instead."

Putting down the cloth I was holding, I lean over. "Not a good place for you to be, darlin'." I ignore Jeannie as I talk to my girl. Her friend doesn't care, her eyes are scanning the room. I recognise that look, see it on most of the hangarounds who come to our parties. All looking for a ride on biker cock and hoping to snag a man.

Moira, though, she's different. Her wide eyes are only on me. She looks like a startled doe, she knows I didn't want her here. At least she's dressed in a fairly conservative style, okay, her white jeans are figure hugging, but the baggy top keeps her other assets from being on display. Jeannie, on the other hand, is dressed to kill, her short skirt and tight, low necked top leaving little to the imagination.

"I'll go."

"Best if you do." I want Moira out of here and fast. "Look, I'll call you later. We'll do something tomorrow if I can get some time."

"For heaven's sake, Mo. Let your hair down for once. Look, there's dancing. I'm in the mood to party, you can't leave me alone."

For fuck's sake, Jeannie. Let her go. I start leaning forward to suggest that in no uncertain terms, when we're interrupted.

"Hey, what's your name, darlin'?"

I tense as Bomber comes over, but he's got eyes on Jeannie, and not on my girl. Thank fuck.

"Prospect! Why's this lady not got a drink yet?"

Because she's underage, I want to tell him. But it's not my place. The MC doesn't give a fuck about citizen shit like that. With his sharp eyes on me, I pour a tequila for her at her request, and pass Moira a soda. Bomber reaches over to pick up the shot, his arm brushing against Moira's friend's breast as he passes it to her. Not receiving any discouragement, his arm loops around her shoulders.

"You here for some fun…?"

"Jeannie," she supplies, her eyes widening as she takes in his ripped chest, his low-slung jeans, his short tee forming a gap where the skin of his lower stomach shows. If I'm not mistaken, he's already sporting a large bulge in his jeans. Of course, my eyes don't linger there for long.

"I'm Bomber, darlin'. First time here I take it. I'll look after you."

Bomber's okay. He's already told me I'll get his vote when my patch comes up at church. I beckon him to come closer. "Bomb, this here's my girl." I point to Moira. "She shouldn't have come to the club. I'm going to escort her out. Can you watch the bar for me?"

His eyes narrow as he looks from Moira to myself. "Hangarounds are fair game. She's yours? Prospects ain't got no rights, son. Best take her out. I'll stay here while you're gone if you make it quick." He pulls Jeannie closer to him. "This one and I have got business to attend to, isn't that right, sweetheart?"

Jeannie's beaming. She's obviously got no more use for her friend now she's used her to get into the clubhouse, bagging herself a handsome biker in the process.

I start to raise the flap of the bar when a voice roars. "Where you off to, Prospect. I need a drink." It's Blackie, my father. His name coming from the black plate he worked with before the steel mills closed.

Sighing, I signal Moira to wait. As I get back into position, she hops on a bar stool. "What do you want, Prez?"

He hadn't missed the look I'd given Moira. His mouth curves. "I think I want me a bit of that," he says as he steps closer to my woman. "Up for some fun tonight, sweetheart?"

Moira's gone white as she struggles to find her voice. "Er, no. I'm with him."

Later I'd come to think that was the moment that sealed her fate. Especially when I confirmed it. Pulling my back straight, I reinforce her words. "She's my woman, Prez. Soon as I get patched in, I'm going to claim her."

"Well, you're not patched in yet, are you, boy?" His grin broadens as he turns back to Moira. "My son's busy for now." My eyes widen as he claims the relationship he usually prefers to forget, but as his head tilts indicating the queue of men forming, I can't deny he's not right. Then he continues, "I'll let him take a break soon, but in the meantime, why don't you and I get acquainted, particularly if we're going to become family."

She looks at me. I shrug. He's acting out of character, but I'm in no position to argue. All I can do is take it at face value, and hope all he's up to is questioning her to discover whether she'll be a good fit for the club. For me, as the president's son.

He doesn't really give her a choice. His firm grip on her arm all but pulls her off the stool.

I have an uneasy feeling as she goes off with him, but while I don't particularly like my father, I'm certain he wouldn't hurt her. I told him she's mine. As my president, and according to club rules, he's right not to accept it. As my father, he should.

It seems everyone's glass is empty. I lose sight of her as I'm run ragged trying to satisfy all their requests. When at last the pace slows, my eyes search the room, I'm unable to see her. But I'm the sole bartender tonight, I can't leave my post, can't go looking for her. Jeannie, I do see, sitting on Bomber's lap, her skirt up around her waist, and though the material hides what they're doing, their mutual groans suggest she's getting what she wanted. A good fucking from a biker.

But where's Moira? Half an hour? An hour? How long has she been gone? I've got an uneasy feeling, so strong it makes me think to fuck with this. It might mean I lose the patch I've worked so hard for, but I'm leaving this bar. Right now. My gut churns with urgency to find her as I slide out from behind the wooden planks which make up the bar top.

Fuck! *There she is.* Christ! She's stumbling down the stairs, moving awkwardly, hanging on to the railing. Completely dishevelled. She's crying.

I head over in her direction fast, roughly pushing brothers aside to get to her. "What the fuck?" I scream as I reach her.

Her eyes meet mine, she flinches, then she quickly looks away. No one stops her as she heads for the door. As she passes me, I can see her white jeans reddened with blood around the crotch.

"Nooooo!" I roar, as everything drops into place. "Moira! Moira!"

My screaming has caused the room to go silent. Even the music's stopped. Jeannie's jumped off Bomber's lap, and is moving toward her friend, her hands straightening her skirt, her own pleasure forgotten in Moira's obvious anguish.

"Moira." I reach her, grabbing her arm.

"Leave me alone!" she screeches, shaking my hand off. "Don't touch me!"

"I'm taking her home," Jeannie snaps at me.

"I'm coming with you."

"No. NO!" Moira is struggling to make her way out. "I never want to see you again."

I try to go after her, Furnace, our VP is holding me back, his face is grim. "Let her go, Prospect."

I shrug out of my cut, disrespectfully throwing it down on the floor. "I'm no prospect for this fuckin' club!" How can I get my head around the only obvious conclusion, that my own father has raped my woman? The girl who was mine. The girl saving herself for me. How can I start to deal with something like that? There's no doubt in my mind, that's what has happened.

If I wasn't in the club, she'd be mine already. He took her. Because I was going to make her my old lady.

If I can't go after her, there's only one thing that can be done. "I'm going to fuckin' kill him!"

My hand goes to my waistband, and I take out my gun, heading toward the stairs that my father is just descending, a satisfied grin on his face as he finishes buckling his belt.

He sneers at me, before shouting, "Why's the fuckin' party stopped? Put the music back on. Prospect, get back to your place behind the fuckin' bar."

I raise my gun and step forward.

His eyes go wide, then he laughs. "You haven't got the fuckin' guts. Couldn't even keep hold of your woman. Hadn't even fucked her, you pussy. Now you'll have to measure up to what I've got. Doubt you can do that. You'll always be wondering, won't you?"

I chamber a round, the sound echoing in the still quiet room. Before I can fire, Furnace's hand covers mine. "Not this way, Son. We do this proper."

"VP?" Blackie snaps.

"You've gone too far this time." Furnace is shaking his head. "Party's over, Brothers. Women out of here. Church. Now."

"You can't call church." Blackie tries to bluster, his back straightening and his face looking like thunder. "You're not the prez."

Furnace stares at him, then says loudly. "Raping a girl? Taking a claimed woman from a brother? You don't deserve your place at the head of the table. Anyone here got a problem with that?"

Apparently nobody has. The murmuring is full of cries of derision for what Blackie has done. No voices of support. Men have enough sex to take when it's offered, seems they're not happy with someone being forced.

Blackie gets pushed into church, he continues protesting. I hang back, my hands quivering with anger, deciding I'll shoot him on the way out.

Furnace beckons me. "What you doing standing here?"

"Fuckin' prospects don't attend church," I remind him.

"Put your cut back on, Brother. And come with me."

I do, unsure what Furnace is up to. Or why he called me Brother. Wanting only two things, to see my father take his last breath, and to go find Moira. Talk to her, comfort her. Fuck! He's taken her from me, and I'm not sure I'll be able to get her back. My own father fucking raped her. Would she ever want to even talk to me again?

I go into the normally forbidden territory, sitting in a chair Furnace brought in and placed at the end of the table. It puts me opposite my father who's gone to his normal seat. The fucker's still grinning, doesn't seem worried at all.

In fact, he starts the meeting off. "I want to know why a prospect is sitting at the table. Boy's got no right to be here."

Furnace isn't the slightest bit cowed. "He's been here long enough. Proved himself. I vote him in."

Before Blackie can protest further, the votes gone around the table. Everyone but my father says 'aye'. All throw looks of support toward me, sympathy too. Looks of disgust go in the opposite direction.

"Brotherhood," Furnace starts, "is what we're all about, Brothers. And brotherhood means looking out for everyone else, having each other's backs. It doesn't include the right to a man's woman, whether prospect or patched member. Anyone disagree?"

"Too right, VP." Comes from all directions.

"Fucking right. Can't take another's woman." This powerful endorsement from Rusty.

"She wasn't fucking willing. Anyone could see that." Bomber sends me a look of apology, as if he's wishing he could have done more. The problem is, even knowing my father could be a bastard, none of us thought him capable of that. Even I hadn't realised how much he must hate me.

"Prospects can't claim women." Blackie protests.

"Whether or not, you raped her. Disrespected her. Disrespected your son. You can do that to your flesh and blood? Makes me wonder how the fuck any of us can trust you."

"Got it in one, VP." Bomber says it first, but others are quick to agree.

"I vote Blackie out." Rusty says it plainly. "Ain't no place for a man like him in this club."

Blackie starts blustering, Furnace shuts him up. "Nothing you can say, Brother. You can't vote on this."

The vote goes quickly around the table. Only seconds later it seems, Blackie's out. As two members force him from his chair, and stand with him held tight between them, Furnace eyes his now empty seat. "Want to take a vote on a new prez now? Or give it some thought?" the VP asks.

"I vote Furnace." Bomber hardly waits until the VP's words are out of his mouth.

"Seconded." Someone shouts quickly.

A full vote's taken. Furnace looks like he's just been passed a burden, but he's quick to rise to the challenge. "First off, Carter's now a full member. I'd say welcome to the table, Brother, but now's not the right time. We'll decide your handle later."

I'm a member. Which gives me rights. No longer a prospect. I stare at my father. "I want him dead."

"Dispatched to Satan? Well, Brothers. Our new patch has put that on the table. Anyone disagree?"

"He's a loose cannon if we let him live. Out bad's too good for him." Bomber's support surprises me. "Man thinks he can take what isn't his."

Another vote. This time I say 'aye' too, but all the time I'm watching my father's face, seeing it go through a range of emotions as it dawns on him this is his last night on earth, finally settling on hatred directed toward me.

Furnace bangs the gavel loudly after pronouncing the death sentence. Then he catches my eye. "You were the brother wronged, Carter. You get a say in how he's dispatched."

It's only then I realise how long I've hated him. I'd tried to be dutiful, done what was expected, followed him into his newly formed club at the time as a result of his plea to make up the numbers. It's as if he'd been jealous of me all my short adult life. I was better looking, younger, faster, stronger. Everything he tried to belittle and put down.

The words come out before I've really had a chance to compose them. "We all know where he'll end up. I want to cut his cock off so he won't be able to rape anyone, even in hell." My voice gets louder, stronger, as my father seems to diminish in front of my eyes. *I could never, ever, forgive him for this. If he lived, every breath he took would remind me.* "I want him to know what it's like to burn before the fires of hell reach him. Burn his tat off. Do what you like to him after that, but let me take the final shot which kills him."

"Rain hellfire down on him?" Furnace's mouth quirks. "Reckon we might have found your road name. Hellfire."

It was messy. It wasn't quick. Blackie was begging for death long before I fired that bullet toward him. But no amount of suffering could make up for what he'd done to me. More importantly, what he'd taken from Moira.

Would I ever have another chance with her?

CHAPTER 7
MOIRA

Present day

It's one of those evenings when it's impossible to settle. Each time I get comfortable my body starts burning, sweat pouring off my brow. So I open the window, standing there for a moment, letting the freezing cold air cool me. Back on the couch, within minutes I'm too cold, so I'm getting up to close the window again. *Fuck I hate this. My thermostat's broken.* Jeez. What a state to be in. It's not long before I'm back to wiping my dripping face. *No wonder Hell can't stand to be near me.*

What's he doing now?

My mind tortures me with images of his still lean ass pounding in to a willing sweet butt. Any of them would go with him without giving a thought to me, his wife. One reason I no longer go to the compound. They'd let me know if they'd scored one over on me, a snide comment here, a knowing look there. I wouldn't be able to bear it.

Thirty-six years we've been married. Lots to show for it. Not least my gorgeous kids. I stare at the photographs on the mantel-piece. There's Demon, looking fine in his cut and leaning against his Harley. That was taken on a ride last year. The last time I remember being on Hellfire's bike.

Then there's Kennedy, my beautiful daughter. She got married a few months back, and I'm hoping there'll be grand-children in my near future. I admit to having breathed a sigh of relief when she finally settled down with a good man. Accountants don't need to be boring, and at least, she has nothing to do with the club. I didn't want that for my daughter.

Then there's Samuel. My, but he was an afterthought. Didn't think we were going to be lucky with another. There's eight years between him and Kennedy, but it saved me having empty-nest syndrome too early. He's at college, brains of the family went to him. He's studying law—Hellfire suggested he concentrate on the criminal side. My lips curve as I recall the conversation. Samuel's a good boy nowadays. Still relies a lot on his mom. Still getting us to bail him out when his student allowance doesn't stretch to feeding him. He'll learn. In time.

Does it upset me that the menopause signals no more babies for me? Nah, not at all. I've done my part to repopulate the world. And got three great kids to show for it.

I just hope Hellfire also appreciates how much he's got, and doesn't throw it away. If I know for certain he's been unfaithful, I'll file for divorce. Couldn't live with this uneasy feeling inside of me. I'm not that woman who would turn a blind eye. There'd be ugly fights, uglier tears. Trying to work on a marriage that's failed wouldn't be worth it. *That's why I don't want to know for sure. Want to hang on to these last few days, weeks, months when I'm in ignorance.* The day he admits it, well, he's not coming back.

How did it come to this?

We'd overcome the worst beginning a marriage could ever have. I'd always thought our relationship was unshakeable, that having survived what we had, nothing could come between us. We were it. For life.

His father had raped me. Had tricked me into his room under the pretext of showing me some old photographs. Said since we were going to be family, I ought to see them. He was the president of the club; how could I refuse? It's only when he shut and locked the door behind me, I realised his intentions were something else entirely.

It might have been thirty-six years ago, but the memories still come back to haunt me, especially times like this when I'm feeling low. I'd turned and looked at him, seeing something positively evil in his eyes, summoning up the only defence I thought I had.

"I'm with Carter," I say, firmly.

"You're a bitch. You don't care whose cock you ride. Came here with the hangarounds tonight, knew what you were asking for."

My heart's beating fast. How do I get out of this? "I'm with Carter." I repeat, wondering why I allowed Jeannie to persuade me to accompany her tonight. I knew it was wrong. Carter had told me it was best I didn't come to the club. Not until he patched in. "I'm sorry," I try to tell him. "I shouldn't have come here. I'll just leave."

It's as if I hadn't spoken. "Prospects can't claim women. Asshole's been lying if he told you other than that." He walks closer, near enough I can smell his perspiration. My nose wrinkles, it's unpleasant. "And why would you want a boy, when you can have a man? The president at that. Doesn't get much better, sweetheart. Now why don't you show me what you've got. Strip."

I refuse. He won't listen. I say no. He ignores it. I scream, the music from downstairs drowns my cries out. I fight him, of course I do. But he's so much stronger, he easily overpowers me, laughing as he does and when each of my weak kicks misses its mark. Then he roughly takes what I'd preserved for so long, what I wanted to give to Carter.

I'd refused to see Carter. Hadn't wanted anything to do with him ever again. My thoughts of him tainted by his father. My greatest fear was coming face to face with Blackie, him perhaps even wanting more. There could be no future between Carter and I. Family dinners? I couldn't even imagine it. I was scared of Carter, was he like his father? Had I had a lucky escape? Would he have become fed up with waiting and forced me himself?

I was embarrassed too, not wanting my parents to know. I had gone to a notorious biker club, where girls only go for one thing. Biker cock. In their eyes, I would have been asking for it. In most people's eyes, I suspect.

Telling my folks only that I'd broken up with my boyfriend, they were sympathetic at least as far as to follow my instructions when answering the phone, telling him I wasn't home, or that I didn't want to speak to him. He came to the door, my father turned him away, and then shook his head at me. *I'd been dating a biker. What did I expect?*

One time I'd tortured myself, and had watched him ride away, noticing his cut no longer read Prospect, but instead had a full patch there. The patch he'd been after. Did he get that because he allowed his father to hurt me? Was that the price he had paid?

"You can't keep yourself hidden away, Mo. It's not healthy."

I'm not sure if I'm glad Jeannie's come to visit or not. That night she'd left her hook-up to come with me, taken me back to her place, looked after me. But the loss of my 'cherry', as she put it, didn't seem such an earth-shattering event to her, while I was completely devastated.

Worse, she seems to have found a boyfriend, the biker she went with that night. She's always at the clubhouse, and reporting back how much fun she's having, while I just wish I could erase its existence from the earth.

She hasn't seen Carter's father around, and there seems to be a new president, but she knows no more than that. When I ask her, she heard nothing to suggest his disappearance is related to me. Bikers live a mysterious life, I'm told. They never divulge their business, even to those they take as old ladies.

"I'm not feeling well, Jeannie. Leave me be."

"How, not well, Mo?" Where men are concerned she's shallow, but she's got a good heart underneath.

"I'm not sleeping. Every time I close my eyes…"

"Oh, hun." She puts her arm around my shoulders. "You've got to snap out of it. There was always going to be a first time, wasn't there? Now it's over, you've got to move on."

She doesn't understand. "I wanted my first time to be when, where and with a person I chose. Not with the father of the man I loved." I sniffle loudly, "I wanted it to be with Carter."

"Carter, or Hellfire as he's now known, keeps asking about you. He wants to know you're okay. You can still be with him if you want to."

"I was a virgin." I tell her again.

She tries to stifle her laugh, but fails. "Everyone knows that."

I shudder. When Blackie had dismissed me, I hurriedly got into my clothes, not realising I was bleeding, and had forgotten I was wearing white pants. Yeah, everyone who'd seen me that night would have been well aware. All those bikers. I bet they're still laughing now.

"Apart from not sleeping, how are you? You look pale, Mo," she observes.

That would probably be from not eating, and not going out. "I keep being sick, I think I'm coming down with something."

Her eyes sharpen. "And it's been, what, three weeks now?"

I nod.

Her lips purse, then she announces she's got to go, but she'll be back. True to her word, it's not long before she returns. With a pregnancy test. Wild-eyed I stare at it, and at her. It sounds crazy, but I never considered that might be the reason I'm feeling unwell. I just put it down to stress. Now she's put the idea in my *head, I'm terrified. Going completely cold, I realise I need to know. Picking it up with shaking hands, I take it into the bathroom. A few minutes later, having done what the instructions told me, I take it back out, setting it down on the dresser.*

When it's time, it's Jeannie who picks it up. The answer is written on her face. I'm going to have a lasting memory of that night.

Unless I do something about it.

"How much money have you got?" I ask her. "Can you lend me some?"

Her expression shows she's joined the dots together. "You want an abortion?"

I can't have the baby of a man who's raped me. Can't have that reminder in my life. Though it goes against everything I've ever thought. It's the only option, as long as I can get the money together.

"Blackie should pay," she tells me. "He caused this. I presume he didn't use a condom?"

He hadn't. He hadn't given me the chance to ask him. I was too busy saying no.

Her mouth narrows. "I'll help. Let me think how to do this. Don't worry, okay?"

Don't worry? Has she lost her mind? What else could I do?

Even now I rub my stomach, the memory of the horror of finding out I was carrying the baby of my rapist returning to me. I was seventeen. Too young to be a single mother, too immature, even had I had a man by my side. Too young to cope. Too young to be able to afford to do anything else. The only certainty was I'd be homeless if my parents found out. They were a dichotomy of alcoholics and religious nuts.

If I'd been sleepless before, it was worse that night. When Jeannie had called and asked me around to her house the following morning, I couldn't refuse to go, I was out of options.

She'd said she would help. All my teenage-self could do was hope she had answers on how I could get the money I needed.

What I hadn't expected was to find Carter, *Hellfire* now, waiting for me.

I spin on my heels, not wanting to speak to him. Now, even more, unable to face him.

"Moira. Wait." *He doesn't give me a chance, following me back down the path, his long legs covering more ground than my own. He catches me, his arms hold me tight, his familiar scent and warmth surrounding me.* "I know it all," *he says fast, as though he's only got moments to speak.* "I love you, Moira. What Blackie did? I've no words to tell you how I feel. But we've both got to work through it, deal with it. And that's best done together. I love you, Moira. I want you to be mine. Nothing's changed except for that barrier my fuckin' father put between us."*

He can't know everything. He'd run a mile if he did. There's no easy way to tell him. "I can't, not now. I'm pregnant, Carter. Pregnant. I want an abortion."

"I know." *His nose nuzzles my cheek.* "I know. And whatever happens, we're in this together. My fault you came to the club, I didn't warn you sufficiently, didn't explain. But I'm a patched member now, babe, the old rules don't apply. You're mine, everyone knows and respects that. Ain't gonna be anyone put a hand on you again."

I don't believe him. Don't want him, or his club. "Your father…"

He interrupts. "He's dead."

"Dead?" *I repeat incredulously, unable to believe it.*

He holds me at arm's length, one hand smoothing my face. "What he did to you? Couldn't be left walkin'."

"You killed him?"

"We all had a hand in it, babe. Not one of my brothers condoned what he'd done. Prospect or not, he'd laid hands on a brother's woman. Hands which weren't wanted."

It was a fucked up situation. There I was, unable to deny I wanted to be with the man who'd said he had already claimed me. A man whose father had raped me, stolen my virginity. A man who'd killed his father because of the actions he'd taken that night. On top of that, I had his brother incubating in my stomach. But somehow he wanted me, and he was going to have me, no obstacle too great to be put in his way. Hellfire proved he had a strength of character, a determination inside him that many other men didn't have.

Fifteen years later it hadn't surprised me that when Furnace came off his bike and was pronounced dead at the scene, that it was Hellfire who was voted in as the new president. Just like that morning when he'd solved my problems, he'd stepped up, showing his strength yet again. A force to be reckoned with, no problem too difficult to be solved.

My decision, he'd told me, about the baby. He'd stand by me either way, he'd deal with whatever road we would take. It might have been just a few cells at that moment, but being able to see a path ahead where I could keep it changed everything. I hadn't had to explain. When Hell had placed his hand on my stomach, I knew the choice, and commitment, had been made without the need for discussion.

We married without fuss a week after I found out I was expecting. Our son, who was to become Demon, born as far as anyone else knew, a month early. I'd moved into the clubhouse the day of our wedding, surprised at my welcome, but then, Hellfire had smoothed the way. Blackie, it seemed, had been wiped out of existence, his name never mentioned, or at least, not in my hearing. The room I'd been raped in, now taken over by Furnace. I'd never stepped foot in it again.

More unexpected, I became friends with the men, quickly they'd ceased to frighten me. They might be rough and tough bikers, but in many ways, were still boys underneath, playing tricks and pranks on each other. Furnace was a good prez, Hell-fire, when he'd got his chance to have his turn, even better.

Demon prospected when he turned eighteen with my blessing, like the man he knew as his father, quickly moving up through the ranks, only a few years passing before he became VP. Hellfire and Demon worked well together, were a strength to the club. Their views coinciding on most things, where they differed, each willing to listen to the other. I'd often wondered whether it was because they were brothers, not father and son.

Though that secret, Hellfire and I had agreed, we'd take with us to the grave.

CHAPTER 8
PALADIN

My gaze follows Jayden as she enters the Tucson club-house. She looks around, spots me, and starts heading over. I can tell by the serious expression on her face that she's got something to get off her mind. There's not much she can hide from me, I've spent the last two years and more watching her, learning about her. Falling ever deeper in love with her.

As she draws closer, I kick out a chair. A quick nod of thanks, and then she sits down, immediately leaning forward and putting her elbows on the table, clasping her hands in front of her. It would be hard not to notice her eyes look sunken as though she's had a sleepless night.

"What's up?" I ask.

She sighs, presses her lips together, then finally, speaks. "Seems I've got to grow up now. Can't be a kid any longer."

Music to my fucking ears. Yet how will I cope if she acts adult, and I'm still required to be hands off?

"What's happened, Doll?" Something has. That's for sure. "You get into it with Slick and Ella last night?" I'd felt like punching Slick myself. Date night, fuck my ass. I could see how angry she was when she'd left me.

"Slick and El were assholes."

She won't be getting any argument from me. Her way of putting it brings a fleeting smile to my face, but it soon slides away. "And?"

"They told me about the Herreras. About the renewed threat." She glances around, drawing my attention to where a pregnant Sam is playing with Eli, Drummer's toddler son. Sophie, with an even larger rounded stomach, is walking in holding the hand of Olivia who's tottering by her side. Her eyes catch those of Marcia who's sitting on the floor with her eight month old twins happily playing on their mats. Then her head turns slightly, taking in Joker and Lady talking with Darcy, Peg's expectant wife who's just come off her firefighting shift. Jayden looks back. "About how me being here is a danger to everyone else."

What? My face tightens. "I'm sure they didn't word it like that."

A shrug. "Maybe not. But that's what it comes down to, doesn't it?"

She's right. It is a grown-up way of looking at it. But I don't want her to feel she's got everyone's safety resting on her shoulders. She's nervous, constantly scanning the room as if expecting the Herreras are going to appear any moment. "Jay, we're not even sure they're going to act on their threat, or even if they actually meant it. We're just being prepared. Doll, there's nothing for you to worry about. Every man here would give their lives to keep you safe."

Her lips thin again. "But that's what I don't like. Of course I don't want the Herreras to take me, but I don't want anyone getting hurt trying to protect me." She glances at her clasped hands which are trembling, then up at me. "They mentioned Colorado."

"They mention why?" I ask, my jaw locked.

A quick look toward me. "Well they are worried if we go off together, they don't think we'll be able to keep our hands to ourselves." The way she says it doesn't sound like it's a particularly attractive option.

In a way, I can understand. Much as I'd like the chance to move our relationship on to the next step, the thought it could happen so much quicker than expected has got me off balance too. I sigh. "Even if we wanted to, Jay, probably won't be as easy as that. Hellfire and his old lady have been married forever. Got grown kids, one I think about my age. I don't reckon we'll have completely free rein. It wouldn't be like we'd be moving in together."

As her head tilts, I see a fleeting expression of relief. "We didn't get around to discussing details. What is the plan, then?"

Drummer had filled me in after his conversation with the Colorado prez. "I'll be patching over as a member and will bunk down in the clubhouse. You'll be staying with Hellfire and his old lady in their house off the compound."

"I'm not sure I like the sound of that." She's shaking her head. "Staying with strangers."

I nod, she wouldn't. Living with people we don't know will be hard for the both of us, particularly at the start. My hand starts to move, I force it to stop. I'd do anything to reach over the table and take hers, but we're not alone in the clubroom. Word will get back to Drummer and Slick, my innocent action could be misinterpreted. I can't wait to go somewhere where we can be ourselves. In Colorado, nothing can stop us physically demonstrating our affection for each other, once the next few months have passed, and Jayden's reached her seventeenth birthday.

As she bites her lip, worried, I rush to reassure her, "Promise you this, Jay. You don't get on with Hellfire's old lady? I'll find somewhere else for the both of us."

"Pal, I…"

"Doll, I'll do whatever you want to keep you happy. Always have. That's not going to change."

"I'm not ready to play happy families, Pal. El will want me to continue school."

"Jay, you're still young. I know that. Your education is important. I want you to continue it too. Get your diploma, then decide what you want out of life."

Once again she looks around at the room filled with old ladies and babies. Heart has just walked in, making a beeline for his wriggling twins, Grunt, the fucking overgrown mutt, bounding along behind. I see her hands twitching as though she's eager to go and help. *She'll make a great mom one day. Fucking loves kids.*

"I'll miss this." She seems to have forgotten about her education.

"So will I," I tell her truthfully. "Hard for me to move as it is for you. The men here? Well, they're all the family I've ever known."

Her look is older than her years, she pales a little as she offers bravely. "You don't have to come, Pal. Slick and Ella have offered to start somewhere new."

"I'm twenty-one, Jay. Young enough to make a fresh start. Only been with the club three years. Slick's been here forever. Be much harder asking him to move. And where would they go? None of the other chapters have had an influx of old ladies and kids like this one. Ella's best here with the support of the other women around her."

There's a moment of silence, her teeth worry her lip again, then, with visible reluctance, she agrees. "El doesn't need the stress of a move. Not before the baby's born."

There's something about her today that unsettles me. Part of me expected her to jump at the chance of us starting some place new together. She's worried. Not just about packing our bags and starting all over again in a new place. "Speak to me, Jay."

"It's just…" Her hands flutter, then she starts again. "You and me, Pal. What are you expecting? Here, we've not been allowed to be anything but friends. If we go to Colorado, can we just continue the same way? I don't think I'm ready for anything else."

I rear back. I had wondered, when it came down to it, she might not want me. But hearing her suggest she's uncertain about progressing our relationship, I realise I hadn't been prepared. It affects me like a knife twisting in my gut. *Perhaps she's scared of going as she thinks I'll be making assumptions?* I'm pleased when she stays quiet and gives me a moment to gather my thoughts.

Raising my chin toward her, I finally answer her question. "I'll be there for you, Jay, however you want me. As a friend? Sure, yeah, I can do that. Got a lot of practice there. Want us to start dating? Absolutely. I'd love that. But you're getting ahead of yourself if you're talking about becoming lovers." I pause, lean forward, and now do take hold of her hands, fuck what anyone might think. "We'll do this as any other couple. I told you I'd wait for you, and I have. Not even been tempted by anyone else. But…" As she takes a deep breath, I tighten my grip as a sign I don't want to be interrupted. "You owe me nothing, okay? If I've waited in vain, that's on me, not you. If you want to go out with other boys instead? Hell, it might hurt, but I'll understand. You need the time and space to make up your mind, I'll give it to you. Can't say I won't be upset if you don't choose me in the end, but I'll deal. Okay?"

Her brow furrows. "Don't you want me?"

That's what she heard? Rapidly I rerun the conversation in my head. Can't see where I said words to that effect. "Jay, I could be jailed for the thoughts I have about you, so get that out of your fuckin' little head, okay?"

I smirk, I can't help it. Her face has gone bright red. She looks adorable, and I just want to kiss her. *Maybe, when we get to Colorado, I can.*

Jayden tugged at every protective instinct I had from the moment I met her. When I'd first heard her story, I'd wanted to gather her up into my arms and never let anything hurt her again. I knew my desires toward her were wrong, she was fourteen, jailbait. While Drummer and Slick had warned me of the dire consequences should I act on my feelings toward her, they needn't have told me. I knew what I felt toward her was wrong. She needed time to heal, to go to therapy, to deal with what had happened to her. To grow, to mature. I'd been determined to wait for her. I knew even then my feelings toward her would never change. All these long months, years, that I've waited, I've watched out for her. Been her friend. It's up to her to indicate whether she wants me to be more.

Maybe in Colorado, we'll have a chance to find out.

It's easy to see she's shocked and overwhelmed with everything being dropped on her like this. I don't want to crowd her or pressure her. I stand, seeing the pool table is free. "Want to let me beat you?"

My suggestion we shelve this heavy conversation for now is greeted with a quick smile, a recognition I'm giving her space to consider everything I'd just laid on her.

"Beat me? In your dreams," she scoffs, as she too gets to her feet.

Our conversation ends up being put on the back burner. Not just for now, but for months. As the days and weeks pass with nothing more than oblique threats from the Herreras, nothing more is mentioned. The suggestion of us moving to Colorado seems to have been put aside indefinitely.

Mouse is here and there at the moment, we never seem to know when he's going to be around. He's got something going on. As concerned brothers, we wish he'd open up so we can help him. Can't fault the man, he still does his job for us. Part of that is keeping an ear out for chatter on the Herreras. If they are indeed coming for Jayden, there continues to be no suggestion of it in the info he's found.

The idea of me taking Jayden away to keep her safe loses the urgency it had. As the days go by, it appears we'd been passed an empty threat. Satisfying myself that the clock is ticking on, if I have to stay in Tucson and wait until she's eighteen, well, that's what I'll do. I'll wait forever if necessary.

Jayden's the one girl I want. As soon as I'd been patched in, the sweet butts started cosying up to me, but eventually gave me up as a lost cause. I wasn't going to betray her. Even the hangarounds that come to our parties hold no interest for me. My fear in the dead of the night is that in the end, she might not want me. But even that thought doesn't make me break the promise I'd made to her that night so long ago.

Life's never boring here in Tucson. Joker and Lady get married, then Joker's brother dies, and Joker becomes the guardian of a baby girl. Another kid on the compound for Jayden to fawn over. It tugs at something inside me when I watch her competently handling every baby and child, knowing that one day I'd like that to be my baby she's looking after.

Sam and Sophie grow big and rounded as they incubate both of their second children. Then, fuck me, Mouse at last opens up and lets us in on his problems, starting when he returns from one of his sojourns off the compound with Drew, a fifteen-year-old boy, brother of the woman Mouse appears to have claimed, even though he barely knows her.

When Mouse tries to explain his unusual and immediate attraction to Mariana, his overwhelming desire to help her, I can fully understand. That was how I felt about Jayden, the first time I'd seen her. Seems men like us fall quickly, and hard.

Drew, well, the lad seems to be okay. Just a few months shy of his sixteenth birthday. I'd like the kid better were it not that he's so close in age to Jayden. I suppose it's natural as two teenagers they'd be drawn to each other, Jay helping him settle in, teaching him to play pool with much hilarity as the kid takes a while to get the hang of the game.

To start with, I watch them grinning, seeing Jay take pride in thrashing him time after time. But then I notice the looks Drew's giving Jay are starting to get more than friendly. Jay won't react, will she?

But fuck me, she's starting to flirt. It could be just a natural feminine response to someone who's clearly showing an interest. But she's mine. I begin to pay more attention to what they're doing. Torn, because in my heart she belongs to me, but my head tells me I need to give her space. If her feelings for me have changed over time, I have to accept it. I'm unable to give in to my caveman instinct which is to whisk her away to my cave and claim her.

"What's got into you, Paladin?" Slick's grinning as he comes over. But when I nod toward the two teenagers, their heads close together as they laugh about some shit or another, his eyes narrow too.

"You going to give him the same warning you gave me, Slick?"

"Fuck," he says, under his breath.

"Yeah, I know." I shake my head. "Kills me to say it, Slick, but if she's changed her mind about me…"

The man who's stood up and taken the role as her father, gives me a long look. "They're almost the same age, Brother. Got things in common to talk about. School and that."

Which makes me feel no better. Have we grown apart? Is it reasonable to think she's looking for someone who could understand her better? But how could anyone comprehend her more than me? I know all her secrets, and still want her.

Slick's hand lands on my back. "Came to find you. Drummer and I want to have a word."

Sounds ominous. Reluctantly, and with one last look at the pair who are animatedly discussing something, grinning and laughing while they talk, I follow him into Drummer's office.

Prez waves me to a chair in front of the desk, Slick sits beside me. I look from one to the other, noticing for the first time, the strain in Slick's face. A cold feeling settles inside me.

"Had word from Chaz, Prez of the Wretched Soulz. He's heard another rumour the Herreras are ready to settle their score with us. This time it sounds serious. I believe him."

"They coming for us?" This wasn't what I wanted to hear.

"They want to hit us where it hurts. Word is they're not preparing for an all-out battle right now, but their single focus is on Jayden." Prez doesn't try to sugarcoat it. "We knew it was on the horizon, know that they blame us, and her, for the massacre that night she was rescued."

Massacre is the right word. We'd hit and taken out five members of the notorious crime family. At the time, with the blessing of the head of the clan who used us to clean his own house. Now there's a new leader, one whose views are clearly at odds with his predecessor's.

"Chaz is going to drop a hint to Los Zetas. There's suggestions this signals the Herreras are getting back into the skin trade, which would step firmly on the cartel's toes. But revenge might be too high up Javier's list to stop anything he has set in motion. It's time we think seriously about protecting her. She's at risk, Paladin."

She is. We do what we can to minimise the danger. She's never alone when she goes off compound, either I or a prospect take her to school and bring her home, but if they hit in numbers, one man isn't going to stop them.

"While Chaz thinks they're not prepared to make a move immediately, I don't know how long their patience will last. If they know she's still in Tucson, I can't, won't rule out an attack on the compound." Prez's eyes have gone steely. "I'd like her gone. Then Chaz can let them know they're wasting their time looking for her in Arizona."

"You think that will solve it?" *Won't they just keep trying to locate her?*

"Herreras are Tucson based so I think it's a safe bet, once she's out of state they'll stop looking. It's certainly better than us trying to wait it out with her here, not knowing when they might strike." *I trust Drummer. He wouldn't feed me a line. If this is what he believes, I'll go along with it.*

"I've spoken at length with Ella. Don't want to uproot my ol' lady now."

I nod at Slick, fully understanding. *Ella must be at least six months pregnant. After a recent small bleed, the doctors are monitoring her pregnancy carefully. Not a good time for them to up root.*

"You're resurrecting the idea of me taking her to Colorado."

"Hellfire's expecting you next week."

My jaw drops. *Fuck, that came at me out of the blue. This is happening fast. Those things we'd spoken about a couple of months ago, now coming to fruition. Thinking about it hypothetically is one thing, now it's set in concrete, I realise how much it will hurt losing my family here. I don't know Hellfire at all. Only seen him in a few meetings. He and Drummer are very different, that's for sure. What will it be like to have a new prez to answer to? New brothers to get to know?*

"Lot to lay on you, Paladin."

"I'm fine." I reassure Drummer fast. "Jayden's safety is all that matters to me." I swallow, pushing down my personal regrets at leaving Tucson. "So, what's the plan?"

CHAPTER 9

JAYDEN

A couple of months ago it was suggested that Pal and I leave the compound, up roots and settle in Colorado. When I first heard, it should have been a dream come true. The resolution of what everyone had expected forever, a chance for Paladin and I to be together. But here, in Tucson, I'd been cocooned, safe in the knowledge that Paladin wasn't allowed to cross the line. In Colorado, there would be no one to prevent him. When the implications of that had sunk in, I'd realised I was unsure whether that was still what I wanted.

I'd been forced to grow up early. Even at fourteen I knew the abuse I locked away in my head wasn't right. After I'd had my innocence taken away, my first thought was to take back control. To be with someone I chose for myself. I'd latched on to the man who, in my eyes, had saved me, even after it was explained he'd only played a small part. I'd fixated on him, and was devastated when he'd explained that he couldn't be with me in the way that I wanted, softening the blow by telling me he'd wait until it was time, for almost four years until I was of age.

At first, I believed him. Had to have something to put my faith in after the hell I'd been through. Therapy had helped me slowly come to terms with the fact that while I'd been naïve, I'd been groomed by experts. What had happened wasn't down to me, but was all on them. I hadn't asked for, or encouraged it.

Therapy also opened my eyes. Words Paladin had said were what I wanted, needed to hear, but perhaps he hadn't meant them.

For the past two years, Paladin has been my friend. My anchor. Always there when I needed him, but never going further than he should. Even if he hadn't been warned off by Drummer or Slick, I don't think he'd have acted differently.

But men have needs, don't they? Needs that drive them, sometimes so strongly, they take even when it's not offered. While I'd never dream Paladin would force a woman to give against her will, I still wondered how he could wait for me. Perhaps he was being discreet. Maybe there was a woman in town I didn't know about, someone who was giving him what I was told I was too young to offer.

I eye the hangarounds who come to club parties with jealousy. Oh, Slick and Ella usually spirit me away before my tender eyes can see too much, but I've seen them arriving, wearing skimpy clothes meant to attract. *How could Paladin resist them?* He's not a boy. He's a man. It's hard to believe he's been true to his promise to wait for me.

My therapy sessions haven't ended, but have just moved away from the crime that had been committed and how I was dealing with it, to pushing me to consider what I want from life. Making me question whether I'm right to keep Paladin tied to me. Is it really him I want? Or am I hanging onto a dream I once used to keep my spirits up, to prevent me falling into despair? Knowing there was someone who knew what had happened, but who could put it aside, saying he didn't care about my abuse. Am I just frightened another man might reject me because of my past? Whereas Pal knows it all, and says he can ignore it.

The assumption of everyone here is that Pal and I will end up together. I've been starting to question whether that supposition is right.

Two months ago, the possibility of the removal of my safety net in the form of Slick and Drummer, led me to do some soul searching. I'm already sixteen, seventeen is approaching fast. Physically I'm probably ready. My body is that of a young woman's now, not a child. Some states, and, according to Sophie, Wraith's English old lady, the whole of Great Britain have sixteen as the age of consent. It's only because of the place that I live that I'm not legally allowed to have sex yet. The Arizona citizen law having been used by Slick and Drummer to set the arbitrary date when they'd untie the leash that held Paladin back.

If I truly felt something for him, surely I'd be jumping with joy at the thought that the time when we can truly be together, had a chance of being brought forward?

Those demons residing in my head though, I can't stop hearing their voices. While another teenager might take small steps toward womanhood, experimenting along the way, I had the veil drawn from my eyes far too early. In my head, sex hurts, it's dirty.

I read Ella's books when she's not around. Women should enjoy sex. There's even numerous mentions of battery operated boyfriends, while I can't even face touching myself. I've no idea what an orgasm is, I've had sex. Too much sex. Yet derived no pleasure at all. In my experience men don't need a woman to be willing or an active partner to reach their own release. Despite the words I've absorbed with my eyes, I can't imagine feeling the desire that the characters find in books.

Then, there's another thought that worries me, that maybe I'm just not turned on by Pal. Over the years, have we become too familiar? Even if I wanted to, is it now possible we could progress to lovers from just being friends?

Pal had shown no inclination to repeat, what had turned out to be a disastrous dinner date, after that one attempt at the

Wheel Inn. On one hand, I could understand it. Who would want to go through that fiasco again? It was worse than being supervised in the clubhouse, every word spoken overheard, every gesture in clear view to be analysed. Slick might have agreed to us dating, what he'd done, was ensure we understood, in actuality, that wasn't going to happen. So when Pal didn't ask me out again, deep down I understood why.

On the other hand, my traitorous mind makes me question, had he found me a disappointment? I'd dressed up, thought I looked good for him, but maybe I'd just shown I was too young. He's nearly five years older than me. At fourteen, when Pal was still a teenager himself, that hadn't seemed to make much of a difference, but now he's twenty-one, and I'm still in my teens. Had the way I'd presented myself betrayed the gap was too much of a difference? The delight I'd shown when we'd first arrived, a demonstration of my lack of experience. If so, going to Colorado will be a matter of duty to him, proving his dedication to the club, rather than to me.

Fearing we could be growing apart, when Drew arrived on the compound I was pleased there was someone else my age. It seemed natural to take him under my wing. There's only a year between us, because of the schooling I've lost, we're in the same grade. While we might not attend the same school, our education is one area we have things in common. I've taught him to play pool—his ignorance a source of amusement for us both.

I'm not blind or stupid, I know Drew feels an attraction toward me. He's good looking enough, his Hispanic looks and colouring, his dark eyes and his tall lithe body wraps his affable yet serious character up in an attractive package. What girl wouldn't enjoy such attention?

But he doesn't affect me either. When his eyes focus on me, it doesn't make me tingle, doesn't make parts of me come alive in the way people describe in fiction. Maybe that's all it is.

Stories to enjoy having no basis in reality. Maybe it's not just me. Or am I suppressing my reactions because of fear?

When I was first rescued from those men, I wanted a loving touch to erase what they'd done to me. Now years have passed, my memories trigger fear. I'm not sure I want any man to put their hands on me at all. The thought of being with Paladin, or anyone, scares me.

After the initial suggestion of Colorado had been brought up, I wasn't sure what to do when I realised the emotion I should have been feeling wasn't there. That instead of being excited that Paladin and I would have more freedom, I was frightened of having to confess and admit I didn't know my true feelings. I'd been pleased when the subject seemed to have been dropped. Now, two months later, it's being raised again.

"Next week's too soon." My eyes flick wildly between Slick and Ella. "I'm not ready."

My sister wipes tears from her eyes. "Me neither. Slick, there must be something else we can do."

Slick's a strong man, but faced with two crying women seems at a loss. "I'm sorry. I don't think it's the right time for us to move, Ella. The baby… Don't want to risk anything now. But Jayden, you can't stay here. You wouldn't be able to go to school, to go off the compound at all. And in the end, the Herreras might bring the fight to us, just to get to you." He turns to Ella. "We've discussed this, darlin'. Agreed it was the right thing."

"There's something she's not telling us." Ella astutely replies to Slick, but her eyes are on me. "What is it, Jayden?"

I can't tell them I'm having doubts about Paladin. Or rather that I can't understand what I feel for him, if anything. It might never have been more than a schoolgirl crush, which would mean for years I've been leading him on. It's crazy. Since I was first brought to the compound, all I wanted was him, now he's being handed to me, I don't know what to do.

"Jayden," Slick narrows his eyes shrewdly. "Paladin is going with you. Someone you know and can trust. I'll be happier he's there, I know he'd give his life to keep you safe. But I also know I can trust him to step away if a relationship with him is not what you want. No one's going to be putting any pressure on you, or making you do anything you're not ready for."

"I should hope not," Ella snaps. "Is that what you're worried about, Jayden? That he'd, he'd…"

"He'd never do what those men did, El. I know that." I bite my lip, not wanting this conversation to continue, knowing I've got to step up and do the right thing. This is not the time to just think of myself. "It's come as a shock, okay? I know it's better for you to be here until you have the baby. I'll go to Colorado, I'm fine. Really." I'm lying through my teeth, while hoping they can't see it. Forcing a lightness I don't feel into my voice, I ask, "So, what's going to happen? It's a long way to ride on Paladin's bike."

Slick laughs, his hand covers mine. "Not asking you to do that. Ella and I will fly up with you. It's only four hours with a brief stop in Denver. Paladin will ride up so he'll have his bike with him."

I frown. "Will he be safe, riding alone?"

A gentle smile from Slick at my concern for Pal. "A couple of brothers will escort him to Phoenix. After that, he'll be out of the Herreras' territory and safe to continue alone. Don't worry about him, he can look after himself."

Now my concern is for my sister. "Ella, are you okay to fly?"

"I'm just at the end of my second trimester, Jayden. The doctor said it would be fine."

Once decisions are made, the time seems to zoom past. The day of my departure quickly arrives. My clothes and stuff I'm taking are packed, emotional goodbyes have been said, and Wraith's waiting with the SUV to take us to the airport.

"We're going to be fine." Paladin's packing a last few pieces into his saddlebags. "I'll see you soon, okay? You want me to come to Hellfire's when I arrive?"

"Slick and Ella are going to stay overnight," I reassure him quickly. With my thoughts all over the place about what he'll expect when he and I have the chance to be completely alone for the first time, I'd rather get settled in a new place without the added pressure.

He stares at me earnestly. "You've got my number, okay? You call if you need me." Talking to me, he holds up his hand to Shooter and Jekyll who are waiting, obviously eager to get going.

"Pal." I say hurriedly, wanting to get this out before he leaves, realising I'm being selfish. I'll have my family with me helping me settle in. Pal's going to a strange clubhouse all on his own. "If you want to talk, you call me too."

His face softens. Approaching me, he touches my face. "Don't worry about me. I'll get in touch, and we can explore our new home. Think of it as an adventure."

Then he's on his bike, nodding at his brothers who'll escort him until he's put a safe distance between himself and the Herreras. As they ride out of the compound, and I realise Paladin's in for a long twelve-hour ride, it hits me. *I'd forgotten to tell him to ride safely.* I want to run after him, worried something might happen on the road…

"He'll be fine." Slick puts a comforting hand on my shoulder. "He knows what he's doing and will stay out of trouble."

I hope he's right.

"I'll miss you, Jayden."

I swing around to Drew and give him a quick hug. "You'll be fine. I'm sure your sister will be too."

He doesn't seem so certain of that, but Wraith's tossing his keys in his hands as though impatient. Slick helps Ella into the back seat, she waves at me to join her. Then, with one last round of goodbyes, we're off.

It's the first time I've flown. I'm unsure whether my nerves are for the flight, or for the unknown I'm heading into. We're all relatively quiet on the plane, Ella sits next to me, Slick on her other side. She holds my hand, I don't protest. It's fairly easy to change flights, and then we're arriving at our final destination.

I know Hellfire's been to Tucson before, but I don't know if I'd remember him. Slick, luckily, knows who to look out for. The man he approaches first with his hand held out, then with a manly hug and much back slapping, does look vaguely familiar, but older than I'd been expecting. *He looks old enough to be my grandfather.* His advanced years seems strange on a biker. There's no one his age in the Tucson club.

A younger man, probably nearer to his mid-thirties like Slick, stands beside him. He looks stern and grim, until he spies my eyes on him, then he smiles. It transforms his face.

"My wife, Ella. And this is Jayden." Slick introduces us.

"Hellfire," the older man says, then indicates to the man beside him. "Demon, my son and VP."

Ignoring the slight hesitancy before the word 'son', when I look closer I can see the familial resemblance. I shake both their hands politely, while thanking God Slick and Ella are with me, and I'm not meeting them alone. *They're strangers. Bet they'll be fine once I get to know them.* The VP, though, looks distracted and distant. When he glances at his father, he frowns. Inwardly I shudder. It's not that I take a dislike to him, he just doesn't seem to be overly friendly.

I find the car journey awkward. Slick sits up front with Hellfire, Ella and I in the back. Demon's on his bike behind us. I'm wondering how they got their road names, the handles Hellfire and Demon not sounding particularly comforting, hoping the possible explanations going around my head aren't the right ones. I don't feel it's my place to ask.

Pueblo. My new home. Pulling my sweater around me it's hard to believe we're in the same country. Tucson at this time of year is growing warmer. Here it must be twenty degrees cooler. The sun still shines, but there's no heat in it. I hope the coolness of the weather isn't an indication of the welcome I'm going to get here. The difference in the weather serves to emphasise how far away I'll be from everything I've ever known.

I hadn't put my phone back on after the flight. Remembering, I do so now. It immediately pings with a text.

Pal: Hope you had a good flight. I'm well on my way and safe.

His words remind me I won't be alone.

Jay: Just heading to Hellfire's house. I'll text you later

I'm so very glad he'll be here with me.

CHAPTER 10
MOIRA

Two days earlier

I'm failing miserably in my first lady's duties. We've got the kids arriving from Tucson in a couple of days, yet I can hardly stir myself to do anything. Hellfire's got the prospects sorting out a room for the new brother in the clubhouse, but young Jayden's going to be staying here, and the house is a complete mess.

I hadn't realised how much I'd let it, as well as myself, go until Hellfire walked in, and looked around him, his lips pressing together. "I'll get a couple of the club girls to come and give you a hand straightening this place up."

My eyes shoot to his, then I turn around, seeing what he's seeing. Dust is everywhere, mess in every direction. "There's no need, I've got it handled," I lie.

"Nah, this place is too big for you to do by yourself," his eyes soften as he contradicts me. "'Bout time they did more than work on their backs."

Why argue? I could do with the help. Hard to get myself into gear nowadays. *Is that another reason he's gone off me?* "As long as it's not Bella," I relent. "I can't stand her." I've always had a feeling she's after my man. Even in my presence she's been all over him.

"Nah, not her," he agrees quickly. *Too quickly?* "I'll send Titsy and Sheila. They can help get the spare room cleared for the girl. Jeannie would jump at the chance to come over and supervise."

"Not Jeannie," I say fast. My memories lately have dragged up everything I wish could stay forgotten. Over the years, I'd managed to put to the back of my mind the part she'd played, but now, unfairly, the blame I attach to her has come back. That she counterbalanced her role in my downfall by getting Hell and I together, sometimes isn't enough to stop me remembering it was her fault I'd been there in that clubhouse. I don't want to see her. It will just bring everything back. Her concern seeing me like this will only remind me of her sympathy the morning after. No, now's not a good time for her to be here.

I change the subject, before he can ask why I've so quickly dismissed my friend, by asking, "You sticking around?" It's unusual for him to be here during the day.

"Nah, just stopped in as I was passing. I've got to go to Tits Up, wondered if you'd like to come for a ride? It's a lovely spring day out there."

"I'm alright," I reply. *You don't want my fat ass unbalancing your bike.*

Various expressions cross his face, I try to read them, uncertain whether it's disappointment or relief I'm seeing. Giving myself a mental shrug, I try to pull myself together. "You got problems there?"

A quick shake of his head. "Nah. Taser's got some ideas for redecorating. Just going to see what he's suggesting. You used to like having input into shit like that."

I did. Now I can't be bothered. Why get involved in something I might not be here to see through? The time is fast approaching when I'll have to confront him, have to find out the truth, whether the suspicions I have are right. One thing I've always known, Hellfire doesn't lie to me. If I ask the question, he'll respond. Trouble is, I can't bring myself to hear the answer.

I'm trying to find my backbone first. In the meantime, he's spending more and more nights at the clubhouse, leaving me here alone to brood.

Too much time to think. Perhaps he's doing it on purpose.

I leave the room, ostensibly going to check I've got clean bedding for the spare room once it's cleared, but really escaping before the questions come out of my mouth, questions I'm not brave enough to have answered. It's not long before I hear the sound of his bike fading into the distance.

Damn it. I tear my sweater off over my head. I'm hot and sweating all over again. *Of course Hell doesn't want to be around me. I'm a fucking mess.* My moods are all over the place, I've no energy or desire to do the slightest things.

It's probably lucky he doesn't want to see me naked anymore. Apart from my sagging breasts, though initially I tried to convince myself it was my imagination, there's been other symptoms of menopause I hadn't expected. I was shocked when I first noticed my pubic hair had started disappearing, convincing myself for a time I was mistaken, until one day I had to admit it. What used to be bush is now bare. Hell's always been a man who doesn't like me to shave, now it looks like I have, with the benefit of no stubble, of course. I'll be embarrassed if he ever sees me again.

He's unlikely to. Why would he want me? Not when he's got a perfect and far younger Bella to entertain him.

The sound of a Harley's roar getting louder, then stopping makes me wonder if Hell's returned. Analysing the sound I realise it's not his bike, it's our son's. Demon.

I shake myself, paste on a smile, and go to see what my eldest wants. It's unusual for him to visit this time of day.

"Demon." I enter the kitchen where he's helping himself to milk from the fridge, drinking straight from the carton. I bite back the admonishment. You can't tell a thirty-five-year-old off in quite the same way as I'd have done twenty years ago.

"Mom." He wipes his mouth on his sleeve, comes over and hugs me, placing a kiss to my forehead.

"What are you doing here? You want something to eat?"

"Nah. Just needed to check something. Hell keeps the old record books here, doesn't he?"

I nod. "In his safe. You know the code?"

He rolls his eyes. *Of course he does.*

"I won't be long."

"Help yourself."

Hell was right. As Demon goes off to the study, I look around seeing the stove is covered with grease, the sink with the breakfast dishes in it. I shouldn't live like this. With new resolve I rinse the plates, stack the dishwasher, then, gritting my teeth, fill the sink with hot water and start tackling the burned on stains. Once started, I've a new determination I'm going to beat this shit. I'm hard at work scrubbing, feeling I'm making progress, when I hear footsteps behind me.

Knowing it's Demon, I don't immediately turn, but as he waits without speaking, curiosity makes me swing around.

His face is white. His hands clenched around one of the old record books from the club. His eyes, unfocused, stare in my direction.

"Demon. Dave," I try again with his legal name when I get no response. "Son, what's up?"

His mouth works, no words come out. He swallows, and tries again, coughing to clear his throat. Suddenly in an agonised cry he asks, "Why didn't you tell me? Why didn't I know?" His tone goes from high to low, then back up again.

An icy hand grips my heart. *What has he found?*

"Demon?" I ask again, my gut telling me this is the moment I hoped would never come.

Suddenly he's moving. He shoves the book under my nose. "Why didn't you tell me? You always told me Grandpa died in an accident. You never told me it was at the hands of his son."

That's all he knows? Okay, I can deal. Pretend ignorance. Tell him it's club business. Send him to have it out with Hell. *Is that fair?* But what the heck do I say?

"It's all here. Recorded in the minutes of the meeting. Blackie *raped* someone, Mom."

I try to take the book away from him before he starts reading between the lines. But it's too late. I hadn't raised a stupid son.

"He raped Hellfire's woman. Though he wasn't a patched-member then. He was a prospect. Voted in only minutes before the vote to dispatch Black Plate, *Blackie,* was taken." I move in fast, trying once more to pull the notebook away from him, but he's quicker, and too tall, holding it over my head. "My grandfather was a fuckin' rapist," he snarls. "And my own father killed him. Why didn't I know this?"

"It's not the kind of thing you boast about or discuss over a family dinner," I yell at him, still jumping up, trying to catch hold of his arm.

He stills. "You knew." His eyes go wide. "You fuckin' knew. You knew Hellfire killed him. And what he'd done."

"You just told me." I think fast trying to backtrack. Oh, we've both made mistakes here today. *Club business.* He shouldn't have spouted everything he'd just read, but I can excuse him. What man can keep quiet once he'd discovered such secrets in the family tree? But me? I should have played dumb. Innocent. Blackie had disappeared. That was all I should have been told. Might have questioned my man, but never should have given away that I knew what crime had been done, nor from my easy acceptance, admitted that not only did I know, I had no concern about my husband committing patricide.

He's shaking his head. His eyes flaring as brightly as the demon for which he was named. He stalks me. I retreat, all thoughts of grabbing hold of that notebook gone.

"What would I find, *Mother*? If I keep reading? What other fuckin' secrets am I going to find out? Do you want to tell me yourself?"

What do I do? Tell him half the truth. Maybe that will satisfy him.

"It was me. Blackie raped me." My hands cover my mouth as the words I never thought I'd ever admit to my son come out. "He raped me. That's why Hellfire was voted in, that's why he was the one who killed him."

Various expressions cross my son's face. Sadness, pain. Sympathy. As tears start to flow from my eyes, his hand begins to reach out to touch me, then his brow creases, and he pulls it back. "How much did I weigh when I was born, Mom?"

My voice, my whole body is shaking. "Eight pounds." I can't tell him a lie or contradict what I previously told him.

"Bit big for a premature baby."

My head moves side to side, my eyes open in horror.

"You were seventeen." He already knows that. It's family history. I'd used it to stop my kids from making the same mistake.

"Got pregnant almost to the day you got married, I came along eight months later. That's the story, isn't it? But Blackie was killed a month before you got married." His voice increases in volume. "I'm not stupid. Look at the fuckin' dates, Mom! I'm not Hellfire's son, am I? *Fuck!*" As a wail comes out of his mouth, I step forward to comfort him, he moves out of my reach.

His own head is shaking now as though with that action he can dismiss the implications. But it's impossible, the thought has taken root. "I'm yours, but not his. He's not my father. He's my fucking brother." The book drops out of his hands onto the floor as he leans over the counter, his head cradled in his arms.

I want to go over and say something, anything, to ease him, to take this new burden from him, but I can't find the right words to use. Tentatively I move closer, putting my hand on his back, he shrugs it off.

"Why did nobody tell me?" he cries. Then, more sharply, "Who else knows? Who else is in on the joke?"

"No one knows," I quickly correct him, "and no one treats it as a joke. Maybe they suspected, the old-timers in the club. It's possible Bomber and Rusty put two and two together. But they can't *know*. They've never said anything, never hinted."

"Why didn't you tell me?" he asks again. "I knew Blackie was bad. Just didn't know I was the result of a rape."

"Dave, Demon…"

"Not now, not now Mom. I've got to have time to process this. Tell Hell I'll be gone for a few days."

I open my mouth to tell him Hell's his father in all the ways that matter, but before I can get out another word, he's already turned his back on me and is striding out of the room. Within seconds I hear his bike fire up, then the sound rapidly fading into the distance.

I sink to the floor, my head in my hands. The day I never expected, would have wished never to arrive, had come. Demon might be a full-grown man, thirty-five years of age, but he'll never stop being my little boy. If I could have saved him this pain, I would have.

My tears falling freely, I reach into my pocket and pull out my phone, saying only when it's answered, "Hell, come home."

He might have taken minutes; it might have been hours. I'm in the same position when Hell comes running through the door and finds me sitting on the floor, a hundred used tissues beside me, my eyes red and swollen.

"Darlin'," he yells when he sees me. Throwing his bike key on the counter, he hunches down beside me. "What's wrong?" he demands. "Are you hurt? What the fuck happened? Talk to me, woman! Moira, talk to me!"

He's beside himself. There's only been one time when he's seen me anything close to this distraught before. Ironically that was the day he came up with a solution to my problems, the day he asked me to marry him.

"Demon." I manage to stammer out. "It's Demon."

Hell's face grows dark. "What the fuck has he done?" He swipes his grey hair back, then his hand reaches out and hesitantly touches my face. "Did he hurt you?" He sounds incredulous, and so he should be. Demon's never raised a hand to me, or any woman.

"No." My voice is stronger as I deny it adamantly.

"Fuckin' tell me, Mo. Never seen you like this. You're scarin' me, woman."

I swallow, wipe the tears, which I can't seem to stop, away from my eyes, then try to get out the words which are going to destroy him. "Hell, he knows. He *knows*."

Hellfire goes completely still. The blood drains from his face. His eyes, wide and wild, burn into me. "He knows... what?" He speaks slowly and carefully, enunciating each word precisely as though speaking to a child. But he already understands what I'm alluding to. Just needs me to confirm it.

I point to the discarded club record book, lying, spine broken, on the floor. "He knows, *everything*. He knows he's Blackie's son."

Hell throws his head back and roars, both hands tearing at his hair. "No, Mo. No." Rocking on his heels, he tries to gather himself together. After a few minutes when the implications set in, he asks the next question. "How?" But when he picks up the record book, he immediately understands.

"I didn't know," I start in a whisper. "He wanted to check some old records. I didn't *know*, Hell. Didn't realise how far back he was looking. Didn't see anything wrong. How could I have told him he couldn't search through old club business? He's done it before. He's the VP, how could I challenge him?"

Suddenly Hell's arms are around me, pulling me to him. "You couldn't have known, darlin'." His hands start stroking my hair, and now we're both swaying back and forth. "I brought the books home so he wouldn't stumble across them. Said we needed space at the club, no one saw anything wrong in that. We keep the last ten years' records at the clubhouse, anything older than that, I keep in the safe." He pauses, and his arms hold me tighter. "You're right, as VP, he can't be prevented access to any of the paperwork. Just never expected he'd need to search things that happened thirty-six years ago."

"He hadn't a clue, Hell. I know he hadn't gone looking for what he found. I don't know what led him to those records. He was so shocked."

"I should have destroyed them." Hell looks distraught and annoyed with himself.

"You couldn't, Hell. They're the official records."

He takes a deep breath, trying to get himself under control. It's only then I notice tears are leaking from his eyes, leaving a trail down his cheeks. "How did he react?" His voice now quiet, full of emotion. "How the fuck did my *son* react to finding out his real father was a rapist?"

"He was upset." My words are an obvious understatement. "He took off, Hell. Told me he needed to get his head around it. Said to tell you he'd be gone for a while."

"Any idea where?" he asks in clipped tones.

"No." I think for a moment. "Have you?" I can feel him shaking, this is one situation he can't control.

"No. Demon has problems; he'd normally come to me. But this? I'm the last person he'd want to talk to. Huh, I'm the man who lied to him all his fuckin' life."

And I'm the woman who lived the lie.

We sit, on the floor, huddled together as the world we'd so carefully built comes crashing down around us. Demon, our son for all intents and purposes, is out there alone, *hurting*. There's nothing either of us can do about it. How he'll cope, how he'll want to proceed from now on, a mystery neither of us can solve. Until Demon reappears. *If he ever does.*

CHAPTER 11

HELLFIRE

I need to get back to the clubhouse. Once he's digested the news he should never have stumbled across, Demon will want to speak to me. Go head to head with me. I know my son. He won't take it out on his mother—she did nothing wrong. She was the victim as much as he was. No, it will be me he challenges, me he comes for. And the place for the confrontation will be the scene of the crime.

Moira's tears are slowing, but I don't take it to mean she's feeling easier in her mind, she's all cried out and exhausted. Gently pulling her to her feet, I lead her into the lounge, encouraging her onto the couch. I pour a vodka, and leave it beside her.

Going into my study, I take out my phone.

"Bomber? Need your help, Brother." I pick up the glass I'd filled with whisky for myself, while knowing a stiff drink won't make this any easier.

"You got it, Prez. Anything you need." Bomber's deep voice vibrates through the earpiece as he doesn't hesitate to give me assistance without asking for details.

I pause, struggling to get the words out. "Demon, is he at the club?" I doubt it, but thought it worth a shot.

"Haven't seen him. Last I knew he was going to your place. He wanted to check something or other."

I swallow a sip of whisky, resisting the urge to throw it back in one, then take another and drink myself into oblivion. But I didn't gain my rank, and have held it for so long, by escaping into a bottle. "He was delving deep into the old club records, Bomber. Too fucking deep. Thirty-six years to be precise." I pause, then dive in, "He knows, Bomb. He fuckin' knows. About Blackie, and Moira."

There's a sharp inhaled breath. "Prez…"

"Moira's in pieces, Demon took off. Fuck knows where or for how long. He'll be coming for me, Bomb. He'll want to confront me, want to know why I hid the truth all these years."

"What can I do, Prez?"

"I need to be at the club. That's where he'll be comin'. Can Jeannie come here? I don't want Mo to be on her own." I know Jeannie and Mo have been distant lately, but she's the only person who my old lady can talk to about this. No one else knows, and she wouldn't want them to.

"Of fuckin' course. No question about it. Where do you want me, Prez?"

Bomber and Rusty are the only two members who were in the club at the time Blackie pulled his last stunt, no one else knows the dirty secret or even suspects. Blackie's death, a stain on the club, isn't discussed. Today's the first time I've let down my guard and all but confirmed Demon's heritage to Bomber, from his reaction, however, offering no questions, he's known all along. Was it that obvious? Or had Jeannie told him?

"At the club, Brother. Demon might want answers from you."

"I'll fuckin' give them to him. Still remember that fuckin' night, Prez. You had no choice but to kill him."

Yeah. Not only had I lied to Demon about our true relationship, I'd killed his real father too, taking away the chance for him to know him. Heck of a lot to lay on the boy—right now, I can't even think of him as a fully grown man. He's my little kid, and he's hurting. Too fucking much. Quickly I wonder if it would have been better to have told him while he was growing up, but dismiss it. There would never have been a good time to explain about the man who'd provided the sperm that made him. I only wish it was a secret that could have been buried along with me.

"I did what I had to, Brother. No choice about it. No heavy conscience and no regrets."

"But Demon might see it differently."

He might. Fuck knows what he's thinking right now, or whether he's even capable of rational thought.

"I'll explain to Jeannie, bring her over. You were right to call me, Prez. Jeannie was there, she knows everything about Mo. Might not know why or how Blackie disappeared, but she'll settle Mo. Mo did right, you stepped up. Made a fuckin' good go of it too. You and the club's first lady? Set a fuckin' good example for everyone else these three-and-a-half decades."

"You too, Bomb. You and Jeannie."

He huffs a quick laugh. "Not that we haven't had our ups and downs, but we're good, Prez. We're good."

Can I say the same thing about me and Moira? Not sure what we are at the present, but need to put our problems aside until Demon resurfaces, and we know where his head's at. Our eldest child takes priority right now.

Bomber's quick to arrive, Jeannie riding bitch behind him. Her face is taut as she enters, that he's already explained the situation is clear. She nods at me tersely, then rushes over to Moira. Seeing her friend, Mo starts crying all over again, and the way she reaches for her shows me I was right to call Jeannie in. All differences between them swept away, at least for the moment.

I grab my keys, then side by side with one of my oldest friends, ride to the clubhouse.

Entering, I stand at the door, my hand holding onto the frame as I peruse the assembled brothers, hoping, but not seeing, the man I wanted to most. I hadn't expected it to be that easy, but in my mind had summoned up my son, *my brother*, as usual, holding court around the bar, a beer in his hand acting like nothing out of the ordinary had happened.

Wishful thinking.

Man's just heard probably the most devastating news anyone could have the bad luck to absorb through their ears.

"Prez?" Cad's waving his hand toward the bar.

Not being in the mood for conversation, I indicate my office, and walk across the room, unwilling to be dragged into anybody else's problems, mine would trump any of theirs. Once in my sanctuary, I pull out my not-so-secret stash of whisky, and pour a glass of pure malt. Then sink into my chair, resting my head back.

What the fuck's going to happen? Will I lose my son? Will the club lose its VP? Will Demon want to throw down against me? Fuck, I worry about him so much. I might not have provided the sperm, but I was there every minute of her pregnancy, held back her hair while she was vomiting, went to every fucking doctor's appointment. Saw my son first on a sonographic screen. He was mine from the minute I heard about him. Never let anyone think anything else. I loved him before he was born—not that we knew it was a him before then—didn't matter to either of us whether the baby would be a boy or girl.

Christ, those first months with Moira were difficult. She'd wake with nightmares in the dead of the night. Took me weeks to get her to trust me fully, even though, by then, she was my wife. Blackie had caused so many issues, it had taken me a very long time to teach her what making love was all about.

Once I'd eventually been able to introduce her to my kind of love making though, she couldn't get enough. We fucked like rabbits, anytime, anywhere. But once Demon was born, we both agreed, she was still young. One baby was enough. I wrapped my shit for the next few years until we were ready for our family to grow. Kennedy was the one we did right. Planned for, *prepared for.* I never treated Demon any differently, even when his sister, my true daughter was born. Not for one fucking moment. He was mine, in all the ways that mattered.

Mo wanted a big family, so I threw the condoms away. As the years passed we didn't think it would happen. Didn't bother us too much, we already had a boy and a girl. When she fell pregnant with Samuel after a big gap, neither of us could have been happier. But hell, if I expected trouble from anyone, my youngest boy would have been the one. He hadn't gone off the rails, but a few times it had come close. He's doing well now, and I've got to the point where I thought I could start to relax.

Demon. Well, he'd been the one to want to follow in my footsteps, and he's doing one hell of a job. He'd become VP on his own merits, a good man to have at my side and at my back.

Or he had been. *What the fuck is going to happen now?*

I can't go home. It's not that I can't face Moira, not that my heart isn't breaking for her. I'm convinced Demon will eventually seek me out, and am determined it would be here he'd find me. Any harsh words spoken between us wouldn't be in front of his mother. She doesn't deserve that.

Knowing Jeannie was there and wouldn't leave her alone however long it takes, I stay at the club. Checking in with my wife the next morning.

"Any news?" She answers the phone without a greeting.

"No, no sign. I've got the boys out lookin' for him. He's not been found drownin' his sorrows anywhere."

"Did, did you tell them?"

"Nah. Give me some fuckin' credit. I told them we'd had a father/son argument, and I was worried. You doing okay, darlin'?"

A pause, then, a whispered, "I just want him to be alright."

Me too. Me fucking too. "I'll keep in touch. Call you as soon as I hear something."

She promises to do the same, then I end the call. Placing my phone back in my cut, it hits me how long it's been since we finished conversations with declarations of love. Too long. Probably time I should remind her. Probably a lot of things I should be doing and haven't done.

The day passes, and there's no sign of him. The next night is the second sleepless one I have. The following morning, I hear a commotion from the clubroom.

"Hey, VP! Prez has been looking for you." Mace's loud voice booms.

I take a deep breath, sit back in my chair, and place my hands palms down on the desk. I wait. I don't have to be patient long.

The door opens, and I feast my eyes on my boy, noticing he looks ragged and drawn, as if he too hadn't slept. I hate that it's down to me he's going through this pain. *Should have burned that fucking record book, then he'd have never found out.*

"VP." I greet him, not wanting to trigger him by using the word, son.

"Prez." He's equally polite as he throws my title back. His expression is guarded; he's giving nothing away.

He closes the gap between the door and my desk, then skirts around the edge. "Stand up," he instructs.

I do. Knowing he's going to take a swing at me. I killed his father after all. *I deserve it.* I let him live a lie all his life.

I tense, waiting for it, trying not to brace myself. *I deserve the pain.*

Time ticks on. Nothing happens. I glance up, my gaze at last meeting his eyes. Like the rest of him, they're inscrutable. Then they close. When they reopen, he lets out a weighted sigh. His hands start to rise; I prepare for the blow. Which never arrives.

Instead his arms go around me, hugging me too him, the extra inch of height he has over me giving him an advantage.

Stunned, surprised, I return his embrace, holding him tightly, having never expected to hold him again.

When his grip relaxes, now I can see emotion in his eyes, and moisture forming.

His mouth twists. "Got a lot to talk about. Got a lot to work through in my head. One thing I want to get out into the open is, Hellfire, you're the best fuckin' brother a man could ever have."

That I didn't expect. "Demon…" I start.

"Nah, let me finish." He lets me go, and now walks back to the front of the desk where he pulls up a chair and sits. He waits until I retake my own seat. "You couldn't tell me. How could a kid cope with knowing what his sperm donor had done? You gave me a home, and shelter, when you could have hated me."

I stay silent, there's nothing more to say.

"Have I got this right? Maybe need you to fill in the gaps." I nod, indicating I'll be happy to. "So, you and Mom? You were already an item?"

"Yeah." I sit forward, placing my elbows on the desk. "Before, well, before, I knew she was the one for me. But I was a prospect. Blackie had strict rules, prospects, especially me, were treated like scum."

"That's why you're easier on them? Wills has got a woman…"

"And I respect that. If that had been the way then, what happened never would have come to pass." I pinch the bridge of my nose. "He was my, *our*, father, but Blackie wasn't a good man. Though clever in many ways. After the steel mill closed, instead of moaning about it, he started the club. Yeah, the money came easily with the shit we were into back in those days, but he still worked hard. What really attracted him though, was the power that came with being sat at the head of the table. Thought he was the fucking king of the club. Thought he owned everyone in it, especially the prospects. He didn't make my life easy because I was his son." I huff a laugh. "That's a fuckin' understatement. He was downright nasty."

"The brothers went along with it?"

"Most were just content having someone to lead them, make decisions on their behalf. Give them something to live for. If the club hadn't been so young, maybe some of them would have stood up to him earlier. Furnace, I think, was becoming uneasy, but I wasn't sure he had the backing of the rest."

"They backed you, that night, though."

"Jeannie had been itchin' to meet a biker. Saw her friend, your mom, as her way in. I'd been dating Moira in secret for a while, already knew I was serious about her. Was going to officially claim her once I'd got patched in." I shake my head. "If I'd dreamed for one moment she'd planned to come to the club that night, I would have made my warnin' to stay away clearer. I'd told her it wasn't the place for her, but not spelled out the reasons why. I was so close to getting my patch, it didn't seem necessary. I had no idea she'd just turn up. She'd always seemed wary of bikers, and until I could give her the protection of being a member's old lady, I didn't want her anywhere near."

"So why did she come?"

"Jeannie persuaded her. Told her it would be fun. Convinced her I'd be thrilled to see her embrace that part of my life."

Demon nods, but his mouth twists. "Sounds just like something fuckin' Jeannie would do." He's grown up with her always being around the club. He knows her as well as anyone. Once again, he meets my eyes, swallowing hard before asking, "So, how did it go down?"

"When Blackie saw her, he read how much I cared for her." I pause, gathering my strength to carry on, needing to make clear how powerless I'd been. The memories so fucking painful, to this day, it's hard to speak about it. Especially to Demon. But he's asked to know what happened, and he's got a right to know. Too many lies between us, I'm not going to fabricate more. "I was on bar duty, Blackie ordered me to stay put as he decided to pull rank. Conned her he wanted to get to know her because of her interest in his son. Told her he was the prez, and that he'd show her the club. He did, but his tour was limited to his bedroom."

Demon puts his head into his hands, I don't bother to spell it out.

"He wasn't discreet. It was clear what he had done. Moira ran off, she didn't want anything to do with me. I wanted to go after her, but instead, Furnace called church, and, well, you've read the notes. It was the turning point for the club. I was patched in; he was voted out." I pause, then scoff, "Seems everyone had become wary of him. No one stood up for him, or what he had done."

He nods slowly, then barks a harsh laugh. "Been thinkin' a lot, Hellfire. Think we're alike, father and son or brother and brother. You did nothing more than I would have done."

A weight lifts off my shoulders as I tell him the rest. I want nothing else hidden between us. "Mo refused to see me afterwards, she was too upset. I tried, but in her mind she connected me to my father, the man who had raped her. I didn't get a chance to talk to her at all." I've decided to tell him everything. "Until it became clear there were lasting implications. She was seventeen, Demon. If her parents knew she was pregnant, they'd have thrown her out. She had no support, no money to her name. When she needed funds for an abortion, she had nowhere else to turn."

His eyes meet mine as the implications hit. If Mo had got her way, he wouldn't be here sitting opposite me. "What happened to change her mind?" he asks through gritted teeth.

"Jeannie got in touch with me. She was after the money. Thought the club owed Mo, that it was responsible for the mess Mo was in. She was right. At last I was able to see her. I knew immediately my feelings for her hadn't changed. Of course, I had to work hard. At first she put my renewed attentions down to guilt."

"You persuaded her to keep me?"

I shake my head. "I let her see she had options. But we had to move fast. I got what I wanted, the girl I'd fallen for. Was able to claim her and walk her up the aisle within a few days."

"How, how could you do that, Hell? Want the baby that rapist had put inside her? That's what I can't get my head around."

"Mo didn't want an abortion, not really, just couldn't see she had any other way out. I was going to have that girl any way I could. It wasn't her fault she was pregnant, or yours. I made the decision you were going to be my son, or daughter if that's how it had turned out. Once I'd determined that, everything else fell into place."

"You've treated me like your son for thirty-five years. You've never done anything to suggest I was anything else." Demon's eyes crease. "I've been racking my brains to find some way you've treated me different to Samuel or Kennedy, and I haven't been able to come up with one fuckin' thing."

I shrug. "You're my son. You always have been. Even before you were born."

He draws his hands down his face. "I've always looked up to you, Hell, as a father, as my president. Now, fuck, I have no words. Not sure I could have manned up in the way that you did."

"You would," I reassure him quickly. "You've just never loved a woman enough."

Suddenly he stands, so fast his chair rocks. His hands clench and open again, then repeat the action once more. "I can't get my head around the man I thought was my grandfather, was my father and a rapist to boot. I carry his fuckin' blood, Hell."

I also get to my feet. "Boy, look at me." I use the tone I probably haven't resorted to since he was a teenager. "You've just said you admire me. Well, I'm of the same blood. Whatever bad our father carried died with him. You hear me?"

He stops pacing. He stares at me. He hadn't looked at things that way. I might not have sired him, but we've got a strong link just the same.

Suddenly he laughs, and points at my whisky. As I get out another glass and top both of them up, he retakes his seat. "Man, this is fucked up. One good thing, I don't need to change what I call you, *Brother*."

That makes me chuckle as well.

"Should we tell anyone?"

I give it a moment's thought. "Bomber knows, he'd always suspected, but he doesn't think anything should change. Not unless you want it too."

"Rusty?"

"Don't know, but it's possible he put two and two together back in the day, but we've never discussed it."

He nods, slowly, a gentle rise and fall of his head. "The old members didn't die easy; things were hard back in those days. You, Bomb and Rust were lucky to survive. The members who aren't the originals know of it, but didn't live the history of this club. They've heard of Blackie, but only as the deceased founder. Don't see the point in telling them of his crime, upsetting the equilibrium in that way."

"I'm thinking of stepping down." I know I'm springing it on him, but it's been going over and over in my mind these past twenty-four hours.

"What the fuck?"

"I've hurt you, Demon. Didn't mean to. But now you have to face up to the fact I've been lying to you all your life. Can you still trust me?"

"Got any other secrets?"

"None," I reply earnestly. "But the club is built on trust. If you, as VP, have any doubts in your head, then I can't continue as Prez."

He grimaces. "Not sure I'm ready to sit in your chair."

"Truth, Brother? There's something going on with Moira. Club's made me neglect her, need to have some space to find out what it is. Invested thirty-six years of my life in that woman, it's about time she came first."

"She thinks you're cheating on her."

I feel my eyebrows rise.

Demon shrugs. "She asks me all the time. Not my place to tell her one thing or the other."

Now it's my turn to speak through gritted teeth. "I have never cheated on her. Never would, never will. Never even think about it."

He gives a half-smile. "Think you're tellin' that to the wrong person."

He's right. I am. "She's worried, Demon. First you've got to get the air cleared with her. She's worried sick you'll blame her…"

"She did nothing wrong. I couldn't have asked for a better mom. You've both been amazing parents to me, Kennedy and Sam. Never gave me a clue I had another dad, or was conceived in such circumstances."

I stand, pick up my keys. "Ready to go see her?"

He grins and follows my lead. "You bet."

As I go to the door, I turn. "I was serious, Demon. Think about taking on the reins of the club. Bout time I handed them over."

"Would need a club vote."

"You think of anyone who'd challenge you?" I can't, I'd brought him up right.

Demon's quiet for a moment. Then he raises his chin. "I'll think on it. But only because I agree Mom could do with more of your attention, not because I've lost faith in you as president of the club." He pauses before opening the door. "Hell, we've cleared the air, but fuck. This is a hell of a thing to get my head around. And you passing the gavel over? Not sure I'm in the right headspace to give that any serious thought."

Placing my hand on his shoulder, I wait until his eyes are on mine. "Hate that you're hurting, Brother. Don't bottle shit up. You want to talk? I'm here. Where it matters," I place my hand over my heart, "you're my son."

CHAPTER 12
MOIRA

Two days earlier

I want my son. Home and safe. Slowly my tears dry up, I'm all cried out. Seeing Hellfire, with such anguish on his face, makes me realise it's not just me or Demon who's hurting. He looks like his life's been destroyed. Which it has. Blackie has found a way to torment us from beyond the grave.

I hear the doorbell and Hell answer it, hoping he'll send whoever it is away. I don't want company. When I hear footsteps, I look up to see Jeannie and Bomber standing there in front of me. Bomber is watching me, wearing a look of commiseration, Jeannie has tears in her eyes. Her hands reach out to take mine.

We've grown apart, Jeannie and I over the past couple of years. Suddenly I see it's my best friend standing in front of me. The person who was there from the start, the only one, apart from Hellfire, who knows everything. If it hadn't been for her, I wouldn't have had my husband all these years. It's not her fault I'm losing him now, yet somehow I've apportioned blame to her.

Maybe it's because she's been so happy with Bomber, while Hell and I have drifted apart. Whatever, I know I'm pleased, relieved to see her.

"Want me to stay?" Bomber looks at Jeannie protectively, then at me. I see a slight warning in his eyes. *Don't hurt my wife.*

Jeannie is staring at me, waiting for me to say something. I let my hands find hers and hold them tight. "Thank you." It's all I can say. Those two words conveying how pleased I am not to be left alone with my grief, showing my appreciation that she was ignoring all the awkwardness between us, coming to me in my time of need.

"I think we'll be okay, Bomber."

I quickly nod, reinforcing Jeannie's words. I've no doubt Bomber knows everything. He'd have to be stupid, which he's far from, not to have put two and two together thirty-six years ago. Even if he and Jeannie haven't spoken about it. But we'll keep up the pretence. I could talk about things openly with my best friend which I couldn't if he were to stay.

I turn away as he takes Jeannie's lips, an expression of ongoing desire and promise that I haven't seen in my own man's eyes for so long. But today's not the time for jealousy to rouse its head. Demon's my focus, not myself.

Bomber leaves with Hellfire. My husband's returning to the clubhouse in the hopes Demon might return there. When they've gone, I step aside, as Jeannie walks through the house she knows almost as well as her own, even though she might not have been here in ages.

"Coffee. I need coffee. Or vodka. What's your choice?"

"Coffee." I follow her to the kitchen. While I may feel like drowning my sorrows, the one glass Hell poured me was enough. I need to keep a straight head in case my son needs me.

"So," she sits at the counter while I pretend to busy myself, "Demon's found out?"

I jerk my head up and down. "He's taken off. Fuck knows where. I'm worried. He's not got his head straight, he's riding…"

"He'll be fine, Mo. He's an experienced rider. I can understand he wants to be alone. Fuck, that's so much shit for a kid to get his head around."

He's not a kid, though however old he gets, it's hard not to think of him still as one. "I wish he'd never have discovered it. Jeannie, how the hell do you cope with the knowledge your father was a rapist?"

"His father wasn't Blackie, Mo. Hell's always been his dad. Demon's not stupid. He'll work that out for himself."

"Hell's gone back to the club. He thinks Demon's going to stand up to him. Take him down for lying to him all his life."

"Demon will work it through," she says confidently. "I don't think you need to worry about that." She waves down at the small bag she brought with her. "If it's okay with you, I'll stay until you've got news."

"Thank you." I place a coffee in front of her, relieved I've got company. I couldn't have asked Kennedy to come over. I don't want my other children to know, not unless Demon wants to tell them. It's his secret as much as mine after all.

We sit for a while in silence. It's hard to talk. All she can offer are platitudes. Neither of us knowing the truth about where Demon is, what he's doing, and what's going through his head. It makes me think of my man. Is he alone at the club? Or is he getting comfort himself? If so, who from? Bella?

Abruptly I put down my coffee. It's making me too hot. Or is it the damn menopause adding to my woes? Why can't my body behave? I can't take it. Getting up, I open a window.

"Hot flash?" Jeannie asks, in a matter-of-fact tone. "I've been getting those myself. Annoying, aren't they?"

"Fuck this getting older." I nod. We share a moment of female bonding, without having to talk.

"Why don't you come to the club anymore, Mo? Miss having you there."

I consider before answering. I've got a lot to be grateful for. I had Demon, Kennedy and Samuel. Jeannie and Bomber wanted kids, but it wasn't to be for them. While I'd been home looking after my children, Jeannie had filled the hole in her life by making a place for herself at the compound. Before we became distant, she used to joke she had more children than me. All the boys in the club were that for her, she'd adopted them all.

"Is Hell cheating on me?" I suddenly spit out, holding my breath for the answer.

Jeannie shakes her head. A moment passes before she answers. "I can't say."

I stand. Almost throwing my now empty cup into the sink. "You're my best friend, Jeannie. Why can't you be straight with me? Why are you more loyal to him?"

"Mo." She's standing too. "I can't tell you because I don't know." Her hands wave, punctuating her words. "Yeah, if I knew, I'd tell you. But you know the score. Bomber and I don't stay around in the evenings. Once dinner's over we go home. All I can say is Hell keeps his hands to himself while we're there. What goes on after? I have no idea."

That makes sense. When the club girls start doing what they're given board and lodging for, Sindy, Jeannie and I used to make ourselves scarce. I can't think of any reason why that might have changed.

"I think he is cheating," I tell her sadly. "He doesn't want anything to do with me anymore." As she makes a noise of sympathy, I wave it off. "Who can blame him, Jeannie? Look at me, I'm a mess. I can't match up to the whores."

"Mo, yeah, we're older. Can't stop time marching on. As for sex, Bomber and I aren't as active as we once were."

"But you still do it? Fuck?" I ask crudely, in case she misunderstood.

"Sure. Yes. But not as often."

"We don't." I tell her gruffly. "He must be getting it else-where. It's the only answer."

With a shake of her head, she refutes it. "Hell loves you, Mo. Fuck, he always did. I wanted him first, you know that, don't you? But from the moment we met, he only had eyes for you."

"His eyes aren't showing him now what they once did. Just look at me, Jeannie. I'm overweight, and bits of me are sagging."

"He's getting old too," she says astutely. "He might attract the interest of the young whores as he's the president of the club, but if he wasn't, they wouldn't give him a second look." She winks. "We've both ended up with *old* men, Mo. Just look at Bomber. Grey hair, where he's got any at all. He's not in his prime any longer. But I've grown old with him. Got no desire to trade him in for a younger model. So I'm not sure why you think Hellfire would."

Men are different to women, though, aren't they? Don't they feel flattered when a younger woman shows their interest? Even if they know it's the power that attracts them, not the man himself?

"Have you spoken to him?" She asks, following me to the living room.

The shake of my head gives her the answer. Then I add, "If I had my fears confirmed, I'd have to leave him."

"Do you ever think you made a mistake? Marrying him?" Jeannie makes herself comfortable.

"Never." Her question makes me think back to myself as a teenager. "Though I never got a chance to live my dreams, being forced to marry so young."

"You wanted to travel, didn't you?"

I did. But getting pregnant knocked that on the head. I'd never had a chance to discover what was beyond the confines of Colorado, except for brief visits out of state to other Satan's

Devils chapters. If I get divorced, maybe I can start all over again. Trouble is, now I might have the chance, I don't feel the urge to go anywhere. Exploring new sights on my own, no longer attractive.

"There's a family barbeque next Sunday. Why don't you come, Mo?"

A strangled laugh comes from me. "You really think Demon would want me to be there? Play happy families?"

"You don't know what Demon might want."

"He might not even be back by then." I snap. Then drop my head into my hands.

Immediately she comes over. "Mo, he'll be fine." Without explaining, she knows what I'm thinking. "Hell and Demon, they get on so well together. Father and son. Brother and brother. They'll work it out."

Jeannie stays with me that evening, I'm glad to have company. Though even her presence doesn't prevent me having a sleepless night, visions of Demon having come off his bike lying dead or dying by the side of the road. I just wish he'd get into contact. He must know I'll be worried out of my mind. Hell, too. Though it remains to be seen how much my son cares about either of us at this stage. We've all been living a lie.

Taking charge, like she does every day in the clubhouse, Jeannie's up early, and is making breakfast when I appear. My eyes are red following another bout of weeping in the small hours, my head pounds, and my stomach churns at just the sight of food. Nevertheless, I try to eat something, not wanting her kind gesture to go to waste.

She tidies up after. I couldn't give a damn what state my house is in.

Around mid-morning, my phone rings. Seeing it's Hellfire, I take it into his office for privacy.

"Hell?"

"Demon's here. He's fine, Mo. He's taken it, well, far better than I'd have thought. We were coming straight over to see you, but Cad had something to discuss with him. We'll be there as soon as we can."

I sink into the chair, hugging the phone to me. Unable to process the words. *My son's safe. He's alive.* And so, it appears, is Hell.

"Glad I had this opportunity to talk to you first. Got to tell you, Mo. I offered to step down."

At last I find my voice, not sure what I think about that. Put the stress my old man carries on the shoulders of my son? "He take you up on it?"

"Nah. But I told him to consider the offer. The VP's got to have confidence in his prez. Now he knows I'm a liar," Hell seems to have trouble over that word, "told him he needs to at least think on the option."

Once again Hell's showing what a good man he is. Putting his son's, no, his *brother's* needs in front of his own. As I put my phone away, I start to wonder how the relationship that now is out in the open, at least between us, will affect the dynamics of the club.

"Well?" Jeannie asks expectantly as I return to her.

I let out a big sigh of relief. "Demon's come back. No blood seems to have been shed."

"Thank fuck!" She looks just as pleased as I am.

"But, Jeannie? Not a word, okay? This is Demon's story. Up to him whether he tells anyone else."

"Mo, sweetheart. You and Hell? Couldn't have been better parents to that boy. He'll know you've always done your best for him. He couldn't have wanted for anything more. You're right. Serve fuck all if it came out now. Most of the members don't even remember what it was like or weren't around in those days. No point rocking the boat now." She purses her lips. "They won't hear anything from me or Bomber. Don't want them to think there might be other secrets waiting to be dredged up from the past."

She's right. It's not just Demon who could lose confidence in Hell as the prez, but the club in general. Trust. Such an important word in the brotherhood. If Hell lost that? He'd lose the club completely.

My man wants to keep the patch on his back? We've got to act like nothing's happened.

I wonder if it's possible for Demon, hell, us, to do that.

CHAPTER 13
PALADIN

Now

When I'd first thought of coming to Colorado with Jay, I'd visions in my head of us living together, of having the chance to become a couple. Of course, I'd recognise there were boundaries until we could cement our relationship when she reaches the age of consent. Whatever my own desires, I respect Drummer and Slick too much to do anything but wait. But I'd expected to be her anchor, as she would be mine, easing us both into our new worlds.

I hadn't anticipated arriving alone, riding up to a foreign clubhouse found only by the guidance of my GPS.

I'm twenty-one years old. I joined the Satan's Devils Tucson chapter when I was eighteen, drawn by my love of bikes and the camaraderie I saw existing between the men. I lost my family when I was young. Not an unusual story. Dad did a runner, Mom couldn't cope, escaped into a bottle and a handful of drugs. Unbeknownst to her, they'd been cheap because they'd been cut with Fentanyl. Luckily my mind has blanked out the finer details of sitting beside her dead body, until someone had investigated the non-stop crying of a five year old and screaming of a baby coming from the apartment.

No family could be found, or none that had wanted me and my three month old sister. Separated, we disappeared into the system. I was one of the lucky ones and wasn't abused, no, just taken in so the family could claim the money, thereafter to be virtually ignored. It was many years before I'd learned my young sister had been adopted. When I was old enough, I'd tried, but have never been able to find the girl who would be around Jayden's age. All I can hope is that she's been loved and cared for, and that, one day, our paths might cross.

The Satan's Devils are the only true family I've ever known, the only place I felt I'd belonged. Now I've given it up to be with Jayden. As I stare at the imposing building in front of me, realising the immensity of what I've left behind, I can only hope I'm doing the right thing. Oh, I couldn't leave her to come here alone, but is my path as aligned with hers as I believe?

As a prospect you know you're an outsider, having to prove to the brothers you're trustworthy. Your sole focus on getting that patch, working your ass off, having no time to yourself and nothing to think about except how best to convince the men around you of your worthiness to call them brother. Neither accepted nor excluded until your time is done.

Here, I won't be a prospect. If I were, I'd know what to expect. No, here I'm entering as an equal, calling men I've never met brother. No guarantee they'll accept me, they'll be as distrusting of me as I am of them. I can see no clear path to earning that trust.

Maybe if I was older, more experienced, I'd better know what to do and how best to fit in, have the confidence that comes with the years. But I'm not. And I don't.

A prospect has come to the gate. I put on my cut when I arrived in Pueblo, but the patch still carries the word Tucson on the back. He stares at me for a moment before sliding the barrier open. *Guess I'm expected.*

He waves across the parking lot to a line of bikes, I back mine in on the end. Getting off, I stretch, flexing my fingers and arching my back. That was a long fucking ride, I'm glad to have made it here, and in one piece. The doorway beckons, but before I make my way inside, I delay a second longer while I send a quick text.

Pal: I've arrived. Just heading in to meet the brothers.

I wait a second, but there's no response. *She's probably busy settling in herself.* Then, bracing myself, I take the first step into my new life.

The clubroom is large and rectangular, the normal bar stretching down one long side. My initial thought is how the prospects must have to run from one end to the other to keep glasses topped up. A range of tables and chairs, are occupied by a number of brothers, scary that there are no immediate faces I recognise. They're all wearing cuts with the Satan's Devils patch on the back, but that's the only comforting thing that I see.

A man's pushed away from the bar. "Well, you coming or going? You're letting the cold air in."

I grin, that's not words often heard in Tucson, normally it's about letting the cold air out, but springtime is decidedly cooler here. Hoisting my duffle over my shoulder, I step toward the man who's spoken. "Paladin." I hold out my hand as I introduce myself.

"Well we weren't expectin' the fuckin' tooth fairy," he responds. "Thunder. Sergeant-At-Arms."

I raise my chin at him, "Thunder." I repeat.

"Drink? Or dump your gear in your room?"

Feeling all eyes burning into me, knowing how important first impressions are, I decide finding where I'll be sleeping and getting my game face on is probably the best way to start. "Drink sounds good, but I'll get my shit sorted first."

"Ink?" Thunder calls out.

I turn, expecting to see a heavily tatted brother, instead a man approaches whose short-sleeved tee shows no decoration on any of the skin I can see. He's probably covered on his chest and back.

"Yeah, Thunder?"

"Take our new member up to the room we prepared for him, will you? Show him what's what?"

"Sure. Paladin, isn't it?"

Says so on my cut, so I just raise my chin.

I follow him up the stairs. On the way he asks the polite things about how my ride here was, how long it took. When he's finished asking and I've offered answers to his satisfaction, he stops in front of a room near the end of a hallway and opens the door.

There's a key in the lock, he takes it out and hands it to me. "Best keep it locked. Else you might find a bitch in your bed. Specially a new, young specimen like yourself. Unless you like surprises waiting for you, that is."

I don't. So I hold onto that key tight. The room's not bad. A window looks out onto the rear of the compound and the desert beyond. No mountains or saguaro in sight, and the vegetation's different to that which I'm used to. A feeling of homesickness washes over me, but I brush that aside. *No looking back. This is my home now.* I'm pleasantly surprised there's a small but serviceable bathroom off to the side. I hadn't expected such luxury. A bed dominates the room even though it's pushed up against the wall, a small wall-mounted flat screen TV can be viewed from the bed, and there's a chest of drawers and suitable closet to hang up my clothes, such as they are. I haven't brought a load of stuff with me. I couldn't carry much on the bike.

The bed looks like it's been freshly made, and if I'm not mistaken, the bedding looks new.

"Jeannie, she's Bomber's old lady, she likes to make sure things are set up for visitors. Or, in your case, new members. Not that we've had someone transfer in before, not that I can remember. Of course, that should be Moira's job, she's Prez's woman, but she doesn't come to the clubhouse much nowadays."

Moira. I know the name. She's who's going to be giving a room to my girl. Idly I wonder why she's become a stranger to the club. *Bad feeling?* Hope that doesn't influence my woman. *Hell, can't think of her like that. Not yet.*

"How many members are there in all?" I need to start learning about this new chapter.

Ink leans back against the door while I throw my duffle and saddlebags on the bed. "Thirteen if you count Prez, fourteen now including you. At least you got us away from the unlucky number." He chuckles. "Three prospects. You met Runt, he's the kid let you in the gate."

"I didn't notice any old ladies…?"

"Bomber's got Jeannie, as I said. Buzzard, our Treasurer is married to Sindy, but that's all of them. Then there's Bella, Titsy, Breezy, Tulia and Sheila, they're our club girls."

Only a couple of old ladies, and no kids by the sound of it. This seems to be a very different club to the one that I left. My immediate reaction is that I'm not going to like it, but know I've got to give it a chance. "Hellfire's the Prez, Demon's the VP," I've met them in Tucson. "Thunder's the SAA. You got an enforcer?"

"Sure have. That's Mace's job, not that he's been doing it long, but he seems to have settled into it." He pauses, frowns, his expression suggesting there might be a story there, but it's obviously not something he's going into now. "Sparky you might have met as well. He's the road captain, we supported your run a year or so back, when you were raising funds for that kid with sickle cell disease."

I nod. I do remember him now. Sparky had been helping Joker along with the other chapters' road captains.

"Probably better if you meet everyone else in person. Helps to put a face to the handle. Talkin' of which. Where d'you get yours from? Sounds like you're a knight in fuckin' shinin' armour."

I grin, he's closer than he knows. "In black leather on a shinin' bike, more like. But yeah, that's the way of it. Young girl thought I saved her."

"Yeah? I'll look forward to hearin' about it."

He'll wait a long time. I frown. I want Jay to have a fresh start here, not be burdened by everyone knowing her past.

Pushing away from the door, Ink suggests, "Why don't you freshen up, then come down and find me? I'll introduce you around." He breaks off, tossing me a sympathetic look. "Can't be easy startin' off in a new chapter. Word is you came up with a bitch. Not your choice to transfer, Brother?"

I shrug. "Circumstances are what they are." I straighten my back as I turn and give him a chin lift. "Gonna do my best to fit in, make a home here, throw in with my new club. You won't find me wanting."

He takes a step forward and slaps me on the back. "Sure we won't, Brother. But you might want to get that bottom rocker changed. Wearing the Tucson patch makes you look like a visitor."

"As soon as I get one, I will," I agree.

"Think Prez wants to hand it to you in church. A formal sort of welcome."

"When is church?" I ask, knowing how ignorant I sound. It was always Fridays in Tucson.

"Tomorrow, Wednesday."

Middle of the week church. That's a new one on me. Still, when in Rome and all that. I'm in no position to complain. "I won't be a minute."

He waves his hand dismissively. "Take your time. We won't be going anywhere, and the bar won't run dry," another pause, then a wide grin, "if it does, you won't be the only one complainin'."

Dutifully I laugh. He exits the room closing the door behind him, and I'm left alone in my new home. Feeling completely disorientated, I start putting the shit I brought with me away. Opening the closet I find there are blankets on the top shelf, things we had little need for in Tucson, I shiver just looking at them. *At least I've arrived in the spring. Got a few months to find my feet before I start having to cope with snow.*

My tablet goes into my bedside table, a photo Sam had given me, of me standing with the Tucson crew, every brother, old ladies and children, and even fucking Grunt in prime position in the front goes by the side of my bed. Huh. I never thought I'd miss a dog. I look at the various expressions. Sam had put her camera on a timer, Mouse is clearly staring as though it should have gone off already, Joker's laughing at something Lady had said. Sam's half turning, trying to get them to be serious. Wraith's standing looking stoic. *Fuck, I miss them already.* Pushing that wave of longing for things familiar back down, I go to the bathroom and take a long piss, noticing towels have been hung ready for me. Which is good, I didn't have room to bring any of that type of shit.

I walk back to the bedroom while zipping my fly, thinking it's time to take the plunge and go down. These first meetings are going to make a lasting impression on everyone. Can't put it off.

Descending the stairs, feeling like an exotic new exhibit in a zoo, I notice Ink waving at me from the bar. I start making my way across the clubroom when a large man stands in front of me. "Buzzard, or Buzz," he informs me. "Treasurer. Keep on my right side, pay your dues and we'll be right."

I grin, as I'm meant to. "Pay me my cut and we'll be square."

"You'll do," he tells me. "What's your line of expertise, Brother?"

I shrug. "Happy to throw my hand in wherever it's needed. Can turn my hand to a wrench, or anything that's going."

"Fucking bitch! Get your hand off my man! Sheesh! How many times do I have to warn you?"

As I start to spin around at the high-pitched voice, Buzzard leans in. "That's Jeannie. She's Bomber's ol' lady. Think the club whores fuck with her on purpose, doesn't take much to get her riled. Think she still believes Bomber's in his prime."

Completing my one hundred and eighty, I see a woman, probably in her middle to late fifties standing with her hands on her hips. A young twenty-something is hovering, yeah, a little too close to a man who's sixty if he's a day. His paunch hangs over the belt of his sagging denim jeans, and his hair is thinning. His beard is so grey it's almost white. His jowls reddened from the wind and over indulgence in alcohol. His face currently split in two by a wide grin as the two women fight over him.

The sweet butt, clearly feeling brave, puts her hand on his shoulder. The old man, who I take it is Bomber, does nothing to discourage her. His eyebrow raises in challenge to his wife.

Jeannie, yeah, that's what Buzz called her, well, she slaps the club girl's hand right off. "Leave my man alone, you two-bit whore," she screams.

"Pal. Good to meet ya. I'm Lizard. This here thing that looks half dead is Cad. You need info, you go to him. He's a whizz at mining for data."

Cad indeed is so pale you can see the veins through his skin. Guess he's Mouse's equivalent. I shake both their hands, wondering if I should correct them on my name, so far only Jayden has ever shortened it. But I let it ride. New place, new handle. Maybe it will stop the knight jokes.

I meet another old-timer, Rusty. Share a beer with Bomber once his wife has calmed down and have the opportunity to thank her for setting up my room. Thunder seems a good guy, so does Mace when I meet him. Not everyone's here, and I'm quite grateful Hellfire and Demon don't put in an appearance.

A few beers, good conversation—when we start speaking our universal language, bikes—I start to feel a little more at home. By the time everyone begins to leave, I've got a mellow glow and have relaxed a tad. But it still doesn't feel like I'm more than a visitor. Guess settling in is going to take time.

I've got to get used to the differences, learn a new set of brothers' quirks and idiosyncrasies. I still feel unsettled when I take myself off to my room and lie down to sleep in an unfamiliar bed, hoping giving up everything to be with Jay hasn't been a dreadful mistake.

The long tiring ride, the beer coupled with the late evening, means my eyes are drooping as I check my phone seeing I've missed a text telling me Jay's glad I got here safe, then I slide under the sheets and take no time dropping off to sleep.

CHAPTER 14
JAYDEN

Although Slick and Hellfire conversed throughout the journey from the airport to the clubhouse, I sensed Hellfire was only providing answers out of politeness. He seemed to be distracted, and it wasn't because he was concentrating on driving as there wasn't a lot of traffic around. I'd picked up on an undercurrent between him and his son at the airport. Selfishly, I hope if there's anything wrong it won't involve me. I don't want to come and stay in a place where there's tension. Leaving everything I've ever known back in Tucson, changing schools, leaving my family behind, that's enough to cope with without adding anything else.

I haven't seen my mom for over two years. No big loss. Ella, my sister has always been there for me. And in recent years, I've lived with her and her husband. I liked the house we had in Tucson, and loved being at the clubhouse. There was always something going on. I'd fallen naturally into the role and had enjoyed looking after the babies and young children.

Sam and Sophie will be due any day. I stuff my hand in my mouth to stifle a groan. I have to stop thinking about what I'm missing. Got to start looking to the future. *Maybe there'll be kids here as well?* I think I'd like to work with young children when I'm old enough. Have a few of my own, maybe. *With Paladin?* Perhaps.

When I was fourteen and rescued, I'd latched onto Paladin. He was my rock. I'd wanted him to take the bad memories away, but he'd refused. I didn't know at the time that Slick and

Drummer had warned him off, just went through hell worrying I was too damaged for anyone to want me. But he'd said the right things, explained. While I didn't like it, I could do nothing but accept it.

Now, two years on, I know he was right. We've never kissed, never been girlfriend and boyfriend, just friends. That was probably for the best. The bad memories have faded; I no longer need to make new ones to replace them. Just start all over again, and do it right.

And I could. Very soon. I'm in Colorado. I doubt Hellfire and his wife would be as restrictive as Ella and Slick, they've no vested interest in a houseguest they've given room too. Here the state law means Paladin and I could legally get together on my seventeenth birthday. I'm sure it's what he's planning on. But the question is, is that still what I want? The idea scares me.

"You're quiet."

Ella's voice breaks into my thoughts. I glance at her as she sits beside me. "Just thinking."

She gives me a hard stare. "I'm sure Hellfire would let me stay on with you. Perhaps just for a few weeks until you get settled in. Don't like the thought of you being alone…"

"I won't be alone, El," I reply fast. She's not had an easy pregnancy; she needs to be settled back in Tucson. They tried so hard for this baby, don't want anything to risk it now. *One more kid I won't be there to see.* I shake my head and bite my lip to force back the tears. *She mustn't see them. Mustn't know I'm upset.* "It's just strange, El. The unknown. Hellfire seems nice." *He actually seems frightening,* but I'm not going to tell her that.

"Hmm." Perhaps I didn't have to say anything. My sister doesn't sound convinced.

It's not long before we're turning down a driveway and drawing up at a pleasant house with a wraparound veranda. There's even a swing on it. All good so far. Though a big part of me wishes I was back with Paladin on the Tucson compound. Here I'll be left on my own with strangers.

Hellfire opens my door, Slick's got Ella's. When we step out I pull my sweater around me. *It seems cold.* Colder than Tucson, anyway.

"Come in and meet Moira. She's looking forward to meeting you." Hellfire sounds welcoming, but there's something about his tone that makes me think his joviality is forced.

He unlocks the front door, steps back, and ushers us inside. The house is homey enough, the door leading onto a short hallway, which then opens up into a large family room. Comfortable looking sofas to three sides, a large TV. Double doors lead through to a big kitchen.

"Moira!" Hellfire suddenly booms out; his voice having increased significantly in volume making me jump.

Slick enters the door behind us, he's got my suitcase in his hand, and his and Ella's travel bag slung over his shoulder. For want of anything better to do, he just sets them down where he stands.

For someone who's supposed to be looking forward to us visiting, Moira doesn't seem very impressed when she enters the room. The look she tosses Hellfire's way is unreadable, but then a smile, somewhat forced I think, appears on her face as she walks across to us with her hand outstretched. "Slick," she greets my brother-in-law and then my sister, "Ella." Now she turns her attention to me. "You must be Jayden. Welcome."

"Thank you for agreeing she could stay with you," Ella starts.

Moira waves her off. "No worries. Be good to have some female company. My daughter's living away from home now. Well, all the kids are." Her face twitches as though disappointed. "Jayden, would you like to come and see your room?"

"Thank you. Mrs…" My voice falters. I can't call her Mrs Hellfire, and I have no idea of their legal surname.

"Oh, call me Moira, please. And it's this way." She turns and leads the way down a hallway, as behind me, Slick dutifully picks up my suitcase and follows.

"This was Kennedy's, my daughter's room. I'm sure you'll settle in fine."

It's a nice room, quite large. I spy a small bathroom off to the side. It's probably as large as my suite back on the compound, and larger than my bedroom in Slick and Ella's house. Outside the window I can see views over a desert. "It's lovely," I tell her, truthfully.

"Slick, Ella. I've put you in the guestroom. It's just along here if you want to drop off your overnight bag." She leads them away. I stay in the room that's been given to me. Wondering how long I'll be here. I know I won't be returning to Tucson anytime soon.

"Do you drive?" A deep voice breaks into my reverie. Swinging around, I see Demon. He'd startled me.

"Not yet, no. I've got my learner's permit, but then we had to return to the compound, and I…"

He doesn't wait for the rest of my irrelevant explanation. "We better get you started. Best if you have a car, then you'll be able to get yourself around."

I hadn't been allowed to be independent back in Tucson. Too much of a risk to go anywhere alone. Getting behind the wheel of a car hadn't seemed worth it. While I already feel homesick, I start realising there might be benefits to me being well out of the reach of the Herreras. Have a car and be able to do what I want? Have the freedom to just go to the shops? To go to school alone?

I give Demon my first genuine smile since I arrived. "I'll have to get used to the idea of freedom, here. I couldn't go anywhere alone back in Arizona."

He's leaning against my doorframe, his brow creased. "Fuck. Knew a bit of your story, but hadn't realised the implications."

I nod. "Not having someone trying to kidnap me is going to take some getting used to."

He chuckles, and comes over, ruffling my hair. "You might not be from this chapter, but you're a Satan's Devils' brat all the same. Got a whole club of brothers who'll look out for you. We'll keep you safe here."

I'm curious. "Is it a big chapter?"

He's happy to answer me. "Thirteen members, well, fourteen now Paladin's joined. Three prospects."

I frown, not sure I ought to ask, but I do anyway. "Is it, is it like the Tucson chapter?"

"In what way?"

I shrug. How can I ask if they're into anything illegal? Tucson wasn't, and I didn't want Pal to be mixed up in anything which could get him arrested.

A quick grin comes to his face. "Satan's Devils have the same rules and regs all over. Wouldn't keep our charter if we didn't abide by them. But there'll probably be a different vibe here. Tucson is quite a family club, here, not so much. Of course, we've got different businesses as well. You can come to the club-house soon and see for yourself."

I thank him, grateful the VP has taken time to speak to me. As he leaves me alone, I wonder about Paladin. How long it will take him to get here, what he'll think of the new chapter he's joined. Where he'll work. What he'll do now his responsibility for babysitting me has been removed. *What I'll do without him.* I've been so used to him being my shadow, I miss him already. But, perhaps this is what I need. Some space. To get my feelings straight in my head.

I heft the heavy case onto the bed, open it, and start to unpack.

I'd been raped when I was a young teenager. Multiple times by multiple men. Made to believe I had to let them use my body, keeping my secret because of threats to my mom. *They'd burn down her house with her in it.* When Paladin, nah, I know better now. When the Devils had rescued me, I'd had a lot of experience of sex and men's sexual desires. Therapy had helped me deal with it, and at first I'd thought Paladin would want payment for his friendship in the same way. Didn't all men want that?

Then, after feeling rejected, I was pleased he'd be my friend without any expectations. I couldn't say I went back to playing with dolls, but I did regain the teenager inside which had been taken away from me. Now I'm sixteen, I've started to think about men, boys, once again. Curious to know what being someone's girlfriend would be like, but my imagination doesn't take me very far. My therapist had explained, in time I'd start to feel desires natural to a young woman. So far, I haven't. I've started to believe something is wrong with me. Something those men had taken, more than my innocence and youth. A chance to ever be normal.

Paladin, Slick, El, everyone. They all expect Pal and I to get together. That's all I've longed for, always considering him mine. That's why he came with me, the promise of a future. But would I ever be able to enter into a proper adult relationship? Were the dreams I once had just those of a child?

Closing one drawer, I open another.

"You okay?"

"Yeah, El. Just getting settled in."

"Moira seems nice." As my sister gives her seal of approval, she comes across and sits on the bed, watching me unpack.

"Uh huh." I give a non-committal comment. I won't pronounce judgement on Moira until I've lived here a few days. Weeks perhaps. How long does it take to really know someone?

"Demon had a word. Said I need a car."

"He just said the same thing to Slick. How do you feel about that, Jayden?"

A genuine smile grows on my face. "I love the idea, El. Oh, I know it will take a while, but to be able to go where I want to, when I want? That sounds amazing." I notice her face dropping. Shoving the last of my underwear into the spot I'd reserved for it, I go across to her. "What's up, Ella?"

Her head shakes slowly. "We were doing our best for you. Keeping you safe and out of danger. I'd lost sight that we were smothering you too. Now you've got to learn independence without me being here to help."

"You did what you had to," I reply, firmly. "And there's the phone, and FaceTime El. We'll speak every day."

She nods. "Just so you know, Slick's going to give Demon the money for a car. He'll sort it out for you. I'm sure Paladin will help you learn to drive."

Slick's been good to me. Treated me like a daughter in many ways. Never made me feel a burden. Part of me thinks though, with their baby on the way, he and my sister deserve to have some alone time, without worrying about me every minute. Even if I've got doubts, I've got to consider them. This is the best thing all around.

There's an undercurrent at dinner. Slick and Ella don't seem to pick up on it, but I do. There's something not quite right between Hellfire and his wife, or their son. It's not that anything's said, the opposite in fact. It's more what's not said. Oh, they talk about the area, what the town's like, about the school I'll be enrolled in, but not until after the summer break as there's no point just going for a couple of weeks now.

They're polite to Slick and Ella, friendly to me. But to each other? I feel I've stepped into a soap opera steeped in family drama.

When my phone pings with a text from Paladin telling me he's arrived safe, I smile to myself, determined to reply later. As I watch the show play out around me, I realise how much I miss him. When Slick and El leave in the morning, I'm going to be all alone.

Just before I go to sleep, I remember I haven't replied to Paladin. I type a quick message to Paladin, hoping we'll can have a conversation. But my phone stays quiet. My lifeline seems a million miles away.

There's not been a day I haven't been close to Paladin.

CHAPTER 15

MOIRA

"Well, that seemed to go alright."

I watch Hellfire sliding out of his cut, placing it carefully on a chair, and then his hands going to the back of his neck and begin to rip his tee over his head. "You think?" I snarl. "And just what do you think you're fucking doing?"

He pauses, mid-action, his hand comically frozen halfway over his head with a handful of material bunched in it. "I'm coming to bed."

"You sleep at the club."

He releases his hold on the shirt, and comes over to where I'm already snuggled under the sheets. "I do sleep at the club. When it's more convenient. But this is my home, and my place is here with you." He stares at me, I stare back. Until I can no longer meet those intense eyes. The ones that used to watch me with such longing, with such hunger. "You're saying I'm not welcome in my own bed? What the fuck, Mo?"

I don't want him here if my suspicions are right, and he's normally warming someone else's sheets instead. But I also don't have the nerve to come out and ask him. My suspicions are bad enough. Having them confirmed, I'd have no choice but to leave him. Whatever his faults, he's still the one that makes my heart beat fast, I still love him. Whether I could turn that emotion off if I knew for sure he was unfaithful, I've no idea. I just wouldn't be able to be anywhere near him.

Instead of answering, I turn over, keeping well to my side. From the sounds, I know he's removing the rest of his clothes.

When he talks next, he returns to the first topic. "Jayden seems a sweet girl. Polite. Mature for her age."

"Given her background that's hardly surprising." I'm sniping at him, but I can't stop myself.

A pause before he replies, "No, I suppose not."

I feel the bed dipping. A familiar sensation that makes me realise how much I missed it. "Tried to make her, and her family feel welcome."

"You don't think we did that?" His voice sounds confused.

"Hell, you could cut the atmosphere with a knife around that table. You'd have to be blind and deaf not to see there was something wrong."

"Not sure I understand what you're getting at Mo…"

I sit up fast, pulling the sheet around me. Wishing I'd put on a nightie, but I'd reckoned on sleeping alone. "So, our son has just found out you're actually his brother and not the father he always believed you to be. He's having difficulty coming to terms with that for some unknown reason," I scoff. Then huff, "And as for you and I…"

His hand snakes out, grabbing onto my arm. "You and I… what, Mo?"

Reaching for my discarded robe, I pull it around me. When I'm decent, I stand, and turn, my eyes blazing. "You're gone more than you're here, Hell. And when you are here, you want nothing to do with me." Tears prick at my eyes. The confrontation I wanted to avoid is steaming down on me like a freight train. It's all my fault, I should have kept my mouth shut. Now I've got to face it head-on.

His head has rolled back onto the pillow. His eyes seem focused on a spot above my head. Taking in a deep breath, he sighs deeply. "It's not what you think, Mo."

"And what do I think, Hell?" I throw back at him. "I'll tell you what I think. What I *know*. You don't want me. You. The man with the huge sexual appetite. You haven't wanted me for months. If you're not getting it from me, you're getting it somewhere else." I reach into my pocket and pull out a tissue, blowing my nose and dabbing at my eyes.

Hell sits up fast. His naked chest taunting me. He might have aged, but I still find him as attractive as the day I married him. "I've not been cheating on you, Mo. I wouldn't, couldn't…"

I don't believe him. "I can't even blame you. I've lost any attractiveness I ever had. You married a fit young girl, you've ended up with an old woman. You just don't desire me anymore." It's only when he shushes me, I realise how loud my voice has become. Although our visitors are down the hallway, I wouldn't want them to hear this particular discussion. Not when it's leading to the end of everything I ever wanted. A good marriage with my man.

"Mo, come here." He holds out his arms. I want nothing more than to be enfolded within them. To seek the security and reassurance I need.

But I have to be strong. Now we've started, we've got to let this conversation reach its conclusion. I've been walking a tightrope for far too long, desperately trying to keep my balance to stop me from falling.

Seeing I'm not making a move toward him, he breathes out deeply, then says in his low, gravelly voice, "Mo. I've not been cheating on you. And I still find you attractive. Fuck woman, never in all the years of our marriage have I looked at anyone else."

The one thing Hell's always been is honest. Even when he's telling me something he knows I won't like. But there's part of me, a big part, that for the first time since the day we said our wedding vows, can't credit him with telling the truth.

He shakes his head and gives a pointed look toward the hallway. "At least come closer. I don't want to have to shout for this conversation."

I'm torn between leaving the bedroom and going to sleep on the sofa, or staying to listen to what I don't want to hear. Sleep? Who am I kidding? Wherever I am, I won't sleep a wink after this. Straightening my back a little, wondering what I can do to prepare myself to hear the words, *I'm leaving you*, realising fast, there's nothing I can do to be ready for that. But I do agree. What we need to discuss isn't for visitors' ears.

I return to the bed, perching on my side, my back turned toward him so he won't see the tears in my eyes.

He moves fast, his strong arms imprisoning me. His words, quietly spoken, direct into my ear. "I love you. I'm not leaving you. I'm *not* cheating on you. Fuck, woman. How could you think it? How could you imagine I don't find you desirable anymore?"

I wait. In times past, he'd have proved it. Have taken my hand and placed it on his thick, hard and ready cock, before throwing me down and sinking into me. He does nothing of the kind.

"Babe, darlin'. Oh, Mo. It's not you, it's me."

"That's what they all fucking say." I huff out. Christ, what a cliché to come out of the mouth of my man.

He snorts. "Yeah, that came out wrong. But it's true, Mo. I've been trying to deal, trying to understand, hoping it would get better. But it really is me." He breaks off, I feel his body tense. Something tells me what he says next is going to be significant. I wait. He doesn't disappoint. "There's no way I can get it up anymore unless I swallow a little blue pill."

Wait a freaking minute. What did he just say? "Hell…?"

I don't know what expression I put into that one word, his name with the inflection that turned it into a question, but suddenly his arms leave me. He throws back the sheets, slides off his side of the bed, and stomps around to stand in front of me. Raising my eyes I see him in all his tattooed glory. He stands, one hand on his very limp dick. He's tugging it.

"See? It's dead as a fuckin' dodo. No life in it anymore. Doesn't matter if it's you, or anyone. Not that I've tried," he puts in the last quickly, "but the live porn in the clubhouse doesn't make it stir. Nor our best strippers on the fuckin' pole." He drops his hands away. His dick, even limp, is impressive. "I don't even get mornin' wood anymore."

Tentatively I reach out my hand. At first he steps back, then, with an exaggerated sigh, he moves forward again, allowing me to touch it. It doesn't twitch. Just hangs there. The cock which used to reach proudly and point up toward his stomach. Idly I notice just how grey his pubic hair has become. He's getting old. He's not the only one.

I sink to my knees, kiss him, *there*, then move my mouth over his cock. *Nothing*.

Grasping my hair lightly, he moves my head away, then he's on his knees beside me. "Have you any fuckin' idea what a failure this makes me feel? What a sorry excuse for a man?"

"You're still all man." I tell him, trying to push my own feelings aside. Despite him telling me otherwise, I still feel this must be some fault of my own. "Perhaps if I was still younger…"

"Woman, stop that. Ain't got fuck all to do with you. It's me." His hand moves under my chin, gripping it gently, forcing me to look him in the eyes. "Up here," he taps his head, "I still find you as attractive as I ever have. It's just my darn cock is broke. What kind of man can't service his woman?" His eyes close briefly, then open again. "I've been scared to tell you. That's why I've been hidin' out at the club. I couldn't face you. I can't give you what you need. I've been so scared you'd leave me."

His fears, so close to my own, make me giggle. He looks at me as though I've lost my mind, then shakes his head. "This," he points at his cock laying lifeless against his thigh, "you think this is funny? Fuck, woman."

I can't hold back the chuckles. Staring at me as if I'm losing it, he starts to rise. I grab his hands in mine, holding them tightly. "Hell, listen to me. Do you remember the last time, Christ, how long ago was it?"

"Ten months," he answers through gritted teeth.

"And two days," I tell him. Well, let's be accurate now. "It hurt me."

He looks confused. "I thought we used enough lube."

"Not the point, Hell. We did. I was sore anyway. So I went to the doctor. Turns out my oestrogen levels are falling, it causes thinning of the vaginal tissues, well, that's how the doctor explained it. She gave me a cream for it."

His face falls. "You're okay, now? If I took a blue pill…"

"I used the cream. For a time. But it seemed to cause migraines. And when you weren't coming near me, it didn't seem worth it anymore."

His head bows. His shoulders shake. Just when I'm about to ask him what's wrong, he looks up with his eyes shining with mirth. "The reason I haven't taken a blue pill? They give me blinding headaches after."

Now I'm giggling uncontrollably. Moments later I'm in his arms. He leans back against the bed, and I'm sitting on the floor on his lap. We probably look ridiculous, but who cares? For the first time in months I feel I've got my man back with me.

"Don't care if we can't get physical anymore," he tells me softly. "I've got all I want in my arms right here."

"Well, it seems we could. If we arrange a time and place carefully, and stock up with Advil."

That gets us both roaring with laughter again.

"If I could take HRT, it might have been easier…"

His arms tighten. "Don't want you even thinking about that shit. Don't want you putting hormones in your body. I was so fuckin' scared."

"It's over now." I say, soothingly. It had been a few years back when I'd had a tiny cancerous lump removed from my breast. They got it early, got it all out. But until I'd received the all clear, Hellfire is right. He'd been scared out of his mind. I'd been frightened as well, but him? It was a demon he couldn't face, couldn't fight for me. He'd ended up feeling so useless.

I pat his cheek. "I'm fine," I reassure him. "*Fine.*" I'd given up smoking, started eating better. It had given us both a scare.

He frowns, "This cream…"

"Is perfectly safe. The doctor assured me. But what about you?"

The lines on his forehead deepen. "Getting old, drinking too much. Smoking. Could be stress." His mouth quirks. "Could be I wore the darn thing out satisfying my woman."

Now that deserves, and gets, a bat on his arm.

He stands, managing to lift me onto my feet. "Now, come to bed, Mo. Let's hold each other like we used to."

That sounds nice. Even that's been a very long time.

CHAPTER 16
HELLFIRE

I'm fifty-seven years old for fuck's sake. That's not old, just middle-aged. Yet as I hold my wife who I hadn't lied to when I said I still find her attractive, unable to give her the loving she deserves, I feel past it. As if my life is as dead as my fucking cock.

Moira's pretending to sleep, I can tell the difference. To be honest, I'm all talked out. It had been so tough admitting my problem to her. What man likes to feel he's a failure? Yeah, I'd been to a doctor, knew that I was far from alone in suffering this problem. Truth is, Mo's getting older, just like myself. Her skin, once smooth, now has wrinkles, she carries extra weight than she used to, and her stretch marks will never fade now. But she's my wife, I love her, love the signs she's given birth to my children, admire the way she's aged with grace. She's still the one my eyes first notice when I walk into a room, the younger women who've not lived a life like she has, somehow not having a fraction of the character that shows in her face. It's her that I want. It always has been.

When I was twenty I would have viewed a woman of her age with disinterest, as I've grown older, my tastes have changed. It's been hard to convince her that she's the only woman for me, especially now I'm not able to physically demonstrate it.

The doctor had suggested things I can try. More exercise than just riding my bike, giving up smoking, cutting down on the drink. But fuck, I'm the president of an MC, responsible for keeping my crew in line and bringing in enough money from our businesses to keep everyone's bellies filled. It used to not be so difficult, drug and gun running being easy money. But we'd lost enough brothers either at the end of a gun or to languish in a jail cell to go back to that.

Stress. Pressure. Yeah, the old days were hard enough, but earning money legit hasn't brought any less of a burden. That's my biggest problem. One that goes with being president of the club. Knowing how hard it is, how could I put that onto anyone else? I wonder if Demon's considering my offer. He'd be a fool to take it on if I'm honest. As for myself? I'd made the offer rashly, despite everything, I know deep down I'm not ready to step down from my place at the head of the table.

These last couple of days have been fucked up. Christ knows where Demon's head's at, and as for myself and Mo, we're forced to face up to issues we'd thought were lost in time. Pressure? Stress? Can't see life getting much easier. Not in the short-term at least. My cock doesn't look like it will have any life in it anytime soon, or not without artificial help. Maybe never. I can only hope I can hang onto my wife.

Eventually I can feel Mo's actually sleeping. I ease my arm out from under her head and try to get comfortable. It's a long time before I drop off myself.

I wake early. Slipping out of the bed I leave without waking her. There's no need for her to get up, not yet. I'll get coffee going, at this hour, no one else will be stirring. Or that's what I believe until I encounter Slick in the kitchen. He's already got a mug of coffee in his hand.

"Morning." I push my bed-head hair back out of my eyes. My nostrils twitch at the aroma of freshly brewed coffee. "Enough there for me?"

"Yeah. Help yourself." Slick grins sheepishly. "It's your kitchen after all."

I pour a coffee, and inhale its life-giving perfume. "Bed comfortable?" I'm wondering if it's not. I didn't expect him to be up this early.

"Bed's great. Thanks for putting us up. Just worried, that's all."

Immediately I guess at the heart of his problem, his concerns forcing me to put mine aside. "Kid will be fine with us, Slick. Honestly, Mo will be glad of the company around here. She's been at a bit of a loss since the kids left home."

He nods slowly. "I'm sure you'll look after her well. It's just, ever since I've known her, we've had to watch out for her, you know? Her safety is so important. Kind of feels like I'm abdicating my duties leaving her with somebody else."

"You're still watching out for her. From what you've said, getting her out of the reach of the Herreras is the key to keeping her safe. You're not abandoning her."

Again, his head dips up and down.

I place my empty cup on the counter. "Now, what's the score with Paladin?"

When he indicates a chair, I expect this to be a long conversation. I put more coffee on to brew, then sit opposite, elbows on the table, my head resting on my hands.

Slick doesn't disappoint, starting immediately. "He got his handle as Jayden seemed to think the sun shone out of his ass, that he was her knight in shining armour. Saw his interest in her right from that time. Drummer and I read him the riot act, he'd risk his patch if he made one wrong move toward her."

"Which, clearly, he hasn't done."

"Nah. I've got a lot of respect for the brother. He's been her friend, her protector. I don't think his feelin's have changed. Done nothing but show he'd wait for her."

"And now?"

Slick shrugs. "In Arizona the age of consent is eighteen."

"Here, it's a year earlier." Not that a designated age made much difference to most teens. "You want me to enforce your original boundary?" I hope he doesn't, I've already got enough on my plate. Don't want to include babysitting a horny teenager.

"Fuck, I don't know." Slick looks confused. "I've interfered in their lives about as much as I want to. They were still under my roof? Then, yes, what I said still goes. But I can't put that on you. It's not fair. Think Ella and I knew we might be pushin' them together by lettin' them both come here. But fuck, didn't want to take away her lifeline."

"You said his feelin's haven't changed. What about hers?"

Slick snorts. "No fuckin' idea. Not something I've spoken about with her."

"Ella?"

"Again, I don't know. She hasn't said anything. Guess it's just as hard to talk about some things with your little sister. Can understand she wouldn't want to poke the sleepin' bear."

"And risk wakin' it."

"You've got it." Slick grins quickly, then his brow creases. "There was a kid back at the clubhouse. A stray adopted by Mouse. He's a year or so younger than Jayden. Kids naturally drifted together. Made me wonder whether being cooped up with Paladin hasn't been healthy, she hasn't had any freedom to explore her options."

I can see his point. "Demon's suggested she gets some independence, learns to drive."

"I know. Already agreed to buy her a car. Something she couldn't have considered in Tucson. We'd never have let her out of our sight."

I stare at him. "Seems she needs to have the ties loosened. Be allowed to make decisions and mistakes for herself."

Slick gazes into the distance. "You're right, Brother. Might not like it. But I think you're right. If, in the end, it brings her back to Paladin, all well and good. If not, he'll have to accept it."

Glancing up at the clock, I startle. I hadn't realised how long we'd been chewing the fat. I stand, pouring another cup of coffee. "I've got to get going, Slick. I'll take this up to Moira, she'll get you some breakfast."

"Thanks, Hellfire. I need to go wake Ella myself. We've got to get a move on if we're going to make our flight."

"One of the prospects will be here to take you to the airport. I'd stay, but…"

"Yeah, no worries. You go and do your stuff. And, thank you, Brother."

I wave off his gratitude, slap his back, tell him I'll keep in touch, then we go to wake our respective wives.

Arriving at the clubhouse I find although it's early, there are a number of members around, mainly in the big kitchen where Jeannie is directing two of the whores, Bella and Titsy, in making breakfast for the men who are eagerly waiting. Kicking out a chair, I take a seat, preparing to get a plate when food's ready to be served.

"You stayed home last night?" Demon has taken the seat beside me. As he bends to sit, he speaks quietly into my ear.

"Yeah, had words with your mom," I reply, my own voice mimicking his low tone. "Got things straight."

"I'll believe that when I see it," he mumbles.

Yeah. He's right to have doubts. I'd let the situation deteriorate for far too long, just because I hadn't wanted to admit to my problem.

"Met the new brother, yet?" He changes the subject.

"Not yet, no. You?"

"Yeah." Demon's eyes flick around. "Hey, Paladin. Here."

Responding more like a prospect, the new guy leaps into action, crossing the room fast. When he draws to a halt, I almost expect him to salute.

"Take a load off, Brother." Using my foot under the table, I push out the chair opposite. When he takes it, I enquire. "How are you settlin' in?"

"Good." He nods. "Got everything I could want here."

"It must be strange," Demon commiserates with him. "But you'll soon find your place. Got any skills we should know of?"

"Willing to go wherever there's a need."

"Strip club." It takes me no more than a split second to make a decision, remembering my conversation with Slick. Yeah, let's front him with naked women, see how long he resists temptation. Test the lad. His self-claimed girl's going to be living under my roof, I need to see what he's made of.

"Fine." Paladin's hard to read. He certainly doesn't leap with excitement, but his pleased nod shows he's happy to be given a job. *A role. A place. Kid will be looking for that.*

"Hey, Taser. Take Paladin here to Tits Up. Show him the ropes."

"Sure boss." Taser, who manages the place, is quick to reply. "Could use another hand."

It's not usual that I get personal service, but Jeannie's crossing the room bearing two plates. When she places them in front of me and Demon, I thank her. Turning my head, I notice a frown on my VP's face. *She knows his story.* She's kept the secret so long, I'm confident she'll never say anything, but it must be affecting him deep inside. Not every day you learn your father's actually your brother. Fuck, I've no idea how I'd start to deal with that myself.

The bacon and eggs go down well. Finished, I stand, take my plate over to Jeannie who relieves me of it, then walk to my office. The day starts well. I manage to get a couple of hours' work done before I have an interruption.

"Prez?"

"Cad. Come in. Everything okay?"

For an answer, he hands me a USB. I plug it into my laptop, pausing while it does its stuff. Before I press play, I ask. "What am I lookin' at?"

"Footage from behind Tits Up. From last night."

On my laptop appears a view of the rear of our strip club. Certainly looks like someone's casing the joint to me. Whoever it is wears a hoodie pulled up over his head, his face virtually concealed by a bandana. In the dim light, it's impossible to make out anything useful at all. But the fact he's there is what's got our security guy worried.

"Have you told Taser?"

"Yeah, warned him before him and the new brother headed out. Young Pal seems to have a good head on his shoulders. Offered to check it out when he gets there. Immediately asked what security is on the girls."

"You think someone's planning something?"

Cad shrugs. "Can't rule it out. I'm going to go back over all the recordings, see if there's anything I've missed before. Pal's right. We need to keep an eye on the girls, and check nothing's been tampered with."

Could be someone planning a robbery, but whoever it is must have balls if they're considering going up against the Satan's Devils. "Let me know if you dig anything else up. We'll discuss it at church later. Beef up the security in the meantime."

Dismissed, Cad leaves my office, my eyes linger on the empty doorway, my nose twitching. I've learned to trust it. After a moment, I pull my laptop toward me, and go back to the spreadsheet I was looking at before.

But I'm not to have long to myself. Another knock, this time it's Demon. As he enters, I close the lid of my laptop, my attention one hundred percent on my son, *my brother*. Fuck, I don't know what to call him, how to treat him. This man I saw birthed, held his hand as he took his first steps, bought him his first bike and showed him how to ride it, taught him how to grow into a man. Yeah, he's my son for all intents and purposes.

From the way his brow's creased there's something on his mind, whether personal or business I can't be sure. "What's up, VP?"

"Lizard says someone's been messing around the shop."

My eyes sharpen. Another of our businesses? This time, the tattoo parlour. I press my lips together. "Cad's just been in here. Someone was at the back of the strip club last night."

Demon's face darkens. He reaches into his cut and takes out his phone. "Rusty. Take a careful look around the bowling alley, yeah? Someone's been eyeing up some of our businesses. See if anyone's noticed anything strange. Yeah. Great." He looks at me and shakes his head, then places another call. "Pyro. You were just going to call me? What's…? Fuck. What's missing? Who the fuck? Yeah. Keep me posted, and yeah, talk to Cad." This time when he ends the call, he answers the question in my eyes.

"Pyro said someone broke into the auto-shop last night. Only just found out. Not sure whether anything else was taken yet, but a few new spare parts that were on special order are definitely missin'. Parts that took an age to come in as well. He hasn't yet found out where or how they got in."

"Inside job?" Last thing I want to think about. We trust our employees, but there's always a chance.

"He's considering it, but fuck, Prez, he doesn't want to go there. And linked with the other reports? Got to wonder whether there's anyone fucking with us. Too much of a coincidence to be isolated attacks."

My thoughts echoed from earlier.

"I'll get over to the auto-shop, help Pyro see what's what. Don't like this, Prez."

Me either. "Pyro said he thought shit might have been taken before."

"Yeah. But Pyro said boxes had been torn open. No attempt to hide a theft. Not a chance this could be accidental." Demon stands. "Oh, and what you suggested? If you're thinkin' of steppin' down because you can't take the heat any longer, if the brothers want me, I'm willin' to take over. But if you think I'm seeing it as my right to sit in that chair, you couldn't be more fuckin' wrong, you hear me, old man?"

I pick up a piece of paper, wad it, and chuck it at him. "Less of the ol' fuckin' man, you hear me, *son.*"

The door closes on the sound of him chuckling. Do I take it that he's bearing no grudge for me keeping that immense secret from him? Sounds like we might be finding a way forward. Doing what we do best, putting our heads together on club business seems to have removed the last of the awkwardness that had come between us.

That's one weight off my mind. One thing going my way. Now just got to find out who's messing with the club. I don't believe in coincidences.

I've also got to find some way to make shit right with Moira.

Stress? Well, I've just got to deal with it.

CHAPTER 17

PALADIN

In Tucson everyone knew my main job was watching out for Jayden. Most days I'd take her to school, bring her home. In between times I'd turn my hand to whatever needed doing. Part of me would welcome having a real job, a place where I could make a contribution by working alongside my brothers.

Naively, having expected little would change, that I'd still have a job looking out for the girl I'd had responsibility for, for so long, I'd promised to see Jay today. But my plans went awry when first thing this morning, Hellfire had teamed me up with Taser, and directed me to the strip club. I could hardly fuck off and see my girl, not when the prez had assigned me a task. When I pick up my phone to send a quick text, I notice I'd missed one from her sent last night.

Jay: Can we talk?

Shit. She'll think I'm ignoring her. Not much I can do about that. I send the message of explanation.

Pal: Got shit to do. Will try and see you later

Jay: Fine

I might not have a lot of experience with women, but even I know when a female says things are fine, they're likely to be anything but. There's nothing I can do about it. Whether she likes it or not, Jay's got to learn the club comes first. Always. I frown, realising while she might know that on an intellectual level, she hasn't experienced that before. Previously keeping her out of trouble had been club business. Now she's in Pueblo, she no longer takes priority, or not in my new brothers' eyes.

"Alright?"

Taser's waiting by his bike. He must have seen the expression on my face when I read the text. I just nod and go to my ride.

Taser's about ten years my senior, he's heavily tattooed and sports a thick beard, maybe to make up for the thinning of the hair on his head. He's got chiselled features though, large eyes with eyelashes girls would probably lust over. I hadn't been introduced to him last night, maybe he was working all evening. I'll have to check what my hours are going to be, might make it hard to see Jay when she starts school during the day, and I'm working at night. Still, got some time yet to figure that out.

We pull up outside a brick building, it's down a side street off the main drag. An unlit neon sign above it, pictures outside leaving no doubt of the scantily clad, or naked women, customers will find inside. I stand back as Taser opens up the building. He gives his version of a tour as we enter.

"Bar over there, stage, private rooms and girls' changing facilities down that way." A wave of his hand punctuates each word. "Manager's office over here."

As Taser flicks on overhead lights, the place looks seedy. As if he reads my mind, he laughs. "Might not look much now, but the low-level lighting is all that they need at night, and covers a multitude of sins. I've mentioned to Prez I'd like to spruce it up a bit. Could do with a lick of fresh paint. But I doubt the customers will care. It's what's on the stage people come here for."

I raise my chin. Much like Angels back in Tucson.

"I want to do a stock check of the liquor today. That will be your job, so I'll show you how to do that. Ever done it before?"

"Helped out," I say truthfully. "But not had the responsibility."

He swings around, his head tilted to one side. "Were you really a full-time babysitter?"

"Pretty much," I respond, though my teeth are gritted. Looking after my girl was no chore.

"Prez won't let you get away with that here."

"Hopefully there'll be no need for it."

He nods. "Right. Doors open at eight pm, we stay open until five in the morning. You okay with being nocturnal?"

Not what I was hoping for, but I'll do whatever I have to. Somehow I'll make it work. "Sure."

"We're open Tuesday through Saturday. We can alternate. Be easier on both of us, but Prez likes someone to be here. Of course, brothers are always popping in, so you won't be lonely. I usually use the daytime to get shit done. Place gets busy at night."

He's given me the details, but I'm wondering whether I should prompt him we need to investigate what Cad had seen on the security footage. But what do I know about which things take precedence? In Tucson, we'd have leapt on any threat immediately. Taser is obviously not giving it such importance. Maybe they don't have to be so on edge here.

At that moment, his phone rings. I give him privacy, wandering over to check the place out. Wondering whether there's a redecorating budget, there are improvements needed I can already tell. And, a cleaner to have a word with if I'm not mistaken. I decide to ask for a rundown of the staff just as Taser comes over.

"Right. That was Demon asking if we'd checked out back yet." He frowns. "VP seems a bit agitated, sounds like it's urgent for some reason. Better get on with what he wants. You comin'?"

It's a rhetorical question, what else would I be doing? I follow him down the corridor he'd pointed out earlier, past bathrooms emitting a predictable odour of disinfectant, then a storeroom, and out through a back door. He leads me around the corner where there's a dumpster. "Cad picked up an asshole on the security recordings from last night right here. Need to see if we can spot what he was doing." He points up above my head. "That's the camera that picked him up."

"Was he waiting for one of the girls to come out?"

"Nah. Place was closed up. Time stamp was six am."

I start looking around. Nothing immediately obvious. I glance at the camera in question, my brow furrowing as I notice while it's not static, its arc only moves from left to right, its focus is on the window and not on… Hmm. I place my hands on the top of the dumpster which would be out of range of the camera and pull myself up, looking in. *Oh shit…* "Fuck, Taser. Oh fuck." Hoisting up fully I place my foot on the edge, then gingerly turn and lower myself in.

Taser's face appears. "What…? Oh, fuckin' hell." He notices fast. "He dead?"

I turn the body over to check, my fingers touching cold skin, then I make the mistake of breathing deep and immediately cover my mouth and nose with my hand. "No question of that. Any idea who he is?"

Taser's gone white as he answers. "Nah. Fuck Pal. I need to call Prez."

I've seen dead bodies before. Killed people too. But I've never literally stumbled across one. There's nothing for me to do now and the smell of the rotting garbage is becoming overpowering. Quickly I get myself out of the dumpster and am brushing myself off when Taser ends his call.

"Prez and VP are on their way over. We're to make sure there's no prying eyes."

He leans over, breathing shallow breaths. "Fuck, Pal. Who would kill someone and leave him behind our club?"

"Presumably he was killed and left here. Looks to me like someone is sending us a message."

Taser looks around as though expecting to see the culprit standing around waiting. But there's no one here, of course. The perp who did this will be long gone. Suddenly his eyes narrow. "This got anything to do with you?"

Me? What the fuck? "What the fuck you talking about?"

"You." He advances, his finger prodding at my chest. "We've never had trouble before. You arrive in town, and this shit happens. Unidentified fucker snooping around Tits Up and someone ending up dead."

"I fuckin' arrived yesterday," I begin through gritted teeth. "Last night I was at the clubhouse. Ask the prospect on the gate if you want, I didn't go off the compound. How the fuck would I have been able to kill the fucker, even if I'd had any inclination. And for your future information, I don't kill people without good reason. Never. You're looking in the wrong direction."

I'm so angry. My cheeks are blazing. It doesn't get any easier when Taser won't give up. "You knew exactly where to look. First thing you headed for was the dumpster. Didn't even wait to check anything else. And if not you personally, you could be in contact with someone. You've been using your phone a fucking lot. Maybe I'll get Cad to look at it."

Now it's me, drawing myself up to my full height and pushing him back. Not an easy task when he must have fifty pounds plus on me, but my rage gives me strength. "Who I'm texting is none of your fuckin' business. And I checked the dumpster first as I've got some fuckin' brains in my head."

"Hey! What the fuck's going on?" Both of us so engrossed in our altercation, we hadn't heard Hellfire arrive. He's here now. One hand on my chest, one on Taser's, and he's forcing himself in the middle of us.

Taser tosses a glare to the prez. "He turns up and so does a dead body. He knew exactly where to look…"

"Paladin had nothing to do with it." I'm pleased as Hellfire jumps to my defence.

"Hold up a minute, Prez. How can we say that? Taser's got a point." Thunder's standing, his arms crossed over his chest. "Leastwise we can get some questions answered. What d'you mean he knew where to look, Tase?"

Hell. Things are going downhill pretty damn fast. I'm a Satan's Devils member. I'm only too aware what form the club's questioning might take. Carefully, with slow movements, I ease my phone out of my pocket and slap it in Hellfire's hand. "Check the calls and texts. I've got nothing to fucking hide."

Hellfire's eyes are on mine. He doesn't even look at my phone, simply passes it back. He lifts his chin slightly. "Paladin's a Satan's Devil. Might not be from here. Might still have to earn our trust. But he's not responsible for this. Has no fuckin' reason to bite the hand that's going to feed him." When he finishes, he looks first at Taser, then at Thunder, then finally, at me. "Get yourself back to the compound, Pal. We'll discuss everything in church later."

I'm dismissed. Probably to give Taser and I a chance to cool down. I don't bother arguing, just take myself off, still angry. I kick up the stand and twist the throttle making my pipes roar as I depart, fast. It's only a moment before I realise I'm going the wrong way up the strange road, heading away from the club, not back to it. As I do a U-turn, I start to wonder whether going in the wrong direction was an unconscious indication that coming here with Jayden had been a wrong move.

Drawing up to the clubhouse and walking inside, I have a strong feeling of being among strangers. When you're a prospect, it's par for the course not to be trusted, and you accept you've got an uphill struggle ahead. It's the reason people aren't immediately taken on as full members. A wave of homesickness washes over me. None of my brothers in Tucson would have questioned me, picked on me. Here I'm the outsider. Seems I've got to gain the confidence of the men around me all over again.

Is Jayden worth it?

Of course she is. I've already been waiting for her for over two-and-a-half years. But today's shown me, stepping into this new life I'd had such hopes for, is going to be harder than I expected.

The atmosphere in the clubhouse is sombre. Someone's been killed. It could be the dumpster was a convenient place to hide a body, but the ownership of Tits Up is no secret. Far more likely it's a message for the club. But why, what for, by whom and what do they mean by it, no one knows. Mace and Buzzard are at the bar discussing it when I turn up.

"You found him?"

"Yeah," I tell the enforcer, knowing there's only one thing he can be alluding to. "Didn't expect to. Thought to check in the dumpster, and there he was."

"How did he die?" Buzzard asks.

I shrug. I'm no medical examiner. "From the way he was lying I couldn't tell." As I speak, I shudder. Those dead, wide-open eyes I'll dream of for a long time.

"Get the brother a drink," Mace yells to Dan, who's behind the bar. "Looks like he could do with one."

"Prez wants church brought forward. Asked me to get everyone in." I'm not in the loop yet. Fuck, I don't even have everyone's numbers programmed as yet.

The enforcer nods. "Prospect, get on that, will you?"

Dan pours my shot of Jack, then takes out his phone. Leaving Mace and Buzzard to it, I take myself off and sit down, and start a text of my own.

Pal: Sorry, Jay. Something's come up. Won't be able to see you until later this evening. Okay if I come about 9?

I stare at the screen, but there are no dots showing she's writing a reply. Shit, this day's gone to fuck already. I'd promised I wouldn't leave her alone, that I'd go see her as soon as I could. But the mystery of the dead man comes first. Problem is, it's club business, and that I can't share.

Club business. The words old ladies understand. But Jay's still a kid. Her lack of response is telling.

Brothers start coming in. I'm slowly sipping my second shot when Hellfire returns with Thunder and Taser, the latter throwing me a dirty look. Prez wastes no time heading into church, and I follow as the rest of them walk in. I'm pointed to a chair at the end of the table.

Hellfire bangs the gavel once we're all seated. He looks around, his face grim. "Had to call it in. Man had no connection with the club, but the location of the body is going to raise questions."

Ink looks upset. "Cops trying to pin it on us?"

Hellfire swipes his bushy hair back from his face. "They'll try. But we've got nothing to do with it. This is one time we can tell the truth."

"I'll pass them a copy of the footage from the security camera," Cad suggests.

Prez nods, then looks at me. "Cops want to speak to you, Paladin. Need your fingerprints as you went into the dumpster."

I hadn't thought of that. "They want me to go to the station?"

"Yeah. In the morning will do. Ask for Sergeant Moss."

All I need. Walking into a police station. But I just raise my chin in acknowledgement.

"What I want to know is why *Pal* here, immediately knew where to look." Taser gives an emphasis on my shortened handle which suggests I'm no friend of his.

Before anyone else can comment, I set him right. "It was obvious. You pointed out the camera. I know the type. It can't rotate all the way around; the dumpster was in its blind spot. It seemed the obvious place to look. If someone was doing something they shouldn't, it wouldn't have picked them up. Seemed the right place to start." I don't explain I've had experience searching for likely places to plant explosives. Seems they don't have that kind of trouble in Pueblo.

Cad's watching me. He gives me a sharp nod. No one questions my explanation. I notice Demon staring pointedly at Taser. I glance at him too, just in time to see him give a resigned shrug. *Not totally convinced.* Of course, he wouldn't like it. He hadn't picked that up.

"Right. What do we know?"

Cad shakes his head at the prez. "Not a lot, I'm afraid. Clearest pics you already have. Bastards are playing us. Anything at the bowling alley or tattoo shop?"

That makes me sit up. I hadn't heard about anything happening anywhere else. I look around with interest, hoping no more bodies had been found.

Both Lizard and Rusty are shaking their heads. "A few footprints, cigarette butts. Someone was there, but no dead bodies thank fuck." Lizard, who runs the tattoo parlour answers. He raises his chin toward me. "Found what we did out of range of the cameras. They knew what they were doing."

"Same at the bowling alley," Rusty confirms. "Could be the same man, maybe not."

"From the timing, unlikely," Cad replies. "I did get a glimpse of movement at your place, Rusty, once I went back and had a better look. Unless one man can be in more than one place at the same time. The intruders hit Tits Up and the bowling alley simultaneously."

Pyro raises his chin. "Found how they got into the auto-shop. Similar problem as Pal just described. Camera's in the wrong fuckin' position, nothing showed on the recordings. Got in through the bathroom window, then closed it after they went out the same way. Didn't pick it up until we looked more carefully and found the broken lock."

A break-in at the auto-shop as well? Looking around, it seems only I was out of the loop. But I'm still a stranger. No one's yet sharing shit.

"Sounds like your security could do with a onceover." I can't help putting in. Sitting here listening there are a ton of things I can see wrong. We'd all have been dead if we'd been this lax in Arizona.

Cad looks at me sharply, his eyes first blazing, then it's as though the wheels start turning in his head, and he lets out a long sigh. "New brother has got it in one. We've become complacent. Haven't had problems before. Relied more on our rep to keep fuckers away. That's certainly one of our next steps."

"I'll take that on," Demon's hand waves. Then, as he's got the floor, continues with a frown. "All our businesses targeted? Sounds like we're up against a gang."

"Still say the timing's a coincidence," Taser snarls, sending me a dirty look. "Got a new member arrive who seems to have acquainted himself fuckin' fast with our lack of security. Now he's here, we have more trouble than we've had for a very long time."

I raise my hands but have no chance to speak as Hellfire jumps in, snarling, "Only fuckin' coincidence is that Paladin may have brought Tucson's bad luck in his luggage. Drummer vouches for him. Might be new to us, but not to the prez of the motherfuckin' mother chapter. I, for one, believe I can fuckin' rely on his word."

After a moment of silence following Hellfire's vehement and welcome comments in defence of me, Sparky wonders aloud, "We tellin' the cops about the other businesses?"

"Nah," Hellfire tells him. "Couldn't keep a citizen's murder from them, but if someone's coming for us, I want to handle it ourselves. I want us to find out who's fuckin' with the club. Once we know we'll send a message that teaches people not to mess with us."

They start having a discussion about who it could be. All I can do is listen and learn. It's like being a new patch all over again, but at least in Tucson, even as a prospect I'd had some notion of who the local players were, long before I'd been invited to sit at the table. Here I've no idea, and don't want to keep asking for explanations of names they're throwing around.

As I keep my mouth closed and my ears open, I notice Taser's not the only one who's been giving me looks of suspicion. Maybe, as Hellfire suggested, they just think I'm a bad omen, bringing bad luck along with me.

It comes as no surprise they're going to have more eyes on all the businesses. When tasks are assigned, I put up my hand to volunteer, but it's telling when I have nothing given to me.

They don't trust me.

Part of me wants to give up and go back to the brothers I know and love. Another part wants to earn the trust of these men, to show who I am and what I can do. Not that I'm free to leave in any event. I'm bound by my promise to Jayden.

I'm not in the best of moods when church comes to an end. An even worse one when I collect my phone to find a reply to my text.

Jay: Don't bother. I've got a headache.

Fuck this shit. I'm stuck here with men who don't trust me. The reason why, Jayden, is giving me the run around. *Fine* and *headache* are female speak for being pissed off. It's not my fault,

I'd have moved heaven and earth to see her, but I can't put her in front of my club. Angry, I decide to have a drink and drown my sorrows now I've no reason to stay sober.

I've seen the way the club girls look at me. I'm fresh meat to them, the unknown. I'm not surprised when I walk into the clubroom that one of the scantily clad women comes over. Breezy, I think her name is.

"Hey, want to have some fun?" Her hand lands on my back, slides down to my ass, and moves blatantly around to my cock.

I snatch her hand away. "Nah," I tell her. As her face falls, I soften my response. "Not tonight, babe."

She huffs, but soon finds another victim. Or lucky guy, I suppose. As I watch what I've just turned down, Lizard now getting an enthusiastic blow job on one of the couches, part of me wonders why I had.

CHAPTER 18

JAYDEN

A tearful goodbye shared with Ella, while the prospect and Slick waited impatiently. I wasn't even going to the airport to see them off. Instead I was staying home with Moira, a woman I haven't got the measure of yet.

I can't wait to see Paladin. We've never been apart so long before. I'd see him everyday in the clubhouse. I can't remember a time we've gone twenty-four hours without seeing each other. He's bound to be missing me too, I'm certain. Perhaps he'll take me to explore this new place on the back of his bike. I've never ridden with him before, Slick and Ella wouldn't allow me. I wasn't stupid, I knew a woman riding up behind a man meant something in the biker world, but if I was going to end up with Paladin, what was there to stop me now?

I'm sad to see my sister leave, but there's also a kernel of excitement bubbling inside, vying to push my sorrow away. I've got so much freedom now. There's nobody coming after me, no threat of kidnap around every corner. For the first time in three years I feel safe, ready to take the next step into my life.

I lost my innocence a long time ago. I grew to be a woman much too early. Ella had done everything she could to give me my childhood back, and although I was grateful, I had felt restricted by the rules that had been imposed. Now Pal and I have the freedom to really explore what we mean to each other. *I can't wait to see him.*

So I watch the car leave wiping tears from my eyes, but looking forward to exerting my new independence. As the tail-lights fade into the distance, my phone buzzes in my pocket.

Pal: Got shit to do. Will try and see you later.

What? How dare he? *He promised he wouldn't leave me alone.* I'm in a strange town, in a strange house with strangers. And he's blowing me off? My first instinct is to run after Ella and Slick, try to stop them, make them take me home. My second, once I realise that's futile, is to be so annoyed I could throw my phone. I don't, messaging him back simply,

Jay: Fine

"You okay?" Moira's looking at me cautiously, and I realise she's reading every nuance of the expressions crossing my face. Sadness, pleasure, annoyance. I wonder how much I'm inadvertently giving away.

My impulse is to stamp my foot and scream. But I'm more mature than that. While she's a stranger to me, I'm no more than that to her. She's been kind enough to give me a place to stay, I ought to at least not be difficult.

"Yeah. I'm fine." She cocks her head and gives a half-smile, managing to convey she doesn't believe it. So I give her more. "I thought Pal was coming over, but he's got things to do."

"Your young man." Her lips purse slightly. "I expect Hell's keeping him busy. He transferred as a member of the club."

Letting out a deep sigh, I reluctantly agree, "You're probably right. It's just that, in Tucson, he was my shadow. There wasn't a day I didn't see him. Even before we had to move back to the compound, we went there every day. I'd look after the children, and he'd always be around. I miss him, you know?"

"Coffee?"

What? It takes a second to process her question, then I nod, and follow her into the kitchen. I take the stool she indicates while she busies herself making us drinks.

As she does, she says conversationally over her shoulder. "Might do you good to have some time apart."

She doesn't understand our relationship. "We came here to be together," I tell her. "Pal's been my friend since…" My voice trails off. I've talked about it with my therapist, but still don't like other people knowing what happened to me.

Moira's quiet for a moment, and then a cup of coffee appears before me, and she sits on the opposite side of the counter. "You're living in my house now, Jayden, and I hope we're going to be friends. I know some of what happened to you, not everything, but enough. I know you're going to miss your sister, but please understand that you can talk to me. Confide in me."

As an opening gambit, it pulls me up. I'm immediately concerned she knows any of the details about my past, then realise, Ella would have had to have explained something about why the Herreras were a threat to me.

My silence encourages her to continue. "I got married when I wasn't much older than you." She blows on her drink to cool it. "I was only seventeen. We've been married thirty-six years now."

Is she telling me a relationship can work even if you step into it early? My brow creases. If Moira is someone I can talk to about how I'm feeling, it could be useful to have a woman I could bounce my thoughts off. I couldn't, with Ella. Any reference to that time and what happened a taboo topic between us. All Ella wanted to know was that I was moving past it. I hadn't wanted to trouble her with how much it still preyed on my mind.

Moira seems to be waiting for me to continue the conversation. "So you were little more than my age when you married Hellfire?" I sip my own coffee even though it's too hot.

"Yes." She throws me a quick grin as she confirms it.

"That's a long time to be with one man."

"That's what you do when you make a commitment. We're married, but I'm first and foremost his old lady. You know what that means to a biker?"

"Commitment to him, and the club." I've seen that with Ella and Slick.

"Yes. To the club. Club's part of the man, can't take that away from him."

"Why are you telling me this, Moira?" I narrow my eyes. I might only be sixteen, but often I feel so much older than that.

Moira's head dips up and down slowly. "I won't say I made a mistake marrying Hellfire, but if I had my time again, would do some things differently. I certainly wouldn't have married so young. That's my concern about you and Paladin. You're only sixteen. From what you're saying, you've been pushed together for years. Being a biker's old lady isn't for everyone. Seems you should use this opportunity to take a step back, consider if he's really what you want."

"He is," I tell her sharply, not admitting I've been having doubts along the same lines. A knee-jerk reaction to her suggestion.

"Is he?" She drains her coffee and puts the empty cup down. "From what you've been saying, he's always been your shadow. I doubt you've dated anyone else. Not had a chance to consider what you really want."

I'm about to contradict her, to say there couldn't be anyone that I'd like more. But something stops me. A notion she might be right. I don't bother to tell her I've never dated Paladin either. That terrible night at the Wheel Inn doesn't count.

"And Paladin? What's his view?" Moira continues, but doesn't give me time to answer, just carries on. "Hellfire told me he committed to a fourteen-year-old girl. Might not know you, Jayden, but I'm certain you've changed over time. Developed in both your body and mind. The girl he said he'd wait for, is she still the same? You, as you are now, are you what he expects and what he wants?"

I have changed, I know that. Grown boobs for a start, such as they are. I've become a woman, rather than a young girl. *Have I emerged as the type of woman who'd attract Pal?*

"The club girls. They're going to be all over a new member..."

I look at her horrified. Paladin had showed no interest in the whores in Tucson. "Pal stays faithful to me..."

"Is that what he says, or the truth? He's a man, Jayden. Face it."

Whether he's said so or not, and while sometimes I have doubts, mostly I believe it. But even if he was faithful in Tucson, maybe there's a chance he wouldn't be here, where I'm being kept off the compound, and have no way of knowing what he gets up to, and no Slick to watch out for me. I doubt whether any of his new brothers would let me know. The thought of him being unfaithful upsets me.

Having dropped that bombshell, Moira stands, collects both empty cups and rinses them. "I wouldn't want you to rush into anything you weren't ready for," she says, staring out of the window. "I never expected to get married at seventeen. While I don't regret the time I've had with Hellfire, I wouldn't have married him so fast if I hadn't had to."

"You were pregnant?" I leap to the obvious conclusion.

"Yeah, Demon's thirty-five."

"And your other children?"

"Kennedy's just thirty, and Samuel came along as a surprise. He's twenty-two."

The discussion of her children sounds a safer subject to keep to. "Only Demon went into the club?"

Her back is still turned toward me, but it doesn't stop me seeing her nod. "It was in his blood."

In her other son's as well, surely? But I don't say the obvious. Maybe she's glad Samuel didn't also follow his father.

Moira busies herself wiping down the already clean-looking surfaces. I sit biting my nails. In Tucson I'd be helping out with all the children, here it's totally different. I'm not in the clubhouse, but in someone else's home. Until I start school next semester, I don't have anything I'm supposed to be doing. It's a strange feeling. I've never felt useless. I miss Ella so badly.

As tears start to prick in my eyes, I try to get my thoughts away from everything I left behind. "Tell me about the club."

"Hmm." Moira pauses. "Much like Tucson I presume. There's the members, prospects, club girls, hangarounds, of course, who come to the parties."

"What about old ladies?"

"Well there's me. Jeannie, she's my age, was my best friend back in the day. She's around the club a lot, keeps the girls in line. And then there's Sindy, she's married to Buzzard."

"Any kids?"

"Nah. Single men for the most part."

My lips press together. Doesn't sound like the family club I got used to back in Tucson. I'd been expecting something similar, had been looking forward to getting to know the women and helping out with babysitting. I hadn't realised just how different this was going to be.

"Do you go to the compound much?"

"Not as much as I used to. If I want to watch porn or fights, I've got the TV for that." She's certainly not making it sound attractive.

At last Moira puts the cleaning stuff away. "You want to go into Pueblo? We could go to a mall. Have lunch out?"

Paladin's blown me off. So what else am I going to do? I agree.

It's not long before we're both ready and heading out. Despite Moira's constant criticism of Paladin, which is strange seeing how she's not met him, she's quite good company. Treating me more like an adult than Ella and Slick, presumably as she's got no parental responsibility for me. We go into town, I buy some new jeans—Slick had set up my own bank account— and Moira then led me to an Italian restaurant for food. As we ordered plates of pasta, I realised I was becoming comfortable with her. When she asked, it wasn't intrusive, and I found myself opening up.

"It was a mall, like this." I wave my loaded fork toward the window. "I was out with some girls my age. Mom couldn't care less what I was up to, where I was or who with. There was this cute boy, Sy, he seemed to single me out. I was flattered."

"What girl your age wouldn't have been? How old were you then?"

"Just coming up to my fourteenth birthday. Sy and I, well, we kept meeting up, minus my friends. He made me think I was special."

Her lips press together. "Giving you the affection you didn't get from your mom?"

She's hit the nail on firmly on the head. "Ella, well, she's a lot older, but we'd been close, you know? But she'd stopped coming around. I didn't know it then, but she was dealing with her own problems. I had no one at home."

I continue eating. Therapy had made me see what had happened wasn't my fault, but it's good to know Moira's understanding that too. That I'd been targeted, a young girl with a single mom who'd got fed up with being tied down with a kid. "After a few weeks Sy took me to meet his uncle. It was him who started buying me presents. Then..." My voice falters.

"He wanted payment." She's right. He had.

"He raped me, but tried to persuade me it was his way of showing affection." Now I lay down my utensils. "Then the threats started. My mom might have become distant, but I never wanted anything to happen to her. They threatened to hurt her if I ever told. I had to do anything they wanted. I was drugged, don't have much recollection of all the things that were done, but his friends…"

Her hand comes out and covers mine. "But you did tell, eventually?"

I shake my head. "Nah. I was too scared. Ella came around. Realised something was up. She already knew Slick, went to him for help, and the Satan's Devils rescued me." My brow creases. "I don't know the details of what happened, but at least I was told the men who hurt me are dead. I do know that they were the Herreras, and that's why they wanted to take me for revenge. Because they blame me for the deaths in their family."

"It wasn't your fault, honey," her fingers squeeze gently. "Not your fault at all."

It's taken me a couple of years of therapy to get to the place where I can accept that, even now, some days I still can't. "I know. But what they stole from me…"

She stares at me for a moment. "Paladin rescued you? That's why you care for him so much?"

"That's what I remember. He was a prospect then, patched in shortly after. When I got to the clubhouse, I was in a state, all I could recall was him carrying me out of that house. I, er, I sort of latched onto him. I didn't want to let him out of my sight."

"Clearly he didn't want to let you out of his. He ever behave inappropriately?"

My jaw must drop. "No. Never. And Slick and Drummer, well, it would never have been allowed."

She shakes her head. "Still think there's something fishy about an older man lusting after a young kid."

"He's not that much older. He was only nineteen when I first me him. And he didn't lust after me." He'd always been the perfect gentleman.

"Not then, perhaps. But now?" I don't understand. My face shows it. "You must have changed, honey. You must have grown up since then."

I shake my head in confusion. "What do you mean?"

Her mouth curves and she winks. "You're a pretty girl, a young woman. He'll have the hots for you just because you're female. But what about you? Does he make your heart race when you see him? You get tingles down your spine?"

I'm confused. "Nah, he's Paladin. I…" My voice falters. "I don't know what you're getting at, Moira?" Then I scoff. "The things you're talking about only happen in romance novels. This is real-life. Pal's a good man. He's a great friend. He's always been there for me." Even if there are reactions I should, but don't get when I see him, that's surely down to my past.

She looks down at her empty plate, her eyes widening slightly as though she hadn't realised she'd eaten it clean. "Gonna say something, Jay, that you might not want to hear, but just think on it, alright? Man you're going to spend your life with? Sure, he's got to be your friend, but more than that. You're sixteen now, in a short time you'll be seventeen and of the age of consent here in Colorado. Boy's gonna be expecting you to take the next step. But if you're not looking forward to that, if he's not the one who turns you on, maybe it's not fair to keep him hanging."

As she pauses to take a breath, my head is shaking. *She's wrong.* Paladin's the one for me.

"I'm not a virgin," I tell her. "I know what goes on."

"I know. That's a pity. But what you were forced to do, you should never be made to, or make yourself do if it's not what you want. All I'm saying is you've got space now. You can start a new life, make new friends. Let yourself see if it is Paladin you really want."

Again, I shake my head. "Want is the wrong word, Moira. After what happened to me, I doubt I'll ever want any man to touch me. But yeah, Paladin will probably expect it. He's a man after all."

Her face flushes as if I've said something to upset her. "Then he's not right for you, Jay."

I shake my head again, but she's put doubts in my head. He is my one, isn't he?

"You ever talk about sex with Ella?"

My eyes widen. "Of course not."

"You want dessert?"

For a second I don't know what she's asking, but when I see she's waving toward the menu, I say, no. She asks for the bill, then looks at me carefully. "Jay, one day you'll meet a man. When he walks in the room your heart will start to pound. When he looks over and your eyes meet, your palms will sweat. When he comes over and talks to you, you'll get tongue-tied. That's what you deserve. Don't settle for a man who you think is safe. Who you think you owe something to. From hearing you speak, I think Paladin's been a good friend for you, but no more than that." She must see from my expression that I'm far from thinking she's right.

But aren't her words just echoing my thoughts before I came here? That Pal might have expectations I'm far from being sure match mine. I'd put that down to the things that I went through, but Moira could have a point. *He doesn't make my heart race, does he?*

"Think about what I've said, okay?"

I agree. I can do that.

After not hearing from him all day, when I get a text later saying Paladin will be over at nine, my reaction is relief he's okay, and annoyance he hadn't bothered to get in touch with me before. I get none of the symptoms Moira had described.

Perhaps she's right. I feign a headache and tell him not to bother.

He doesn't reply. If I was as important to him as I'd thought, wouldn't he try to persuade me to see him? Or is he relieved I don't need him to come over? Have I pushed him straight into the arms of one of the club girls?

I realise I don't like that thought one bit.

CHAPTER 19

PALADIN

I feel unsettled. Don't like not seeing Jay. It's been my job to take care of her for years, and now I'm feeling restless. I text her the next morning.

Pal: You okay? Settling in? How's your head?

I wait for the response, but there's none. The idea that I might be losing her hits me, followed by the thought if she doesn't want me here, there's nothing to stop me from returning to Tucson. A longing to shoot the shit or play pool with Shooter and Road comes over me. Shooter, when he was known as Spider, and me still going by my real name Marsh, prospected together. We'd worked side by side through some shit, a bond that's hard to break, and which I'm unlikely to find here.

It's like being a new boy at school, viewed with mistrust. I walk into the kitchen for breakfast, it's even worse than the day before. Yesterday I was a mystery, the stranger. Then, when everything went to shit, someone looked on as at the very least, responsible for bringing bad luck to the club.

I take a plate of breakfast from Jeannie. It smells and looks fine, but I eat mechanically, feeling eyes upon me. *Nobody would miss me if I upped and left. Least of all, it seems, Jayden.* It's all become fucked up. Our new start together. I haven't even seen her since we arrived.

"Want a word."

With a mouth full of bacon, I acknowledge Demon and hastily swallow. "Sure VP."

"Finish up. Then come find me."

Having handed my empty plate to Jeannie, I go off in search of the VP. He's sitting at a table at the end of the bar, an open bottle of beer in front of him even though it's early, and papers spread out around.

"VP?"

"Pal. Sit." He waves toward a chair.

"What can I do for you?"

"Wanted to pick your brain." He puts down the pen he'd been holding, and leans forward, his elbows on the table, his chin lightly resting on his clasped hands. "The trouble you had in Tucson, that brought you and the girl here. Could it have followed you?"

I don't have to give it more than a moment's thought. I shake my head and say adamantly, "No."

He raises an eyebrow. "You sure about that?"

"Logistics," I reply. "No one outside the club knew we were coming here. Well, not unless there were leaks from this end."

He sits up straight again and jots something down. "Doubt it. But I'll have a word around. We haven't got brothers known for running their mouths. I trust them."

"And I trust my brothers in Tucson." *More than I trust the ones here.* "Jayden's safety depends on no one knowing where she is."

He half stands, getting into my face. "Reading an undercurrent there, *Brother*. What the fuck do you think has gone down? They might not have known the details, but we don't fuckin' advertise when someone's comin' for protection. You think a brother here blurted it out? Who would they fuckin' tell? Who, in Pueblo, would be interested?"

I start to shake my head. Put like that, it does sound ridiculous. I open my mouth, but he hasn't finished, though he has sat back down.

"You don't like that you've got to earn trust. Works both ways, Brother. Seems you need to start giving some to receive it."

I hear what he's saying. As hard as it is for me to get the measure of my new brothers, if they're feeling the same, I need to cut them some slack. I return to his earlier question, this time offering in a more reasonable tone, "If we'd picked up a tail, then it would be too fast to get a team together. One man, perhaps, but it seems there were disturbances at all your businesses the night before last. That would take manpower. Smacks of something local to me."

Demon nods. "We've got street gangs, 'course we have. Pimply faced kids for the most part who have difficulty finding their noses to pick, let alone getting organised and coming after us." He pauses. "Could the Herreras have links to any of them?"

Again, I reply in the negative. "Herreras are a Tucson based crime family. If we were in Arizona, maybe, but I don't think they'd cross state lines to step on somebody's toes. They're not known for getting into bed with other people. They keep themselves to themselves."

As he thinks for a moment, I slide out my phone and glance at it.

"That there," he points to the device in my hand. "Taser says you're always on the phone to somebody."

I roll my eyes. "Right now I'm checking the time. Need to get to the police station to get my fingerprints taken. Not that I'm particularly happy about them going into the system, but neither do I want to be caught for a murder I didn't commit." My eyes narrow. "I presume Taser is going to back me up when I say I jumped into the dumpster not knowing what to expect?"

Demon rears back, then comes forward, again up close to my face. "Taser may have taken a dislike to you, but we put brothers before cops any day."

I raise my chin. "That's certainly how it worked in Tucson."

"You're a Satan's Devil. Might not have put the patch on your back ourselves, but you're one of us."

"Yet there's that little thing you mention, trust." I state the fact.

He scoffs. "More that we don't know you. All we know is you've had a cosy time of it babysitting a bitch."

I bristle at the word he's using. Jay's just a kid. Well, not so much nowadays. I lose my focus as I think about how she's grown and changed. *Almost time to move our friendship up to the next level…*

I realise I've zoned out when his hand crashes down onto the table. "Pay attention, damn you." He waits for a second while I snap my eyes to him sharply. "You're with me today, okay?"

My plan to go see Jay, demand she sees me and tells me what the hell's going on disappears in a flash. I can't say no to the VP. "Sure," I reply, trying to inject enthusiasm into my voice.

"My mom's looking after your girl." Astutely he gets to the root of my problem. "Might do you both good to have some space. Look, Pal. Reason why I want you with me? You're a sharp lad. Things you came up with in church? Would welcome your fresh eyes on our security. Our cameras came out of the Ark, and need updating, more maybe, and better placed." He breaks off, places his hand against his mouth and looks thoughtful. "Fact is, Brother, I've been thinking about a new business." He gives a short laugh. "Fuckin' stupid idea it's now turning out to be. Security. When we can't even mind our own premises."

"Easy to get complacent and rely on a reputation." I give him an out.

"Well, it's just at the idea stage. Whatever you might think, I happen to have taken to you. Like that head on your shoulders. You and I do okay today? Then let's think about both of us throwing in with Cad and getting a new business off the ground." He gives me a wink. "Get's you away from Taser at least."

Wow. I hadn't expected that. "Security was a priority in Tucson," I respond, eagerly. "We were all hot on that shit with the Herreras and others gunning for us. Learned to spot weak points. I'm all up for that. Thanks, VP." I'm excited. A new opportunity for me. A chance to get in on something from the start. A challenge I could get my teeth into. Part of me had been worried I'd just be a lackey for one of the brothers running the other established businesses.

"Let's get going, shall we?" Demon puts his paperwork away and stands.

As we go out to the bikes, the VP throws an amused look my way when I start to enthusiastically talk about vantage points and computer monitoring systems.

He's coming with me to the police station first. It could be moral support or just practical as I don't yet know my way around. When we get there, I'm pleased to see it's all been organised as I'm immediately introduced to the club lawyer, a man called Sykes, who's already there. While Demon waits, glaring at the officers in the reception area, Sykes takes me to a quiet corner and has a few words with me. Then I'm soon called back to go meet with one of the detectives. Initially he seems as suspicious of me as the men in the club.

"Dominic Marsh."

My government name takes me by surprise. I haven't been Dom in years. During school and my prospecting days I was just called Marsh, then Paladin over the last two plus something years. It seems an alien handle now as though it belongs to somebody else. I realise even Jay doesn't know it.

"Yes, sir." I decide to show respect. The lawyer beside me nods as the detective consults his notes.

"You came up from Tucson two days ago. You ever been to Pueblo before? Got contacts with anyone here?"

"I've met some of the MC, the Satan's Devils before, when they've come down to the Tucson chapter, but otherwise, no. I've no contacts with anyone in the city."

"Why did you, what do you call it, transfer?"

I shrug, unable to tell him I've come with a girl who needed to get away from a criminal gang in Tucson. "Just wanted a change of scenery. Hellfire had an opening, I jumped at the chance." Sykes had already coached me.

"Got a dirty record in Arizona?"

"Nah, I'm clean."

"As you'll see if you check." Sykes leans forward. "Mr Marsh has no convictions. Not even a ticket."

"Hmm." The detective looks between me and Sykes, then leans back and folds his arms. "Tell me how you found the dead body? Take me through it from the beginning."

I tell him the truth. No need to hold anything back. "The security footage of Tits Up showed some suspicious activity at the back of the club. I was assigned to go along with Taser…" I break off as the detective raises a brow.

"Jesse Devin," the lawyer supplies.

I resume at the nod. "We looked around, didn't find much. A few cigarette butts which could have been left at any time. There was a dumpster. The security camera wouldn't have been able to cover it, I thought I should have a look inside."

"Why you? Why not this," he consults the notes in front of him, "Devin?"

"I'm younger, more athletic. Didn't think twice about hauling myself up. Didn't expect to find anything inside."

"One look would have showed you the dead body. Why did you jump in?"

"I'm clearly not as familiar as you are with dead bodies. Thought there could be a chance he was still alive."

"Did you touch the body?"

"Yeah. I turned him over. He could have been drunk, hurt, needing help. But one look at his face showed me he was gone. His skin was stone cold."

The detective again moves his eyes toward Sykes who's sitting impassively, then they come back to me and narrow. "Now, the thing is, Mr Marsh, I've got to consider that you were responsible for killing the man, and that you conveniently were the one to find him so any fingerprints could be explained away. What have you got to say to that?"

"The truth, sir. I didn't kill him. I didn't know him. More than that, I didn't have the opportunity. I was at the clubhouse and didn't go off the compound all night."

"Have you got any evidence to the contrary, Detective? How about time of death? Do we know that yet?" Sykes butts in.

The detective raises and lowers his shoulders. "Medical Examiner is backed up with cases. He's not given this one priority."

"Have you ID'd the man yet?" Sykes asks.

"Not yet. You sure you don't know him?" That's to me.

"I'm certain," I stress. "Never seen him before. He looked like a bum to me, but of course, the smell and staining could have come from the dumpster." I'm trying to be as helpful as I can.

It's hard to stay silent, not adding more protestations of my innocence. A guilty man is more likely to do that. But as the time stretches out and no other words are spoken, I realise the detective's waiting for me to let my mouth run.

I start to comprehend just how bad my position is. I'm a stranger in town. A biker. A member of a one-percenter club, and my fingerprints are all over that dumpster and body. *I'd rolled him over, even touched the man's face to make sure he was cold.* If they find no one else, I could be facing a murder charge. All I can hope for is that the man was killed, or crawled into the dumpster and died, before I arrived in Pueblo. My concern grows that I'm going to be arrested. Fuck this. I start to grow angry.

As if he can see my body tensing, Sykes speaks. "My client has come here voluntarily, Detective. He's told you all he knows. He's willing to give you his fingerprints for the purposes of elimination. I suggest you tell him he's free to go."

The detective stares at my face, clearly searching for signs of guilt. After another pregnant pause stretches out, he finally sighs, then his eyes sharpen. "You're free to go. For now. But stay local. I may want to question you again."

I'm taken to another room where I obediently press the tips of my fingers against the tablet screen. Doing so, I wish once again I'd never left Tucson. My fingerprints are now in the system. Something all of us try to avoid. Fuck it.

Demon's still waiting, and not very patiently. He jumps to his feet as soon as I appear. I don't miss the flicker of relief that I'm walking out of here a free man. The club might not trust me, but no Satan's Devil wants to see a brother behind bars.

Then we're all outside in the fresh air. I'm taking in a deep lungful as Demon gives me a nod and discreetly steps aside as he begins a quick head-bowed discussion with Sykes.

When that's done, as we go toward the bikes, the VP turns to me. "Two days you've been here and you're already costing the club. 'Bout time you got working and earned back the lawyer's fee."

I suddenly round on him. "You saying Taser wouldn't have jumped in to check if he'd seen the body first? It could have been him here, not me. You seriously think he'd have let that shit go?"

The VP shakes his head. "Taser would know enough not to touch a dead body. You've got a lot to learn, Brother."

"I didn't know he was dead…"

"Fuckin' obvious, wasn't it?" He's shaking his head. "Get on your ride and follow me."

"Where we going?"

"To the bowling alley. Let's go check out the set-up there."

At least I'm not going back to the strip club and Taser. Rusty I've not had a lot to do with yet. All I know is that he's older than the others, one of the originals who founded the club. I can only hope he, at least, is prepared to give me a chance.

Unlike Tits Up the bowling alley is a family place. Brightly lit lanes, a food bar with a licence to one side, arcade games with lights flashing, and four pool tables. Already there are a few people knocking down pins. Music is playing, but it doesn't drown out the sound of the balls rolling down lanes or the clattering of the pins falling then the machinery churning as they're reset.

"Rusty!" Demon calls out to get his attention. When the older man approaches, I notice he walks with a slight limp. "VP. What can I do for you?"

"Want to check out your security system. Can you take Pal and I through where the cameras are?"

"Sure can. You helping out the VP, kid?" I bristle at the term; it must show in my eyes. "Brother," he hastily corrects. But I suppose I could let it go. He's probably old enough to be my grandfather. "What kind of experience have you got?"

I hate having no skills to speak of. I dredge up memories of some of the stuff I've done. Helping to bury dead bodies probably isn't a great resume. "I helped out with setting some of that shit up back in Tucson. Installing cameras and the like. Checking positioning."

Rusty's eyes gleam. "Sounds like you could be useful." His eyes meet the VP's. "Where do you want to get started?"

Demon's brow furrows. "I can take the inside. Can you take Pal out back?"

As the VP moves off, Rusty eyes me up. "Okay, then, lad. Let's go see what you're made of."

CHAPTER 20

JAYDEN

I'm beginning to think yet another day will pass with no news from Paladin. A dozen times I've picked up my phone, only to put it back down. I'm still angry at him and don't see why I should be the one to make the first contact. It's him who keeps putting me off.

It's hard to accept I'm not his priority any more. I'd got used to having him at my beck and call. Slick, too, at my back, often stepping in to make sure Paladin could drop whatever the club had wanted him to do, to take me where I needed to go. Biting my lip, looking at it through older eyes, I suspect the kindness I received from all the men in Tucson was because everyone knew how I'd come to be there. Some even witnessed my abuse first hand. I hate thinking about that. But it did mean I felt loved and supported, as if they were all my real family. Even the gruff sergeant-at-arms, Peg.

I wonder what this club's like. Now Moira's explained the set-up, I won't, as I'd previously thought, be just changing location, but meeting a completely new and very different group of men. At this rate, though, I'm not sure I'll ever see the clubhouse. I'm also not certain that's a bad thing. I know the reputation they've got, and that not all bikers are good people.

I'd offered to help Moira with dinner, but she ordered in. Just pizza, but that was fine with me. I rinsed and put the plates in the dishwasher afterwards, then escaped to my room. I like

Moira, but don't feel comfortable being around her all the time, still feeling an intruder in her space.

I've just finished FaceTiming with Ella, when a message comes through on my phone.

Pal: Can I come over?

I might not be feeling the tingling Moira spoke about, but I'm excited all the same as I tap out my response telling him he can. Now that I've had to wait for what seems like ages, I'm looking forward to seeing him again.

I'm downstairs ready when his bike pulls onto the drive, and opening the door ready and waiting.

He's standing there, his eyes raking me over from head to toe, before saying, "Fuck, I've missed you."

"Me too," I respond breathlessly. That's the truth. Then, "Are you coming in?"

He nods as a voice calls out from behind me. "Beer's in the fridge."

I cock my brow at him. "Want one?"

"Yeah. Love one."

Standing aside, I let him pass, then my eyes catch Moira standing outside the family room. Suddenly I'm embarrassed letting my friend into another woman's house, unsure of the formalities.

"I'll be in here," she informs us. I might be mistaken, but her words seem to convey a warning.

Interpreting she probably wouldn't be on board with the idea if I took Pal up to my room, I nod at her. *Message received and understood.* Then lead Paladin through to the kitchen area.

"How are you settling in, Doll?"

"Good. Moira's okay." Or is when she's not criticising Pal. "Haven't seen much of Hellfire." I go to the fridge and take out a beer. Handing it to him, he pops the tab. There's so much I want to say to him, but I'm feeling tongue-tied. It's also hard knowing Moira's in the next room, probably listening to every word.

"You won't see a lot of him. He takes his role of prez pretty seriously."

"Like Drummer."

"Yeah. Like Drum."

There's something about the way he says it, a wistful tone that makes me wonder whether he's missing Tucson. I've been selfish, thinking about myself. It must be equally strange for him. My fault he's been uprooted.

"What's the compound like? How's your room?"

He huffs a mirthless laugh. "Different from Tucson that's for sure. Hey, you won't guess what happened last night." As I raise my eyebrow, he continues. "Yeah, was warned to keep my door locked. I forgot. Went to bed to find Bitch already there."

My hands go to my hips. "A *bitch?*" I squeal.

"Not a bitch. Bitch."

"There's a club girl called *Bitch?*" And why is he telling me this? Is he listing all the conveniences on offer? And just how far did it go with Bitch?

"I'll tell you this. Bitch has got sharp claws."

My palm starts to itch. The type which can only be relieved by slapping it hard against a person's face.

I'm just starting to raise my arm, when he adds with a smirk, "Fuck knows why someone would call a cat, Bitch. Though it suits her. Was about what I called her when I tried to carry her out of the room." He pulls up his sleeve to expose deep scratches.

"Pal!" I admonish him, giving a snort of highly relieved laughter.

He bumps his hip against mine. "Yeah, if your door's not locked, Bitch jumps on the handle and opens it apparently."

A cat called Bitch. I've heard it all now.

Paladin raises his beer to his mouth, I watch as he chugs it down, muscles rippling in his throat as he swallows. A sight I've seen a million times before. The familiarity of it touches something inside me. I've been with strangers a couple of days, now I feel more relaxed than I have since I arrived in this strange town. I wave over to the stools either side of the counter.

Watching him carefully, I lower my voice and ask, "How you really doing, Pal?"

He gazes at me just as intently, then slowly shakes his head. "Harder here than I expected. Nowhere near learning the dynamics yet. They might be Satan's Devils, but there's a world of difference between the men here, and the brothers we left in Tucson."

I'm no psychologist, but I pick up on the words 'men' and 'brothers'. It betrays he doesn't think of them as family yet. That's what I've caused him to leave behind. His two hands are placed on the counter; I reach over and cover one with my own. "I'm sorry, Pal."

His eyes flare, "What are you sorry for?"

"Tearing you away from the one family you've known." Over the years we've spent time talking. I know he was brought up in a foster home, just another body so his foster parents could get the money. He says there was no abuse, but there was. I know as well as him how hard it is for a kid with no one to support them. But it was different for me, while Mom had been distant, I'd always had Ella. Pal had had no one, until he joined the Devils.

"Babe. It's not your fault, and," he looks so earnest, I have to believe him, "wherever you are is where I want to be."

With that statement, he washes away my resentment that he hadn't made time for me before now. It hadn't been his fault. "Hate that I can't see so much of you."

"Me too, Doll. Me too." He looks down at where my hand still lies, turning his over and squeezing his fingers around mine. "At the moment I'm finding my place, got no routine to talk of. I've got to pull my weight here, still hard discovering how best to do that. But I'll get something sorted." His lips press together, then his whole expression changes and he gives me a sneaky smile. "Got something on order. Should be arriving tomorrow. Think it's something you'll like."

I tilt my head.

He doesn't disappoint me. "A double seat with a sissy bar."

My eyes gleam. "You going to take someone on the back of your bike?"

"Didn't get it for anything else." He smirks.

"Got anyone in mind?"

My stomach churns with excitement when he answers, "Sure have. And stop playing games, Jay. You know there's only ever going to be one girl on the back of my bike."

I have to remember that means something to him. Now it's my turn to look down at our joined hands. "Pal, I…"

"Jay. Not asking you to commit to anything. Told you that before. But I know I want you riding up behind me. Not going to push you for anything more."

I've got butterflies in my stomach, but my internal analysis doesn't help me understand why. *Is it the thought of riding on his bike? Or, the realisation of how significant that is to a biker.*

"Pal, you won't take anyone else, will you?"

"Thought I just told you that." He looks exasperated. "You can trust me Jay. I know it was easier back in Tucson. Here, apart, it's harder. But there's never going to be anyone else riding behind me. And I won't be going with the whores. I promise you that, babe."

As he stares at me so earnestly, I have to believe him. Perversely, I begin to feel guilty. "But is that fair, Pal? I'm making you wait, when I'm not sure I'll ever be ready."

"Haven't I told you before? I don't care how long it takes, and if it never happens, I'll deal with it." His brow scrunches. "Seeing you with another man wouldn't be easy, but I'd step away, Jay. I just want you to be happy. Fuck knows, you deserve that."

What I don't deserve is him. "Pal, I might never be ready for you or any other."

He stretches out his hand across the counter, laying it gently against my cheek. I lean into his touch. "I think you will, Doll. But we'll take things slowly. No need to twist the throttle just because we've got more freedom now."

I don't disillusion him, but with Moira as my babysitter, I've doubts I've got much more liberty than I had in Tucson. As I watch him drain his beer, a thought comes to me. We'd started off as teenagers having fun, him nineteen, me five years younger. We joked, laughed, played pool. Swam in the pool back in Tucson. Gradually he became my confidant. Without me noticing, our relationship has been gradually changing. Perhaps if I just let it run its natural course, we'll either end up together or, he'll give up waiting. But either way he's right. No reason to speed up now. We don't need to take advantage of our new situation.

"So nothing needs to change?"

"Your pace, your needs, Doll. I'll be here and will be whatever you want."

But for how long?

"You looking forward to starting school? Getting back to normal?"

It's Paladin, no reason to put on a brave face. "Not really. I won't know anyone, and I'll be a new girl. I'll be in a lower grade than others my age, and I won't want to tell anyone why."

"Hey, Doll. You're beautiful and intelligent. Might have fallen back on some of your schooling, but you've a good fuckin' head on those shoulders of yours. They're going to love you."

I have no illusions about how cruel teenagers my age can be. Find a weakness and pick up on it.

"Hey, first day of semester, how about I take you there on the back of my Harley? Make a grand entrance and a point that you're under the Devils' protection."

I grin. "And, a point that I'm taken? My boyfriend dropping me off?"

He chuckles, "Doll, you see right through me. Thought I was hiding it better than that."

I don't mind. I don't want to fend off unwanted male attention. Showing that I'm spoken for would make it easier.

"Thanks Pal." I smile. "It would be like old times. And, if something comes up and you can't make it, I'll understand, okay?" He won't be able to drop everything here like he was able to do back home. I need to grow up and understand that. I've said the right thing, his face relaxes.

As if on cue, his phone pings. He takes it out, reads the message, and shakes his head.

"You got to go?"

"Dynamics babe. Said I don't know what they are. Cad's asking to see me."

I interpret what he's saying. In Tucson, he knew which brothers he had to jump and respond to. Here, he hasn't yet figured that out. "You have to go then." I paste the most genuine look I can on my face. "It's okay, Pal. I really do understand."

His crooked smile is both of appreciation, and of regret he's having to leave. He softens it by asking, "Want to go for a ride, when I get my new seat fitted?"

Do I? Of course I freaking do. Trying not to bounce up and down in anticipation, showing my eagerness like a young child,

I keep my voice as even as I can when I reply to his question, "Sure. Why not? Sounds fun."

He stands, leans over and plants a gentle kiss to my forehead, then picks up the empty beer bottle and looks around for the trash can. I already know where it's hidden away, so I stand and take it from him. Being so close to him, I take advantage, driven to do something I've never done. Going up on tiptoe, I press my lips against his cheek.

His smile is worth it. "Thank Moira for the beer for me, will you?" Then, after one last lingering look, he's gone.

"So that's your young man?"

Abruptly turning, I see Moira standing in the door way. I nod at her question which doesn't need an answer. Her speedy appearance proving what I thought all along. *She's been listening to every word.*

CHAPTER 21
HELLFIRE

Walking into church I take my place at the head of the table. I'm the last in. While the brothers settle, I use the moment for myself. Glancing around, I don't miss that Paladin's sitting quietly at the end of the table. Other brothers are talking, sharing a joke, but ignoring him. Takes time to find your place in a new club. He's wearing a pensive expression. I hope he's not considering he's made a mistake in coming here.

I pick up the gavel and knock it against the wood, then wait for the boys to quiet down. It's not my way to shout or growl at them, except when it matters. When Taser and Lizard continue their conversation a little too long, it's Demon who stares down the table. Catching his eye, they stop talking, sheepish looks on their faces.

"Sorry, Prez."

I raise my chin at Lizard. "Ain't no problem if you're discussing a solution to bring to the table."

The guilty look he gives back suggests they hadn't been.

"The detective in charge of the case has updated me on the man in the dumpster at Tits Up." Paladin's eyes shoot to mine as soon as I start speaking. Of course he'd be worried. Cops would love to pin something on one of us. I put him out of his misery fast. "Body was that of a vagrant, died forty-eight hours before. Which puts you in the clear, Pal, as you weren't even in Pueblo then."

As I expected, a visible wave of relief comes over him and some of the tension leaves his face.

"Still say it was stupid puttin' his hands on the body."

"What if he hadn't been dead?" I'm pleased to see Pal's not letting Taser get away with the implied criticism. "What if he'd been alive?"

Taser shrugs. "Probably have been dying in any event."

I resist the urge to roll my eyes. "If he'd have been alive we wouldn't have had a dead body on our hands and fingers pointing at us. Cops still trying to determine if that's where he died, initial signs from the forensic evidence suggest the body might have been moved." Gazing at them one by one, I add, "While the heat's off Paladin, it's on the rest of us now. Tase— do you know when it could have been placed there?"

Taser looks up sharply as though he's just coming to the realisation fingers could be pointing at him. I watch as he starts to take it seriously. "I'll ask the cleaners. They'd have been the last to throw the bags in. But it's high, Prez. They might have just chucked the trash over, and not looked inside."

"No bags on top of the body," Pal puts in. "If we know when the trash was last discarded then that sets the start of the time-frame."

Taser scowls as though he's wishing he'd made that point.

"If I can, Prez?" I nod at Pal. "What was the cause of death?"

"Seems like natural causes. Sent some samples off, waiting for them to come back." I confirm.

"Then the most likely scenario is someone found him dead and moved him to fuck with us," Paladin continues.

The sergeant-at-arms is nodding. "Agree with Pal."

"But why?" asks Pyro. "What's the point of going to the trouble of leaving a body behind one of our businesses?"

Cad's shaking his head. "If I hadn't seen movement on the cameras, we wouldn't have gone looking. Dumpster could have been collected before the body had been found, and it might have been discovered when the contents were tipped out. Would have taken more investigating, but would still have been linked back to us. More heat then, too, as it would have looked like we'd hidden it."

"Fuckin' sloppy way to dispose of a body. We've got the desert for that." A few smirks go Mace's way.

"If it was natural causes, surely they'd just have thought he'd climbed in and died there?"

"We'll never know Lizard. I agree with Cad though. I'd rather know it was there and face the implications head-on, than have it come up and blindside us when we're involved in other shit."

"What do we tell the cops if they come prying?"

"Same as last time, Taser. The fuckin' truth. Or will that be too hard for you to remember?" Demon snaps.

"Er, Prez? Can we get on to the auto-shop?" Taser sends his friend a quick look as if to thank him for taking the attention away.

"Sure, Pyro. Anything new?"

"Just those few hundred dollars of parts stolen as you already know. I've explained to the customer they're going to have to wait an extra few days. Had to pay express delivery for replacements. Oh, yeah, Pal, ordered your new seat in with that."

Pal nods his thanks.

"Any idea who we're dealing with?" *Who is fucking with us? One thing I know, I don't like it.*

"Cad took fingerprints."

"I can't get into AFIS, Prez. I'm working with Mouse, Keys and Token to see if one of us can break in. But we've got the prints there as something to refer to when anyone gets in our sights." As he mentions his counterparts in the other Satan's

Devils Chapters, I realise he's missed one. "No one from Utah helping?"

"Don't think they've got someone like me." They're losing out then. Couldn't do without our computer and technology expert.

"Lizard?"

"Nothing new at the tattoo parlour, Prez. Just want to know who these fuckers are."

"What we all want, Ink. What we all want."

"So who the fuck wants to mess with us?" Demon throws out to the table. "Whose toes have we stepped on?"

"And is it against the club, or one of the members?" Thunder growls. "Could be one of us fucked with the wrong person."

As everyone looks pensive, all end up shaking their heads, I feel frustrated. I want an enemy I can fight. "Cad? Anything come up while you've been looking into the new police chief? He seem one to want to clean house?"

Cad shrugs. "I've looked at his record, Prez. No cop likes a one-percenter club, but if he was behind messing with us like this, he'd be a dirty cop. No sniff of that so far."

"Well, keep looking. Coincidence we've got problems when he rides into town. Okay everyone. Keep your fuckin' thinkin' caps on. Anything that occurs to you, doesn't matter how small, bring it to me or the VP, alright?"

After a round of nods, I turn to my left. "What about improving security, Demon?"

Demon nods down the end of the table. "I suggest Pal leads on this bit. He's been comin' up with some good shit."

Pal looks startled, but jerks his chin, then starts to come up with suggestions. "Your security cameras could do with an update. They're old, just detect motion, and at night the pictures are grainy. There's new shit on the market that doesn't cost a fortune."

"What would we get if we replace them?" Lizard, presumably making up for his previous lack of concentration asks.

Pal's face suddenly looks years older as he sits forward. "To start with, your current system relies on you knowing there's a problem and then looking at the recordings. Or Cad, using up time going through the triggers that set it off each night. That's old hat now. You, we," he quickly covers his mistake, "ideally want a system that sends alerts out as soon as an event occurs."

"So we could have got to the shop while the thieves were still inside?" Pyro looks interested.

"That's it," Pal agrees. "It gives us a chance to catch the fuckers red-handed."

"And who would monitor the alerts?"

Paladin's voice seems to be gaining in confidence as he responds to Bomber. "Anyone, or all of us."

"Fuck, I don't want us all to set out in the middle of the night just because a squirrel's gone investigating." Ink throws out.

There's a curve to Cad's lips as though he already knows how Pal's going to deal with that. Guess the technical guy and Pal have already had their heads together.

"New cameras would have far better night vision so you'd be able to see if it was some rodent scratching for food. We'd all have an app on our phones. Can view in real time, or check what triggered it. You'd get an alert, call up the system, and see if it was anything you had to leave your bed for." Pal takes back the floor.

"Needn't even take your cock out of your bitch," Mace observes.

"Like it wouldn't put you off your game, Mace?"

"Mace would probably have finished anyway by the time he picked up his phone."

The enforcer glares at Sparky and Thunder.

"As I was saying," Pal's lips twitch. "It's possible that with the new cameras and their better definition we might have got a decent picture of the man at Tits Up the other night." He frowns. "With the current system it's not even possible to see clearly whether it's a man or a woman."

"What else?" It's time I show my interest as well.

"The current system is hard-wired. That relies on phone lines. Anyone wanting to fuck with us would just need to cut them, and no notifications would be sent. There's a lot of benefits in a wireless system. Cameras can be placed where we want them, moved around if need be. They're fairly cheap, so we can have more of them. Oh, and one other thing, most now have heat sensors, so can give early warning in the event of a fire."

"We've got fire alarms."

Paladin takes Taser's comment seriously. "Sure. But a camera can show where the fire actually is."

"Okay. So what about cost? Gismos like this sounds like they'd be fuckin' expensive."

Pal runs through some estimates he's brought with him. It's certainly not as much as I thought, and that seems to be everyone's impression. Cheaper than putting the original system in ages back to the best of my recollection.

As the new member appears to have run out of steam, I turn to Demon. "Anything you want to add?"

"Nah, Prez. Pal's covered about everything. If we go ahead, he'll be workin' with me on the installation."

"Cad?"

"Yeah, Prez. Pal and I have been discussin' this. Personally, I can't wait to get my hands on the new toys, and it will save me a lot of time reviewin' the recordings. Having spoken to Pal, that's old hat now. I'll be workin' on the technical side. I particularly like the idea of more cameras which can be easily moved around and hidden."

"Hang on," Lizard's brows are drawn down. "If you're putting in more cameras, does this mean all areas will be covered?"

"Liz?" I ask, not sure of his meaning.

Now his eyebrows waggle up and down, "You know, the dark corners where…"

"… we take girls and fuck 'em," Taser completes the sentence for him.

As laughter ensues along with predictable discussions of sexual antics being broadcast in real time to all brother's phones, with most for and only a couple against the idea, I pull my smokes out of my pocket, glance at them, then put them away. My mind drifts to Moira and my little problem. Maybe cutting down on the drink and cigarettes might be a start in the right direction.

Demon's head tilts in question, I shake my head. There are some things not up for discussion between father and son.

"I still say I don't want to see Cad's pasty white ass on my phone." Mace is grinning. "Now that would put me right off my rhythm."

"Could there be a voting system? Thumbs up or thumbs down?"

Ink raises his chin toward Pyro. "Or marks out of ten."

"Thirty," Thunder joins in. "Ten for effort, ten for technical skill and up to ten for how horny you get."

"What do you think, Pal?" Bomber, sitting next to Paladin, asks him with a nudge to his arm.

"Depends on what you want to *come* on your screen." Pal says it so seriously, the emphasis he uses takes a second or two to sink in. When it does, the whole table erupts in laughter. I throw him a chin lift. *That's the way to fit in.*

While the merriment continues, I let them have their moment of fun, raising my eyebrow at Buzz as he studies the estimate Pal had passed to him. A practiced unspoken conversation between us. *Got the funds? Yes.*

I bang the gavel for attention. "I'll okay the upgrade in security. Demon will lead, Pal and Cad with him. Get that shit installed as soon as you can, then we'll have a meeting to go through it. In the meantime, try to think of anyone you've come across who may have taken a disliking to us, doesn't matter how small, even if you've cut in front of someone when you've been riding. Cad. Look into the new police chief some more."

Pal raises his hand. "Any street gangs wanting to cause trouble?"

Thunder is the one who replies. "I'm lookin' into that. Can't rule out the little bastards getting too big for their britches. I've got meets set up with the leaders."

Raising the gavel I glance around, but it seems everyone's said anything they needed to.

"Prez, before you bring that down." Demon waits until I raise my chin. "Family barbeque Sunday. Best behaviour as Pal's young girl will be there."

As Bomber bumps Paladin's arm again and says, "Interested to see this girl you followed from Tucson. She must be fuckin' something." I bring the gavel down. Meeting over. I'll let Paladin fend off any other witticisms himself.

CHAPTER 22

MOIRA

Switching on the small hand-held fan, I direct the air toward my burning face. Sometimes it seems this will never stop, that I'll be going hot then cold for the rest of my life. I know it does end, eventually. But from what I've read, I've years still to go through.

I get so irritable. It seems as my internal temperature rises, so does the ability for things to get on my nerves. I'm constantly getting angry or overreacting. Right now, I'm getting wound up replaying in my head the conversation I'd had with Jayden at the mall. She seems like a good kid, perhaps a little mixed up about that boy who came with her. While I'd been speaking with her, I'd become sympathetic that she's not had a chance to be a teenager before. From what I can make out, she's spent all her time helping with the babies and young children, unable to enjoy the freedom of other girls her age. A situation that pushed her into the sights of the man closest to her age on the compound.

Well, we'll see about that. I huff as I wipe sweat from my brow. While she's living under my roof, I'd like to show her she's got her whole life spread out in front of her. She should be allowed to follow her own dreams, not be trapped in those of someone else.

I'm biased, perhaps. I'd had my goals stolen, saw them disappear in a blink of an eye. Rather than travelling, seeing the world, I'd become pregnant and trapped. I wouldn't want that for anyone. Not that I'd wish away Demon, just wished he'd come along in my time, and been the son of the man I loved, and not the one I hated.

Jayden's young, she's got choices. I want to help her see that. From what she's told me, she believes she's tied to a man who doesn't even attract her.

I pour my undrunk coffee away. A hot drink now is not what I need. Instead I pour a glass of cold water. That lad, Paladin, seems to have been Jayden's shadow, taking her and collecting her from school, and being her only male friend. She seems to have been brainwashed, or has brainwashed herself into thinking she's his, set up to be his old lady. I haven't had a chance to speak to the young man, but I already dislike him. Oh, he said the right things when he'd been here the other night and I'd been shamelessly eavesdropping, but saying the words and what he really means by them are two different things. As for her sister and old man? What were they thinking? Fine, they had to keep her safe, but holding her to the decision she made at the worst time of her life? What fourteen-year-old sets her sights on a man she wants to be tied to forever?

She might be waiting for him. But I know men, and what they get up to. I have strong suspicions he's not waited for her. He was nineteen when he promised he would, an age when testosterone would have been raging. In a clubhouse full of whores, what young man would have been able to hold back? Nah, her expectations of him are too high, and if I'm right, when she finds out the truth she'll be devastated. If I do nothing else for her, I'll make her see her expectations of him are unrealistic.

Hmm. Jayden will be starting school next semester. Plenty of boys there her own age. Hopefully one might catch her eye. She doesn't want to do what I did, jump into a relationship far too early.

I'll remind Demon about getting her a car. Girl deserves some independence and some fun in her life. Maybe she'll meet someone who'll treat her as she deserves. She's a pretty kid, won't take long for the boys to notice her. Yeah, someone else would be better. Someone not connected to a motorcycle club.

Emptying my glass, I rinse it. I'd made certain to get a good look at Paladin when he'd visited, quickly noticing, before me was standing a boy who appeared he's only just grown into a man, not yet battle-scarred or war-weary. He was quite fair, his hair short, scruff around his chin looked like he was trying to grow a beard but not quite succeeding. His arms resembled sticks, no muscles at all. In all, a breath of wind would likely blow him away. When I'd heard Jayden's fella was five years her senior, I thought at her age the age difference was too much. But seeing him, they wouldn't look such an odd pairing.

Even so, he's going to have to do something to impress me before I think he's right for her. I remember what I'd thought when I saw him and my lips press together. I saw someone who, though he hasn't taken advantage of a young girl yet, definitely wants to. I've more than enough reason to hate a man who thinks they're entitled to something they shouldn't have. Nah. I'm not going to help push them together. I won't make it easy for them.

Was her sister out of her mind? Letting them both come here together as though him taking advantage of her was a foregone conclusion.

I straighten the cushions in the already tidy lounge. After the club girls had had a good clean and tidy up, there wasn't much for me to do. Ah, Jay's left her cup on the side. I'll wash that. Damn, I'm burning up again… throw open the window, splash cold water on my face. Take off my cardigan. I've got used to wearing layers of clothes. Damn the menopause. *No, fuck it!*

I stand in the cool breeze that's blowing in. Hellfire hadn't come home again last night. He'd called, let me know shit had gone down, but after our heart-to-heart I'd expected things would get better. Looks like I'm going to have to stay used to sleeping alone. Now Hell's eased my mind on the reason he's been distant, I'm starting to worry about him. He's been the prez for twenty years now. It's a stressful job, and one which is taking its toll. Trouble is, if he steps down, our son is the most likely to step up in his place. Would I wish the same fate on him? Saving the father might ruin his son.

As if I've conjured him up, the sound of a bike arriving reaches me with the distinctive sound I'd know anywhere. It's Demon.

I'm putting on the kettle and checking what food I've got in the fridge as the door opens.

"Mom." Demon walks in, his arms surrounding me in a tight hug. It's not the first time I've seen him since he discovered the revelations, but the first that I've had him all to myself. As I stand back, holding him at arm's length, he starts to fidget. "I got something on my face?"

"Just checking you're okay."

He doesn't pretend not to know what I'm asking. "Truth? Still trying to get my head around everything. But Hell and I are fine, okay?" His eyes soften. "I'm more grateful than angry, Mom. What you both went through? Never had a fuckin' clue."

"Do you think it's possible we can move on? Put it behind us?"

Looking thoughtful, he shrugs. "I'm glad I know. Would rather it hadn't happened. But it did. Just got to deal with it. Anyway, how's Pal's girl?"

"She's not his girl." I snarl.

His brow furrows. "What the fuck? That's not how he tells it. She said anything?"

I shake my head. "Jayden's only sixteen," I hiss. "Far too young to be claimed."

A shrug from my son. "She's seventeen in a couple of months as I understand it."

"Still not old enough for the likes of him."

Demon looks surprised. "That's her business, surely?"

Placing my hands on my hips, my words come out before I can filter them. "If I hadn't had had a biker interested in me at that age perhaps I wouldn't…" My voice trails off.

His face has darkened. "What happened to you was bad, Mom. But you can't dislike Pal because of what happened to you."

I can't explain my thoughts to him, he wouldn't understand. If I hadn't gone to the clubhouse when I was seventeen… *I wouldn't have him and maybe not Hell.* Christ, my thoughts don't make sense even to myself. I settle for telling him, "Just want her to know she's got options."

"I think Pal already knows that. Kid's having a hard-enough time adjusting. He needs his friend."

"As long as he knows that's all she'll be. While she's sixteen." And while she's under my roof if I've got anything to do with it.

Demon opens the fridge and pulls out a pack of bacon. "Okay?"

I nod. He busies himself opening the pack. He's thirty-five, but still always as hungry as any teenager.

"Club barbeque on Sunday. Family one. You coming? We're all expecting to see Jay. Introduce her to the club."

"Family?" It's obviously the one Jeannie had mentioned.

"You know what I mean. Daytime, no live porn shows."

"Knowing your lot that would surprise me." I mumble.

"What was that?" Bacon cooked and enclosed in bread, he speaks through a mouthful.

It's not the first time I've shaken my head at him for the very same thing. I content myself with saying, drily, "No need to worry about you getting into a relationship with a woman."

He stops. His hand in mid-air. "Whatcha talking about? You saying I'm gay? I can assure you I'm fuckin' not."

"I'm saying no woman in their right mind would go out with a Neanderthal like you."

Grabbing the dish towel he goes to swat me. I jump out of his reach.

When another motorbike approaches the house, no one needs to tell either Demon or I who it is. As my old man parks up, Demon asks quickly, his brow creased in concern. "Got things straight with Hell?"

I feel myself blushing. I had. But I doubt Hell would want the reason explained to his son. I settle for telling him, "We're getting there."

Hell comes in, Demon finishes the late breakfast he'd helped himself to and leaves. Shortly after, Jayden comes down from her room and joins us.

She's excited to hear about the barbeque. I wouldn't have said anything, preferring to keep her away, but Hellfire invites her himself. She's clearly looking forward to meeting all of Paladin's new brothers. I stand, my lips pressed tight together. Already feeling responsible for her, the fact she's going means I have to too. I know all too well the dangers of a young girl walking into the compound. It's not where I'd be if I had my choice, but there's no way on earth Jayden will be at that place unsupervised.

Club business is obviously keeping Paladin busy and away from her, so when Sunday arrives, she can't wait to get going and see him again.

Hellfire takes the SUV; I'm pleased not to be riding behind him on his bike. Things between us are still strained, neither of us knowing how to move forward. We've lost something, and while my new knowledge means the obstacles have been identified, I'm not sure how we proceed from here. I can't stop the menopause continuing its course, and I don't have a cure for Hell's problem.

At least there's something I can do. Despite getting headaches, I've started medicating myself again, to be prepared. But even with that, how does this work? Do I ask Hell to take one of those pills? What if he takes one and I'm not in the mood? Do we have to arrange a time and place? Coordinate our schedules? Whatever happened to spontaneity? Seems we need to have another discussion; I just suspect neither of us knows how to approach it. One thing for certain, for us to have the heart-to-heart talk we need, he has to be with me, not at the club.

Jay's quiet on the short journey. Another thing I lay at Hell's door. He's not been around enough for her to get comfortable with him. When we arrive and park, she hangs back, her eyes wide as she takes in the compound. I've been to Tucson before, and this is an old converted industrial building, miles removed from the only other clubhouse she knows. I see the brick building through her eyes. It's bound to look a little foreboding. A far cry from the ex-vacation resort in Arizona. She'd been spoiled there. Though, I suspect, once she gets inside, it won't be all that different.

Paladin's clearly been waiting for her. He comes out of the clubhouse as soon as we're parked, his enthusiastic welcome slightly ruined by the fact a scantily clad Tulia, the youngest club girl, is tearing after him.

"Pal! Wait up. Aren't you coming to the barbeque? Thought you and I could..."

Pal turns and glares at her. His long strides, her short but more speedy ones, mean they're both near the car when Jayden steps out. "Tulia," he says sharply. "Get back inside."

"But Pal…"

"Pal?" Jayden's stepped out. Her eyes wide, her nostrils flaring as though sensing a rival. "Who's this?"

"No one," he replies sharply. "Just a club whore who doesn't know what's good for her."

The two girls stand, their eyes shooting daggers at each other. I wait, interested to see how this plays out. Jayden's going to have to find some backbone if the club girls see her as competition, especially if it's a man they've already had.

Paladin steps between them, his back toward Tulia. "Get back inside. I've already told you I'm not interested," he tosses his instruction over his shoulder. "Jay, it's so good to see you." He holds out his hand. I inwardly give an exasperated sigh as Jayden reaches out to take it. *She trusts him.* I wish she wouldn't.

"Scat," Hellfire steps to my side, slipping the keys to the SUV into his pocket, and scowling at the club girl.

"Whores are going to be at the barbeque?" I question him. They never were allowed in the past, not when the kids were around. But then, my children haven't been kids for a long time.

"Under sufferance," Hell replies. "Brothers asked for them."

"They can't keep their hands to themselves for one afternoon?"

"They've been told to behave." He nods pointedly at Jayden who's walking hand in hand with Paladin, the latter talking animatedly. I wonder whether he's explaining Tulia's presence, and, whether Jayden believes him.

The sun is shining. It's a pleasant spring day. I follow my own man around to the back where the grills, set up in the remains of the old furnace, are already emitting aromas which, despite my reluctance to be here, are making my mouth water. Eyeing the picnic tables, the preponderance of males, the smattering of scantily clad females, I uneasily wonder what the afternoon will bring.

Two people I don't see are Jayden and Paladin. I frown. *Damn it.* Where have they gone? *I should have warned her to stick by my side.* Only been here a minute, and I've already failed as a chaperone.

CHAPTER 23

PALADIN

Fuck these club girls. There are five of them, and each one seems to have trouble understanding when I say no, I mean it. They look on me as someone new, someone they haven't yet taken for a test ride. My only qualifications are that I'm a biker, and unfamiliar, a challenge. I've had to fend each of them off.

I'd been looking forward to Jayden arriving, giving her a tour of where I'm living now, and showing her off to my brothers. She looks fucking gorgeous today, figure-hugging jeans, knee-high boots, and a leather jacket Ella had bought her in recognition of the lower temperatures here. Her long blond hair brushed until it shines, flowing around her shoulders. I'm proud to walk in with her, but hope it won't be long before I get that scowl off her face.

I was going to take her straight outside, but decide to detour. "Want to come see my room?"

"Oookay," she agrees, the strung-out word betraying her hesitation.

Damn it. I don't want her scared of me. Just wanted somewhere where we could talk uninterrupted. I'm also too embarrassed to say anything in case I'm misreading her reluctance. If she thinks I'm going to take advantage, she's on the wrong track. Tugging a little on her hand, I don't give her time to take in the bar area, before leading her to the stairs and then up and along the hall until we reach my room. *Oh, shit.* I left it unlocked and now the door's ajar.

As it opens fully, Jay bursts out laughing when she spies a very large feline taking up the middle of my bed. First time I've actually been pleased to see Bitch. Her presence has broken the tension.

Quick as a flash, I tell her, "And that, is the only female that's been in here."

Her eyes shoot to mine. I'm telling her the complete truth, and can only hope she believes it. "Keep forgetting to lock the darn door. Cat must know who's got a mind like a sieve. Hey, be careful…"

She's crossing to the bed, her hand outstretched. Holding my breath, I wait for that paw to strike out, but damn Bitch is actually purring as she starts getting stroked. Jay's attention on the cat, she asks over her shoulder, "What was that, outside?"

"Fuckin' club girl not taking no for an answer." I scowl. "Honestly Jay, sometimes I don't think we talk the same language."

Jay giggles.

"It's not funny."

"It is. And it's a compliment, isn't it? They want you?"

Gingerly, trying not to disturb Bitch and keeping away from her claws, I sit on the bed. "They want to try a new cock. They're having a competition to see which of them can get me first." Mace had explained to me. The brothers think it's a joke and have been placing bets as to how long I'll hold out. "But no one will, I promise you, Jay."

When her eyes meet mine, I can see a maturity there as she asks in a serious tone, "How long can you keep refusing, Pal?"

"With you waiting? Forever."

Stroking the cat, her hands having something to do, seem to make the conversation easier. It suddenly hits me we're alone.

In a bedroom. For the first time ever. "What if," for a second I wonder if she's speaking to Bitch, as that's where she's now looking. "What if I can never give you what you want?"

"I won't be going with a bitch, Jay. Just want what's best for you." I love her. Have done for quite a while now. The feeling having gradually grown, morphing from being that of a friend or a brother into something else. As she's matured, so has the way I feel about her. But I can't tell her. Don't want to scare her off.

I watch, intrigued, as Bitch gets up and stretches, then rubs herself against Jay's arm. Even the darn cat is entranced by her. I hold my breath when Jay scoops her up in her arms and cuddles her. *Don't let her claws come out now.*

Then Jay's standing, carrying her to the door, placing her outside. "Sorry, Puss. I'm not sharing my man." She closes the door, but not before eyeing the scratches under the door handle. A slight grin comes over her face as she realises how the crafty feline gets in.

"Better lock it. She'll only be back."

"I can see that. Clever cat." She locks it. Another first. Her and I behind a locked door.

We both laugh as we can hear Bitch throwing herself at other rooms along the hallway. Then Jayden's face grows serious, as she glances at the barrier between us and the outside world, then at me. She's biting her lip, making me want to soothe it with my tongue. My cock thickens in my jeans. It has to be because we're behind a locked door, hundreds of miles away from Drummer, Slick, Ella and all the men and women who'd watch us like hawks back in Tucson. For the first time, I'm allowing myself to have a very masculine reaction around her. There's no doubt of my feelings toward her at all.

Now the cat is no longer between us, I allow myself to move closer, pushing for something I never have before. "Can I kiss you, Jay?"

She rears back, looking startled. I hope it's because my request came out of the blue, not because she finds it distasteful. Again, her teeth worry her lip.

"Never mind," I say softly. "We'll just go join the others. Food should be ready soon."

"Pal," she puts out her hand and touches my arm. "I've, I'm…"

"It's not the right time." I get it, I do. I'll just live with my disappointment.

"I'm not sure whether it is or not. Sounds crazy, doesn't it? I know you expect things to change between us, now that we're here." She glances around. "Alone." A quick grin. "I can't help but expect Slick to jump out of the closet."

"With a shotgun," I laugh. Understanding exactly what she's thinking. We've both been conditioned not to respond to each other.

She inches closer to me. "Pal? I, I think I would like to kiss you."

I inhale sharply. A moment I've anticipated for so long. I've kissed her forehead before, even her cheek, but until that peck on the side of my face the other day, which barely counts, she's never taken the initiative. I'm nervous, I've kissed girls, of course, but no one who means as much to me as Jay does. All of a sudden I regret suggesting it, wanting the dream to go on a little longer rather than risk disillusioning her. *What if I'm not what she expects?* What if I do something wrong? Knock my teeth against hers? What if it's awkward? Fuck, I'm scared I'm going to push her away.

Her breathing has sped up. How do I read that? Is she nervous too? Fuck, she has to be. *Has she ever kissed anyone before? Did the fuckers who… No, don't go there, Pal. Don't even think it. And never ask.*

I'm the man. I'm expected to make the first move, aren't I? My hands are shaking as gently I raise my right, placing it against her left cheek. I lean in, oh so slowly, giving her every chance to move back. She raises her head slightly, her lips aligned with mine though inches still separate us. A gap which narrows too fast, yet at the same time, torturously slow. I can feel her warm breath against my skin, only a fraction of free space remains between our lips.

Bang! A hammering on the door. Both of us jump apart, my heart's thundering in my chest. Jay's hand covers her own, as shocked as I.

"Pal? Jay? You in there? Food's ready!" It's Demon. He's trying the door handle.

"Coming!" I yell back, then, when I've unlocked the door, I raise my chin defiantly at the VP. "Bitch got in." I tell him, explaining the bolt.

He grins. Accompanying his words with a wink. "Mo, Mom, sent me. Think she was worried what you're getting up to." Jeez. Perhaps it's not Slick we need to worry about here. Seems we're still not allowed time to ourselves. He leans in conspiratorially, "I won't tell her you locked yourselves in. Don't think she'd believe you about Bitch. Hi Jay." He nods the last over my shoulder.

Looking around, I see Jay's face is flushed as though I really had kissed her. That she's embarrassed is putting it mildly. But I'm proud as fuck when she jumps to my defence. "The cat was just in here..."

"I'm messing with you," Demon laughs. "Fuckin' cat gets everywhere. Only tolerate her as she catches the mice." He stands back, waving his hand. "Come on then."

Swallowing back the request that he leave us alone to finish what we started, I hold out my hand for Jay to take, then lead her back down the stairs, across the clubroom, and out to where picnic tables are already filled. There's still a short queue by the grill. Interestingly, it's set up in what I've been told is the remains of the original furnace.

Jay's grip on my hand tightens. I'm not surprised. It's the first time my new brothers have seen her. Cad, already eating, catches my eye and gives me a thumbs up. Working closely with him, he's one of the brothers I know best.

Thunder's manning the grill, Runt and Wills, two of the prospects helping out. Both, close to my age, eye Jayden up with interest. For some reason, there's no bar on prospects having a girl here, and something about the way they're assessing her has me placing my arm around her waist and pulling her into my side.

"Might as well piss on her while you're at it," a voice, unmistakable as Lizard's, says in my ear. "Hey, I'm Lizard. Seems your man's too rude to introduce me to his lovely lady."

As Jay gives a nervous laugh, she takes the hand he holds out to her. Instead of shaking it though, he raises it to his lips and kisses the back. Jay blushes, as my body goes rigid. Lizard laughs, using my confusion to step up and get ahead of us in the line. Turning, he winks at me over his shoulder.

Asshole.

We fill our plates, Jayden grabs some salad shit that doesn't interest me, then I lead her to a table where there's space, pretending I don't see Moira beckoning us over. In order to avoid her, I belatedly realise I've joined the table where Pyro and Taser are sitting.

Both men's eyes immediately go to Jay.

"Jay, this is Pyro and that there is Taser." This time I take the lead.

Taser's giving her a long assessing look. Too long for my liking. Suddenly he speaks, "So you're the baby Pal's been sittin'."

Pyro slaps him around the back of his head. "Doesn't look much like a baby to me."

"What I was thinkin'," Tase replies, rubbing his skull. "Now I see what Pal's been makin' such a fuss over."

Is it wrong that I want my property patch on her? Or, if not that, a fucking big neon sign flashing over her head, *mine*.

Jay takes a delicate mouthful of food. It is good shit, Thunder can cook. But I don't much care for her appreciative groan which goes straight to my dick. I can only hope it doesn't have the same effect on anyone else, or I might need to kill someone. She swallows, then looks around.

"Anything here to drink, Pal?"

"Sure. Soda?" I start to stand, then waver.

"Go ahead, Brother. We'll look after your girl."

Which is what I'm afraid of. Jay in no way looks like jailbait. *They know her age, don't they?* Fuck me, but I can't remember. I hurry away, almost pushing brothers out of my path in my hurry as I go back to the coolers to get our drinks. Bottle and can in hand, I start to return to the table, when Sparky steps in front of me, impeding my progress.

"That's her, is it? Nice lookin' kid."

"Yeah, that's Jayden." I confirm.

"You bringing her on the ride the weekend after next?"

"Might. Haven't asked her yet. She's not had any experience ridin'. Need to get her on the back of my bike to see how she takes to it." I think for a moment. "Will there be any other women along?"

Sparky shakes his head. "Prez, Bomber and Buzzard may bring their old ladies. You're the only other fucker who'd let a bitch up behind him." He laughs and walks off. I swear he's muttering no one else would be crazy enough.

I speed up, keep my head down, and end up back at the table without being stopped again. Jay's laughing at something Pyro has said. At least she doesn't seem to feel I've left her adrift. But then, she's used to being around bikers.

"Sorry, got caught up."

She smiles as she takes her soda. "Pyro and I were just getting acquainted. So Pyro manages the auto-shop, and you, Taser, what do you do?"

"I run the strip club." If he's said it so bluntly to shock her, it won't work. She knows all about Angels in Tucson, the strip club Satan's Devils own there.

She grins. "Always fancied trying my hand at pole dancing." I'm not sure how I stop myself spitting out the mouthful of beer I've just taken.

"You're not fuckin' pole dancing." I tell her.

Almost about the same time Taser points out, "Got a pole inside if you want to give it a try? I'm sure Titsy could give you some pointers."

I growl, they laugh. Jay looks like she's giving it careful consideration. Then she glances at me and smiles, managing to convey she was pulling my leg. A wave of relief goes through me. Her looking the way she is? Don't want to see my brothers watching her slide up and down a fucking pole.

CHAPTER 24

JAYDEN

I'm having fun. I don't know what I expected coming to a different club. I knew it wasn't going to be like the Tucson chapter, that a family barbeque was a misnomer as there wasn't much family here. But the men I've met so far have been alright. The problem I'm going to have is learning all their names.

It had been strange upstairs in Paladin's bedroom. The first time I'd been alone with him. The first time he was going to kiss me. As I eat the food on my plate, I wonder what it would have been like if we hadn't been interrupted. Would it have made the tingles that Moira had described go through me? The anticipation had almost been enough. Talk about bad timing, we'd been *that close* before Demon had knocked on the door.

Part of me wishes he hadn't stopped us. The other part is glad, in some ways, that he had. It's not that I don't trust Paladin, I don't trust myself. I don't know the boundaries, when to stop, when to encourage him. I'm scared of him taking advantage and going too far like those men had in my past, but likewise, I haven't any experience of successfully saying no. Would I have known when to stop? Or would he?

In two months, I'm legal. Many kids my age have already lost their virginity, obviously, mine went years ago, but I left school friends in Tucson who were sexually active and not ashamed of it. What does a date on the calendar matter? Particularly when different states, different countries, have different interpretations. Do I feel old enough? I feel ancient in many ways, a nervous kid in others.

I chew, swallow, then pick up my soda and take a sip, trying to analyse my feelings when I'd first seen Pal today being chased by that whore. She's around here, somewhere. While Pal had been getting the drinks, I'd seen her glaring at me. She, and the other club girls, are immediately recognisable due to their lack of clothes. The sun is shining, but it's nowhere near warm enough to be prancing around almost naked. I suspect they're on the lookout for a male body to keep them warm. *As long as they're not expecting to get their hands on my man.*

My man? Since when have I felt possessive about Pal? I suppose I've never been challenged. Have always accepted he was mine. Yet, once Tulia had been sent on her way, and Pal had taken me up to his room, the green-eyed beast inside had fully woken up when it appeared someone had got in there first. The sense of relief that I'd felt on seeing that clever cat had surprised me. But it had also brought home, this is where Pal lives. He could be getting up to anything, and I'd never know. He could tell me whatever he thought I wanted to hear, as for what really goes on, I'd be none the wiser.

A nudge to my ribs. "You're quiet. You okay?"

I nod, smile, and don't let him into my thoughts.

"Mo said come and join us." I glance up. A woman, Mo's age, is standing beside us. Pal's smiling at her. "Jeannie, this is Jayden. Jay, Jeannie. She's Bomber's old lady, and looks after us like a mother."

Jeannie's wide smile suggests she's flattered, rather than upset by his description of her. She waves to where two or three picnic tables have been pushed together. Along with Mo, there's another woman sitting there, properly dressed for the cool day, so I assume she's another old lady and not a whore.

When she sees who I've spied, Jeannie explains. "That's Sindy, she's Buzzard's woman." From here I'd guess she's about forty. Suddenly Jeannie's body stiffens. "Oh no, you fucking don't," she snarls, then turns and stomps off.

My eyes follow her to see her heading toward an older man who currently has one of the scantily clad women's arms looped around his neck. To be honest, he seems to be ignoring her, but that doesn't stop Jeannie storming up and ripping the club whore away.

Looking up it's to see Paladin grinning. "Bomber, I presume?" I ask.

"Yeah. Whores love to fuck with Jeannie. Come on then. I'll introduce you."

Making a mental note not to look too friendly with Bomber, I let Pal take my plate.

When we arrive at the table, it's another round of introductions. I already know Hellfire and Mo, of course, but now I meet Jeannie's man, Bomber, Sindy, Buzzard who's the money man apparently, and a man called Rusty who runs the bowling alley. I smile broadly at the latter.

"Free entry for brothers and family," he tells me, when he sees my interest. "You any good?"

"I've never tried," I say, surprising him.

"It wasn't exactly safe for Jay to do normal teenage things in Tucson," Pal explains.

"Well, fuck me. Bout time you learned, isn't it?"

"She plays pool though," Pal lets him know I'm not entirely pathetic.

Rusty's eyes sharpen. "Any good?"

As Pal goes to speak, I place my hand on his arm and lean over him. "How about you judge for yourself?"

He laughs heartily. "I've got a suspicion I might end up playin' against a ringer. But I'll take you up on that. Anytime you want, kid."

Like Bomber, he seems older than Hellfire, so I don't get upset when he calls me that.

"You finished?" Pal points at my empty plate. "Want anything else?"

Rubbing my stomach, I shake my head. "I've had plenty." When he stands and holds out his hand, I take it. I pause a moment, looking around at the men. Even the older guys seem to keep themselves fit. Satan's Devils all over seem to be a good-looking bunch. Remembering my thoughts about Pal, disloyally I look around seeing if any of the younger men here would cause my heart to race, and then glance back at the man by my side, realising he comes out on top. There's just something about him. I wonder again what it would have been like had our kiss not been interrupted.

As he walks around and introduces me to more of the men, I realise I have never done this before. Oh, back in Tucson, Paladin was never far from my side, but we never gave off the vibes that we were a couple. It's comforting in a security blanket way to have people assume we're together.

"So," the man called Sparky asks, "you up for the ride out?"

I glance at Paladin. He hasn't yet asked me. He makes up for that now. "We'll have to make sure first that you're comfortable on the bike, but assumin' you are, would you like to come?"

"Where to?"

It's Sparky, who's apparently the road captain, who gives me the details. "Royal Gorge Bridge. We're going to ride our bikes over it." Remembering I'm new to the area and that the information hasn't told me much, he expands, "It's a high-suspension bridge nearly a thousand feet above the Arkansas River. Cars aren't allowed, but our motorcycles will be. I've arranged it with the park management. It's about an hour and fifteen-minute ride from here."

My eyes light up. "Sounds fun. I'd love to." I can't wait to be out on the bike behind Pal knowing it would be amazing. The bridge sounds exciting too.

Pal's watching me closely, then he smiles, his whole face brightening. "Looks like you better count us both in, Sparky."

Sparky winks at me before walking off. "I hope you're okay with heights," he throws over his shoulder ominously.

"Are you?" Paladin asks, curious.

I have absolutely no idea and tell him so. He laughs. "Guess we're both going to find out."

Music is playing, but not overly loudly. A couple of the club girls are dancing, their moves clearly aimed at enticing the men. I notice two brothers I was introduced to as Ink and Mace eyeing them up. As I watch, Ink moves closer, moving in behind one of the girls, thrusting his hips behind her. As they pivot I see he's got his hands over her boobs.

Hmm.

Quickly I turn away from the X-rated display, noticing Paladin frowning. "Thought this was a family affair," he grumbles, while taking my hand and leading me back over to where Moira, Jeannie and Sindy are sitting.

"You enjoying yourself?" Moira asks.

"Yes, thank you," I reply politely. It has been interesting meeting the men, and seeing where Paladin's living. If I'm honest though, it makes me homesick for Tucson, and the people I knew there, emphasising how very far away I am.

I seem to have interrupted a conversation which resumes when Sindy asks Moira. "You coming along on the ride?"

Moira doesn't look very enthusiastic. "I don't think so. Been a long time since I went on the back of Hell's bike."

"Oh, come on, darlin'. It will be fun. If it gets too much, you can ride back in the crash truck." Hellfire tries to persuade his wife.

"We'll talk about this later," she tells him in a voice that allows no argument. I notice he just raises his eyebrows in response.

"Well I'm up for it," says Jeannie, leaning back into her man. As Bomber puts his arms around her, she continues, "It sounds fun."

"Yeah. Riding over a suspension bridge a thousand feet above the ground?" Sindy shudders. "I'll come along, but whether I go across or not I'll decide on the day."

As Sindy puts it so starkly, Jeannie's eyes widen as though she's reconsidering.

"I'll look after you, sweetheart," Bomber, noticing, says into her ear. I love seeing their relationship. I've picked up that they've been married almost as long as Hellfire and Moira, yet seem so much more at ease with each other. He's still protective after all this time. That's the type of relationship I'd like to have one day.

Demon comes over. Two bottles of beer in his hand, one he passes to Hellfire. Hellfire is just in the process of taking it when shots ring out.

For a second, everyone's stunned. Then controlled panic. The men start shouting and gesticulating. Pal's already got his arm around me and is pushing me in front of him toward the clubhouse. Bomber's herding Jeannie and Moira, and Buzzard has run over and is dragging Sindy.

"Stay with them, Pal, Bomber." Hell yells, then disappears.

"What's going on, Pal?" I ask, panicked. "Is anyone hurt?" Why I'm querying him I don't know. He'll know nothing more than I do. *Could it be the Herreras? Could they have found out where I am?*

The club girls have also come in. Titsy looks white, the others a combination of animated and perplexed.

"This happened before?" Pal asks Bomber in a low voice.

Bomber's reply is a shake of his head.

The place seems to be in confusion. Brothers are rushing in and out. I can't make sense of the things I'm hearing. I tug Pal's arm. "What's going on? Who shot at us?"

But he knows nothing more than I do, until Hellfire and the men all flood back through the main door. "Women to stay here. Prospects keep an eye on them. Everyone else, church now." Two prospects jump to attention, guns ready in their hands. I'm sure there was a third one, maybe he's still outside.

As Hellfire storms past, Moira puts herself in front of him, her hands on her hips. "What the fuck is happening, Hell?"

"Drive-by," he says quickly. "We're going on lockdown, Mo."

"No, Hell…"

He grabs her by the shoulders. "*Yes*, Mo. We don't know who or what they'll be targeting next. Until we do, everyone is to stay here. You got me?" Having told his wife, he makes his voice louder, and repeats. "Lockdown. All old ladies, whores and brothers will be staying in the club."

Jeannie gasps beside me. "Hell, we haven't been on lockdown for years."

Bomber speaks up, his tone firm. "Well it seems like we're going to be now. We're staying here, Jeannie." Like Hellfire, he sounds adamant.

As the brothers are walking past into church, Pal seems reluctant to leave me. I want to stay close to him too. I know what lockdown is, it means I'll be staying here for the duration. I was supposed to live with Hell and Moira, now I'll be here at the compound instead. I'm too used to that, I'm disappointed. I had been looking forward to having some independence. My eyes flick to Pal's, I can see he's torn.

I need to step up here. "Go," I tell him, prodding him in the direction of his brothers. Part of the reason is selfish. If he finds out what's going on, maybe he'll tell me too.

He places his lips to my forehead, nods, then steps away.

Hellfire's still here, I overhear him. "Mo," he hisses, "You need to step up. You're the prez's ol' lady."

She's looking horrified, but at last straightens her back and nods.

Hell raises his voice slightly. "Jeannie. I want you and Mo to make a list of what we're going to need."

Jeannie says drily, "It's been a long time, but I can remember how this goes, Hell. If you think it's really necessary."

Hell stares at her. "I'm hoping we're overreacting, but I want everyone here. Safe."

CHAPTER 25

HELLFIRE

We haven't been on lockdown for fifteen years. No wonder Mo was so shocked. I could be making too much of this, but I'm going on gut feel here. Won't take any chance of anyone else becoming hurt. I haven't told the women, but the prospect, Runt, had taken a bullet. He'll live, but this shit is serious. He could have been killed.

I'm out of practice at this. Since we got out of the drug and gun running business, and have been earning our money clean, the club's had no real enemies. Or at least none that brought trouble right to our front door. Then we have a dead body turn up, planted outside our premises. Other odd things happening, our shop broken into. Now a drive-by shooting.

Mo's going to hate being here. She didn't want to come today; I'd had to persuade her. Jeannie will be fine, as will Sindy, but Mo? Christ, keeping her here is going to be hard.

But she, the other old ladies and the club girls are all my responsibility. It's my decision they stay here to be safe, while I have to send men out to try to hunt down an enemy we currently can't identify.

Who is fucking with us? That's what I don't know, and what we've got to find out.

Everyone's already in church. Mace lights up and slides the pack toward me. I toss him a grateful nod and take out a smoke. For once, everyone quiets as I flick the lighter. While they're not talking, their body language shows how agitated everyone is.

Not bothering to bang the gavel, I open the meeting. "Don't want to waste time lookin' for answers we already know we don't have. What I want is ideas on how to find out who these mother-fuckers are."

"Runt didn't get the license plate."

I'm not surprised Cad's already asked. "Everyone else was out back I presume?" Yes. Of course we were. Our only witness, and casualty, was the prospect who was out front taking his turn watching the gate, and who, as a result, had been shot.

"Runt going to be okay?"

"Yeah, Thunder. It was just a scratch even though it bled a lot. I just cleaned it, put a couple of stitches in." Rusty's medical skills come in handy at times.

"What's the plan, Hell?"

I glance around. Everyone's looking to me. Christ, I'm tired, and they're all expecting me to have answers. "Demon, Thunder and Mace. Get out on the streets. Keep your eyes and ears open and start tracking down those gangs. I want to know if anyone's heard any whispers of people moving in, looking to take us down."

"Take what down?" Mace asks, incredulously. "Who's got anything to gain from closing our businesses? Shooting up our club and takin' us out? It's not like we've got a gun trade to take over anymore. We don't even deal in fucking drugs."

"Someone's got a beef with the club. It feels personal," Demon proposes. My eyes shoot to him. "What if we're not looking for a gang, but one person?"

"Could one person fuck us up like they've done? All the activity on the security cameras had the same time stamp that night." Pyro, like the rest, is looking worried.

"Two," says Cad, adamantly. "I went back over them. Checked the timings again. Two people would have been all that was needed."

Lizard's looking thoughtful. "Been trying to think of who might have a grudge against us. What about Smithy?"

"Nah," Demon says quickly. "Good suggestion, but word is he went to LA."

I raise my eyebrows. Demon shrugs. Man didn't cut it here, maybe he learned from how he'd fucked up. We'd let the prospect go some months back.

"It's worth following up," Cad proposes. "I'll dig deeper, check he actually left and see if I can find what he's doing now."

"Thanks, Brother. Probably a dead end, but we can't rule anything out."

"Any progress by the cops on the dead man?" Taser asks.

"We haven't been told..." I break off, raising my eyebrow, again putting Cad in the spotlight.

"I'll hack into the police database. See if there's anything that's not being passed to us."

"I want half of us here at all times. We keep the businesses running, but women and club girls are to stay at the compound until we've got more info."

"You think they'll come after us in our homes?"

"Can't rule it out, Buzzard." I wipe my brow. "While we remain ignorant as to who or why, I don't want to take the risk that they might." After pausing for a breath, I lay it on them. "I'll want to talk to all of you individually." I glance around the table. "Any shit you don't want to discuss openly, you can fuckin' tell me in private. I want to know if anyone's pissed someone off. Slept with the wrong wife, for example. I'll be speakin' to everyone. If it doesn't affect the club, that shit stays with me. But for the sake of your brothers' lives, don't keep anything to yourselves."

All of them start looking at each other. There are shrugs, shakes of heads. I'm determined to find out if anyone's stepped on anyone's toes.

Pal's frowning. He raises his hand. "I'll get in touch with Drummer and Mouse back in Tucson. See if the Herreras might have found out where Jayden's gone. A long shot, but we can't rule out it's her that's the target."

A murmuring starts to grow but I shut that down fast. "Unless anyone here has a loose mouth, can't see how anyone could know. But thanks Pal, doesn't hurt asking the question."

Taser's glaring at Pal, but then he normally does. "What about the girl herself? Could she have given away where she was going? Seems mighty suspicious you and her turn up, and all hell breaks loose here."

Pal puts his hands to where he'd have a beard if he was able to grow one. Slowly he shakes his head. When he leans forward to speak, it's in a measured voice, but carries the weight of scorn with it. "Let me think about that. Girl threatened with being taken and raped, sold on as a sex slave. Her life made intolerable as revenge on the Satan's Devils. Yeah, quite possible she'd be loose-mouthed and tell everyone where she was going. You might have a point there, *Taser*."

Eyes go from Pal to the man he's addressed. Taser looks sheepish, but doesn't give up. "Can't hurt to ask."

Demon's fingers are drumming on the table. I glance at him; he's got something to say. "While I think Taser's barkin' up a blind alley, I think we ought to talk to the women too. See if they've been fuckin' someone they shouldn't."

"See, we're not sexist at all," Mace grins broadly. "Equal suspicions here."

"Jeannie's not stepped out on me," Bomber snarls.

I jump in as Buzzard's face grows dark. "I think the VP means the club girls, not the old ladies." When that's appeased the married men, I start to sum up. "We look at the club as an entity, consider who might have a beef with the Satan's Devils. At the same time we look at each of us individually and that includes the women. We get eyes and ears on the ground. We keep our businesses running with maximum security." I break off, looking between Cad and Pal. "How long until the new cameras are up and running?"

"Got it on order," it's Pal who responds. "Installation is easy. By the end of the week?"

I nod, then resume. "Everyone not out investigatin' stays on the compound. Women to be protected at all times. Two men out front on the gate." I glance at Demon, sending him a silent message, *have I forgotten anything?*

Demon steps in. "No brother to be ridin' alone, that goes without sayin'." His glare, a copy of my own, lands on each of the brothers. "If you've got something you're hidin', you need to come clean to the prez or me. We won't share shit that has no bearin'. You been dippin' your wick where it shouldn't have been? I want to know it."

Fuck me. There are several of them who look guilty. Well, bikers attract tail. Always have, always will.

"I'll look into any names you give me," Cad offers.

"You really want a list of people I've fucked?" Ink's eyes look wild. "What if I didn't know their names?"

Demon's forehead crashes down on the table. Turning sideways, he gives me a look. And a sly grin. *Seems like he'll be giving me a list too.*

"Cad, you might have your work cut out." I'm shaking my head as I tell him. "Might be easier to ask who hasn't fucked someone they shouldn't."

It's pure accident, but my eyes fall on the newest member sitting at the end of the table. Everyone else's do too. It's Lizard who puts a label on him. He points straight at Pal, "Not him, he's a fuckin' virgin."

It was a figure of speech. But instead of giving us the finger or some other gesture, the lad goes bright red. It's the fact he says nothing that gets us incredulously laughing.

"Fuck me, you fuckin' are, aren't you? You're waiting for that bitch." Thunder roars with laughter.

"Hey, come to me if you want some pointers, Brother," Mace offers.

"Have you even got a dick? It work?" That's from Ink. "Probably fallen off by now if you haven't used it."

Poor Pal looks like he wants to slide under the table.

I take pity on him. "Well the rest of you assholes who overwork your dicks, I'll see you in alphabetical order." I raise the gavel. "Meeting fuckin' dismissed. Bomber you're up first."

"Haven't got anything to say, Prez," Bomber protests.

I glare at him. "Everyone, Bomb. That includes men with old ladies."

Demon holds up his hand. "One last thing, Prez?" I nod. "Jeannie and Mo will hopefully have got together that list you asked them to of supplies we're going to need. Volunteers to go get them?"

"I'll go," Pyro offers. "With Taser. Will take you some time to go through the brothers by the expressions around this table."

He's right. I'm just wondering how long this list of people they've fucked is going to be.

"Prez. Just before we break. Been looking into the police chief some more."

"What you got, Cad?"

"Zilch. Can't dig anything up. If he's targeting us, from his record he'd do it legal."

"This doesn't have the feel of a set-up," I raise my chin to Cad. "Thanks, Brother."

Cad nods.

"Okay, assholes. Let's get this shit done."

As everyone stands and leaves, Bomber hesitates. "You want me in your office, Prez?"

I nod to him. "I'll be there in a moment."

When he leaves, it's just me and my son. Demon's head is moving from side to side. "Reckon you know what you're in for?"

I don't, that's the problem. "My gut feel is it's personal. Against the club. We've either got a common enemy, or someone gunning for one of us. Seems too haphazard to be something organised by a gang."

"Runt was the one who got shot."

"Speed of the attack meant they were aiming for the poor fucker on guard duty. Could have been any one of us. We were rotatin' the prospects so they all got food at the barbeque. I can't see how Runt could have been the target."

"Maybe you're right." He doesn't sound convinced.

"You any other ideas?"

"Other than you acting as father confessor?" Demon grins. "Nah."

Bomber's waiting for me in my office as instructed. I walk in and go to my chair, with the desk in between us. Behind me hangs the flag that's in all our chapters, the insignia of the Satan's Devils.

"Got fuck all to say, Prez."

"Whoa. Let me get my ass in the chair first, Bomb." I sit, then lean forward with my chin resting on my hands. "No judgement, Brother. But are you fucking around on Jeannie?"

Instead of an instant denial, my old friend starts to shake his head, then his eyes crease as thought he's remembering something. The silence seems to stretch out. Bomber made Jeannie his old lady a few months after Mo and I married. A year later they'd made it legal. Seemed solid as fuck all these years. Even today I'd noticed they were still demonstrable toward each other, a closeness still shared that I seemed to have lost with my wife.

"Brother," I say in encouragement. "I need to know."

His lips thin as they press together, his hands are clasped between his legs. He takes in a deep breath, then says firmly, "I don't fuck around on Jeannie."

I stay quiet. Something else is coming. Despite what he said in church, *does she fuck around on him?*

Suddenly he sits back, folding his arms across his chest defensively, then looks at me with a challenge in his eyes. "You know what it's like. Thirty-five, thirty-six years is a fuck of a long time to be with one woman. To stay attracted to each other? Well that's fuckin' hard. Things become so familiar, making love becomes practiced. Hard to put the spice back in it."

I know what he's talking about. Fuck, do I.

Again I don't speak, letting him continue.

"Well, Jeannie and I decided we'd do something different. We *don't* cheat on each other. Or not in our eyes. We, er, we joined a swinger's club a few years back."

I feel my eyes open wide. Like me, Bomber and Jeannie have a house off compound, we don't live in each other's pockets. But I never would have guessed that about him. Now I'm quiet as I don't know what the fuck to say. I couldn't have predicted I'd hear that.

He takes it as unspoken criticism, and glares. "We don't cheat. We do fuck other people. But only when we're doing it in the same room."

Could I do that? Let Mo be fucked by another man while I was watching? Fuck no. He'd get a bullet in his ass before he could get his dick close to her cunt. *She's all mine. No one else's.*

I try to gather my thoughts, to put my prez hat back on. "You do what you have to Brother. Ain't no business of mine. What I need to know is, were all the parties willing? Anyone not too happy seeing you fucking his old lady?"

"Nothing immediately comes to me, but I'll give it some thought, Prez. Make a list of names and addresses."

Just how many on that fucking list?

"Appreciate that, Bomb."

"That all?"

"Yeah."

He stands to leave. "Don't tell Jeannie I told you. Unless, you and Mo?"

"No way, Bomber. Sorry." I'm proud I can keep my voice even.

He chuckles. "Didn't think so. Pity."

When my office door closes behind him, I have to wonder whether he's just told me he wouldn't mind fucking my wife. I'm not stupid, I've always known Jeannie had her eyes on me from the start.

No way. No fucking way.

Hold on. Hadn't Bomber suggested Jeannie, him, I and Moira get together one evening? Yeah. He had. An innocent request? Fuck, he's got me thinking now. Before I take him up on that offer, I'll have to make sure I know exactly what he does, and doesn't expect. *No way. No fucking way.*

CHAPTER 26

MOIRA

I can't believe this is happening. Glancing around, I see the club girls sitting at the bar. They seem to have composed themselves now the immediate threat has gone and are doing shots. To my disgust, Sheila's pouring hers into Titsy's bare cleavage, the ample breasts that frame it are being held up in the latter's two hands. Sheila then proceeds to noisily slurp, suck and lick the vodka or tequila, who cares for the details, all up.

Runt, who's appeared with a bandage on his arm, is resting on the couch soaking the sight up. The other two prospects, supposedly on guard are also distracted.

Not my first rodeo, certainly not the first time I've seen something like this. But Hell had promised me a family afternoon, and it's turned into a freak show as normal. Worse than that, he's forbidden me to leave and go home. Fuck that. I'd prefer to take my chances, though I've still got my brains. As old lady to the president, if someone's coming after the club, I might be a target.

"You'll be with Hell in his room. Bomber and Buzz have rooms here, so Sindy and me will be fine." Jeannie's mouth narrows as she looks at Jayden. "Haven't got any spare rooms, so Jay will need to bunk down with Pal."

"No," I tell her. "She can take Pal's room. Pal will have to sleep somewhere else."

"For goodness sake, Mo. She's not your daughter. I've seen enough of that boy to know he wouldn't take what wasn't on offer."

"I told her sister I'd watch out for her," I insist, disliking the idea immediately. "Putting temptation in her way isn't taking care of her."

"Well you can tell Pal he's sleeping on the sofa." Jeannie doesn't seem to understand.

"I will." I respond, my temper rising. "Not going to have that girl taken advantage of. I'll give Pal a piece of my mind. Pal won't…"

"Hey, what's all this about Pal? Pal won't…?" I hadn't realised Jay had come up behind me.

I open my mouth, but Jeannie gets in first. "There are no spare rooms, Jay, so you'll have to stay in Paladin's."

"Paladin will sleep on one of the couches," I get in, tossing a glare at my friend.

Jay looks around. Her jaw setting when she sees the lumpy, filthy, worn out couches. When she turns back to me, her eyes are sparking. "No he won't. If that's the way it has to be, I'll stay with him. In his room."

"No you won't." I contradict. "I promised your sister."

"What Mo?" she challenges me. "Just what did you promise her? All I heard was you offering to give me a room in your house. You promised nothing about defending my honour, nor keeping Pal and I apart. My sister *trusts* Paladin. And so do I."

"You're not seventeen yet…"

"I will be in two months. Sixty days. And that's going to make how much of a difference? You gonna call the cops on me? Get Pal arrested?"

"So you will be sleeping together," I throw back, through gritted teeth. "You want to throw your life away? Hitch up with a biker at sixteen?" I notice Jeannie's staring at me in confusion as the words keep tumbling out of my mouth. "You're going to jump at the chance to fuck?"

Jayden's looking equally taken aback, but unlike me, she's able to speak calmly. "I'm not saying that. What I am saying, is that whatever I do, it's my business. Not yours." She turns to Jeannie. "Thank you. I'll discuss the arrangements with Pal."

When she swings on her heels, the men are exiting their meeting. As soon as she spies him, Jay's straight over to talk to her man. Being on lockdown hasn't seemed to have upset her at all. But then, I suppose she's more used to that, than being able to get on with her life free of constraints.

"What the fuck is wrong with you?" Jeannie hisses. "I was fifteen for fucks sake when I lost my virginity, never regretted it. That girl's already lost hers. Now you're keeping her to a mythical age limit. Lots of places she'd already be legal anyways."

"I don't want her to repeat the mistakes I made."

Jeannie's eyes soften. "You made no mistake, Mo. If anyone did, it was down to me. I plagued the hell out of you until you gave in and came to the club. That you were Hell's put a fucking target on your head. Neither of us had a clue what was going to happen, wouldn't have come within a mile of the place if we had. Jayden's not you. You, shit, me too. We were both naïve and clueless. Jay's been living in a club for two years. She's known Pal for that long too. I say we leave those young folks alone and let them work it out by themselves."

I don't know what the hell to think. *Am I being unreasonable?* "I'll talk to Hell. Maybe there's a spare office Pal can sleep in."

My friend is shaking her head. "You're not going to let this drop, are you?"

My eyes swing back around to her. "*I can't.*"

Seeing Bomber leaving Hell's office, I take my chance and pop my head around his door. "I need to talk to you."

For some reason, seeing me makes him grin. Then he stands. He walks around to my side of the desk. He steps, no prowls toward me. A look on his face so intense, I take a step back. "Er, if you're busy…"

One hand goes around my waist, the other goes to the back of my head. With a gentle touch he slides his fingers into my hair, and angles my face up. His eyes search mine, his flaring. *Oh my.* Suddenly his lips are on mine. This is no gentle polite kiss, the type we've been satisfied with for a long time now. This is a kiss of possession, as though he's reminding me I'm his.

I let him lead, he's fully in command. His tongue demands entry, I let him have it. He's controlling, he's making parts of me come alive that I thought were dead. Slowly, almost reluctantly, he pulls back. "Not time now, Mo, but I warn you, might take one of those little blue pills tonight."

"Might be a good idea," I agree.

"Mo, my Mo." His eyes gentle as they smile at me, his fingers smooth across the skin of my face, he doesn't seem to care about the new wrinkles. *He's not wearing his glasses; he won't be able to see the details.* Nor am I mine, I realise, as I stare back at his still handsome face. *There's a reason why you lose your close-up vision in old age.*

His forehead comes down to touch mine. "What was that about?" I ask.

"Just reminding you who you belong to, Mo."

Who else would want me?

"Now," he pulls back, holding me at arm's length. "What did you want to talk about?"

I can't remember. Oh, hang on, yes. "Jay can't stay in Pal's room, Hell."

He looks puzzled. "Then she can sleep somewhere else."

"Jeannie says there's nowhere. All the rooms are full."

"I'll have a word with Pal." Hell grins, as if he knows something I don't. "I think she'll be safe enough with him."

"I don't want to push them together, Hell. She's too young."

"Mo, darlin'. They both are. But they're old enough to know what they want."

"I don't like it. There must be something…"

"Nah, Mo. Jayden stays in Pal's room."

"Hell, you're not listening to me. I…"

He taps me on the nose. "Jayden stays in Paladin's room. No, let me finish, Mo, you haven't heard what I haven't yet said. She'll stay there, but on her own. I've got plans for Pal, he'll be somewhere else instead."

Resting my cheek against my man's shoulder, he cradles the back of my head. We stand like that for a moment, sharing a closeness that we haven't enjoyed for a long time. I realise I've only been thinking about myself, and how much I hate being on lockdown. I haven't given a thought to him and the problems he's dealing with. Like finding out who the club's enemies are.

"Are you okay, Hell? Do you know who's coming after us?"

He draws in a deep breath, then lets out a loud sigh. "No fuckin' idea. Not yet. But I'm working on it."

"How can I help?"

"Just be my ol' lady."

I haven't felt that for a very long time. Maybe I should stop focusing on me and think about him instead. I don't know if I'll be very successful, but if he's expecting me to step up, perhaps the least I can do is try.

"Okay."

One last kiss, and I leave him. Buzzard is waiting outside, I step back to let him enter, and then go into the clubroom again. Approaching the bar, I hear a commotion.

"Well this is plain fuckin' stupid. I had plans for tonight." Tulia's getting riled.

"I wanted to go shopping tomorrow. I need some new clothes," Sheila's joining in. "I don't see why we should have to be available twenty-four seven just because the men can't go out."

Before Bella can open her mouth, I'm in front of them, while part of me wonders why they want to go shopping when the lack of clothing seems more their norm, I raise my voice. "Do any of you understand what a lockdown is?"

"We're not stupid." Bella's expression makes me want to slap her face, but I refrain. "The men have obviously fucked up. They need to stay out of sight. Someone's gunning for them."

"Someone's gunning for the club," I correct. "And what are you?"

"Whores," says Bella, putting it plainly, obviously having no concerns with the term.

"Club girls," says Tulia, making it sound more gentile.

I point at her. "You're right. You're part of the club. Same as us old ladies. Someone wants to hurt the club? They could try and take any of us. Lockdown's for everyone's benefit."

Tulia's mouth opens and shuts. Bella huffs. As I turn around, Jeannie raises a glass toward me. I grin back. Actually, I'd forgotten I used to enjoy keeping the girls in line. Before I stopped coming to the club.

Hellfire's demonstration, the promise of what might happen later tonight, makes me view things in a different light. When Jeannie drags Titsy and Breezy away to help her in the kitchen, I go along too. The leftovers are brought in from the interrupted barbeque, saran wrapped and covered up, sandwiches cut for brothers who'll be hungry later, then the place is cleaned up.

As we go about our tasks, Jeannie and I reminisce about old times, our laughter attracting an audience.

"He didn't?" Bella puts her hand to her mouth and gives a very unfeminine snort.

"He did." I nod toward Jeannie for confirmation.

She giggles. "We hadn't meant it to go so far. But Mo had prepared a bowl of food. Rusty assumed it was for the kids."

"Kid. I only had Demon then."

"Yeah, well, he picked it up and started eating it."

"He said it was great. Finished the plate and wanted more…"

"Walk it back, Mo. He actually asked for a slice of bread to mop up the gravy."

I'm laughing so hard I'm holding my stomach. "And you said…" I point at her, hardly able to get the words out.

"I asked him," she takes over, "whether he wanted it heated up."

"He said no, it was fine."

"Oh God, what was it?" Tulia asks.

"Cat food." Both Jeannie and I shout out together.

"You're never going to let me fuckin' forget that, are you?" A booming voice interrupts us. But Rusty's got a huge grin on his face as he walks over and gives me a big hug. "You know, Mo? I was thinking we don't see enough of you nowadays, but," he rubs his stomach, "maybe that's a good thing."

"Hmm. You like the food I give you, old man?"

Rusty swings around to Jeannie quickly, his face falling. "You haven't… you wouldn't…"

"Oh, stop complaining." Thunder steps in. "Whatever it is she serves up is fuckin' tasty."

"The rattlesnake cooked well, didn't it?" Jeannie asks, innocently.

Both men cover their faces and gag.

Jeannie winks at me and we crack up. *Why did I think I didn't miss this?*

Later that evening, Pal, who'd been out most of the day after the barbeque ended so abruptly, returns to the club. Hell calls him over for a word, and then, after grabbing a bite to eat and a quick word with Jayden, Pal goes back out.

Taking me into a corner, Hell speaks quietly. "I've asked him to provide extra security at the strip club. His shift will last until five am. By the time he gets back, he'll be dead beat and Jayden just waking up."

"You're a genius. Thank you. But isn't the strip club closed today?"

A tap to my nose. "Closed, yeah. But we still need to take precautions. As to why, Mo, that's club business." He pauses. A smirk slowly covers his face. "Now do you want to stay down here and party?" Hell turns me around so my back's to his front. Ink's getting down to business with Titsy, Bella's on her knees in front of Pyro. And I can feel a hard cock pressing into my back.

I don't need asking twice. I follow Hell upstairs to his bedroom, only a quick sideways glance toward the storage room on the way, the room which used to belong to Blackie. He stops me as I walk through the door, pulling me against him once again, whispering in my ear, as though to remind me this place holds good memories as well. "This is where Kennedy and Samuel were conceived."

"Ain't going to be more babies conceived tonight." I huff. "That's one thing for certain. Getting old has some benefits."

"Hmm," he nuzzles my ear. "Good. Skin on skin. No condoms."

I turn around. Going up on tiptoe I kiss him. "No condoms. Unless…" I frown.

"Not been with anyone Mo, I told you that. Only woman I want is the one here with me."

He kisses me as he's done many thousands of times before. Then he undoes the buttons of the blouse I'm wearing, and slides it off my shoulders.

"Fuckin' beautiful, babe."

"Can we turn the light off?" There's an edge of pleading in my voice which makes him still.

"You really want to?"

"I'd like you to imagine what I was like before. Not as I am now."

Ignoring my request, he removes my bra in a move he's perfected over the years. My tits, no longer perky, drop out. His eyes flare as he touches my nipples, rolling them between his fingers and thumbs. "Love these, always have, always will," he pronounces before he lowers his head, taking one hard nub into his mouth, and then the other.

While paying attention to my breasts, always skilled at multi-tasking, one of his hands moves to the zip of my pants. I place my fingers over the top to stop him.

"Please turn the light off," I beg.

"No," he refuses with just one word. "Need to see you, Mo. Need to show you I don't give a fuck about wrinkles, stretch marks, cellulite or whatever fuckin' shit you women worry about. I need to see the body that's mine. Only mine."

I've got all of those, and worse. For a moment my worry is greater than the feelings his administration to my breasts elicits. What happens if a man who's taken Viagra is turned off? Or does he remain ready to perform even if his head's not entirely on board? Guess I'm going to find out.

Moving down my body he trails his tongue over my stretch marks, tracing each one. He caresses the no-longer flat tummy, then starts dragging my pants down, my panties along with them.

I wait. Not disappointed when I hear him gasp. "What the fuck have you done to yourself, Mo?"

I suck in a breath, feeling the tears pricking at my eyes. *Guess I'm going to find out how Viagra works.* "It's the menopause, Hell. I can't fucking help it."

He hasn't stopped. Kneeling and moving down the bed, he pulls my pants off entirely, then sits back, examining what the harsh overhead light has revealed. He's seeing, for the first time, what I see every day in the shower. My mound is now almost completely bare, just a few straggly pubes remaining around the edge. I keep them trimmed and tidy, but it looks a mess. There's a little more hair still on my labia.

"Fuck, Mo." His exclamation could be one of pleasure or disgust. Knowing how much he appreciates a neatly trimmed bush, I'm going with the latter. I risk a glance at his face, he looks like he's thinking. Suddenly he leaps up. *This is it. I disgust him.* "Wait there." *What?*

He's got me naked, he hasn't revealed himself yet. My jaw drops when he stands and barefooted, leaves the room.

Do I get dressed? Slide under the covers? Is he coming back or has he gone to find a whore to take care of his medically induced rock hard cock? I put my fist to my mouth, trying to stop the sob escaping. *Hell's gone.*

But before a moment has passed, he's back. He goes into his bathroom returning with a towel and something else.

"Up." He instructs.

Bemused, I lift my hips and let him place the towel under me. *Oh shit.* "Hell?"

"Want to see all of you. Looks fuckin' sexy, Mo. Can't fuckin' wait until I slide my tongue into you and you're completely bare."

I half sit up. *Christ. I haven't seen that leer on his face for years.* "Hell," I screech when I realise his intention. "You can't…"

He slaps my ass lightly. "Fuckin' can. And will."

"Where the hell did you get shaving cream?" He doesn't use it himself, he's got a beard.

"Oh, Mace had some. And a spare razor."

"Mace? You went and asked him?" My voice is an octave higher than normal. "You tell him what you were using it for?"

"Think he'll guess when he sees I've still got my beard in the morning, babe."

As he speaks, I go still. Cold cream covers me, and the even colder steel starts scraping against my tender parts. "Hell, be careful." I hope his hands are still steady, waiting to feel him cut me.

"Relax. I'm not going to hurt you."

"Mace won't be able to keep his mouth shut. It will be all over the clubhouse by morning." I'm so embarrassed.

"That I'm making love to my woman? Oh, they'll know that anyway, babe."

Christ, this shouldn't be sexy. But the way he's biting his lip, deep in concentration as he removes the remaining hair, is proving a turn on. But I'm worried about his statement. "You gonna boast to prove your virility?"

"Nah. But everyone's going to hear you screaming, Mo. They're going to know I'm giving my ol' lady a good fuckin'."

"Sure of yourself?"

"You looking this damn sexy, Mo? Fuckin' right I am. There. Finished. Stay there." He disappears into the bathroom, returning with a damp washcloth. As he wipes the shaving foam away, his eyes seem to glow. He goes and rinses the cloth, then returns and cleans me again. Then sits back on his haunches. "Christ Mo," he palms his dick, "fuck, woman. Fuckin' amazin'."

If I knew it would cause a reaction like this, I'd have shaved myself years ago.

"Thought you preferred a neatly trimmed bush…"

"Babe." His eyes meet mine and hold them. "I did. On you. Before I met you, the whores went bare. You were different, *my woman.* I didn't want you to look like a whore."

Has he just insulted me?

"Nah, whatever you're thinking, stop it right there. Haven't seen a bare cunt for over thirty-six years, Mo. What I'm considering is how my beard's going to feel when I do this."

Without waiting, he lowers his head and licks me from my slit to my clit, the rasp of his beard alien, and… totally sexy. When he does it again, my back arches. When he places his fingers inside me, closing his mouth around the hard nub at the same time, I can't stop the cry coming from me. *It's different. It's amazing. And at the same time, familiar.* I know all his moves; he knows my reactions. He plays me like a darn fiddle. It's not long before my muscles are stiffening, waves of sensation starting to build. Whether it's that it's been so long, whether being bare makes that much of a difference, but when I come, my body jerks forward and yeah, he was right, I do scream.

"You, naked." I demand, breathlessly, when at last I return to myself.

He moves off the bed and gives me my very own strip show. His tee-shirt's removed, revealing a smattering of silvery grey hairs on his chest. When he undoes the zip of his jeans, he's gone commando. His hair is as thick there as ever, but his pubes are near white. His cock though, that's what makes me lick my lips, it juts out proudly.

Seeing me watching, he palms it slowly, sliding his hand up and down. He eyes my mouth, saying, "Not tonight, not gonna waste this." It reminds me we only have the one chance.

Then he's taking the lube I'm not even sure I now need, slathering it over his cock. When he applies it to me, his movements are erotic, he ramps up my desire then kneels, pulls my hips over his thighs, presses himself to my entrance and pushes inside.

My hands grip the covers. Months have gone by when I never believed I'd feel him inside me again. As I relish the sensations, tears fall from my eyes. *I love him so much, I always have.* He's the only man for me.

When he starts to move, I stop thinking anything. He found my sweet spot decades ago, he knows exactly what gets me going. His hips start thrusting, he reaches forward, resting his weight on one arm, he looks into my eyes as one hand encircles my throat lightly, just enough to show me who's in control.

"Eyes on me, Mo," he reminds me how he likes it.

Christ he's good. He's hitting that spot time after time. His face is contorting as he chases his own pleasure.

"Fuckin' come for me, Mo."

As though my body was waiting for his instruction, I explode.

He cries out, his movements become frantic, the depths he's plundering extend my orgasm, my muscles clench down on him, then again and again.

"Fuck! I'm coming babe," he roars.

I swear I can feel him releasing inside me. Squirt after squirt of his hot cum. My arms wrap around him, holding him to me, enjoying the closeness, the security of being held by my man, being connected so intimately.

We lie without speaking, until I feel his cock softening. Then he rolls to his side, his arm thrown up over his eyes. A slight groan comes from him.

"You alright, Hell?"

"Get me some Advil, will you, darlin'?"

CHAPTER 27
PALADIN

Right at this moment, Jayden's where I've always dreamed of having her. *In my bed.* Problem is, I'm not there. Nah, I'm with fucking Taser at the strip club. It's Sunday, it's closed. Nothing to do but patrol around, checking out every noise and sound.

I'd half expected Taser to stay inside monitoring the cameras, but to give him his due, he's outside with me.

I'm stamping my feet. It might be spring, but the night's turned chilly, and standing around, or just walking a few paces isn't enough to keep me warm.

I've checked the cameras are still working, and their positioning for the umpteenth time. It's cold, and it's boring. Seems like it's getting to the man with me too.

"So, Pal. You certain nothing's followed you to Pueblo from Tucson?"

I shake my head before I reply, "Can't be certain about anything. But a drive-by's not the Herreras' style. They wanted us? They'd come in guns blazin'."

"You'd know, I suppose," he says grudgingly.

"So, Prez will be questioning everybody. You got any skeletons maybe rattlin' their bones?"

"Nah, nothing from me."

His tone makes me cock my head questioningly. "You're going to speak to Hell, though?"

Throwing me a sneering look, he confirms, "He's speakin' to everyone, isn't he? If there's anything he should know, I'll tell him."

I'm wondering about having a word with the prez. Taser is edgy about something. Mind you, the way single brothers screw around, I expect Hell will get quite a lot of information.

The night continues, time dragging. The most excitement is when a rat runs across the parking lot, the movement catching both of our eyes. I replace my gun in its holster sheepishly.

"You certain you got nothing to do with that body?"

"Let it drop, Taser, will you? I've told you before. Know nothing about him. It's most likely the body was moved and planted here, so what about you? You're the manager of Tits Up. Message for you?"

"Message for the club," he growls impatiently. "Nothing to do with me personally."

He's getting on my nerves. "I'll check around the front again." I do, just to get a moment to myself. But there's nothing there. No movement this time of night on the quiet roads of the city. Everyone else is in bed. *Where I want to be.* Next to Jayden.

My pillows, sheets, are going to smell of her. My cock twitches. I will it to behave. Got my girl where I want her, that's enough for now. I'm not going to take things further. I may not have much experience, but I know things have got to proceed between us slow. *What if I'm a disappointment to her?* I make myself think of something else, and not about the fact, when it comes to it, I won't know what the fuck to do. *She does.* Nah, she was never an active participant before.

She's asleep in my bed. Perhaps it would be better if she wasn't. It's putting thoughts in my head that shouldn't be there. *Think of that new exhaust you want, Pal.*

The sky is lightening by the time Thunder and Lizard arrive, relieving us from the night shift. I get on my bike, and side by side with Taser, ride back to the clubhouse.

It's quiet inside, just a prospect and Ink watching over the compound. Exhausted, I climb the stairs. Unlocking my door as quietly as I can, I open it.

She's sprawled out, in my bed. Sheets kicked off where she's too warm. With my back to the door, I just stand and watch her, drinking in the most beautiful sight of my life. Checking out the colourful pyjamas she's wearing, covered in unicorns. I've got a child-come-woman in my bed. Her clothing, the innocence that radiates off her sleeping body, makes me realise I shouldn't be thinking the thoughts about her that I am.

She's appropriated most of the bed, and is lying in the middle. I slide out of my cut and tee-shirt, leaving my jeans on. Yawning widely, I bend down and take my boots and socks off, then step forward to the bed. I'm so tired, if I don't lie down, I'll keel over where I stand.

There's a small space I can just about fit into on the left-hand side. I lift the covers, ease my body down gently, freezing as a small moan comes from her mouth. Then moving again when she's quiet once more. Managing to find enough space, I lie on my back, my hands secured under my head. My nostrils breathe in her perfume. As I close my eyes, I feel the warmth radiating from her.

This feels so right.

I wake, too hot. I'm being smothered. Jay has rolled over. I don't want to disturb her, but fuck, I'm burning up. Her body is flush against mine, her leg thrown over my thigh, her arm over my chest. She's treating me like a teddy bear. I'm uncomfortable, sweating, but I've never felt so good in all my life.

When I wake for the second time, it's movement that's disturbed me.

"Oh, God, Pal. I'm sorry. I…"

My hand shoots over hers, anchoring her to me. "Ain't got nothing to apologise for, Doll."

"I'm taking up all the bed."

"I'm comfortable," I lie. "Just don't move your leg…"

"Oh!"

Too late. I try to will my morning wood to go down. Fuck, who am I kidding? It's not the time of day, it's her, in my bed that I'm having a very normal male reaction to. I still, wondering what she's going to do. Not wanting to scare her.

"I, er, I'll get up now. You must be tired."

"Yeah, I'm going to sleep on a while." See? I can have a perfectly normal conversation with my dick throbbing, the object of its desire so fucking close and yet so far. *She's too young.* Once she's out of the room, I'll take care of it for myself. Will be far from the first time I've thought of her while I've been jerking off in the shower.

She doesn't seem in a hurry to move, even when I let her hand go. She leaves it lying on my chest, then her fingers start moving, tracing my muscles.

"Doll," I protest.

"Can I kiss you?"

Jeez. She's playing with fire. But what can I do, but give her permission?

"Sure, have at it, sweetheart."

Her leg, *thank fuck* moves away from my hips as she pulls it down to her side, giving her leverage to sit up and lean over me. Her blue eyes sparkle as she looks down. She seems emboldened that I'm lying next to her, keeping still, unthreatening, leaving everything up to her.

I watch as her hand approaches my face, tentatively, then faster, until her fingers make contact with my skin. Then she traces my features as if learning them. Finally, she touches my mouth. I open it slightly, unable to resist flicking out my tongue to taste her salty digit.

She grins.

Now her lips approach mine. A gentle touch, she pulls away. Then moves her face back down, this time applying more pressure. When she licks at the seam, I open my mouth. Her tongue touches mine, I play with hers gently. Morning breath should be horrible, it's not.

I can't get enough of her touch, her taste, her feminine aroma. But I force my hands to stay where they are, tamping down my impulse to take over the kiss and control it.

Suddenly she moves. She's straddling my chest. Her mouth descends again, and this time, both palms caress my cheeks as she kisses me. *She's killing me and she doesn't even know it.*

"Am I doing it right?" she whispers against me.

Fuck if I know. I've not properly kissed a woman before. A few fumbled attempts in high school, but I was more interested in staying alive than being laid. Then I was a prospect, the club girls forbidden to me. By the time I was patched in, I'd already committed to her.

"Feels right to me," I say softly. "Fuckin' good, Jay."

"You want me to stop?"

"No, but you ought to." I wiggle my hips, my cock's twitching automatically, pressing painfully into the zipper of my jeans.

My movement catches her by surprise. She looks down at those innocent-looking unicorn pyjamas, and then at my face. "Pal, I…"

"You go get dressed babe. Breakfast's probably ready downstairs. I'll get some more shut-eye."

If she doesn't go, even her unicorn armour might not be enough to stop me.

"How long will the lockdown last?"

Please, Doll, get off me. I try to stop them, but my hips flex again. *If she moved a bit lower, she'd be sitting where I want her…* "I don't know. But we're doing everything we can to end it." My voice sounds level. Almost normal. I'm not sure how.

"Will you be in danger, Pal?"

I grab hold of her hands, look into her eyes, and tell her, earnestly. "Not if I can help it."

A thoughtful look, much older than her years. A quick nod, then, thank fuck, at last, she moves off me. First back to her three-quarters of the bed, and then out that side. Then, grabbing some clothes, she disappears into the bathroom.

I want to call her back. I don't. But I touch my hand to my lips, remembering the feeling of her there. Something I want to repeat. And soon.

I'm asleep before she comes back out. It's mid-afternoon when I finally wake and go downstairs. Jay's deep in conversation with Mo, so waving my hand to show I won't interrupt her, I go straight to the kitchen and make myself a sandwich. I'm just finishing my last mouthful when Lizard puts his head around the door.

"There you are. Prez wants everyone in church."

Putting my plate in the dishwasher, I follow Lizard. This time when Jay catches my eye, I grimace slightly and indicate I'm following the rest of my brothers who are heading into the meeting room. She nods to show she understands.

The first thing I notice is Cad. He's always struck me as very laid back. When I worked with him selecting the security cameras, he'd not get frustrated when we couldn't find the ones we were after, trying store after store until we found them in stock. Today, for the first time I've noticed, there's some colour in his face, spots of red in his cheeks.

Prez takes his seat at the end of the table. With trouble surrounding us, everyone shuts up as soon as he sits down.

Instead of immediately speaking, his head shakes side to side. He catches Cad's eye and raises his chin. It's only then he opens his mouth. "Okay. Except for Paladin who was catching up on his beauty sleep, I've spoken to everyone now."

"Pal won't have any info to give you. He's a v-i-r-g-i-n. He won't have been fucking around." Ink looks like he's made a big joke.

I just sit fuming.

"Be that as it may, I still need to talk to him." Hellfire glares around, stopping any other comments dead. Luckily.

"Hope he fuckin' hasn't," mild-mannered Cad actually growls. "Got more than enough work as it is."

"Yeah, well. Can understand that, Brother. It's a shame none of you other fuckers have the willpower our new brother has."

"Hey, don't include me in that!" Buzzard glares at him. "I'm faithful to my wife."

I wait for Bomber to confirm he is too. He doesn't. Oh fuck. I'd never have guessed that, seeing him and Jeannie together. But I do notice him scowling at Hellfire and wonder why.

Prez looks around, his gaze settling on each of us one by one, ending up with Cad. "I've just fuckin' given Cad two hundred and twenty names. Two fuckin' hundred and fuckin' twenty names of people you assholes have fucked in the last six months. And that's only those whose names you can remember."

"Fifteen were mine." Pyro's fist bumps Taser's proudly.

"Hey, the odd twenty were mine," Ink puts in.

"I couldn't remember most of their names," Sparky is frowning. "Or their faces. I could probably recognise their cunts though."

"Not much help," Demon says, drily. "Not unless we have a naked line up of all the bitches in Pueblo."

"A lie down, not a line up," suggests Ink helpfully.

Cad thumps the table. "It's going to take me some time to narrow down the possibilities."

"Yeah," Hellfire nods at him, then raises his chin at the rest of the brothers. "Need you to think on those you might have forgotten to wrap it up with."

Demon jerks his chin at the prez, then looks down the table. "Any you might have left with a reminder. A kid or a fuckin' STD? Or any that might have an angry husband or partner."

Most don't look bothered. Pyro and Taser look a bit worried to me.

"Do we need to have the convo with everyone about keeping their shit covered?" Demon asks, quite seriously.

The expression on Hellfire's face is comical. His fist comes down hard on the table. "I run a fucking MC," he shouts. "Not a fuckin' sex-ed class."

That Demon mentioned it to lighten things up becomes obvious when his hand goes over his mouth to smother his laugh. Chuckles come from around the table.

Hellfire stands. "Just wanted to let you know Cad's got his work cut out to get answers. And that's if we're even on the right track. If he finds anything he wants investigated, we'll have to speak to any and all the women he identifies."

"They're all women?" Thunder asks.

His question is greeted with wide-eyed stares as brothers look at each other. I notice everyone puffing themselves up and trying to look manly.

Before he moves toward the door, Hellfire looks around evilly. "Mostly," he replies.

Well, fuck me. Then everyone's looking around wondering who might like to play for the other team. Lady and Joker were great guys back in Tucson. I'd stand up for any man if that's his preference. Doesn't matter none to me.

Prez is making his way past. "Pal, a word."

Well, he said at the start of the meeting he needed to speak with me. I've nothing to hide, nothing to worry about, so I follow him into his office.

I take the seat he waves me to. Before he can speak, I let him know. "Can't say I'm particularly happy it coming out in front of the brothers, but yeah. I've had no woman. Got no one hiding in my closet. And I can't believe the Herreras are behind this. The trouble we're having seems almost juvenile to me."

"Feel you there, Pal. That's my gut instinct too."

Okay. So can I go now? But I wait for my official dismissal. It seems Prez hasn't finished though. "You okay to go to the strip club again tonight? The night shift?"

"Taser going?"

His eyes sharpen. "You got a problem if he is?"

Quickly I shake my head. "Not at all. Just wanting to know I'm not the only fucker being deliberately kept away from his bed."

He rolls his head around on his neck, lifting a hand and rubbing the back of his skull. "You're not slow on the uptake, are you, Brother?"

I knew I was right. "Keepin' me and Jayden apart won't stop anything happening. In fact, it's more likely to start if there are obstacles put between us."

Hellfire stands. "My wife," he begins, then pauses as though not knowing how to proceed. "Well, Moira's taken a liking to Jayden. Sees a lot of herself in her. Doesn't want her to make a mistake."

"Everyone makes mistakes, Prez. Don't do it knowingly, but they happen all the same. Jay trusted the wrong person when she'd just turned a teenager, that was her error. And one she's still fuckin' payin' for. Anyone got Jay's best interest at heart? Well that's me. Jay knows where she stands. She wants me? She's got me. She doesn't? Fuck, that would tear me apart, but

I'd stand aside. Here in the clubhouse, where I haven't got the measure of all the men yet, I want her by my fuckin' side. I need to be there with her, so I know she's safe."

"You're still protecting her?"

"Fuckin' right I am. And I always will. Whether we're together or not." I try to wipe the glare off my face. "Look, Prez. Demon's, what, thirty-five? Moira can't have been far off Jayden's age when you got together. You telling me you didn't know what you wanted then? That your relationship's been wrong all this time?"

"Watch your tone, Brother," Hell snarls. But he returns to his chair and sits down, putting his elbows on the desk. "I'm not saying that. Best fuckin' thing that ever happened to me, never wished it any other way. You got the same feelin's I had for Moira, and your girl feels the same way? Then I hope you'll be half as happy. And no, it wasn't a fuckin' mistake."

"I know how I feel, Prez. I hope Jay feels the same, but ain't gonna pressure her. But I need space. Yeah, she's sharing my room, and I feel better for knowing she's there. Under my protection. But to do that job properly? I need to be with her. Send someone else tonight, please?"

I watch his face, hoping my pleading tone gets through to him. I don't want to beg, but I'm getting close to it now. Time seems to pass slowly until he lets out a deep sigh.

"Mo's gonna kill me," he mumbles under his breath, then to me, "I trust you, Pal. Just don't hurt her. You do? I'll let Mo at you first then finish what's left of you off."

CHAPTER 28

JAYDEN

Last night I was disappointed to sleep alone in Paladin's bed. I'd snuggled under the covers, placing my head on the pillow that smelled of him. Even though he hadn't been there, I'd felt closer to him than I ever had.

All evening Mo had been saying things that were eating away at me. That a young man like Paladin wouldn't have waited, suggesting Bitch couldn't possibly have been the only female to have been in his bed. That nearly three years was too long for a biker like him to be satisfied with his hand, not with all the willing pussy around him.

When Pyro, one of the men left in the club to protect it, had come over and offered to play pool, I'd accepted, if only to get some space to clear my head. Ignoring some of the stains on the pool table, I'd thrashed him three times. I'd then beaten Buzzard. The computer guy, Cad, put up more of a run for his money. By then, time had passed. The club girls had started dancing around the pole, showing off their bodies in ways I'd be ashamed to. The old ladies, what there were of them, were making moves to make themselves scarce. It was my cue to leave this strange party.

That the compound was shot at didn't particularly upset me, no one had been badly hurt and I was thankful for that. I'm no stranger to this lifestyle. I'd been on the Tucson compound when a bomb had gone off, and Slick had got badly injured. I'd been there when a wildfire was approaching. I know what a biker's life is like and the risks that they take. That we take, the women who choose to throw their lot in with them.

As I started making my way to the stairs, out of the corner of my eyes I saw Titsy had now got her top off. When she writhed on the pole, interest flared in the men's eyes. The words Mo had been throwing at me all evening had come back to me. Perhaps she was right. With all this temptation around him, how would Pal be able to resist?

Before I'd settled down to sleep, I'd done something I never thought I would. When I'd gone up to his room, I'd shamelessly searched it, smelling the sheets, seeking anything, a note, letter, something to show he hadn't been honest. I'd found nothing. No signs the bathroom had been used by anyone else. The only sign a female had been in here, a few stray cat hairs on the bed cover.

It's was then I knew I was being stupid. Pal would be mine if I reached out to take him.

Mo's been treating me like a kid who doesn't know her own mind. Yet she was only a few months older when she met Hell. If it worked out for them, why wouldn't it for me? They'd even started their family immediately.

Paladin knows my story, he lived part of it. Was there during my recovery, was my rock to lean on when things got hard.

Take my bad memories away I'd begged him, when I was just fourteen. Like the gentleman he is, he wouldn't. He became my friend, giving me no sign he'd push to be anything else. Until now, when we've been given the opportunity.

Do I want him? Or is it just my expectation of the natural progression of what I wanted all those years back.

I fell asleep eventually, thoughts still whirling around my head.

I wake to find I'm sprawled over a body. How Pal's not fallen off the edge of the bed, I don't know. I've managed to move from the side I'd taken, traversed the middle, and ended up taking over most of the rest. My leg's over his denim clad thighs, my hand resting on his chest. His breathing alters, *he's awake.*

I keep my eyes closed, enjoying the feeling of his beating heart under my hand, feeling it speeding up as I leave it there. A strange emotion comes over me. A sense of possessiveness. *He's mine.* Now I know I hadn't just been searching for signs to prove him unfaithful and unworthy, I'd been making sure no one else had claimed something that belonged to me.

I don't want to move, I'm too comfy. I'm also embarrassed. The first time I'm in bed with him and I'm wearing my most comfy pair of pyjamas, with decidedly non-sexy unicorns on them. I should have worn a sexy negligee, but I don't even own one. Putting off the moment when I have to talk to him, not knowing how to handle this situation, I concentrate on my breathing, gradually feeling him relax again, and then, like him, return to sleep, my lips curling. *I like this.*

When I wake again, he's staring at me. "Oh, God, Pal. I'm sorry. I…"

He traps my hand that's still on his chest under his fingers. "Ain't got nothing to apologise for, Doll."

He doesn't mind me lying on him? "I'm taking up all the bed."

"I'm comfortable," Now that must be a lie. "Just don't move your leg…"

"Oh!" I suppress a self-conscious giggle, and my face burns red. I can feel he's hard underneath the denim he's still wearing. Is that down to me? Or is it just the state I've heard all men wake up with? I ease my leg down so I can no longer feel it. I'm certainly not going to draw attention to his cock. "I, er, I'll get up now. You must be tired."

"Yeah, I'm going to sleep on a while."

He lets my hand go, I still don't want to move. Without me ever having admitted it, this is exactly where I want to be. It feels so good, so natural, as though we were made to be together. He doesn't protest when I leave my hand where it lies, nor when my fingers start moving, exploring his muscular chest. There's something tantalising about touching his naked skin, though I'd be hard pushed to name it. I don't want to stop.

"Doll," he protests after a few minutes.

Whoops. I'm taking liberties. But he's taken none. Unlike the men who'd taken advantage of me. It makes me want more. There seems to be a disconnect between my mouth and my brain, as suddenly I find myself asking, "Can I kiss you?"

He's quiet, as if I've stunned him. Then, "Sure, have at it, sweetheart."

I don't hesitate. Sitting up, leaning over him, placing my hand against his face. If he'd moved, trapped me, I would have been scared, but he does nothing to concern me, leaving me completely in charge. It's what I want, *need*. I giggle slightly as I slip my finger into his mouth and he licks it, but my mirth fades fast as I hadn't counted on nerve endings in my forefinger being able to send tingles down my body. Such a small thing, but how sexy.

I can't wait any more. I kiss him chastely. *It's not enough.* I kiss him again. He opens for me. Our tongues touch. I've imagined it, dreamed of it, but never experienced it, that exciting tingling caressing him like this invokes. He must have more experience than me, but he lets me take the lead. I explore his mouth; he returns the action. His hands twitch, he does nothing to take charge.

I need more. I move, throwing my leg over him so I'm sitting across his chest. I kiss him again, using my hands against his bristly cheeks.

"Am I doing it right?" I ask, hesitantly.

"Feels right to me," he replies softly. "Fuckin' good, Jay."

"You want me to stop?"

"No, but you ought to." His hips move. I feel a hardness against my ass.

Suddenly I remember I'm wearing these decidedly unsexy and childish pjs.

"Pal, I…"

"You go get dressed babe. Breakfast's probably ready down-stairs. I'll get some more shut-eye."

Sitting up, I try to inject some normality into the situation, asking him about when the lockdown will end. I'm probably putting the wrong pressure on his stomach or something, but I feel his hips move again. He groans, I don't think he's even aware of it.

I better get up. Wishing again I was wearing something sexy, I slide off him, grab some clothes, and as nonchalantly as I can, as though getting out of a man's bed isn't something strange, I take my clothing into the bathroom.

Once inside, I shut the door and slide down the wall, sitting on the floor with my back against it. My fingers go to my lips, caressing where our mouths had touched. Right now I'm feeling like a giddy teenager who's just had her first kiss. Which is exactly what I am. Oh, sure, my abusers had forced their mouths on me, but I'd hated both it and their wandering hands. Paladin, though, kissing him had blown memories of that away. It was… what words can I use to describe it? Incredible.

My fingers cover my mouth as I realise, my breath must smell, I hadn't brushed my teeth. *But I hadn't minded his, nor his taste.* I think it could become addictive.

He needs his sleep. I don't know what time he came to bed, but it must have been only a few hours ago, as I'd been told he was going to be out all night. Even though I'd like to wake him for more, it wouldn't be fair.

Lockdown's not finishing any time soon. Until then, he and I will be together. Time enough to explore. The notion no longer scares me, but instead is exciting.

When I emerge from the bathroom, I'm disappointed he's lightly snoring and is fast asleep. But I don't mind going down into the clubroom on my own, I've lived among bikers long enough. The men I've met seem nice, and the women will all be there.

The smell, and people walking out with loaded plates leads me to the kitchen. Both Jeannie and Mo are at the stove. As I'm walking across to them, Mace gets in front of me, and puts his hand on Mo's shoulder.

"So, I was expecting to see Hell without his beard this morning." He glances at her, and I don't miss his wink.

Moira's cheeks flame and as I look curiously on, notice she appears mortified as she replies, "He chickened out and decided he'd just make do with a trim."

"Sure he did," Mace smirks.

"You going all ol' lady on him, Mo? Hell wouldn't be Prez without that thick beard of his." Pyro calls out.

Mace chortles. "I don't think it was himself Hell wanted the shaving foam for. He seemed a bit too excited for that." As Mace doesn't give up, I see Moira redden even more.

What else could Hell have been shaving? Oh. I put my hand to my mouth and turn away choking back the giggle that's about to escape. *He wouldn't, would he?* Aren't they too old to get up to stuff like that?

Titsy leans over and helpfully switches a burner off. "Bacon's burning, Mo." Then, oh no, she continues, "Prez does like his women bare."

"You've no idea what he likes," Moira snaps. "Stop lying, you slut."

Jeannie puts herself in between them, giving Titsy such a look, the club girl makes herself scarce pretty quickly. Then Bomber's ol' lady catches my eye. "Jay, want some breakfast?"

I'm not sure I do anymore, but I nod, grab the plate she hands over, and disappear into the clubroom. The choice is sit by myself or at the table with a couple of club girls. I choose my own company. After a while, a slightly calmer Moira comes to join me, relaxing after she scans the room to find Titsy's not there.

"So," she sits down beside me, "how did you sleep?"

"Very well," I reply honestly. Thinking it's best not to add how I awoke.

"I'm sorry, Jay. Lockdown must seem very restrictive to you."

"Not at all, Mo. I've been on lockdown before. In fact," I nibble my lip as I think, "I've probably been cooped up on a compound longer than I've not." When she throws me a look of sympathy. I shrug it off. "I've lived this life for years. Of course it's different here, it's not such a family club, but the vibe's pretty similar. I know the biker types."

Now she's shaking her head. "You don't know about this club."

Reaching out I pick up a slice of toast. "Bikers are bikers, aren't they?"

"This club is not the same as what you're used to. Oh, not so much nowadays, but back then, when we first came to the club, it was very different." Jeannie settles a tray of coffee on the table in front of us and sits down. "There are only a few old-timers left."

"Let me guess. Hell, of course, Bomber and Rusty."

"Correct."

"What happened?" Toast consumed, I lean forward to pick up a coffee.

"Ancient history," Mo tries to dismiss it.

Jeannie hip bumps her. "Less of the ancient, Mo. Makes me feel old." She turns to me. "Furnace was the VP, when the old Prez, Blackie died, he took over. Eventually made Hellfire his VP, then when Furnace crashed and burned, Hell became Prez. Lost brothers over the years because of the shit we were into. Brothers were a different breed then, harder, they had to be, they lived life on the edge. Wasn't unusual when they returned from a run without everyone with them. Hell wanted to take the club in a new direction, and when he took over, he seized his chance. He'd met up with Drummer, who'd become Prez of the Tucson chapter when his dad, Bastard had died. They both had ideas about starting a clean MC, so Hellfire brought this club into the Satan's Devils."

"Oh?" I had wondered how the two clubs had joined up.

"Best thing Hell ever did," Mo agrees with a shudder. "Hated those days. Lockdowns were the norm for us then. Brothers getting killed or arrested. Those were dark times."

"Thank fuck Bomber and Hell survived."

"I'll drink to that." Mo raises her coffee cup. She looks around. "Is it getting hot in here, or is it me?"

"Must be you, I'm cold." I'm with Jeannie. I'm not that warm myself. "It's because you're going through the change, dear," Jeannie pats her friend's arm as she continues, then adds with a wink. "Either that, or something got you all heated last night."

Again Moira goes red. A short time later, Hellfire puts in an appearance. Surprising me when he crosses to the couch, leans over, places his hands either side of Moira's head, and gives her a kiss worthy of a romance novel. I've not seen her stunned into silence before.

"Wow," Jeannie says when he walks off, watching him enviously. "I could have me some of that."

Moira slaps at her, and growls, "He's mine, hands off." Her evil stare has me giggling.

We talk about this and that. I help them with lunch, then we're sitting back down. I'm a bit bored. In Tucson, the kids would have kept me busy. At last, out of the corner of my eye I see Pal walking by, but as Moira's talking to me, I can't be rude and leave her to go to him. A little while later, he's walking past me again, this time, acknowledging me, but clearly indicating, he's off to yet another meeting.

CHAPTER 29
HELLFIRE

My list was quite short in comparison." Demon stretches out his legs and sits with his arms folded. There's a twinkle of amusement in his eyes.

"Twenty? In the last six months?" Unlike me, who married young and who's remained faithful to his old lady, my son is still very much single at thirty-five. Still sowing his wild oats too. I'm beginning to doubt there's a woman out there for him.

An unrepentant shrug. "What can I say? I like variety. Those are only the ones where I asked their names."

"Are you ever going to settle down?" The corners of my mouth turn down. He doesn't answer. I didn't expect him to. Instead, I ask what worries me most. "Was it anything we did, Demon? Me and Moira?"

I'm worried when his head dips up and down. "Sure is. All your fault." Just as I'm opening my mouth to ask what we've done to cast such aspersions on the institution of matrimony and monogamy, he continues, "You and Mom? You set a very high bar, Hell. Sure, this past year or so you seem to have drifted apart, but what you've found with each other? I've always doubted I'd ever come across that."

"I knew Mo was for me, the first time I saw her," I admit.

"That's what I'm looking for too," he says, seriously. "I'm always hoping I'm going to find her. Not got anything against committing to the right woman, just running out of hope I'll ever come across anyone who'll make me feel what you did."

I pull a very long list toward me. "In the meantime…"

"In the meantime I'm getting the practice in." He chuckles. "Can't deny I'm enjoyin' it too."

Looking at the list which seems to go on forever, it's my turn to shake my head. "Why the fuck do we keep club girls when brothers go elsewhere? I didn't know there were this many single women in Pueblo."

"There's not," Demon leans forward, tapping on the paper. "Lot of the names there are duplicates. Once a bitch gets a taste of biker cock, she goes back for more. Least a couple seem to have gone through all the brothers." He sits back again. "Bit of a surprise Bomber's name's there. Thought him and Jeannie were solid."

He's my VP. Anything happens to me, it's likely he'll take over. Wouldn't tell this to anyone else, but he's got the right to know. "Shocked me too, Brother. But he's not being unfaithful to Jeannie, or not in the way you're thinkin'. They're swingers."

A loud snort is startled from Demon's mouth. Both his hands sweep back his hair, then he shakes his head. "Well I'll be fucked."

"Accordin' to this list, you have been," I can't resist putting in, drily.

"Very funny. But Bomber and Jeannie? Would never have believed it."

Surprisingly I would. It's hard to keep spice in a marriage that you've been in for thirty plus years. They're just coping with it in a different way.

"Mom know?"

"No," I reply fast. "And she mustn't. Um, Bomber, well, he made an offer…"

He catches on quickly. "A foursome with you and Mom? Fuck, Dad. If you ever take them up on it, that's one thing I don't want to know." He looks horrified, then chuckles incredulously again. "Yeah, Dad. Best to keep that from Mom."

"You've got no worries there, Son." I try not to show how hearing him call me Dad again has affected me.

"So." The pursing of his lips, the lines on his brow are indications he's returned to the matter in hand. "Cad had any luck with the list?"

"Cutting out duplicates we're down to about a hundred and thirty. Mostly girls picked up in clubs, banged around the back, then let go. Many have no names to go on. Brothers insist they made no promises."

"Let's talk this through. A dead body left where it would likely bring us to the attention of the cops. Want my suggestion on that?" The jerk of my chin conveys I do, indeed, want to know his thoughts. "A homeless person found dead isn't unusual. Could have been opportune rather than premeditated. Someone stumbles across him, someone who already wants to do us harm. Plants him to cause mischief."

That makes more sense than killing a random guy or combing the streets looking for someone who's recently died. Another chin raise shows my agreement.

"Then we've got the theft at the auto-shop," Demon resumes. "Now that, I think, could have been targeted. They were after something in particular."

"You think?" I frown, because following that train of thought has implications.

My VP leans forward, placing his hands on my desk. "We both know the problems with that. If they wanted those particular parts, they needed to have inside knowledge they'd just been delivered."

There's the rub. That points to either a member of the club having a loose mouth, or one of our employees. "Pyro's questioned everyone. Short of trying to torture the truth out of them, no one's fessed up."

"They wouldn't. But I'd be tempted to keep my eye on everyone who had knowledge. Which brothers knew, Prez?"

We're definitely in focused-work mode when we both use our titles. "Pyro, Sparky and Mace. They're the other two who put time in at the shop."

Demon's brow furrows. He pinches the bridge of his nose. "Those three are brothers I put one hundred percent trust in."

"Look at it the other way around. Which wouldn't you?"

"The prospects. They're the only ones who haven't proven themselves yet."

"Any contact with the shop?"

"Runt was there when the delivery was made."

So fingers would point in his direction, but, "Runt was the one who got shot."

"Leave that for a moment," Demon suggests. "Let's talk about the drive-by. One car, one gun. Okay, a semi, but one pass wasn't going to do much harm unless we were all congregated out front."

"Lucky we were at the barbeque."

"Indeed it was." He rubs at his temples. "Either someone knew and wanted to cause fear, not fatalities, or they were unlucky not to take down more."

I hadn't looked at it that way. "Runt…?"

"Could have set himself up."

It's my turn to frown. "Hell of a risk, VP. An automatic fired from a car? Those bullets could have hit anywhere. Runt could have been killed."

"Or he shot himself."

Is that any more fanciful than anything else we discussed? I'm not going to dismiss it out of hand. "Did anyone check his wound? See what calibre bullet caused it?"

Demon's head moves left and right. "I'll ask Rusty, but I doubt he'd have looked. He just wanted to close it up to stop the bleeding."

"The bullet. Can we search outside? See if we can find it. It went straight through."

His mouth twitches, "If Runt was involved. If he did shoot himself, he'll have picked up the evidence."

I stand and start to pace. "Fuck, I don't like this VP. We all know it's why we make men prospect. So we can see what they're made of. Sniff out a plant. Runt's been here, what, nine, ten months? He's close to getting his patch. Surely something would have shown up in the time he's been with us. I've never had suspicions about him before."

"Me neither. But the brothers? We've not had anyone patch in recently. Ink was the last, and that was two years ago. Smithy didn't make the grade."

As he refers to a prospect we parted company with, my head tilts. "Smithy?" His name has come up before. "Cad check him out? Are we sure he didn't leave sour?"

Demon scoffs, "I'm certain, Prez. He was more relieved than upset. Thought he was going to ride his bike all the time and not turn his hands to work. When he realised he'd have to actually work for his cut, he didn't think what we did was so glamourous. Anyway, yeah, Cad's confirmed he's gone."

"And?"

Demon chuckles. "Headed off to LA last I heard. Think he was going to try to get in with the Wretched Soulz. A club, as he put it, with more guts."

Well, if he failed with us, he's unlikely to make it with the dominant club in California, and most of the Southwest come to that. It's not the first time someone's been enticed into the brotherhood after watching too much Sons of Anarchy.

"Fuckin' hell." I shake my head, then Demon and I exchange glances. Smithy fucks up with the Wretched Soulz he won't be leaving with a polite handshake. Still, seems my VP's right. Smithy has to be ruled out.

Demon jerks his chin. "Which makes everything come back to Runt. What do you want to do about him?"

That's a very good question. Man's worked hard. He's determined to get his patch. But then, he would if he's got an ulterior motive and wants to infiltrate the club. But some things don't add up. "If Runt was a plant by the cops, he wouldn't be so stupid as to fuck with us in the ways we've been fucked. It's almost childish retaliation."

"Childish? Shooting up the club?"

I wave my hand. "You know what I mean. Runt *could* be a plant for personal revenge. This is what this feels like." I'm the prez. I need to make decisions, sometimes ones I don't like. "Get Cad looking into his background. Yeah, I know he'll already have done a check, but see if he can dig deeper. Ask Rusty about the wound, could it have been caused by a handgun?"

"We pull him off duty?"

"Leave him for now. Watch him. Once we get more from Cad and Rusty, then we'll question him." If the man's innocent, he'll have nothing to tell. But I'm not naïve. To make sure he's telling the truth, we'll probably have to hurt him. Only when a man's at his limits will we believe him. If he's not against the club already, our treatment could turn him.

My VP knows the implications. "We could lose a good man, Prez."

"Or we could find out the truth and be able to get the club off lockdown. My gut feel, VP, is that we haven't seen the last of this. Whoever is behind it, isn't going to stop. I want just you, me, Thunder and Mace in on this. Keep our suspicions about the prospect to officers only for now. Give us a chance to get to the bottom of what Runt has to offer before everyone knows which direction we're looking in." I grimace. "Brothers would be unable to hide their distrust."

Leaning forward, Demon places his clasped hands between his knees. "Which might be completely unwarranted. Yeah. Don't want to rush this, Prez. Keep Cad going through the list of names. And let's just watch Runt for a while."

"Time we wait we could have something else heading for us."

"So, we keep Runt locked down. He's injured. We can excuse him from duties. Make sure one of us is always close to him. Get Cad to monitor his phone calls."

"Whoever it is isn't working alone," I remind him. "Much as we can keep an eye on Runt, can't rule out something else is already set in motion."

"A few days at most," Demon's eyes stare at mine. "That's all I'm asking. If he's innocent, what we do to him might turn him on the club if he hasn't gone against it already. Even as a prospect he knows too much. We could be signing his death warrant, even if he's not guilty. Don't want to go down that route if we don't have to take it." His tone is pleading.

Lowering my head into my hands, I know he's right. If we take Runt to the basement, guilty or not, there's a very good chance he won't be walking out. We could lose a good man for nothing. End up killing an innocent man because he's been wrongly accused.

"Look at it this way, Hell. *If* Runt was behind it, he made sure the drive-by happened at a time no one else would be injured. That suggests he's not looking to kill or hurt anyone else."

"And if it's not? We've got people gunning for us who didn't give a damn if there were women or brothers outside at the time. As most times there would have been, were we not having a barbeque that day."

Demon raises his chin. "So, we're at more risk if we're barking up the wrong tree. If it's not Runt, and we divert our attention away from the real culprits, something could blindside us. Something serious leaving some of us dead."

It's times like this I hate being the prez. Having to make decisions and hope that they're right. If we accuse Runt, could be I'm responsible for killing an innocent man. I'm sitting here, discussing that, feeling no remorse. Am I more like Blackie than I thought?

My son and I are close. Closer maybe through the bonds we share. He was born my brother, but I've raised him as my child. Through both nature and nurture we've got strong links. Is it any wonder at times it's as though he can read my mind?

He's staring at me intently, giving me a moment to pull my thoughts together, before saying, "We've both got a bit of Blackie in us. Sometimes we might need to call on it, Prez. Can't run a one-percenter club without breaking a few heads."

Barking a laugh, I set him straight. "If Blackie was here, he'd already have Runt in the basement. He'd be a dead man walking by now."

I turn away. Am I showing my weakness by not being able to make a decision? All my life I've tried to be the opposite of my father. Am I taking it to extremes, and leaving the club exposed as a result?

Demon stands to leave, pausing to pat my shoulder. "A few days, Prez. If there are no other leads and fingers still point toward Runt, then he's visiting the basement."

CHAPTER 30
PALADIN

This evening has been like old times. Jayden and I playing pool. Already the brothers here seem wary of taking her on, but I don't mind being beaten by a woman. Teaching her pool had been my way of getting her out of her room, back when she first arrived at the Tucson club, giving her something to focus on rather than feeling everyone was looking at her, wondering how she was doing. It had also been a way of me being able to keep close to her, without attracting criticism. I'm proud as fuck when she beats me.

"Yay!" She's jumping up and down. "Ready to concede, Pal? That's three times in a row."

I lean down, speaking into her ear, "You just got lucky tonight. Ouch." I jump back as the minx bats at my arm, pretending to rub a sore spot that doesn't hurt at all.

"Lucky? You have to admit I'm the better player."

That she might be. But wild horses wouldn't pull that fact from me. "Nah, that's me, Doll."

During the evening Jay's talked to a lot of my new brothers. Pyro vowing he'll never play against her again, making me laugh. I got a few slaps on my back for being brave enough to take her on, and was cheered when I did beat her—before her final winning streak. She seems comfortable here, more animated and like her old self, than she'd been at Moira and Hell's, it's almost as if being on lockdown gives her a sense of security. Watching her talking to Runt who's sitting on the sofa, checking he's comfortable, I frown. I haven't considered it before, but maybe her independence and freedom will be more of a challenge for her. For more than two years she's lived with the fear of being taken again. Something I'll need to work on. After the lockdown is lifted I'll need to buy her that car, teach her to drive, and help her get to the place where she can enjoy her new freedom.

Fact remains, though it's a strange club to her, she's relaxed here. *She'd make a great old lady.*

Slow, Pal, slow.

She's sitting beside Runt now, laughing at something he's said. A kernel of jealously starts to burn inside me. I've always said if she ends up not wanting me, I'll accept it. *I lied.* Seeing her with another brother? *Nah, couldn't take it.* Perhaps it's time to stop pussying around. Step up and show her what I've got to offer. This morning had certainly been a start in the right direction.

When I'd first seen her, when she'd put her trust in me, I knew she was going to be mine. My feelings have only become stronger as she's grown into a woman. She's it for me. If I'm not the one for her, I need to know.

Fuck it. Runt's got his hand on her knee as he leans forward to whisper into her ear. Throwing the cue stick on the table, I march over. "Ready for bed, Jay?" If there's a double entendre in my words, it's meant to be there. A strong message for the prospect.

Runt catches my eye. Grinning, he leaves his hand exactly where it is. His eyes find mine in challenge. "We were talking." A definite message that I was interrupting.

I eye the prospect. Runt was obviously named as he's a scrawny kid, probably around my age. He's tall, but built more like a runner than a fighter. Though I've not got much more when it comes to muscles, I still think I could take him on, even if he weren't injured. In Tucson, it would have been easy. He's a prospect, I'm a fully patched member. But here, for some reason, prospects are allowed to claim women.

He's not claiming mine.

Jay's looking between us. I'm sure she's totally innocent, and unaware of the undertones between Runt and myself. She's only showing concern for somebody injured. While his interest is clearly deeper.

"Jay." I hold out my hand.

"If you want to talk to Runt, you stay where you are, Jay." I swing around, glaring at Moira who's come up behind me.

Jay's starting to look confused.

Runt smirks and pats her fucking leg again with the hand he's about to lose. "That's right. You stay where you are, Jay." Then to me, "You haven't claimed her."

He's right. I haven't. But everyone knows that she's off limits. Don't they? Just in case, I make it clear to him. "She's mine, Runt."

"She's not yours, Pal. She's her own woman with her own mind." It's Moira again. *Why can't she butt out? Why is she pushing the prospect and Jay together?* "Mo, I know you mean well, but this is between Jay and me."

"I'm looking out for her. Just like I promised her sister," she explains. Her eyes challenging.

I hadn't noticed, but the room's gone quiet as our voices have got louder. Jay's looking confused. She starts to stand; Runt pulls her back down. That's enough for me. I start to move forward; my progress is halted by a strong grip on my arm.

"What the fuck is going on here?" It's the VP. As Runt opens his mouth, Demon shuts him down. "Not you, Prospect. Pal, explain."

"Prospect's got his hand on my woman."

"Your woman? You're claiming her?"

Jay's eyes are wide open. She looks at me, then at Runt. Then at the hand that's still on her fucking knee.

"I'm claimin' her." There's no doubt in my mind. The sight of another man touching her has brought all my possessive instincts to the fore.

"He can't fucking claim her," Mo all but screeches. "She's not seventeen yet."

"Citizen fuckin' rules, Mo." Oh shit, Prez is involved now. "And claimin' and fuckin' are two different things. If they're committin' to each other, none of our fuckin' business what goes on behind closed doors."

"I'm not having it!"

"It's what me and Jay…" *Fuck!* My hand goes to my cheek as the sound of the forceful slap that's just landed echoes in the sudden silence. My fists clench, my muscles tense. But not only was it a bitch who slapped me, it was the Prez's old lady. I can't retaliate.

Moira's sharp intake of breath makes me suspect she knows she's gone too far. I look over her head to see Prez raising his chin, letting me know he'll handle it. Me? I don't trust myself to speak to either him, or her.

"Jay, come with me," I turn to her instead, holding out my hand. "We've got things to talk about."

"No…" Runt starts to protest.

Demon steps past me and up to him. "Prospect. You don't question a member."

"It's up to the girl…"

He clearly doesn't know when to shut up. Despite his mother's views, Demon appears to be on my side.

"On thin ice, there, Prospect," VP snarls out. "Now let the girl go."

At last, Runt lifts his hand away. Jay stands, comes slowly over to me. Her beautiful eyes on me the whole time.

"Pal?" she says, hesitantly, wincing a little as her eyes focus on my cheek where I suspect a reddening handprint is appearing.

"We'll talk in private." I place my hand at the small of her back, and lead her to the stairs, feeling Moira's glare burning into my back every step.

I'd forgotten to lock my door again. There, in the middle of the bed, is Bitch. Her presence breaks some of the tension between us. Jay steps quickly across the room, ignoring my sharp warning about staying away from her claws, and sits beside the cat, lifting her into her arms. The fucking cat purrs. Me? I'd have got scratched.

Using the cat as armour, Jay nuzzles its fur, then looks at me. "What the hell was all that about, Pal?"

I pace toward the bed, stopping just short as Bitch is watching me with her calculating green eyes. "I got jealous when you were talking to Runt, okay? He was pushing my buttons. He shouldn't have put his hand on your fuckin' leg."

"I didn't really notice. He was just being friendly. Asking what I thought of the club and how different it was from Tucson."

"Friendly? He's a man, Jay. And you're an attractive woman." I sweep back my hair in exasperation.

She peers up through her eyelashes. "You think I'm attractive?"

"Of course I fuckin' do." Once more, I eye the cat. "Jay, please, put Bitch outside."

"Why?"

Because I want to hold you. "Because she's glaring daggers at me. It's distracting."

With a giggle, she stands, cat in her arms, walks to the door and puts the feline outside. With a better memory than mine, she locks the door behind it. Then turns. "Now what?"

I pace toward her, rest my hands on her shoulders, and lower my face. When my lips find hers, she responds. Her arms go around my back. Unlike the kiss earlier, it's me taking charge, taking control. Moving one hand so it's around the back of her head, I hold her to me. If she makes the slightest move to pull away, I'd stop, but she doesn't.

I'm learning her, she's learning me. Our tongues mate together, teeth smash, we back off, angle our heads better. The taste of her I could get drunk on. She's perfect.

At last I pull back, resting my forehead against hers. "Lost it when Runt was pushing me, Jay. Made me realise, if I don't make a stand, anyone here could try and take you from me. Wanted, needed, to claim you. Make those fuckers understand you're mine. Put you off limits."

My cock's hard, throbbing. I press closer to her, knowing she can feel it when she gives a small gasp.

"Pal, I..."

"I know you're not ready, Jay. I'll wait until you are. But I need to know if it's worth waiting. If it's not, tell me now. Fuck knows, it will kill me to watch you with anyone else. But if that's what's going to happen, if I've not got a chance, tell me now, please, Jay."

"I don't want anyone else," she says softly.

The words I want to hear. But I can't forget what happened downstairs, nor how Moira had me sent to the strip club last night. Something's happening that I don't know about. "What's Moira got to do with this, Jay? What's she been saying to you?"

It's her who takes the lead. Holding my hand, she leads me to the bed and sits, When I lower myself down beside her, she draws one leg up under her, sitting sideways to face me. My hand still in hers, she looks down at it, entwining her fingers with mine.

"I don't know what's got into Moira. Ever since I've been here she's been making me question what I feel for you."

I can't suppress my snarl. "What the fuck has it got to do with her?"

"She seems to have it in her head that you're going to force me…"

"She thinks I'm going to rape you? For fuck's safe."

"No," she says quickly. "She just thinks you'll pressure me. That I'm too young to know my mind, that I should explore my options…"

"Explore your fuckin' options? Is that what you were doing with Runt? You got the hots for him, Jay?"

"You asked, Pal. Now you're not letting me explain." Her calm words, in response to my burst of anger, make me take a deep breath. "We've known each other for ages, have never been allowed to be more than friends. We, everyone, expects us to take the next step, eventually. I don't know how to go from being what we are, to getting physical. Moira's said you probably haven't waited for me. That you're a man, with needs. I need to know if that's true. I need to trust you. Since I met you, since you promised me, Pal," her voice grows shaky as though afraid of the answer, "have you ever been with anybody else?"

I close my eyes. If I move too fast, I might scare her. Move too slow, she might not think I care and I'll lose her. Tell her the truth, she might run a mile. I realise I've got no option. I turn her hand over and hold it tight. "Jay, I haven't been with club whores or anyone."

Her lips press together, her eyes find mine and hold them. "Since when, Pal? Since we met? Since you said you'd wait? Or since we've been here?"

"Since ever," I admit in a low voice. "I've never had sex."

She looks at me sharply. "What?" Her tone is disbelieving.

"I've got no experience, Doll." A few ideas. I might not have done it myself, but I've certainly been exposed and I'm not ignorant.

"You're a virgin?" She sounds incredulous.

"Yeah." I can't read if that's a good or bad thing.

Her eyes grow big. As a tear slides from one, I can't help myself, gently touching my forefinger to her cheek, I wipe it away.

"I'm not," she admits.

I move fast. My hands holding her arms, I stare at her until she looks at me. "What did I tell you, Jay? That you might have had sex, but you've never been made love to. In all the important ways, you've never had a first time."

"Neither have you?" she questions again.

"Neither have I." I confirm.

When I thought about us taking the next step, when I'd allowed myself to imagine it, it had been me taking things slow, moving things on gently. Taking my time so as not to scare her. Waiting, I don't know, until at least her seventeenth birthday, treating her like a queen, making her see how special she is to me.

What I never expected was for her to stand up, take a deep breath, then rip off her tee, and stand in front of me in her plain white bra. I'd seen her around the pool in a more revealing bikini, but something about the innocence of the garment she's wearing goes straight to my fucking cock which swells almost unbearably, as I feast my eyes.

"Jay." I can only say her name, completely lost for words. It's an invitation, pure and simple. My head shakes side to side, my whole body's trembling in anticipation.

Moving fast, as though wanting to complete the action before she can regret it, she takes off her jeans.

"Jay, for fuck's sake." My heart's pounding. I can't take breath into my lungs.

Seeing my chest heaving, she misinterprets my non-verbal communication. "You don't want me?"

I stand, our bodies inches apart. "Fuck, Doll. I want you more than I want my next fuckin' breath." My hands itch to reach out and take her. My brain says it's too soon. Too fast. My own fear of doing the wrong thing coming between us. "Doll, why did you get undressed?"

"To force a reaction from you, Pal. You're always the gentleman. Never touching, never taking advantage. Never giving me an indication that it's me you really want. I wanted to see what you'd do."

I grab hold of her hand, place it on my cock. "Is this reaction enough for you, Doll? One chance to get dressed. You don't? I'm going to be taking this for a test ride very soon."

Fuck me, she giggles. I move my hand away, hers stays on my throbbing, aching cock, squeezing it gently, exploring it, making me hiss. "Test ride? Trust a biker to describe it like that."

Maybe not the best terminology, but I chuckle back. "Just hope you're going to decide to buy afterwards."

Her hands go to the bottom of my own tee. I help her, sliding out of my cut and grabbing the back of my shirt behind my neck. Once my top half is naked, her hands land on my pecs, her fingers exploring my small nipples. Again, air whistles in through my teeth.

"Fair's fair," I say softly, as I reach behind her to undo her bra.

She giggles again, putting her hands on the *front clasp* of her bra and undoing it herself. "Guess you're kinda proving you don't have experience."

"I know enough what to do," I threaten, remembering a bizarre conversation around the table in Tucson. Can't remember who said it, but it sounds apt. "Part A," I touch her hand over my cock, "Goes into slot B," I touch her, *fuck me*, damp panties.

"That's all there is to it?" She chuckles, but her eyes flash in challenge. Her breathing has sped up; her face is flushed. Could be because I've now moved my hands and am playing with those gorgeous tits. Pinching her nipples slightly between my fingers and thumbs. The first time in my life I've had an almost naked female that's mine to do what I want with.

Her hands move to my jeans. She undoes the button, then the zipper.

"Careful." I place my hand over hers and take over. I've gone commando, don't want any accidents with those zipper teeth.

Once I'm free, she's in charge again, pushing my jeans over my hips, sinking to her knees as she eases them down. Her teeth nibble her lips, perplexed as she meets my boots. Then, as though solving a puzzle, she taps my leg, indicating I'm to lift it so she can get my boot, sock and jean leg off. She then does the same to the other.

I expect her to stand up, she doesn't. Instead she leans forward, her nose inhaling the musky scent of my balls, then she runs her tongue up my shaft. When she closes her mouth around the head, I almost lose it. Taking hold of her hair, I pull her gently back.

"On a hair-trigger, here, Doll."

With my encouragement, she stands. It's my turn to sink to my knees, sliding her panties down her legs. This time it's me taking the opportunity to inhale her perfume. I've smelt her feminine musk before, but not up close. In full strength, it's intoxicating. Using my hands on her hips, I back her up until her knees hit the bed, then a slight pressure on her stomach has her moving backward.

She's lying flat on the bed, feet still on the floor. A slight resistance, then she's opening herself to me, letting me see everything in all its glory.

I breathe in sharply. "Prettiest cunt I've ever seen."

She chuckles. "You've got nothing to compare it to."

I lean in closer. "Porn, Doll. Porn."

I'm not sure if her gasp is a reflection on my reading and viewing material, or down to the fact I've just licked her, delving into her slit and licking up her cream. Wow, her taste. Best thing I've ever had on my tongue in my life. "You'll have to tell me what you like, Doll. I'm just experimenting down here."

Another sharp intake of breath, then, "Just keep on doing what you're doing, Pal. Oh, God, yeah. I like that."

"How about this?" Closing my lips around her clit, I suck, then rotate my tongue in little circles. The music of her groans, sighs and little moans fill my ears. Right now I feel like the most powerful, luckiest guy in the world.

"Pal!" *Guess I'm doing something right.* While I continue to lick, suck and blow on that nub of nerves, I ease a finger inside her. *Fuck. She's tight. Hardly seems my cock will fit in there.* Trying to get my brain to focus on two things at once, I add another finger, curling it around, trying to find that soft spongy spot I'd heard about. Well, some men can't seem to find it all their lives, probably be too lucky to hope…

"Pal! Oh my God! Pal." Christ. If she gets much louder the whole clubhouse will hear. And who am I to give a fuck?

Her feet have lifted off the ground, her strong thigh muscles clutching at my head, her hands are grasping the covers tightly. Suddenly she goes rigid, sucks in a deep breath then screams again.

I feel the walls of her cunt rhythmically clutching at my fingers. I continue to suck, gentling my mouth, until her hand comes to my head. "Stop, it's too much."

I pull away, shifting myself so I can lift her legs onto the bed, then I lie on top of her. Taking a risk, I lower my mouth to hers and kiss her, tentatively, in case she doesn't like the taste of herself on her mouth.

Her eyes widen in surprise, I can see doubt flashing across her eyes, then she's kissing me back, her hands coming up and holding my head to her.

After a moment, I pull back, checking that she's doing alright.

"Pal, that was, that was… I never dreamed."

I feel relieved. Proud as fuck of the first orgasm I've ever given to a woman. Can only get better from here, can't it? As I learn what she likes.

"Don't have to do any more, babe." I nuzzle her cheek.

"But I want you. The way I always wanted you," she admits. "I thought I'd be worried, scared. But I'm not. I want more."

"I don't want to hurt you. You're so tight." I growl. That's the last thing I want.

"You won't." It's her who's reassuring me. "We'll fit."

She lifts her knees in invitation, flopping her hips open. I'm hanging on by a thread. "Doll, I'm not going to last long." It's my first time. Christ, why didn't I think to practice for the big game and jerk off in the shower first? What a fucking disappointment I'll be.

"It doesn't matter." As I stare down into her eyes, I see emotion shining out. A reassurance, a promise, a lack of judgement. "I just want to feel you inside me."

Who am I to argue? I go to position myself, my rock hard cock nudging at her entrance then… *Oh fuck. What am I thinking?* "Jay, darlin'. I haven't got a fuckin' condom."

Before temptation can tease either of us anymore, I roll off her, falling to my back, taking my unruly dick in my hand trying to calm it. He's just been the closest he's ever come to his rightful place, now I've had to deny him.

She leans up on one elbow, her other hand batting mine away from my dick, taking its place, starting slow, gentle sliding movements. Covering her fingers with my own, I squeeze them tighter, showing her the action I like. It doesn't take long. Soon I'm gasping, as white ribbons of cum decorate my stomach.

Fuck me. She's reaching out her finger, scooping up a few drops, bringing them to her mouth and tasting them.

While my breathing returns to normal, I can't help but laugh at the expression of distaste on her face. "Guess you're not going to want to swallow."

CHAPTER 31

MOIRA

I can't remember Hellfire ever looking so angry. In thirty-six years he's never raised his hand to me, so I don't have any fears he's going to start now. But the way his body's vibrating suggests I'll get a tongue lashing at least—and not the kind I got last night.

It's telling, that as Hell directs me into his office, Demon's following close behind. A good son trying to protect his mother. Well that's what I think until we get inside. All three of us stay standing. Demon has his back to the door.

"What the fuck were you thinking, Mom?" It's only now that I notice Demon's furious. "You do not speak to a member, any member, the way you just spoke to Paladin. Doesn't matter whether you like them or not."

"You got a problem? You speak to me and I'll sort it." Hell slams his hand down on the table. "Respect. That's what the club's built on. After all these years, you should know your fuckin' place. And that's not telling a member who he can or can't have sex with."

"You disrespected Hell, Mom. Me, as well as Pal."

I straighten my back, feeling sparks flying from my eyes. "Know my fucking place? You wonder why I don't like coming to the compound. At home I can ignore it. Here you're both misogynistic dicks. You might be okay taking your brothers' sides at all times, but I'm not going to stand by and watch that lad ruin that girl the same way I was ruined."

Demon rolls his eyes as dramatically as I've ever seen. "Have you watched them together? If you think he's going to rape her, you're very much mistaken."

Hell chuckles, but it's not a happy sound. "Kid doesn't even know what he's doing."

An almost smile crosses Demon's face, but clearly they're not going to let me in on the joke.

"Sit down, Mo." Hell waves to the chair while walking around his desk. "Fuckin' start talkin'. What's got into you?"

I'm still mad. My voice betrays it. "Give or take a few months, she's the same age as I was when I came to the club."

"Go on." I don't miss the look of worry that crosses Demon's face at the tone Hell's using. But I know my husband.

"I had hopes, dreams, Hell. I was going to travel the world or as far as I could. Instead I ended up pregnant and married. Same thing's going to happen to that girl. She won't have a life…"

"You didn't have a life, Mo?" Hell asks, his voice deadly calm.

"Mom," Demon starts warningly.

But I'm on a roll. "Of course I didn't have a life. Cooped up with bikers. Living on the compound for years until we bought the house when Kennedy was born. Having to face up to what Blackie did every fucking day."

"What did Blackie do, Mom?" Demon growls.

Why the fuck's he asking? He already knows. He wants to hear it; I'll spell it out. "Raped me. Got me pregnant. I was only fucking seventeen. He took all my choices away. WILL SOMEONE OPEN THE FUCKING WINDOW?"

Demon looks shocked at the bile in my voice. He staggers over and sits in the second chair, while Hell, used to my ways, not surprised by my abrupt change of subject, turns, undoes the latch and at last lets the cooler air in. I fan myself.

"You regret having me? You regret *me?*" Demon asks. It's only then I notice his face has paled. I can throw things at Hell, not at Demon.

Immediately I try to repair the damage, to backtrack. "Of course not! It's the circumstances I regret."

"Mom," his voice sounds slightly calmer, but he's almost emotionless as he speaks. "What happened to you was awful. What Blackie did, despicable. He hurt you both. But, he was my father. If it wasn't his undiluted blood running through my veins, I might not be the same person. I don't think I've turned out to be a disappointment to you, have I?"

Somehow, his softly spoken words get through to me, more than if he'd been shouting. They both give me space, time to let clarity come to my thinking. Now it's my turn to stand. I walk over to the open window, appreciating the breeze coming in.

"I'm sorry," I say at last. "Look, Hell knows, you've probably guessed, I'm going through the change." Demon's mouth shuts fast as though it wasn't an admission he wanted to hear from his mother. Hell, in contrast, parts his lips. "No, let me speak, okay? I'm getting old. I'm not the person I was."

"You're still beautiful, Mo."

"Put your glasses on, Hell." I smile at him briefly. "It's not nice for a woman who knew she used to look good to be losing her figure and there's nothing she can do about it. Getting wrinkles, broken veins. Knowing inside she's drying up, unable to have children anymore."

"You wanted more kids?" Demon asks, a worried look thrown toward Hell.

"Of course not," I laugh, then look at him slyly. "Couple of grandkids wouldn't go amiss."

"I'll work on it, Mom."

"In wedlock, not out." I pretend to slap him around the head, he pouts. "Anyway, I don't know. It's got my brain all screwed up. My body's telling me I've left it too late. I'll never follow my dreams. Sometimes all I can think about are lost chances, everything I'd missed out on. I just wanted to stop Jayden from making the same mistakes."

"Did you have counselling, Mom?"

"What are you thinking Demon?"

"PTSD," he replies to Hell.

What? "I'm fine. I haven't got PTSD."

"You might have," Hell contradicts. "It doesn't have to manifest itself immediately. You had a kid, me, the club. Now, and it's down to me, I know, you've got too much time on your hands. Fuck, I don't know what a woman goes through. All I can say, getting old is having a toll on me too."

Demon rests his elbows on the desk, lays his head down between them, then looks up. "It's fine knowing getting to the root of what's wrong. But how are we going to move forward? We've a club full of brothers who all heard Mom."

"She apologises to Paladin," Hell says.

I glare. *Like fuck I will.*

"Paladin's not Blackie. Fuck, Mo, he's more like me. He's loved that girl forever. Anyone can see that. Just like I fell in love with you. And Jayden's not you. Any dreams she's got are hers, and not yours. She didn't have your shitty family. She's got people who care for her."

"They're not here."

"Still not up to you to look out for her. We weren't told to keep them apart."

"I don't like being here, Hell. I want to be in my own home. I only came to the barbeque because you wanted me here, now I'm stuck. I'm playing the part of the prez's old lady, and that's not me. Not anymore. I'm not that person."

Hell draws his hand down over his beard, more white than grey now. His blue eyes, so similar to Demon's, stare at the man he's proud to call his son. "One solution," his focus is back on me. "That you're not the prez's old lady anymore."

Demon breathes in sharply, looks up at the ceiling, then back down. He seems to have cottoned on faster than me.

It takes me a moment to wonder how what Hell's suggested could come about. Then it hits me. "You want a divorce?" *Had I fucked up that badly?*

Hell gets up, walks around the desk, and comes to crouch in front of me, his knees cracking as he does so. "Nah, Mo. Never, ever that. You and me babe? We're for fuckin' keeps." As I tilt my head to one side, he continues. "The club? I've given thirty-seven years of my life to the men I call brothers, and I can't change that either. I'll be a Satan's Devil until I can't ride anymore. But, they've also had some of the best years, the last twenty, of me leading them. I'm tired, Mo. It's not just you getting older, it's me too. I think we both deserve to follow our dreams for a while."

"Dad?"

Hell swings around so he's facing our son. "I'll stay in the chair until we've got this situation sorted, but after that, you can step up."

"Hell, you can't. Not for me…"

"Not for you, Mo, for us. You're right. When have we had time just to be with each other? Christ, for the first few years, after Demon was born, it was a struggle just to stay alive. I'm lucky to be here, so many brothers aren't. You had to live with that, not knowing whether your old man was going to come home." He's right. I had. "We deserve some time off. When did we last have a vacation?"

Er. Never?

"Let's take some time for ourselves. Go to places you dreamed of. Just you and me. What do you say, Mo?"

"You mean it?" My heart skips a beat as excitement bubbles through. He's talking about a different type of future than I'd been expecting. Maybe it wasn't too late for us after all. Perhaps our time together is only just beginning, not ending.

Hell leans forward, speaks under his breath directly into my ear. "Without all this stress, might get my cock working again."

While he's been speaking, my eyes have been watching Demon. There's worry there, concern he might not match up to his father, but also a hunger. "You alright with this, Demon?"

I watch as he pinches the bridge of his nose, then looks up and nods. "Not what I would have wanted nor expected. Dad offered when I found out he wasn't my father, but I'd turned it down. Thought that was the end of it. Blindsided me if I'm honest. But after you've done your Grand Tour or whatever, you'll be back, won't you? Back at the club and by my side."

"Your club," Hell emphasises. "Not mine when I step down. I'll be a member. Always have your back, as my son, brother, and my prez."

"Christ." Demon shakes his head. "Don't start yet, Dad. You're still wearing the prez's hat for now."

Am I selfish? Taking my man away from the club?

It's as if Hell can read my mind. "Would have to step down sooner or later, Mo. Would rather it be on my own terms, and while we're both young enough to enjoy ourselves." He stands, his bones protesting audibly again, and holds out his hand to me. "Think you need to make an apology, Mo."

I nod, and first turn to Demon. "I'm sorry."

"Nah," Hell scoffs, "Not to me or the VP, to Paladin. Near tore his head off out there."

Before agreeing, I take a moment. Maybe my dreams weren't abandoned, just delayed. Jayden's life might pan out different, she may get exactly what she wants. Perhaps she doesn't have the same expectations that I had. And maybe, just maybe, if

Paladin's half as good to her as Hell has been for me, maybe he is right for her. I've never been one for platitudes, never said a word if I didn't mean it. Finally, I nod. I can say my apology, and as sincerely as I can make it.

I stand, take my man's hand, following him to the door. Then I swing around. "For goodness sake, shut the window before Hell freezes in here, Demon."

We leave the room to his bark of laughter.

Neither Paladin nor Jayden are in the clubroom. Brothers seem awkward, eyeing us carefully as we make our way across to the stairs, heading to Pal's room to try to find the young couple. I'm gripping Hell's hand, pleased he's still with me, knowing how much I'd pushed him tonight. Eating humble pie is never nice, but I feel better now I've got the weight I'd been carrying off my shoulders, and the promise of a future where I won't have to worry every day about Hell.

We walk down the corridor, past all the closed and locked doors. I notice Bitch jumping up at one, expertly swinging on the handle, but it doesn't open. Taking pity on the long-haired fluffy tabby, I crouch down, holding my hand out.

"Be careful," Hell warns, "she's got one fuck of a scratch to her."

But she comes straight over to me. I stroke her for a moment and soon have her purring. "Poor girl. No one wants to share their bed with you?"

"Can you fuckin' blame us? Look." He holds out his arm, showing me the scabbed over scars from his last encounter. "Only thing she's fuckin' good for is catching mice."

I laugh, standing unscathed. "Don't think she likes men."

"You think?" He shakes his head. "Come on."

A step or two in front of me, he pauses in front of a door, but his hand stops in mid-air, and his other reaches out to halt me. "Er, think we better leave the apologies until the morning."

From the noises coming from behind the door, well, fuck. Seems my outburst hadn't deterred them.

Hell's looking at me strangely, heat in his eyes.

"What?" I take a step backward.

"Come here, *old* lady."

I take another step back.

"*Woman*." He snarls warningly.

I step away again.

Suddenly he launches himself on me, pulls me up in his strong arms into a fireman's lift over his shoulder, slaps my ass and turns in the direction of his, *our*, bedroom.

"You might have to give me a moment for the blue pill to work, but the way I'm feelin', woman, that shouldn't take too long."

"Perhaps, *old man*," I giggle into his ear, "there's things you could be doing while we're waiting."

CHAPTER 32

JAYDEN

I slept held safe and secure in Paladin's arms, a deep dreamless sleep. When I woke, I felt his hardness against me. As memories of the previous evening come back to me, I know I'm feeling happier than I ever have before. What had happened between us was so right, so easy. No awkwardness, no embarrassment, no bad memories returning to haunt me. Any doubts I'd had that he was the one for me had been swept away.

Learning Pal was a virgin had made me brave. The knowledge I didn't have to compete with anyone, that we were doing things our own way, learning together. I wasn't an inactive participant; I didn't let things just happen to me. Sex had been fun, something I hadn't been expecting.

This morning, I want to surprise him. While leaving him sleeping, I slide down under the covers, taking his cock first in my hands, then daring to place my mouth on it. I explore with my fingers while my tongue swirls around his uncircumcised head, finding the slit and licking up the drop of pre-cum that's escaping.

It tastes salty and not too bad. One hand cups his ball sac, covered in hair. I'm thoroughly enjoying myself exploring his body when the covers are thrown off and I hear a loud groan, then a hand lightly covers my head.

"Fuckin' good way to wake up, Doll."

"Good morning," I murmur around his cock, the vibration of my voice and my hot breath causing it to jerk.

Using my hands to hold the length I can't get into my mouth; I pick up the rhythm he'd shown me the night before. I try to get more of him inside, I gag, and pull back.

"You okay?" he gasps.

To answer, I just go back to what I was doing.

His sounds of appreciation, his grip on my hair, give me a powerful feeling. This man, right now, is completely under my control. It doesn't take long before I feel him swelling.

"Fuck, Jay, I'm gonna come." The words are staccato, his voice strained.

Remembering how horrible his cum tasted, I pull back, continuing to jerk him off in my hands. Once again his stomach is covered. I'm fascinated by the white strands, cupping it in my hand to stop it running onto the bed sheet.

"Babe, that was fuckin' amazin'." Leaning over, he picks up the tee he discarded last night, and wipes himself clean.

I look at him apologetically. "I'm sorry, I couldn't…"

"Fuck, Doll. That doesn't matter. Wow. What a way to wake up. You wanna do that every morning? Ain't gonna stop you."

I giggle. Suddenly I'm thrown on my back. I'm the recipient of a lewd leer, then he slides down my body, pausing only to play with my nipples before he's between my legs, parting my thighs, and putting his mouth *there*. My head rolls back on the pillows, my fingers grasp the sheets. I'm already turned on and wet from administering the blow job.

He licks, his fingers are inside me, it makes me want more. *Today he's buying condoms*, I think quickly, wondering how what he's doing to me could get any better. *That place he's found inside me…* As soon as he touches it, I lose all control. I wail, try to breathe, *I can't*. My muscles clench, the tingling builds, I need, I need… Christ, I see stars as I cry out loudly.

"Pal, God, Pal."

"Just me, babe," he raises his head just at the point when I can't take anymore. "Just me here."

"You are a god, Pal," I assure him. "I'm sure I had a religious experience just then."

He rests his chin on my mound, his fingers toying with my trimmed pubic hair. "You know, first times aren't supposed to be amazing, it takes time to know one another. It should only get better from here."

"Don't think I'm going to survive, Pal. Anything more would kill me."

He chuckles, I can feel the vibration. It's arousing me all over again. He slides up the bed and holds me, my clit is throbbing now, feeling neglected. Shyly, I can't find the words to ask him, but take hold of his hand, and try to move it downwards. He picks up on my unspoken message, moving his fingers to the spot where I need them.

It doesn't take long before I'm pulsating and crying out all over again.

"Hmm, like that I can give you multiple orgasms. You got any more in there?"

I place my hand over his fingers to still them, I'm too sensitive now, but it's not long before the tingling restarts. The next orgasm takes less time, and isn't as powerful.

"Fuck, I can't wait to be inside you."

Neither can I. But there's something to be said for learning each other's bodies before going all the way. I feel so much more comfortable with him.

He pulls his hand away and sits up unashamedly naked. His cock is again erect, but he ignores it. "You know what the best thing is? We've got a whole fuckin' lifetime to explore and get to know each other." Tapping his head, he continues, "Got lots of ideas in here."

I grin cheekily. "From the porn you've been watching?"

He places a gentle tap on my ass. "Am I going to regret tellin' you that?"

Not if it means he knows what he's doing. For an answer, I smirk.

Reaching over me, he picks up his phone and checks the time, he sighs. "Better get showered and dressed, Doll. Rather stay here, but I've things I need to do."

I sit up, going to pull the sheet around me, then realising I've no reason to hide from him now, leave my breasts on display. I'm rewarded by a hungry stare. "Doll, it's fuckin' hard to leave you."

"Do you have to, Pal?"

He looks reluctant. "Unfortunately, yeah."

Tilting my head, I query. "What types of things do you do, Pal?" I've never asked him before, but now we've been so intimate, surely there's no need for secrets between us?

Rolling his head on his shoulders, he looks uncomfortable at my question. "I can't tell you club business, Jay."

"Why not?"

"If you don't know anything, you can't tell anyone what you don't know." He purses his lips, thinking. "If the police ever questioned you, all you need to say is the truth."

My brow creases at him mentioning the cops. "Are you doing things that are illegal?"

"Don't intend to," he replies, looking serious. "Normally most things we do fall on the right side of the law. But this situation we've got now. We find the man who shot up the club? Won't be handing him to the cops. And," he taps my forehead, "that's the most I'm going to say about that."

"Will you be finding out why we're on lockdown and putting an end to it?"

"Hopin' to, Doll."

I watch the myriad of expressions crossing his face, trying to read them. Last night seems to have changed me, I no longer feel just the girl who needs protecting, I'm also a woman who needs to look after her man. And not just sexually. It's like a dam has burst inside me; I've grown up overnight. My newfound awareness tells me he's uneasy.

As he walks around naked collecting fresh clothes, for a moment I'm distracted by the way the muscles in his ass flex. As for the Satan's Devils tat on his back… The only way I can continue this conversation is to force my eyes to focus on something else.

"Pal," I start, staring at my fingernails. "I'm not asking for details, but something's bothering you."

Out of the corner of my eye, I see him straighten. "You're not wrong there, babe. Can't tell you what they are, but I've got suspicions. Can't put my finger on them, but something doesn't seem right."

"Talk to Hellfire?"

"Yeah. In Tucson, I would have gone to Wraith or Drummer. Problem is, here I'm the new boy. What I'm picking up might be wrong. Don't want to make waves when I've only been here such a short time. And especially if I'm not even clear myself whether personal feelings might be influencing me." He's chosen a fresh tee and jeans, and is carrying them over his arm. "I don't know the brothers in the way the rest of them do."

"You're suspicious about a particular person?"

"Yeah. But the reason I don't trust him, could be the wrong one."

I can only think of one man. "Runt was just playing you last night, Pal. He was pressing your buttons and it worked."

"I didn't say it was Runt, did I?" He swings around fast.

I shrug, he didn't have to. I want to help. "Is there anything Mouse could do? Look into him for you?"

"Mouse? Jeez, Jay. You don't understand this shit. I've transferred to another chapter. I can't go running back to the Tucson brothers for help. It would be a betrayal."

I don't get annoyed or angry, he's clearly walking a tightrope. Instead, I explain my thoughts. "You said yourself you don't know the brothers here." Ignoring the fact I'm still naked, I pull myself onto my knees. "Look, the shit that's happening is serious. Runt could have been killed. Anyone could have been in that shooting if we hadn't all been around the back of the club at the barbeque. I don't know what else has been happening, but lockdown means there's danger out there. If you've got an idea, I say you run with it. Explain the situation to Mouse. If he turns up something of interest, then you can speak to the brothers here and get them to follow it up. If he clears the person you're fingering, no one need to ever know."

He's over beside me in a second, his lips smash down on mine. When our kiss finishes, my mouth feels bruised. I look at him in wonder, a cheeky grin on my face. "What on earth did I do to deserve that?"

"You're a fuckin' little genius, that's what."

My grin widens. "So I'm not just a pretty face?"

Seriously, he replies. "No, you're definitely not." He caresses my cheek. "But now, Doll, I've got to head for that shower else I'm never going to get out of here."

I chuckle as he goes to the bathroom, understanding exactly what he means. Sex, it seems, is addictive.

While he's gone, I take the opportunity to grab some clothes from the bag the prospect had brought from the house. I'm going to run out of clean things soon. But I've one more clean tee I can use, and my jeans will do for another day. When Pal comes out, I take my turn in the bathroom, which unfortunately means, washing away the scent of him from my skin.

He's waiting for me when I come out, tapping his phone against his chin. I nod at it. "You ring Mouse?"

He stares at me for a second, then his mouth widens. "Club business, babe."

I dry my hair quickly, tying it back into a ponytail to keep it out of my face. When I finish, he's standing behind me.

"You alright, Jay?"

"I'm worried about facing Moira," I admit. "She really went off on one last night." I'm certain she'll be able to read that we've taken the step she'd warned me against taking. I'm sure it will be written all over my face. Our new easiness together, our new relationship, is going to be difficult to hide.

"She says anything to you? Leave her to me," he replies, gritting his teeth. "Not lettin' anyone spoil this for us, babe."

I am feeling nervous as we descend the stairs. It doesn't help when Mace shouts out. "Hey, the lovebirds have decided to put in an appearance. Heard you had a good night." He waggles his eyebrows and I know my face has gone bright red.

Pal shows him his middle finger, then with his hand on the small of my back, encourages me into the kitchen. When I smell bacon, I realise how hungry I am. Hmm, guess I worked up an appetite. My face flushes again as I remember just how, and that from the enforcer's comment, probably everyone else knows as well.

The kitchen is normally a hubbub of conversation, but today, while it's still crowded, the atmosphere is subdued. Hellfire's sitting at the big table, Moira by his side. Both seem to have finished eating, just have coffees in front of them now. Hell's hand is on the table, covering that of his wife. At least there appears to be no awkwardness between them.

As soon as I walk in, Mo catches my eye. She leans over and says something to Hellfire and then stands. Hellfire gets to his feet alongside her. I'm hoping they'll just walk past us, but they don't.

"Jay, Pal, can I have a word?" I've never known Moira to sound so timid.

Pal looks at me, concern in his eyes. He's leaving it up to me to decide whether we'll hear her out or not. "Sure." I reply for the both of us.

"Hey, take these with you." Jeannie has hastily assembled a couple of plates. I can't refuse, but right now, my appetite has left me. I walk out into the clubroom with my plate and utensils in hand and then follow the prez and his old lady into his office.

Uncomfortably, Pal and I place our plates on the worn wood of his desk.

"Eat, before it gets cold," Moira suggests. "I'll do the talking."

Pal's not so affected as me, and he's soon taking a loaded fork to his mouth.

Moira nods in satisfaction. "I have to apologise for last night. I was out of order." She glances at Hell who nods encouragingly. "Haven't got an excuse, except, there are things that happened to me in my past that's been affecting how I look at things. Jay, I only wanted to stop you from making a mistake."

Pal chews, swallows, then looks her in the eye. "We're not making a mistake, Moira. And you didn't stop anything."

For the third time this morning, I blush.

Moira resumes. "I don't regret having my first son, but I do regret having him so young. I saw myself in you, Jayden, and wanted you to have the life I couldn't."

Pal swallows again, then lays down his fork. "Jay can have any life she wants, Moira. Just I'll be there to support her. Agree with you, kids are a long way in our future. We'll be taking care they don't come along before time," he breaks off to wink at me, a reference to our lack of condoms. "Whatever Jay wants, she'll have."

"I spoke out of turn," she repeats. "I'm sorry."

"Moira, I'm just happy you care." My eyes soften as I smile at her. Her reasons might be fucked up, her way of going about it wrong, but she is someone in my corner. I reckon I can live with that.

Hellfire? Well he just looks relieved as I pick up my fork and proceed to demonstrate that my appetite has returned.

CHAPTER 33

PALADIN

I don't like doing this. The feeling that I'm going behind my new brothers' backs is an uncomfortable one, but the Jay had made a good suggestion. I'm certain there's something I'm missing, worried I'm letting personal feelings influence my suspicions. But Jay was right. This lockdown is serious, if the actions against the club escalate, then someone could be killed. When it could be a matter of life or death, if there are actions I can take which might potentially help, I've got to do what I can.

I'm in on all the church meetings, but no one else has hinted that they are thinking along anything close to the same line as myself. I've considered discussing my thoughts with Prez or the VP, but they might dismiss them out of hand. I may well be looking in completely the wrong direction, but owe it to everyone here to check things out.

While Jay was showering, I had indeed placed a call to Mouse.

"Mouse, it's Paladin."

"Well I didn't expect to hear from you so soon. Missing us already? How's it going in Colorado?"

"Good, Brother. Mainly good. I need to talk to you in confidence, Mouse. I might be completely wrong here, would rather it was kept away from Drummer's ears for now as technically I'm going behind Hellfire's back. But it could be important."

There's a sound which suggests Mouse is lighting a joint. "Depends what you want. I don't like keeping Prez out of the loop. But talk to me and I'll hear you out."

That's rich from him, considering how long he kept the club in the dark about Mariana, but I let it pass. I suppose his was a personal matter, what I'm asking could set chapters against each other. "There's trouble here. Someone gunnin' for the club. I've got an idea where fingers should be pointing, but because I'm new here…"

"You don't know who to trust." Mouse isn't slow on the uptake.

"Got it in one. Need to delve into someone's background." I break off, wondering how to put this delicately. "I've not taken to him, Mouse. That could be influencin' me."

"Paladin, always thought you had a good head on your shoulders. Trust your gut. Give me the name and I'll look into it for you. I turn anything up? Just promise you'll take it to Hellfire and take any flack for keeping him in the dark."

"That's what I intend to do, Brother." Christ, I miss him and my other brothers so much. I give him the name; he promises to get onto it. "Any news on the Herreras, and how are Mariana and Drew?"

"Heard nothing new from the Herreras. Mariana's recovering slowly, but getting there. Drew's missing Jayden."

After last night, I recognise Drew was never any competition. He might have had a teenage crush, what's between Jay and me is the real thing.

Before I end the call, I again stress the need for confidentiality.

"Never spoke to you, Brother. Now go do your shit. I'll start lookin' into it for you."

I've just finished the call when Jay comes out of the bathroom. She looks so fucking beautiful. I'm damn proud to be her man.

Sitting through Mo's apology was awkward, but at least it seems to have cleared the air. Jay's not one to bear a grudge against anyone, and if she can let it drop, I'm happy to take my cue from her. It also means, when the VP crooks his finger and beckons me over, I can leave the clubhouse without worrying.

"Mo certainly went off on you and Jay last night, didn't she?" Demon and I are checking the positioning of the new camera's behind the auto-shop.

Reaching up, I slightly alter the angle of one, squinting my eyes to make sure the area's going to be totally covered. "She's apologised. Time to move on."

"From what I heard, what she said didn't make any difference at all." He nudges me in the side hard and winks suggestively. *Damn. Those walls in the clubhouse really are paper thin.*

I feel myself flush. "Truth be told, Moira escalated matters. Well, her and that fucker Runt."

"Yeah," Demon frowns. "He was well out of fuckin' line." He pauses, and looks around, then leans in and speaks quietly. "What do you make of him, Pal?"

"Runt? After that display last night you could say I'm biased," I reply carefully.

"Can understand that. Hey, is that camera working?"

"Should be. Why?"

"Can't remember seeing this view earlier." Demon gets out his phone. "Ah, my mistake. It's there. Back to Runt. Apart from last night, what are your feelings?"

"He's a prospect. I've not been here long enough to form a view, VP."

"Well, think on it. If there's anything you come up with that's made you look at him twice, let me know."

He's got Runt in his sights? Interesting. But I say nothing more, just nod. "I will. Right now, apart from makin' an unwanted move on my woman, nothing stands out. If he hadn't been injured, I'd have taken him on last night."

"No one would have blamed you, Brother. Hey, you makin' Jay your ol' lady?"

"That's the way I'm thinkin'. Need to ask her first. She's still young." Moira's words had got me considering. Jay deserves to have the best in her life. I just hope I can be that for her.

"Jay's mentally older than a lot of women her age. She's been through a lot."

He's got that right. My phone rings. Looking down at the screen, I see it's a call I'm expecting. I wave the device in the VP's direction, he nods and concentrates on what he's doing as I go around the corner to answer.

"Mouse. Whatcha got?" I'm hoping I'm wrong and he'll say nothing.

I'm to be disappointed. "Fuck," I exclaim, half to myself, half to him. Wondering what I'm going to do now. In fact, that's the next question Mouse asks me.

"Even with this, I haven't got enough." I'm thinking out loud.

"Thought you'd have a problem." Mouse clears his throat, "Look, Brother, I know you didn't want him involved, but I'm fuckin' worried about you. I've spoken to Drummer. He agrees you shouldn't tackle this by yourself."

"I don't know who to trust…"

"Taken that into account. You're going to have a visitor."

"Yeah?"

"Uh huh." When he tells me the name, my face splits into a grin. Be good to have backup from someone I can trust.

I must still be beaming as Demon stops what he's doing. "Good news?"

I haven't thought this part through. "Uh, well. Yeah. I know we're on lockdown, but one of my Tucson brothers is passing this way and wanted to come for a visit. You okay with that?"

"He handy with a gun?" Demon seems interested.

"Very," I smirk remembering how he got his handle. "His name's Shooter."

"He know we've got trouble?"

"That's hardly likely to put a Tucson brother off," I scoff.

"True that." The VP gives a quick grin, then he looks thoughtful. "We don't know what we're up against. Not going to turn away an extra pair of hands that could help. Only problem, space is tight, as you know. He'll have to be on the couch or in your room."

I'll sort out the logistics later. After the info Mouse had dug up, it will be good having someone at my back as I dig deeper. Someone I definitely can trust.

After Demon and I meet up with Cad and Pyro to discuss the fine tuning of the new security system, the VP goes to his bike.

There's an important stop I need to make before returning to the compound. "VP, I've got to make a slight detour. I'll meet you back at the club."

His eyes narrow. "You're not riding alone, Brother. You know the rules."

My face starts burning. "Er, I need to visit a pharmacy. There's some shit I need to pick up."

"Some shit, eh?" Instead of mounting up, he leans against his bike with his arms folded. My reddening cheeks must betray me. "This have anything to do with last night? Need the morning-after pill?"

"No." I reply fast, not wanting that rumour to get about. "I need fuckin' condoms, satisfied?"

He chuckles. "Why didn't you just come straight out and say so?" Now he does throw his leg over the bike. "I know just the place. Follow me."

When he pulls up, it's not the type of store I was expecting. It's a place with the windows blacked out. I park alongside him, raising my eyebrows. "Really?"

An unrepentant shrug. "Thought they'd have the best selection."

It's a fucking adult store. Knowing he'll just jerk my chain even more if I protest, I kick down the stand, get off, and straighten my shoulders before stepping inside. Demon, to my relief, stays with the bikes.

The array of merchandise is astounding. With the VP waiting outside, I try not to get distracted of the thought of Jay in hand-cuffs, and instead go straight to the display stand I'm after. Quickly, I realise, I've no idea of what I'm buying, especially when the store has such a bewildering array. I've never previously had reason to purchase condoms, and I'm certainly not going to be asking the advice of the female assistant.

Instead, I nonchalantly peruse them, as if I've done this a hundred times before. Flavoured? Hmm. Would that mean I get to come in her mouth knowing she doesn't like to swallow? Great idea. Now, what would she prefer? Strawberry? *Bacon, for fuck's sake?* Chocolate? All girls like chocolate, don't they? I grab a pack of those.

Glow in the dark? Now that would be decidedly creepy. Who wants to look down and see their cock glowing green? I put those back on the shelf. Studded? Inside or out? Nah, maybe some time in the future we'll experiment.

There's pleasure-shaped, warming, *mint?* Tingling with a spearmint lubricant. Coloured—which would she prefer? In the end, I impatiently pick up a couple of packs of the ones they seem to have most of, assuming they're the most popular brand. Then, knowing the VP is waiting, hurry to the counter and act cool as my purchase is rung up and I hand over my cash.

"You took your time." Demon grins knowingly as I head for my bike. "Find what you needed?"

It's best to ignore him.

As soon as I get back to the compound, I find Jayden. When I tell her about my phone call, she's delighted at my news.

"Shooter? Coming here?" Her face lights up. "It will be amazing to see someone from home."

I share her enthusiasm, but in truth it makes me feel guilty. Jayden and I should be embracing our new life, not looking back to old friends and places. Once lockdown's ended I resolve to find out what Pueblo has to offer us. There's no point continuing to wish for what we left in Tucson, the Herreras aren't going to disappear anytime soon. Fuck knows when, or even if, they'll stop looking for Jayden.

Later, when we've retreated to our room, I close the door, standing with my back against it. As Jay looks at me with one eyebrow raised, I put my hand in my cut and bring out the packets I've bought.

She comes closer to see. "Chocolate?" Her eyes sparkle with mirth.

I smirk. "Thought you might give me more blowjobs."

The minx reaches out her hand and traces my already lengthening cock. "You liked how I woke you this morning, then?" she asks cheekily.

"Fuckin' ace, babe." I press my lips to hers.

"You like chocolate then, do you?"

"Mmm mmm," I agree, nuzzling her cheek.

"Could get some chocolate paste and smother my pussy."

Fuck. I like the sound of that. "Trying to sweeten me up, Doll?"

"Is it working?"

"Uh huh."

"I balked at the glow in the dark ones." As I go on to describe the various types available, Jayden's holding onto her sides as she laughs. It's when I talk about the studded ones, she looks interested.

"What about a cock piercing?"

"How about I just give you my cock for now?" Christ, I don't desire a needle anywhere near my dick. To get her mind on other things I back her over to the bed, watching her eyes light with desire.

It seems easy, natural between us. Our hands move together, her helping me out of my clothes, mine helping with hers. Both of us breathing faster, heart rates speeding up. In our impatience, it doesn't take long before we're both naked. She lies back when I encourage her, more than happy to allow me to give her a couple of orgasms with my tongue to get her in the right mood.

Then I'm fumbling, trying to get the condom over my dick.

She raises her head at the delay and watches. "Did you buy the right size?"

"Not helpful, Jay." I toss the one I've just torn a hole in away. My eagerness is making me clumsy. I try again, this time with more success.

"You didn't get ribbed for her pleasure?"

I send her a look. But I do love her teasing. I'm more than conscious that mine isn't the first cock she'll have inside her, but the first time she hasn't been forced. I'd rather she was relaxed and laughing at me than tense and scared.

"Are you ready yet?" she taunts, exaggerating an exasperated sigh.

"Sure am," I tell her, positioning myself, while watching her face. A slight look of apprehension as I start pushing inside, gently, hoping I know what I'm doing.

She gasps, I pull out slightly, then try to advance some more. She was tight enough for my fingers, she's strangling my cock. I'm going only on instinct, holding back when all I want to do is thrust inside. Not even her hand or her mouth, nothing has ever felt so good around my cock. Her tight, warm sheath that I can feel even though I'm covered in that thin barrier of latex.

Her fingernails are digging into my shoulders, but I ignore the pain. On impulse I pull her leg up around my hip, which opens her to me, allowing me to gain more ground. She makes that little gasp again, checking her face, it's with shocked pleasure. If I was with anyone else, I'd be nervous. But this is Jay, *my* girl, the one I've waited for what seems like forever.

"Are you there yet?"

One more push and I am, "Yes. Oh fuck, Jay. You feel so fucking good." She squeezes her muscles. "Do that again." She obeys.

"Pal, can you move now? I need…" Her breathless moans and sighs encourage me.

Fuck yeah. I pull out, push in gently. As she pushes back against me, I thrust harder. Trying to remember that spot I'd found with my fingers. I angle my hips differently, and when she groans, I know I've found it.

"Pal," she cries out in encouragement, and again I fasten my pace, putting a snap and a swivel into my hips, making sure to catch that special place over and over again. Whatever I'm doing, it seems to be working.

"Pal, Pal, oh God, I need…"

I reach my fingers down between us, strumming her clit, determined to hold off on my own satisfaction before, oh, fuck. She's tensing, her muscles pulsating, she's screaming, coming all over my dick. That's it, I can't hold back. Tingles down my spine, my balls draw up, I've lost all control and any sense of rhythm for the last final strokes as cum shoots out. Shivers run down my spine and I realise I've never come this hard in my life.

I drop down over her, only when she pushes at me do I realise I'm crushing her. Well, hey, I'm not practiced at this. "I'm sorry."

"Couldn't breathe," she huffs out, but the smirk shows she's fine.

When I get my own breath back, I go deal with the condom. Suspecting she'll be sore, I get a warm damp cloth and take it back to her. When she tries to close her legs, I shake my head. She's got nothing to hide from me.

Finally, I lie down beside her, pulling her into my arms. "Jay, on your seventeenth birthday, I'm gonna ask you to be my old lady."

"You are, huh?"

"You gonna say yes?"

"You're giving me two months to think about it?"

I'm a bit concerned she's not jumping in with both feet now. But I try to be reasonable. "If that's what you need."

"I think," she starts, distracting me when her nails graze over my nipples, "I need to see more of what you can offer before I make up my mind." Her tone suggests she's teasing.

"You do, huh?"

"Yeah, I do."

"I haven't scored ten out of ten yet?"

She bites her lip; I think it's to stop herself grinning. "There's probably room for improvement."

"You reckon?"

"I think you need more practice." She's trying not to giggle. "Perhaps quite a lot more."

As I pull her to me, and our lips meet, I'm thinking I'm more than happy to oblige.

CHAPTER 34
PALADIN

"Spi… Shooter."

Having received a man hug and a slap on my back, Shooter steps back and touches his fist to mine. "Hey, asshole. You ain't been gone long enough not to be able to remember my fuckin' handle."

Yeah, I shouldn't have forgotten. It's been nearly three years since he lost the name Spider, not that he was that lanky lad anymore. He's muscled up a lot. Still the same in many ways since we prospected together, still that twinkle in his eye. You form a bond when you enter the club more or less at the same time, working all the shit jobs, trying not to complain in earshot of the members, but laying it on the one who'd understand. Hank had been our third prospect back in those days. Hank had ended up being the first to patch in, unfortunately posthumously as he had died protecting Sophie. Luckily Spider had kept her safe too, survived and patched in and had been given a new handle due to his sharp-shooting skills.

"I'm glad you're here, Brother." I tell him earnestly, waiting while he gets his saddlebags and shit off his bike. "Want to come inside and get a drink?"

He pretends his tongue's hanging out, I punch his arm. Fuck, I've missed someone I can just relax with. Apart from when I'm with Jayden, my guard has constantly been up since I came here.

As soon as we go inside, Jay comes running over, throwing her arms around Shooter. I stand back grinning, not in the slightest bit jealous of my brother. Tucson brothers all know where I stand. When she steps back, it's natural for me to put my arm around her, pulling her into my side.

Shooter grins knowingly. "Didn't think it would take you long, Brother."

Jay speaks up fast. "Let us tell Slick and El, okay?"

He makes a motion of zipping his lips. "Your secret to tell." He whistles. "Wouldn't want to be in your shoes, Paladin."

There may be some benefits to being in Colorado.

He follows me to the bar, Runt, with one hand in a sling, and a slightly wary look in his eyes, hands us two beers and a can of soda.

"Shooter, isn't it?" Demon holds out his hand.

"This is Demon, the VP." That starts a round of introductions, queries as to Shooter's ride, and how he found the journey. It's a while before we can get a moment to ourselves. Then it's Jay wanting to know how all the babies are doing.

When at last she's satisfied, Shooter catches my eye. "Can I dump my shit in your room, Brother?"

Jay gives me a knowing look. "I'll give you some time to yourselves."

Shooter follows me upstairs. Inside what counts for my home here in Pueblo, I quickly pull the comforter and sheets over the bed and straighten them up. Guess neither Jay nor I are the domesticated types. He ignores me tidying, just waits patiently until there's somewhere to sit.

Leaning over he picks up something from the bedside table, looks at it and snorts. "Really?"

I snatch the chocolate flavoured condoms out of his hand and shove them into the drawer.

He grins, then tells me without preamble. "Mouse got you an address. I'll text it to you."

I close my eyes. "Thanks."

"You sure about this?"

"I'm not sure at all." He's sitting, I stand. Pacing the room. "Apart from the people who work there, only a couple of men knew about the parts that had been delivered."

"Custom parts for a ninety-nine Dyna Super Glide," Shooter confirms.

"Yeah. Only about three hundred dollars' worth, if that. But they'd had to be ordered in. Brass foot pegs and passenger pegs, grips, solid brass gas cap with Fuel Hole written on it, and matching oil cap. Oh, and brass throttle holding."

"Nice, if you're flashy like that."

I stop my pacing. "What d'you reckon they'd be worth second hand?"

"Possibly two-thirds if they're sold as new. Not a lot to risk getting caught by the Satan's Devils."

"And a Satan's Devil wouldn't be able to put that shit on their own bike."

"His," Shooter taps the phone, "cousin just happens to own a ninety-nine Dyna Super Glide."

"Bit of a coincidence, isn't it?"

"So what's the plan?"

"You and I go to the address Mouse gave you, check it out. If the parts are on the bike, then we've solved the garage break-in."

"Have you considered that might be all you solve? That it was just coincidence that happened on the same night the body was left in the dumpster?"

Shooter's got a point. I'd been worrying about that too. "Apart from the drive-by, it was mainly mischief. And even that was timed when there was no real chance of anyone getting hurt."

"Except for the prospect."

"Except for that. Yeah. But two people could have done everything. The timing fits."

"Him and his cousin. But for what reason?" Shooter's challenging me. I'm glad. It's good to be able to talk it through with a trusted brother, while anyone here might think I'm nuts.

That's also part of my problem. "I don't know, Shooter. Perhaps he's been slighted by the club? Passed over? Things aren't happening fast enough? Got a personal beef with one of the brothers?"

Shooter rests his elbows on his knees. "You're on lockdown. You're chasing your asses trying to find an enemy outside the club who could be non-existent. You're suggesting the mischief might have been done by someone inside. To sow seeds of discontent? We know what lockdowns can be like. People livin' in too close proximity, tempers getting frayed."

I've been going over and over in my head what the perpetrator could hope to get out of it. "If it's someone in the club, that might be enough. A sort of fuck you. He could be standing laughing at us, getting his kick from seeing us chasing our tails. If that's all it is, there might be nothing else happen at all."

"Or you're completely wrong. And it's a gang who wants to take over territory. In that case the incidents will escalate and likely end with blood on both sides."

He's right. "That's why I want to investigate this quietly. If those parts aren't where I expect them to be, I can rest easy, and I won't have distracted the club from searching for who's really out to cause trouble. If they are, I'll stay sleepin' with one eye open."

"I don't blame you. Talkin' about sleepin'…"

"On the couch downstairs, or in here with us."

"Floor suits me fine." His face splits into a grin. "I can enjoy the live porn." He rears back out of reach of my punch, laughing his ass off.

"Not gonna be any show." I inform him, seriously. Jay and I will just need to keep our hands to ourselves. Sucks, but it is what it is.

The next morning Shooter and I leave early. I'd cleared it with Demon we were going to check out some security shit, instead we rode well out of the city, heading to the address which Mouse had found for the cousin, Drayton. We found it easily, parking discreetly down a side road and walking the rest of the way.

"How d'ya want to play this?"

To be honest, I've no idea. Walk up to the door and ask to see his bike? Yeah, like that would work.

Shooter's arm comes out to stop me mid-step. "Listen, it's a Harley."

As the unmistakable sound of the bike's pipes reaches us, we pull back under cover of some shrubbery. As the rider rides it onto the driveway, I point at the Dyna Super Glide. "That's him." My eyes narrow as I spot the unmistakable new parts.

The front door opens. "How did it go? Any better?" A woman stands in the doorway, leaning with one hand on the doorframe. She's grinning as though amused.

"Like the shit." The man who resembles his cousin kicks down the stand and gets off. "Got some admiring looks too. Jealous assholes."

"You and that damn bike." The words are censoring, but his wife, or whoever it is, is smiling.

"Just look at it, Sylvie. See how the sun hits it? Makes it one of a kind." Even from my vantage point I can see it is a beast of a machine, one already heavily customised.

"Well, there's your proof," Shooter whispers.

I need more. "Hold this." I slide out of my cut and pass it to him. Now I'm just wearing a black leather jacket and jeans.

"What you doing?" He asks as I go to my bike.

"You stay here. I'm going to ask a few questions."

"What? Like are those stolen parts on your bike?" he hisses.

"Come on, you know me better than that." I think my plan will work. Nothing bikers like more than discussing their ride with a fellow biker.

"Let me come with you," Shooter insists.

"Nah. Best just one of us go. Less threatening."

"Well, let me go instead. Come on, Paladin, you've got a fuckin' brain, use it. If you're right, there's a chance he might have seen you in Pueblo. Me, he won't know at all."

I don't take more than a second to realise he's right. Having got this close, I can't afford to blow it now. As he slips his own cut off, I put mine back on. "Be careful," I warn him.

"Always am." He waves away my concern with a grin.

As I stay put, he runs back to where we've left the bikes. In no time at all, from my vantage spot I watch as he rides down the road, braking and slowing when he passes the gleaming Dyna Super Glide, which indeed does sparkle in the sun, still parked on the driveway. He makes a U-turn, then comes back, stopping at the curb.

"Nice ride," he calls out. His voice dripping with admiration. "Mind if I take a look?"

Drayton stands from where he's been crouching. "Sure." I can see his smile from here. "She's a beaut, ain't she?"

"She is that," agrees Shooter. "Wow. I like those brass parts. Bet they take some cleaning to keep them lookin' like that."

"I expect so. They're brand new."

Shooter laughs. "Fuel Hole," he points at the filler cap.

"Matching oil cap too," Drayton helpfully tells him. "Oil Hole, see?"

As Shooter bends over, I know he'll be cataloguing the rest of the missing parts. "Where'd you get them, man? Could do with some new shit myself. Got my bike recently and looking forward to makin' it mine."

Inwardly I chuckle. Shooter's had that bike years, prides himself on keeping it as it came out of the factory looks wise, performance, now that's another matter. He prefers having a wolf in sheep's clothing.

It might be my imagination, but Drayton looks shifty. "Went to the Harley store in Boulder."

"Special order?"

"Well, I've got places to be, I'm afraid. You'll have to excuse me now. Need to put this baby away." Drayton pats the saddle as if it were alive, then starts to wheel the bike into the garage. Shooter takes his cue to leave.

"Thanks man."

"No worries." Drayton waves his hand over his shoulder.

I'm back at my bike by the time Shooter's returned. He's got a satisfied grin on his face. "Think that's everything we need."

"Sure is. I got a few pics as well." I suppose it might not stand up in court, all we've got are identical parts to those that were stolen suddenly turning up on his cousin's bike. Enough evidence, though, for Prez to start asking questions I would think.

"He got a bit shifty when I started to probe where he got them from."

"Noticed that." I pass Shooter his cut.

He slides it on its rightful place on his shoulders. "Ready to get back?"

"Yup."

As we start our engines, I breathe a sigh of relief that this part of the puzzle has been solved. Now I just need to decide how, and who to deliver the evidence too.

It's taken an hour to get here, the same amount of time to get back. But now I'm riding with more urgency. There's a man in the club I haven't found myself able to trust, and now I've got proof I was right all along. I want to get back, somehow, without giving too much away, I need to warn Jayden.

Have I got enough to take to Prez or Demon? Who should I talk to first? Should I run it past Mace, or Thunder? I'm still new to the club, I'm unsure who would be the best person to approach. As I ride, my thoughts are racing. My anger at anyone in this Satan's Devils Chapter being involved seeps through me. What do they hope to gain? What plans have they got? Have they done enough, or is there still more yet to come on their agenda?

I don't notice my hand twisting the throttle as my rage grows, forgetting this road is unfamiliar. Fuck, the bend's tighter than I thought. My rear wheel starts to slide out from underneath me, I try to throw my weight over, but I'm too late, I can't right my bike. Continuing to fight the inevitable crash that seems to be approaching in slow motion, my time with Jayden flashes through my head, my hopes for our future…

CHAPTER 35

JAYDEN

Earlier

I love seeing Shooter, a familiar face from home. Pal and him have always been close. It's a shame, though, that him sleeping on the floor of our bedroom last night obviously meant I wasn't going to have a repeat performance of my amazing experience the night before. Truly making love with Pal had been incredible. A far better first time than I could ever have hoped. Everything between us had just been so easy. Fun. Just what I needed. There had been nothing to trigger bad memories from my past.

Now it's morning, and Pal and Shooter clearly have plans.

"You two going for a ride?"

Pal shoves a piece of toast in his mouth and swigs down his coffee. While Shooter snorts with laughter, making my eyes narrow, Pal simply tells me, "Club business."

"Always hated that." Jeannie pauses before opening yet another pack of bacon. "But you can't do anything about it, girl, best you get used to it from the start."

"Why's Shooter going with you?" I try to weasel it out of him, tackling it from another direction. "He's here for a visit."

"He's a Satan's Devil too, Jay. You know this." That he says nothing else suggests Shooter's been roped into Colorado business.

I toss my hair back over my shoulder, my eyes blazing. Looking around, I see Taser, Mace and Pyro all looking amused. Runt's sniggering into his coffee. Before I get told my place in stronger terms, I huff. "Well I guess I'll see you later."

"No goodbye kiss, Doll?"

Before I act on my impulse and slap him to wipe that smarmy look off his face, I turn on my heels and start walking away. Before I'm out of the kitchen, Pal reaches me, his hand grabbing hold of my shoulder, he pulls me back against his chest. "I'd tell you if I could, Doll, but I can't. What you don't know…"

"…can't hurt me." I finish, still annoyed. But I do turn my head when he nuzzles my neck, and my lips do meet his but only briefly. "I'll see you later."

Of course, Paladin and Shooter didn't give me any idea of where they were going. I'm not even an old lady yet, but already I detest the words *club business*. I was the one who'd suggested Pal contact his brothers in Tucson, that Shooter's here as a result of that is obvious. He's come to watch Pal's back. Which means what they're doing might be dangerous. Doesn't Pal know how much I worry about him? Surely he must.

I go up to our room, busying myself putting Shooter's blankets and pillow away. I've no idea how long he'll be staying. I like him, it's great to see someone from home, on the other hand, I want to continue to explore Pal and my new relationship. It's like something's been turned on inside me. I've started to feel horny all the time. He doesn't even need to be here, as soon as I start thinking of him, I want him. I wonder if he knows what a monster he's created. *Does he think of me too?*

The small room's tidy, I can at least walk across the floor now without tripping over Shooter's saddlebags. Lounging on the bed, I pick up the Kindle that Ella had given to me as a going away present. My lips curve as I remember her saying that I won't have to sneak read her books anymore. Then I frown, realising how much I miss her.

No point moping, things are what they are. Making an effort to put regret for a situation which can't be changed behind me, I open the cover. Great! One of the books I pre-ordered has been delivered. I download it, then start to read. It's by one of my favourite authors, she has me hooked by the end of the first page.

So much so, when a knock sounds at the door, I don't hear it. Until the knock comes again.

"Jay? You in there?" A male voice hisses.

The door's locked, of course, to keep Bitch out. I go and open it. "Taser?" *What's he want? I just want to get back to my book.* He'd interrupted at a crucial point.

"Jay." Something about the way he says my name sounds wrong. "Jay, there's been an accident."

Book forgotten, my hand covers my mouth. "Pal?" I ask around my fingers, hoping to hell it's not him.

"Yeah, I'm sorry, Jay. He's come off his bike. He's badly injured. Come. I'll take you to the hospital."

"Oh my God, no. Shooter?"

"Shooter's fine. He's with him. Come, quickly, there..." his worried eyes meet mine, "there might not be much time, Jay."

No! This can't be happening. Not now we've taken that step. Not now I've admitted to myself, if not expressed it in words to him, how much I love him.

"Hurry, Jay."

Automatically I slide my arms into the sleeve of my jacket that Taser's picked up from the chair and is holding out. I close the door, not bothering to lock it. What does it matter if Bitch gets in when my man might be dying? My heart's beating so fast I think it's going to leap out of my chest. I turn to walk down the corridor.

"This way," Taser grabs my arm. "We'll go down the fire escape, it's faster."

I didn't even know there was one. Obviously health and safety's not a priority at the club as no one had pointed it out. Taser knows this place better than me, so I follow him to a door I hadn't noticed at the far end of the corridor, almost running down the external metal steps. A motorcycle is parked waiting at the bottom.

Taser doesn't give me a helmet. Now's not the time to protest that I'm under eighteen and, by law, need one.

My first bike ride, and it's up behind another man, it feels so wrong. As Taser roars out through the gates of the compound, I sob, wondering if I'm ever going to know what it's like to ride with Paladin. *How badly is he hurt? How did it happen? He can't die, can he?* All I can do is pray I'm not too late. *He can't die. He can't. Not now.* More sobs come one after the other. I'm blinded by tears.

I don't know Pueblo, have no idea where the hospital is, nor how far away. All I can hope is that we get there soon, and in time. *In time for what? To say goodbye?* I couldn't bear that. It would destroy me. *I can't lose him. Not now. I can't.* Every nerve in my body is screaming.

I close my eyes, trying to picture his face. Trying to conjure up every detail. Trying to remember the feeling of his arms around me. When the bike starts traversing rough ground, I open them.

Where are we? This doesn't look like a hospital parking lot.

Taser swings the bike around, spitting up gravel beside a muscle car.

"Where are we, Taser?"

His terse reply is just one word. "Off."

Are we taking the car the rest of the way? That doesn't make sense. But with the majority of my brain focused on Paladin, I do what he says.

Suddenly I'm face down in the gravel, Taser's heavy weight on my back, my arms wrenched behind me. Something's tied them together. *Shit. Has this been a trick? Is he working for the Herreras?*

"Paladin?"

"Don't know where the asshole is or care. But I can't wait to see the motherfucker's face when he finds you gone."

Paladin's okay. He didn't crash. Oh, thank God!

My wave of immense relief is short lived. Almost immediately I focus on what's happening to me. If Taser gets his way, Paladin will be hurt, though maybe not physically. His devastation if I've gone missing will equal mine when I thought he was lying injured. I have to do something.

Escape. Get away. My mind races. *I can't let the Herreras get their hands on me again. There's no other reason Taser's got me tied up. I can't let him put me in that car. Can't let him take me to them.*

He pulls me up expecting a weak woman. But knowing what lies in store for me, I'm going to fight. Taking him unawares, I throw my head back, hitting him in the face. Then I turn, kneeing him as hard as I can in the balls and then take off, running toward the road. *Have I incapacitated him enough?*

The loudly roared, "Bitch," from behind shows he can still breathe, and the sounds of his heavy boots on the gravel pounding after me suggest I haven't. From somewhere I find another burst of speed. Suddenly I feel immense pain between my shoulder blades, and I fall to the ground unable to control my twitching muscles. I can't breathe, I'm screaming but making no sound. I don't know how long it goes on, the pain's awful, I feel like I'm dying.

The pain stops, my muscles still jerk uncontrollably, I'm flapping around like a landed fish.

He takes his time getting to me. When I at last can gasp air into my lungs, he crouches in front of me, showing me something. "Wonder what hit you? You've been tasered, *bitch*."

He drags me up by my bound hands, pushing me in front of him. I try to struggle but I still haven't got control over my limbs and know I lost control of my bladder. *He must have had the taser at full strength.*

As he opens the trunk, I've at last regained sufficient presence of mind to stiffen my body to try to stop myself being pushed inside. He takes hold of my hair, pulls my head back, then smashes my face, hard, into the bodywork. Half-stunned, he has no difficulty shoving me in, folding my still weak limbs and slamming the trunk down.

I'm dazed, my muscles aching from the long burst of the taser, my head hurting. I'm scared. *He must be taking me to the Herreras. Are they paying him?* What else could he want with me?

But instead of the car starting, I hear the motorcycle engine instead, then the sound of it pulling away. After the noise of the exhaust pipes fades, there's silence.

He's left me here.

I start screaming, kicking futilely. I'm scared of the dark, scared of closed-in spaces. My voice goes hoarse, my legs hurt where I keep knocking them against whatever's kept in this trunk, tools and something sharp that's cut me. I can only hope I'm not bleeding to death.

How long will he leave me?

Is there a way to get out of here? Some sort of mechanism to release the trunk from inside? I force myself to calm down, concentrating on slowing my breathing. *Pal, help me. What should I do?* Am I looking for a lever? How should I know? My education didn't include how to escape from a locked car. A hysterical giggle bursts forth when I think perhaps it should.

Calm down, calm down. But it's dark. *Ignore that. The dark won't be what kills me.* Hampered by my hands being tied behind my back, awkwardly using touch only, I trace the seams around the trunk closure, finding nothing that appears might be a mechanism which would open it. It would be better if I knew what I was searching for, but even trying everything, nothing works. *If this had been his plan to leave me here, he might have removed anything which would help me escape.*

At last deciding getting out the way I was put in isn't going to work, I try to kick at the back seats, but there's not enough room to manoeuvre. I can't get sufficient weight behind my legs to kick, and my hands, tied so tight that I'm starting to lose feeling, are becoming next to useless.

It's getting warm in here. It's getting harder to breathe. You shouldn't leave dogs in hot cars in the sun, let alone people. For the first time I'm glad I'm not in Tucson, in that heat, I'd already be dead. But even though the outside temperature might be twenty or thirty degrees cooler, and the sun's rays a little weaker, the end effect will probably be the same. It might just take a little longer.

I'm already thirsty, dehydrated. *Not yet you're not. But you will be.*

I'm so scared, I start screaming again.

What's his plan? If he's handing me over to the Herreras, he'll be back before I'm dead, else he wouldn't get any money.

What if I'm wrong? What if my brain just went to the one enemy I knew I had? What if he's got nothing to do with the Tucson crime family? Perhaps it's closer to home. Perhaps he wants nothing for me. Only to take me away from Pal.

Why would he want to hurt his brother?

If anything about Taser had seemed off before today, I may not have believed him. Wouldn't have been tricked by him, and certainly wouldn't have gone anywhere with him. But I'd not had a clue. If Pal suspected anything, he hadn't warned me. Had he been wrong? Was Taser the man he'd had suspicions about? Was it what I didn't know that had ended up hurting me? *Had he known about Taser?*

I think back to the few short hours ago in the kitchen. There was no indication anything was amiss. Taser had seemed friendly enough with everyone, even Paladin.

Pal. Tears roll from my eyes. We had our whole lives ahead of us. Now, I don't know how much of mine I have left.

CHAPTER 36
HELLFIRE

I give Demon a nod as he walks into the clubroom. Much as I hate doing this, it's time. Nothing further has come to light, we've no more information as to who could be fucking with us. In the absence of anything else, all fingers seem to point to Runt. He hasn't done himself many favours, playing on his injury as if it had been near fatal. He's even got the club girls waiting on him hand and foot. When I insisted he take up bar duties again, he'd made such a song and dance I almost relented. But he can pick up a bottle with one hand. He's right handed after all; he was shot in his left. Rusty assured me it's nothing more than a scratch.

Had I been able to claim Moira, she would never have been raped. Because of my past, I'd allowed the prospects more latitude than they'd have in any of our other chapters. If they want a girl, they can have her. That doesn't extend to trying to poach the woman of a patched member though. I'd lost even more respect for him when he'd gone head-to-head with Paladin.

Christ. What a fiasco that had been. Moira's still working through that shit that happened with Blackie, guess I'd hoped that as thirty-six years of water had passed under the bridge, she would be able to put it behind her. It was a slap in my face to find some wounds remain as fresh as the day they were inflicted. After all this time, it still influences her thoughts and actions.

That Runt hadn't helped, had orchestrated the situation to inflame her, only added to the dislike I was beginning to harbour for him. I was loath to accuse a man of something he might not have done, but if he was inclined to cause mischief in the clubhouse, it had made me wonder, what else might he have done?

Two days I'd given him. Time had run out. With no other suspects on the horizon, Demon's bringing him down to the basement now.

I raise my chin toward Mace who immediately leans over the bar, speaking to Dan. The prospect nods, and the music is turned up, AC/DC thumping out through the speakers.

Thunder gets to his feet, and follows Mace down the stairs, Demon and Runt only just ahead of them. I wait, but nobody seems to have noticed.

Runt is used to being given shit jobs. He knows what we do in the room beneath the clubhouse, he's been responsible for laying out plastic sheeting and doing clean up before. Catching up with them as Demon unlocks the door, not unexpectedly I hear him complaining.

"My arm's killing me, VP. I'm on light duties."

"Don't worry," Demon replies. "You're not going to have to lift a finger."

Runt glances around him, noticing for the first time the enforcer and sergeant-at-arms have followed him and the VP down. When his eyes fall on me, they widen. He starts to back up. "Hey, what is this?"

It's clear the penny is dropping.

"We just want to have a chat with you, Prospect," Demon assures him. He points to a chair sitting on top of a clean section of plastic sheet. "Sit down."

"I've done nothing wrong." Runt eyes the chair nervously. "Look, I was just fucking around with Paladin's woman. I was bored, okay? Was just a joke, didn't mean anything. How was I to fuckin' know it would start World War Three?"

"Not here about that," Demon tells him. "We want answers to a few questions."

Mace steps up. He pulls Runt's arms behind him, expertly zip-tying his wrists together. I nod. Over the last few months Mace has grown into his role. His face is impassive, and I know he'll do everything necessary.

"What the fuck, Mace?" Runt struggles against him, then asks, hopefully, "This part of the initiation for prospects?"

"Just sit down." Thunder growls.

"Prez, what's going on? I ain't done anything."

He could be right about that. Lazy bastard that he is. But that's just one more thing to suggest he's not giving his all to the club.

"Sit," Demon instructs, his loud voice booming. When Runt doesn't obey, he says louder, "For fuck's sake, do what you're told. Don't make this any harder than it has to be. Either you sit, or Mace and Thunder will put you in the fuckin' chair."

As the sergeant-at-arms flexes his not inconsiderable muscles, Runt, lacking in that department, has a look of defeat in his eyes. He takes the couple of steps necessary, his feet tapping against the plastic, and, at last, sits, perching on the edge of the chair looking decidedly uncomfortable.

I lean against a workbench. It's covered in tools, all used for one purpose. To get information. I'm only hoping we won't be using them on an innocent man. Folding my arms across my chest, I let Demon take the lead.

He doesn't waste time in asking his first question. "Why did you leave a dead body behind Tits Up?"

Runt startles. Whatever he'd been expecting, it wasn't that. I examine his face, watching for any sign of guilt.

"What the fuck are you talkin' about, VP? I didn't."

"Where did you find him? Did you go lookin', or was it just opportune?" Thunder asks questions of his own.

I'd like to know if it was premeditated too.

"I didn't find him. I didn't go lookin'. Why the fuck are you asking me these questions?"

Demon looms over him. "Who are you workin' with?"

If I hadn't had such strong suspicions, I'd have believed his half-sobbed response. "I don't know what the fuck you're talkin' about. I'm workin' my ass off for this club to get my patch. I don't understand what you're asking."

The prospect's eyes are flicking wildly between us. It's debatable how much damage he's doing to his ass with the amount of work he does, but he's still trying to get us to believe all he wants is that patch he's chasing.

"Fuckin' funny way to try to get your patch, Prospect," Thunder approaches him. "Causin' trouble for the club."

"I'm not causin' trouble for the club." Runt's voice rises. "The dead body had nothing to do with me."

"Who did you sell those parts to?"

"What fuckin' parts?" Runt cries out.

"The parts stolen from the auto-shop. You knew they'd been delivered. You were the fuckin' one to unload them."

Runt looks distressed. "I did what I normally do. I helped Pyro when he added them to the stock. Then I didn't touch them again."

Demon leaves him and crosses to me. "Without an admission, we've got nothing concrete on him."

I wipe my hands over my face, drawing my cheeks down with my fingers. This isn't something I'm going to enjoy. "Won't get anything from him without persuasion, VP." I spare a glance for the man in the chair. "He's not stupid. If he admits it was him doing that shit, he'll end up hurtin', or dead." We don't take betrayal lightly. We can't. It would make us look weak to simply banish him from the club. "We're on lockdown because of what he's done. Need to clear this up so people can start living their lives again."

"It might not be him," Demon reminds me.

"It might not. At the moment, I don't believe him."

My son, *brother*, stares at me, then after a moment, he raises his chin. "I've not heard enough to make up my mind one way or the other. Thing is, it all points to him, doesn't it?" He lets out a sigh. "Let's fuckin' hope we've got this right." Without turning, his eyes still on me, he calls out. "String him up, Brothers."

"What? *No!*" Runt starts protesting loudly. "I've done nothing wrong. You've got to believe me. I'd never hurt the club. No, please." The last is almost a scream as Mace and Thunder, none too gently, loop a rope through his already bound hands, and winch his arms up behind him.

As Thunder kicks the chair away, Runt's leaning forward. In that position it won't be long before his shoulders are screaming.

"I've done nothing wrong," he shouts. "Nothing."

"Need the fuckin' truth." Demon's now moved over and is facing him. "Might not have anything to link you to the body, but you were one of the few people to know those custom parts were delivered, and you were the only person who was out front when you got shot."

"I was shot," Runt repeats in a screech. "You can't be suggestin' I put myself in the line of fire? The way those bullets were flyin' I could have been killed."

"Could have shot yourself." Thunder shakes his head. Yeah, Demon and I had shared our suspicions. "Fuckin' lucky the drive-by happened when everyone else was out back."

Demon nods at Mace, who yanks the winch.

Runt screams in pain. "My shoulders. You're fuckin' dislocatin' them. Oh, man. Let me down. It fuckin' hurts."

"One way to get us to stop, Prospect. Give us something to make us believe you."

"I can't," Runt sobs, then cries out, "I don't know anything. I didn't do anything. Oh, fuck, no. Please stop." Tears, either of pain, or in realisation of the seriousness of his situation, start to leak from his eyes and roll down his face.

Mace steps over to the workbench. The look he gives me is full of distaste for what he's about to do. Christ, torturing our enemies is bad enough, but one of our own? Someone we thought we could trust? I acknowledge the expression he's wearing, then step to the side to give him room to choose which implement he's going to use.

"No!" Runt screams as my movement has brought his attention to the tools I'd previously been hiding. "No, please God, no!"

The VP holds out his hand, motioning Mace to stay where he is. "Runt. A dead body on our premises, a theft of a few hundred dollars of shit. A shootin' where only you got hurt. Apart from the resultin' lockdown that's been inconvenient, you haven't brought serious damage to the club yet." He pauses, to let that sink in. "Admit it was you. Give us the reason. Tell us who you are workin' with. You won't make a patched member, but you'll leave here alive. I promise you that." Another brief period of silence. "Tell us the truth and this stops right now."

Runt's shaking his head. Demon indicates Mace to come forward. Suddenly Runt's shouting again. "I can't fuckin' tell you what isn't true. I can't make up the reason I did what you accuse me of as I didn't fuckin' do it. I'm not workin' with anyone so I can't tell you their fuckin' name. You're going to kill me for no reason. However much you hurt me, I can't say anything you want to hear.

"I've not been the best prospect, I know that. But I fuckin' love this club. I'll do anything to become a member. This is the life I want. I'd never do anything to jeopardise that." He pauses, looks between us, pleading eyes resting on us one by one. "Don't do this. There's nothing I can tell you unless I make shit up. You don't want me as a prospect? Will fuckin' kill me, but I'll leave today. You just got to believe me, I'd do nothing to hurt this club."

I don't believe him. That's the problem. Demon looks at me, sadly I shake my head. Then Mace is moving forward again. Seeing what he's holding, Thunder nods, moves behind Runt and takes a firm hold of his hand.

The enforcer's carrying pliers. "One last chance, Runt. Or say goodbye to your fingernails. Hurts like shit, or so I'm told."

Runt's sobbing loudly, aware there's nothing he can say to convince us. Reluctantly I'm impressed as his resolve to stay quiet.

"Wait," says Demon. Mace pauses. "Anyone got a hold over you, boy? Someone you're afraid of more than us? You working for someone with a grudge against the club?"

As Runt's mouth opens and closes, for a second I wonder if Demon's on the right track. But when he shakes his head, I can't tell if there is someone who he's not naming, or if he's innocent of everything we're accusing him of. It's that doubt that turns my stomach. But there's only one way to find out.

"Get on with it, Mace," I instruct.

CHAPTER 37

PALADIN

"Jeez, Brother. You okay?"

I take the hand Shooter's holding out, gratefully accepting his help to get to my feet. Gingerly I shake out my arms, and check out my legs, flexing my limbs. I'll have a good selection of bruises to come I expect, but nothing's broken or permanently damaged.

My bike though, that's a mess. It's scraped up badly. As I've been checking out my limbs, Shooter's picked it up, and kicked down the stand. It leans forlornly.

"Looks rideable," Shooter says.

"Stupid fuckin' thing to do," I curse myself. Should have been riding more carefully. But I'd been so anxious to get back to the club. The bend had been sharper than I'd expected.

"Got a fuckin' graze on your face, Brother. You bang your head?"

Probably, yes, if the ringing in my ears is any indication. But I brush it off. "I'm fine to ride. Need to get back."

He looks at me carefully, then, clearly seeing nothing to worry him, goes to his bike. "Let's get going then. We'll take it easy. You feel dizzy we'll pull over and stop. Not any real need to hurry, Pal. Taser won't know we're onto him."

Touching my hand to my scalp, I'm not surprised to feel the stickiness of blood. I ignore it, paying attention instead to the sense of urgency that's eating away at my gut. Despite what Shooter's said, I feel a strange need to get moving. *I've got to get back. Point the finger in Taser's direction.* Let everyone know he's gone bad. I have no idea of the reason, but expect there's something in his closet that maybe others who've ridden beside him for longer will be able to find.

Grimacing as I see the dent on my tank and fender, I start the engine. It roars, nothing, luckily seems wrong with it. Ignoring the various pains in my body, knowing they're just superficial, I take off again, this time, keeping the speed down.

I need to take this to an officer. Mace or Thunder. Demon if he's around. I'd rather not go straight to Hellfire, but will if I have to. The burning intuition suggests there's no time to waste. I've never trusted Taser, now I know he's responsible for at least the break-in. The body dumping makes sense as well, he'd have fucking known those cameras weren't showing the dumpster. As for who he was working with? Probably his cousin who bene-fited from the parts.

While I don't know why, I suspect his actions are going to escalate to something worse. No one goes against the club without good reason. It's far too risky. Once started, it's some-thing that needs to be finished. He's got some plan, it's down to me to make sure he doesn't complete it.

Wills opens the gate allowing Shooter and I onto the compound. We park.

"Got to make sure someone knows about this, Brother."

My chin raise is the only answer he gets.

Hellfire had called church for later, so the number of brothers milling around doesn't surprise me. Pyro acknowledges me with a raise of his hand. Taser's holding court by the bar with Lizard and Ink. One by one my eyes roam over my brothers, but I see none of the four men I want. I do notice music is playing loudly.

Shooter raises his eyebrow; I shake my head. Rusty is sitting by the end of the bar, his sharp eyes have spotted my injuries.

He stands and approaches leaning in close so he can be heard over AC/DC. "What the fuck happened? What does the other guy look like?"

Shooter grins. "The ground came off best."

"Huh. Landed dirty side down?" Rusty's hand lands on my shoulder, and his eyes examine me. "You alright, lad?"

I don't respond wanting to waste no time reassuring him, neither have I time for him to check me out. I brush away his touch and concern. "Rusty, I need to speak to one of the officers. Is Hell in his office."

The old-timer tilts his head. "Urgent?" It must have been in the tone of my voice.

"Nothing more."

He leans in closer. "These old eyes see a lot. Can put two and two together. Reckon Prez has found our traitor. Saw him, Mace, the VP and Thunder a while ago, looks like they had their man." He taps his head. "After all these years, not much passes me by."

But Taser's at the bar with a drink in his hand. Unless there's more than one, Prez is questioning the wrong person.

"Rusty. I need to see them. Now. Where the fuck are they?"

His hand points downwards. "In the basement. Doubt they want to be disturbed."

"Shoot, you with me?" Then I leave Rusty with his jaw dropping, and push my way through brothers and women, heading for the cellar that I know is set up in a remarkably similar way to our storeroom back in Tucson.

With my brother at my heels, I race down the steps. The door's locked. I bang on it loudly. When that doesn't work, I try to kick it down.

Just when I'm wondering about the ricochet if I try to shoot the lock out, the door opens. Prez is standing there, a thunderous look on his face.

"No interruptions," he snarls.

Looking past him I can see Runt strung up, tears rolling down his face, Mace, Thunder and the VP surrounding him. Their faces, turned toward me, all look furious.

Leaning forward, I tell Prez, "You've got the wrong fuckin' man. Runt's not behind this. Or not the lead, anyway." Belatedly I admit he could have played a part.

"Who the fuck is then?" Prez's eyes blaze. "You better have something to back yourself up."

"Oh, I've got evidence," I tell him. "It's Taser."

He rears back. Then gets into my face. "You've had a fuckin' downer on Taser since you've been here."

"I need to tell you what I know, Prez. Shooter was with me. He can back me up."

"What the fuck's holdin' us up, Prez?" The VP's walked over.

Hellfire turns. "Pal thinks Runt is innocent. Says he's got shit to prove it's someone else."

"Yeah?" Demon turns, looks at the man who's strung up and weeping. He pinches the bridge of his nose as he spins back. "Think we ought to hear it, Prez."

I wait. Hellfire thinks. Then he calls to Thunder and Mace. "Get him down. Tie him to the chair so he can't escape, then come to my office."

Only minutes later, Shooter and I are standing in front of Prez's desk. The spare chairs occupied by Demon and Mace. Thunder's standing at my back. From the things they've been saying, I got back just in time to stop Runt being tortured. Now I know what that feeling of urgency driving me was. I may not like the prospect, but he doesn't deserve to be put through a fuck load of pain if he's innocent.

"Talk to me," Prez instructs.

It only takes a few minutes to go over my story.

Demon lowers his head into his hands. "So," he glances again at the pictures on my phone. "You're pretty certain these are the parts that were stolen." He looks at the Prez. "Only proves he was responsible for the break-in. The other shit happening the same night could be a coincidence."

Hell's shaking his head. "How much were those parts worth again?"

"Two, three hundred dollars."

Thunder speaks up. "Not a lot in monetary value, Prez. But we lost business because of it. Promised a customer we'd deliver, didn't have the parts to put on his bike. Loud-mouthed asshole, been bad-mouthing us across the city. Says we're a bunch of cowboys who don't know shit about running an auto-shop. He wanted those parts as he was showing his bike the next weekend at some festival or other."

"Bad luck it was him, or…"

"Or Taser knew the effect it would have."

Prez doesn't seem convinced. "Pal, you're new here. You might think you've added two and two together correctly, but you don't know our brother like we do."

"Hang on a moment, Prez." Mace raises his hand. "Taser was pretty cut up when he didn't make Enforcer."

"But he's moved on. Got over it," Thunder objects.

"Has he?" asks Demon. "He was quick to throw his hat in the ring after Ingot died."

"Ingot was your old enforcer?" Shooter asks.

Prez throws him a look as if wondering why he's spoken. But Drummer always encouraged all members to speak up. He answers him anyway. "Yeah, we lost Ingot about six months back."

"How did he die?" Shooter continues.

"Fuckin' hit and run. Never found the fucker who killed him." Mace sounds like he's still upset about it.

Oh fuck no. Jay's inside. Pushing him roughly out of the way, I reach in and pull her out. She hangs limp in my hands, so still it looks like she's dead.

How fucking long has she been left here, in a car, in the heat of the sun in the fucking desert?

Now it's my turn to be pulled aside after I lay her gently on the ground. My mind numb, my brain unable to process I've lost her forever. I fight, wanting to hold her, unwilling to let her go, even in death. Pyro's arms are around me, keeping me away. I struggle, but his grip is too strong. It's Ink who's there fast with his knife, cutting the zip-tie which holds her hands together. Rusty places his fingers to her throat.

"She's alive. Just."

My own heart starts beating again. Elbowing Pyro in the gut, he frees me. I fall to my knees beside her.

"Pull yourself together," Rusty snarls, then shouts, "Anyone got water?"

Ink has. Seems he carries just about everything in those saddlebags of his. Rusty sits himself behind her, raising her head, and dribbles water into her mouth. He removes his bandana and wets it, then drapes it over her forehead.

"Are the keys in the fuckin' car?" Rusty yells. "Or can you get it started?"

Assuming we're going to be driving her to a hospital, I stand, ready to pick her up.

"I'll give it a try." Pyro runs to it.

"Get the air conditioning started."

"What air conditioning? It hasn't got any."

"Fuck. We need to cool her." Rusty starts lifting her tee-shirt. When I growl, he demands. "Take her fuckin' jeans off, Pal. What's worth more, her dignity or her life?"

Put like that, there's no choice. As I pull down her jeans, they're stiff with dried urine. What the fuck has she been through? I'd have done anything to save her from this. *If* she survives I'll spend my life making sure nothing else ever hurts her. When she's lying in just her bra and panties, my brothers stand around, shading her from the sun. Tee-shirts come off, Rusty squirts water over her body, and the clothing becomes makeshift fans.

It seems like forever, but suddenly there's a little sound from her lips. Her eyes flicker, then open. Rusty sits her up more. "Take a drink, sweetheart. But slowly, just a sip." He holds a bottle to her lips. Dropping to my knees I crawl over to her, take hold of her hand and squeeze it.

"Pal?" She says croakily.

"You're going to be fine," I tell her, with a cautious glance at Rusty who nods, and confirms it.

"Yeah, sweetheart. We got you now. You're going to be fine."

CHAPTER 39

JAYDEN

I'd tried to stop myself losing consciousness, but it was something I had no control over. As I lay in that car, accepting I couldn't get free, knowing my feeble attempts were doing nothing more than to exhaust and overheat me. Though it went against the grain, I knew lying still would help me to last longer. Gradually, I knew I was losing the fight.

I started to hallucinate, felt insects walking over me. At one point, I could have sworn there was a snake in the trunk slithering around my legs. Then my eyes closed again, and this time, I no longer had the strength to open them.

There's moisture on my cracked lips. My tongue flicks out greedily to wipe it away, without thinking where it came from. I open my mouth slightly, in the hope that there's more. *Is it raining?*

I'm hallucinating again. I'm hearing voices. My hands no longer seemed tied behind me, maybe I've lost all feeling. Must have done in my head too, it no longer feels like it's resting on metal. There's also a cooling breeze flowing over me.

I attempt to open my eyes which are darn near swollen shut and sealed with dried tears. As more water dribbles into my mouth, I at last manage to see out. It's one of the bikers, Rusty.

"Take a sip, sweetheart. But slowly."

Someone grabs my hand, holding it tightly. "Pal?"

His mouth moves, I don't hear his words, but that doesn't matter. I'm just overjoyed that he's here and I'm no longer locked in that car. I try to reach for him, but my arms are dead. I can't move my legs. Rusty helps me sit upright, holding that bottle to my lips, taking it away when I take a big gulp.

"Slowly, take it slowly. Too much too soon and you'll be sick."

My limbs start tingling. "Oh," I gasp.

"Pal, start rubbing her legs. She'll have cramps from dehydration and from lying in the same position for so long. Ink, Pyro, work on her arms." Then into my ear, he says, "Sorry, darlin', your muscles are crampin'. It will hurt. We'll get you back to the clubhouse and I'll get you some painkillers once I know you can keep them down."

"I can't ride," I tell him, seriously.

"Fuck, no," he chuckles. "Got the crash truck coming." He smooths his hand over my forehead, I think it's a comforting gesture, but he disavows me of that when he says, "You're not burning up so much. Your temperature has started to come down."

At last I think I can move my arms. I struggle to sit straight, Rusty helps. It's then I notice I'm not wearing clothes, well, only my underwear. And there are men all around me. "Pal, my clothes?" I gasp.

Rusty snorts a laugh. "She's going to be fine if that's what she's worried about." Then to me, he asks, "You got a bikini, darlin'?"

"Yes, but…"

"Probably less decent than what you've got on now. Hey, Pal," his voice has hardened. "Fuckin' look at this." I'm leaning forward, Rusty's now able to see my back. "She's been fuckin' tasered."

"He's going to die."

Hoping Pal knows who it is, but so there can be no doubt, weakly I grab his arm. "It was Taser."

"Yeah. We've sussed that already, Jay." The expression on Pal's face would be frightening were it not that I know it isn't directed at me. He's planning retribution for Taser. Good.

A truck has appeared. I'm lifted in arms I'd given up thinking I'd ever feel around me again. Pal lifts me into the back, then slips in beside me. "Put the air conditioning on full while you load my bike, Wills," he instructs the prospect.

They know what they're doing. It only takes a couple of minutes before Pal's Harley's secured and we're driving. Once back at the clubhouse he carries me straight up to our room, Shooter following close behind, Rusty too. Pal goes to place me on the bed, then stops abruptly, making me fasten my arms around his neck.

I grin when I see why. Bitch is comfortably stretched out in the middle of the comforter.

"Just put me down, Pal. She won't hurt me."

"It's me I'm worried about," he growls. But he places me down carefully. Bitch gets up, arches her back, then stretches her front paws out. She comes and cuddles beside me, butting her head against my arm, purring loudly.

"Jayden gonna be alright?" a gruff voice asks. It's Hellfire.

I pull on Pal's arm. "A tee-shirt would be good," I tell him.

Pal starts, seeming annoyed he hadn't thought of that for himself. Quickly he opens a drawer, grabbing the first thing he finds and passing it to me.

Once I've put one of his long tees over my head, pulled it right down until it covers my backside, I take the tablets Rusty hands to me, swallowing them with a fresh bottle of water. Everything hurts. My head, limbs, my back. Overshadowing all that, though, is the fact I'm alive. Bravely I stare Hell in the eyes. "I'm going to be fine."

The prez steps closer. "How did Taser get you to go with him, Jay?"

I scrunch my eyes shut, remembering my terror, swallowing hard. "He said Pal had come off his bike, was badly injured, probably dying, and was in the hospital."

Pal swears loudly, his hand grasping mine and squeezing as though he knows I wouldn't have been thinking clearly after hearing that. Raising my hand I touch the graze on his cheek.

"Yeah," he starts sheepishly. "I may have landed dirty side up. But he didn't know that, Jay. He lied."

"That's the final nail," Hellfire murmurs.

"I, er, I want to see him." I sound weak, but it's a result of what I've been through.

"Nah, Doll. You don't," Paladin contradicts, softly stroking my cheek, treating me like porcelain. "Why the fuck would you want to do that?"

I narrow my eyes at Pal, then use them to plead with Hellfire. Trying to put more strength in my voice, I ask, "He got his taser with him?"

"We took it off him, Jay. You'll never have to worry about him again, I promise."

They misunderstand, seeing me as a frail young girl. I'm not. I've survived worse than Taser. This time, I'm in a position to get revenge. Gently moving Pal's hand away, the ire comes through as my voice deepens. "Hellfire. I want to use his own taser on him. Let him know what it feels like." I speak louder, "I want to watch *him* piss himself." Pulling myself upright, I try to make them understand. "I need this, Hell. Please."

"You know what?" starts a voice from the doorway. Looking around Pal I see Pyro. Raising his chin toward me he continues, "Had my doubts whether you were ol' lady material." He chuckles. "Don't have any doubts left now. Give her this, Prez."

Hellfire isn't convinced. "No, Jay. You don't want to see him like he is now. We've already had… words… with him."

Beaten the shit out of him more like. As long as he's still breathing, I want payback of my own. "He left me to *die*, Hell. Alone. He nearly succeeded. I don't know why, don't understand it. Know you won't tell me because it's club business. But let me see him hurt for myself. Please. I need this."

When I was just a young teenager, men hurt me. I had no control then, like I'd had none today when Taser kidnapped me. I want to make him pay for what he did. I'd like to lock him in a trunk and have him die in the sun. But if I can't do that, I'll make him hurt instead.

Pal's looking at me strangely. Then he says over his shoulder, "Prez. Let her. She does need this. Give her some power for once."

"If I could have hurt Blackie, I'd have done it." A female voice sounds. *Fuck. Is everyone coming into my room?* "I wouldn't have had regrets. He took something from me, I wasn't there to make him pay." *Why's Moira talking about the old president?* I park that thought as I don't understand it, just listen when she continues, "Taser took Jay's freedom at the least. Put her in a nightmare situation. She could have died had you not found her in time."

"Lucky for the tracker," Hell says. "Taser wasn't saying shit about her. Wouldn't even admit he took her, just tried to put all the blame on Mace." He thinks for a moment, then turns away from his wife and looks at Pal. "You know Jayden the best Pal. If you think this is right, I'll go along with it. Just remember, he isn't looking pretty."

"I'm not looking my best either." I run my finger around my cracked lips. My wrists are bleeding and bruised from where I fought against my ties. I've not looked in the mirror, but I've a lump on my head, and my eyes still feel swollen. "When I look at him, I hope it will be like seeing my reflection."

"You look beautiful," Pal breathes. He's got blood in his hair too, and a graze on his cheek. He had come off his bike, though Taser hadn't known it, that part was actually the truth. But that I'm here, alive, and he is too, makes me comprehend what he's saying. Seeing each other again, is what matters the most. Our injuries will heal. While it will take time to move on from what's happened, our fear of never seeing each other again, both of us are still here and have a future to look forward to.

The thought makes me want to put him out of his misery. "Yes," I murmur, so low only he can hear.

"Yes?" He knows what I'm saying, that I'm answering the question he asked the night before last. What I didn't expect were the tears that appear in his eyes. He hadn't cried when he found me. Nor when he got me back here. But me agreeing to be his old lady?

"I thought you'd be pleased, not sad," I tease him.

He places one hand over me, resting it on the bed so he can lean in to give me a kiss. Unfortunately, he's got too close for Bitch's comfort. She strikes out with a hiss. As he whips his hand away, I start laughing.

"Fuck knows what's up with young people today." Hellfire puts his arm around his wife while shaking his head. "Come on. If you're up to it, come and do your worst to Taser now."

I slide to the edge of the bed. Pal hands me my unicorn pyjama bottoms he's picked up from the chair. I slip them over my legs, and discreetly, covered by his long tee, up over my butt. Sliding my feet into my bunny slippers I realise how ridiculous I must look. But what does one wear when about to face their kidnapper?

I get to my feet, wincing in pain. My legs are stiffening, my back and arms feel bruised as hell, and my head is still throbbing. But I don't want to miss this chance. I have to do it now while the memories are fresh. Given time, I won't forgive him, but my resolve to face him might weaken. I hadn't lied. Something inside tells me I need to make him hurt. To take retribution for myself.

Hellfire catches my arm at the doorway, he stares right down into my eyes. "You sure about this?"

"I'm sure. He hurt me, Hellfire."

Hellfire leads the way. The steps down to the basement are dark, plain concrete. Nothing's been embellished here. At the bottom, a door appears to be hanging off its hinges, and there, right in front of me, ropes around his wrists attaching his arms to a beam above, is the man who left me to die.

Blood's flowing freely from a cut above one eye. His chest is bare, and there are dark bruises and burn marks on him. He's breathing shallowly as though in pain, but when he hears footsteps approaching, he opens the one eye he can. His mouth turns up in a snarl as he sees me.

"You're alive."

"No thanks to you." Faced with my abductor, my voice shakes. The last time I'd seen him he was pushing me into the trunk of Mace's car. The flashback takes me back there again.

"You don't have to do this, Jay." Paladin's arm comes around me. I shrug it off and take a step forward.

"Why?" I ask. "Why do you hate me so much?"

"I don't give a fuck about you either way. You were a means to an end," he wheezes.

That's even worse in a way. That I mean so little.

Hell passes something to Pal, who places it into my hand, wrapping my fingers around it. "Aim it at him," he instructs. "Keep your finger on this button. Thirty seconds is recommended."

"Is it turned up high?"

"As far as it will go."

Taser's eyes have widened, then he laughs. "Like that will hurt me."

Oh, I'm determined it will make him hurt. Like I hurt and ache. All I want to do is lie down and rest, but first I need to see him lose his dignity just like I had lost mine. Without delaying any further, I aim, fire, and when those barbs land in his chest, keep my finger pressed down hard on the button, so much pressure my fingertips are white. He goes rigid, then his legs give out, he's hanging by his wrists, his body jerking, his mouth open wide but no sound coming out. I keep the power on.

I don't know how long it is before Pal pries my fingers away. "That's enough," he says gently.

I let him take the taser out of my hand, then I turn, burying my face in his chest. "Kill him," I plead toward Hellfire. "I want to know he's gone so I don't have to worry about him."

I'll always be haunted by the thought the Herreras are still coming for me. I don't need another threat around.

CHAPTER 40

PALADIN

Needing to take Jay away I sweep her up into my arms. She's shaking so much; I worry how what she's just done might have affected her. I know why she wanted to hurt him, could understand it completely.

"Pal?"

"Yeah, Doll?" I'm crossing the clubroom and pausing with my foot on the first step.

"Did he piss himself?"

My face scrunches as I tell her. "Sure did, sweetheart."

She gives a strange, twisted grin. It's the type of expression I hope never to see again on her face. "Good."

As she turns her head into my shoulder, I continue up the stairs and along to my room where Moira and Jeannie are waiting. Somehow they've got rid of Bitch, and there's hot soup ready for her on the bedside table. I stay for a while, watching her eat, watching her do something normal to prove to me she's still in the land of the living. When Pyro comes up and knocks on the door, letting me know everyone's in church, I'm assured by Moira that Jay will be fine with her and Jeannie.

Glancing toward my girl, she raises her chin and looks at me bravely, reassuring me for herself.

It's a sombre meeting room that I enter. Pyro and I are the last to take our seats. Shooter's been given a chair alongside me.

Hellfire half-heartedly bangs the gavel.

"Today is one of the worst days there's been for the club in thirty-six years." He pauses as though to let the seriousness of what he's about to say sink in. "One of our own has turned traitor."

Lizard brings out his cigarettes, takes one, then passes his pack around. Today there are a number of takers. He lights up, inhales, blows smoke out, then asks, "Care to enlighten us, Prez? Most of us only know half the story."

Hellfire takes a cigarette when the pack reaches him. It's the last one, he raises his eyebrow at Lizard who shrugs. Prez takes it as permission, then scrunches the empty packet in his hand. "Okay, some of you already know some of this shit, others don't. So I'll go through from the top. Let's start with Ingot."

As he mentions the deceased enforcer's name, fists thump over hearts. I do the same as a mark of respect though I can't recall ever meeting the man. All I need to know is that he was a brother.

"Ingot was involved in a hit and run, as you already know. The driver left the scene. Neither us, nor the cops, ever found anything to point a finger at the culprit."

"It was Taser?" Ink asks, his voice full of emotion. Sadness and anger combined.

"Yeah." Hellfire says the word that makes the table erupt.

When at last single voices can be distinguished, Bomber snarls, "He still breathin'?"

"Just," Hell confirms. "Club vote is needed to take him out. For those who like closure, the vehicle used was driven to Blue Mesa Reservoir and dumped in one of the deepest parts. That's why it never turned up."

"Fuckin' long way to go. That's a four-hour drive," inputs Sparky. Being Road Captain he seems to have an encyclopaedic knowledge of where places are and how long it takes to get to them.

"Yeah. His accomplice, his *cousin*, followed him and drove him back here. Taser wanted that truck to disappear completely. Wanted to make sure it could never be linked back to him."

Thunder's tapping his mouth. "I recall he was one brother who wasn't around the day Ingot was killed. But then, we weren't expectin' one of our brothers to be murdered, so there was no reason for any of us to stay close, and we weren't suspicious of any absentees." He sounds like he's choked up as he adds, "Never looked inward. Didn't see the fuckin' need."

"I was at a Comic-con that weekend," Cad puts in. "Taser wasn't the only one missing."

"Well we never fuckin' suspected a brother." Pyro's got tears in his eyes. "I'd never have believed it of Taser. Still can't get my fuckin' head around it now. Prez, do we need to go any further? I vote we dispatch the fucker to meet Satan. Don't like breathin' the same fuckin' air." The murmuring suggests others feel much the same.

"I hear you, Brother," Hellfire replies sounding tired. "But I want everyone to know what's been going on. More importantly, why."

"There's no excuse to justify murder." Lizard throws in, looking disgusted.

"In his head, there was," Mace contradicts. "He might have kept quiet about where Pal's girl was hidden, but wanted to boast about everything else. Seems he had his eye on an officer role. Saw himself as Enforcer. Just had to clear a space at the table to make that job his, or so he thought. He was beyond angry I was voted in in his place."

"He hid it fuckin' well."

Pyro's frowning. "He did say you wouldn't be in the role long, that he didn't have faith in your abilities. That the club will soon see you weren't up to the job." He shrugs apologetically. "His words, Mace, not mine."

Mace nods to show he realises that.

"Listen up," Hellfire takes back the floor. "Whatever he thought of Mace's abilities, any weakness he hoped might eventually be exposed, wasn't coming fast enough for him. His next plan was to create trouble for the club. Thought it would test Mace, reveal a weakness."

"Mace ain't weak," Rusty objects.

Hellfire raises his chin. "He's not. He's a fuckin' good enforcer. But in Taser's head, he wasn't good enough. It was pure accident Paladin got in his sights. He thwarted Taser's plans to have a murder pinned at our door. He wanted us to think there was a gang involved, which is why he got his cousin to cause other disturbances that night."

"For which his cousin got paid in auto parts. Three hundred dollars' worth for aiding and abetting a murder."

Hell shakes his head, "Abetting, covering it up, yes. But Taser swears blind his cousin didn't know why he needed to dispose of the vehicle."

"Is this cousin thick?" Buzzard's eyes go wide. "You don't dump a car for no reason."

"Not the sharpest tool in the box, it would appear," Hellfire confirms, then pauses, and looks straight at me. "Cousin's name is Drayton. Pal's already got proof of his involvement. Seen the stolen parts already on his bike. But let's continue. Taser got part of what he wanted, the club on lockdown. Brothers getting frustrated, chasing our tails trying to find an external enemy. He was laughin' that no one was looking within. But of course, we didn't find anything. That's when he decided to escalate matters. Not just, in his mind, exposing Mace's incompetence, but to set Mace up."

"I made that fuckin' stupid comment about Jayden," Mace groans.

"Fuck, no one took it seriously," Sparky's lookin' perplexed. "Tempers were getting frayed, no one likes being cooped up."

This time it's Rusty who gets out the cigarettes. Smoke hangs over the table as half-a-dozen men light up. "What did you say, Mace?"

That's what I want to know too. Tilting my head, I watch the enforcer, interested.

"That if it was the Herreras on our backs, our problems would be solved if we got rid of her." His eyes find mine. "I *meant* send her away to see if that ended our problems. I didn't mean it any other way, Pal, my nerves were on edge so I worded it badly. Was going to ask Hell if you could take her to Vegas for a bit, see if that quieted things down."

"But you said it. And in Taser's hearin'."

"Yeah, Rusty. That's about the gist of it."

Hellfire glares, silencing everyone. "Taser took Mace's car. He'd got rid of Runt on some pretext, so no one knew he'd driven it out of the gates. With so much comin's and goin's as brothers were doing shifts protecting our businesses, no one bothered checkin' the recordings."

"Because we were lookin' outwards for something comin' in, not going out," Cad clarifies with a frown. "I was focused on watching what was outside the gates." He glances at me. I nod. Interpreting there's more security we'll be tightening up in the future. He's already said he values my opinion, someone with fresh eyes. I get a warm glow inside me when I realise my contributions are starting to be valued here.

A glow which disappears immediately with Hellfire's next words. "Taser got Jayden off the compound."

I jump in. "He tortured her from that point. The story he told her was that I was dying or already dead. Jay was distraught. She'd have done anything to get to me, had no reason not to distrust him. When she was left in that car, she had to think he could have been telling the truth. Her physical suffering was obvious, but the mental anguish on top? He's one cruel mother-fucker."

"And that was the man I called friend. *Brother*." Pyro's looking disgusted with himself.

"Wasn't just you, Brother," Demon, quiet up to now, puts in. "He's a narcissistic conman who only thought of himself. Bastards like that can hide in plain sight. All along he thought he was better than us, that we were a bunch of idiots he could fool. And he's still trying to do that."

With all eyes upon him, the VP continues, "He's downstairs trying to justify himself. Telling us of his loyalty to the club, that everything he did was for our benefit. That if we couldn't see how bad Mace was doing, he'd show us how much better he could do when we promoted him to enforcer." He pauses, his head moves side to side. "Doubt it would have stopped there. He said some pretty bad things about my weakness as VP, and Hellfire as the prez."

"Thank fuck the asshole's so stupid," Bomber says. "If he was smarter he'd have gone through all the officers. Would have found a way to get rid of them all until he was seated in the top spot."

Everyone's quiet for a moment as that sinks in.

"Anyone got anything else to add, or shall we get to the vote?"

"Who was he working with, Prez?" I ask. "Anyone other than his cousin?" If there's someone else I want any fucker who helped him to feel our kind of retribution.

Hellfire nods, acknowledging my question and why I'd asked it. "Only Drayton. Very much a follower, just acting under instruction."

"You satisfied with that, Prez?"

Hell glances at Demon who gives a quick nod. "Yeah. Taser didn't have much time for the fucker. Thick as shit, he said. Just did what he told him without asking questions. Lives for that fuckin' bike. Would do anything to get a new part for it."

Pyro grunts. "So that's where the missing shit was going to. Reckon the club probably owns most of that Dyna Glide."

I reckon he could well be right.

Hell bangs the gavel, his face set. "No more fuckin' around. Let's move this on."

"I vote aye," Lizard says immediately. "Haven't changed my mind."

"I haven't announced what we're voting on, yet, Liz. Give me a fuckin' chance," Hell inputs drily. A ripple of chuckles goes around the table; he waits for it to die down. "Brothers, despite all the evidence against him, this is a serious situation facing us now. Haven't had a vote like this for thirty-six years, never needed to. Never been a traitor to the club since Black Plate, Blackie. Whatever your immediate reaction has been, think on your answer. We're discussing killing a patched member." Again he pauses, and looks around, looking as presidential as I've ever seen him. All eyes watch, a pin dropping would sound loud. "One motion on the table. Do we dispatch Taser to meet Satan?"

Demon starts off with an 'aye', others quickly follow. I say it fast when it gets to my turn. Shooter gives a nod, but he knows his vote won't be counted, he's not part of this chapter. Aye's ring out. Thunder's is the next-to-last voice, then Hellfire doesn't hesitate. He bangs the gavel and turns to Buzzard.

"So voted. Taser meets Satan. Record that, Buzz."

The treasurer holds the record book up to show it's already done.

When Hellfire raises the gavel, Bomber clears his throat. "Prez, I'd like to make a suggestion." A head dip in his direction gives him permission. Bomber leans forward, looking down the table at me. "Pal, here. Well, I don't feel we gave him enough of a welcome. Didn't know how to treat him. A member, young, yet to prove himself to us. Nothing like taking on a new prospect, in Pal's case we were expected to accept him immediately. Taser fed into our mistrust of him, his first days weren't made easy."

Embarrassed I feel my cheeks burning, I shrug to suggest it wasn't a thing that concerned me, and exchange a quick look with Shooter. His commiserating glance in return shows he understands how I've had it hard.

Bomber resumes. "We're all hurt by Taser's actions. Ingot was a fuckin' good brother. I'm angry Taser was responsible, and while his admission does bring closure, I came to terms with losing my brother after the funeral."

There are shakes of heads, perplexing looks as brothers wonder where he's going with this.

"Paladin here, he had the most injury. His ol' lady, already recovering from a traumatic past, was kidnapped and left to die. It was fuckin' luck we found her in time. It could so easily have been today we were mournin' her death. I propose Paladin is the one to dispatch Taser."

It's hard to tell how many others agree. Me? Yeah, I'd like to have that responsibility, but I'm just a lowly member, a newcomer at that.

"Seconded," Demon calls out.

"Agreed," calls Pyro.

"Pal's proven himself. I'm proud to call him Brother." That from Cad.

As other comments go around the table, that glow inside me returns. There's no dissenting voices before Hellfire raises the gavel. "Paladin deals the fatal blow," he announces. "Now meetin' fuckin' over."

As the brothers leave the room, Shooter holds me back. "You okay with this?"

I can't even believe he's asking. "It was my fuckin' girl," I hiss. "What the fuck do you think?"

Bomber taps me on the shoulder, pointing me in the direction of the back of the club. We walk through the old and decaying buildings of the steel works until we reach the desert behind. There are targets set up here, for shooting practice.

I wait, alongside my brothers, until at last Taser appears. How he's managing to come forward on his own two feet is a miracle considering his blood loss and the way he's been worked over.

Demon and Mace drag him to a target and tie him against the post. Hellfire nods at me. I take my gun from my cut and approach.

Taser raises his head and spits on the ground. "Fuckin' pussy. You'll never amount to anything. You haven't got the guts to shoot an unarmed man."

He's wrong. I have. "This is for Jayden, and for the club." I say forcefully, stepping forward. "On behalf of my brothers, I'm sending you to Satan." I pull the trigger and the bullet goes straight into his brain.

We leave it until the next day before mopping up the rest of the mess, brothers needing the night to come to terms with the betrayal. His work done here, able to leave knowing my new brothers were now at my back, Shooter could have returned to Tucson. But when Prez came up with a suggestion Shooter had grinned, and quickly accepted.

The whole club wanted to go. So, early in the morning, fourteen bikes rumbled out through the gates, and off on their fifty-mile journey. When we approached the housing development, Shooter zoomed past and took lead spot, and it was only he who parked on the driveway.

This time, proudly wearing his Satan's Devils cut, he approaches the front door.

It's opened fast. Fourteen bikes and a truck have probably woken up half the neighbourhood.

"You!" Drayton, Taser's cousin and accomplice, steps out. "You were the one who was here the other day, asking about my bike." His eyes flick nervously to where the rest of us are parked in a semi-circle around his house.

"Me," Shooter agrees. "I particularly admired the parts you stole from the Satan's Devils."

Drayton's eyes widen. "I didn't. I never. I bought them. I said… They were from Boulder."

"Prove it," Shooter snaps. He sounds so much like Drummer I almost laugh.

"I don't keep receipts." Drayton puffs himself up as though proud he's thought of the answer. "No point."

"Dray? Who is it?" His wife's face appears around the door. "Oh my God. Who are these people?"

Hellfire clearly wants to move this along. He steps down from his bike and goes to stand beside Shooter. "We're here for the bike," he informs man and wife. "We're taking it in payment for the stolen parts."

"Hey, man. Those parts were only a couple of hundred dollars." Drayton's quickly changed his tune, seems to realise there's no point in denying it anymore. "Here, let me pay you…" He starts getting his wallet out.

"You can't take his bike. That's his *everything*," Sylvie protests in a screech. "He's been working on it for years. Restored it."

"You know who we are?" Hell asks lazily. "You any fuckin' idea of what it means to cross the Satan's Devils?"

The way I can see Drayton gulping from here shows he certainly does. His hands now held up in submission.